I0709192

Tuppence and the Devil

Tuppence and the Devil

Boris L. Slocum

2023

3B Independent Publishers

The Sequel to Wergild: A Heartwarming Tale of Coldblooded Vengeance

Copyright © 2023 by Boris L. Slocum

All rights reserved. No part of this publication may be reproduced, distributed, or transmitted in any form or by any means, including photocopying, recording, or other electronic or mechanical methods, without the prior written permission of the publisher, except in the case of brief quotations embodied in critical reviews and certain other noncommercial uses permitted by copyright law.

Printed in the United States of America

First Printing, 2023

ISBN 978-1-7335425-3-1

3B Independent Publishers
347 W. Franklin Street
Paxton, Illinois

www.3bpublishers.com

Other Stories by Boris L. Slocum

Wergild: A Heartwarming Tale of Coldblooded Vengeance (2019)

Skiathos (2020)

1. The Vicarage

It was her curiosity that got the better of her, as it almost always was.

In recent nights, the Fiend several times had slipped off and not been back to their lodgings until the wee morning. There was nothing unusual in his being away—sometimes the creature would absent himself for days at a time—but for his customary disappearances there always were clear explanations.

Here? There was nary a word these last few evenings when the Fiend edged off toward the docks, not returning until the sun first peeked over the horizon the following morning. On those reappearances, he acted very much like an old alley cat fresh home from a revel.

It was a side of the monster that Deirdre hadn't yet seen.

On the fifth such occasion, she got it into her head to follow along in order to see what the rascal was into. The Fiend always had his schemes and his plots. She didn't begrudge him those. How could she? But she'd been travelling with him in his various guises for almost nine months. She felt that fact granted her a certain license when it came to knowing of the reprobate's shenanigans. And who was to say? His nightly perambulations might just concern her in some way.

So, not long after sundown, she left the vicarage, headed through town, and made her way down toward the docks. It was late winter, but Westport was along Albion's balmy southwestern coast, and even after sunset it wasn't dreadfully cool. A thick sweater and a long cloak did the trick— that and a few carefully concealed weapons.

It wasn't that she was afraid so much as cautious. The walk from the cottage to the city gates posed no real dangers, and most parts of Westport were safe and well-lit at night. So what if the docks had an unsavory reputation? She'd seen much in her scant 15 years, and nothing truly scared her, not anymore. She was off to find the Fiend, and she'd settle for nothing less.

What she hadn't counted on was how dark it would be amidst the buildings and warehouses near the docks. Finding the Fiend wasn't always a snap, given how easily he could slip from one form to another, and there being no moonlight and few public lamps in the area around the port didn't make it easier.

So she searched, and searched, and searched.

In the end, as events often did, it fell to the Fiend to find Deirdre rather than for Deirdre to find the Fiend. A voice sounded somewhere not far off as she approached the eastern warehouses.

"What's a lass gotta do to get desecrated around here?" The exasperated and somewhat salty voice she heard was that of a youngster, a mere slip of a girl from the sound of it.

Deirdre followed that voice, knowing it could be none other than the creature she sought.

Now, where exactly was she? If her sense of direction was correct, and she thought it was, there were a number of shabby taverns just past the alley that she approached. It seemed right. A few shadowy figures moved here and there in the distance, and there was the sound of drunken laughter not too far off, but save for the continued disgruntled mutterings of the young voice she followed, the street otherwise was quiet.

Deirdre very soon made out a tiny form in the umber and dared to venture closer, urged on by a voice that simply was not apropos to such surroundings. Hazy though it was, the image attached to the voice was that of a petite and fresh young thing of about 10 years, with long silken hair and a flawless complexion. Even in the darkness, the child stood out.

In sum, it was the type of clean-cut and innocent kid one never saw in such an unwholesome part of town, the type of bait a monster might use to entice its degenerate quarry. This was the creature, no doubt.

"What are you doing?" Deirdre's voice, it irked her to realize, held the same strain of exasperation as did that of the phony child.

"Tuppence!" said the Fiend, as if the two were old friends bumping into one another after some long and unwarranted parting of ways, "what brings you to this little nook?"

"Looking for you," said Deirdre. And then, as if it weren't obvious, "What are you doing?"

"Just taking in the evening air."

"Really?"

"Don't you find the sea breezes bracing?"

"Really?" The stench of the air that close to the docks would've led a barnyard rat to retch. "Can we cut the nonsense? If bodies begin stacking up, the city watch will have to start asking questions."

A sweet and innocent giggle cut through the dark. The child's voice shifted to a tone of mirth and pure incredulity. "Here on the docks? It's hard to walk 20 paces down here without treading on a corpse. One or two more won't go noticed in a city this large, especially a city with such a lively port."

"What happened to 'I only eat chitlins once or twice every 10 years?'" she asked, mimicking the Fiend's high-minded and wounded tone of eight months past. The creature really could be careless at times and sometimes appeared thoroughly indifferent to the consequences of his actions.

"You would have to remember I said that, wouldn't you?"

"And bring it up? Yes."

"Oh … very well. I wasn't getting much attention tonight. Curious. One would've thought a city like Westport would attract a more unsavory throng of pederasts and human jetsam."

"Pity," Deirdre added as they began to walk toward the Port Gate and back in the direction of the city proper.

"Yes, actually," said the creature. "I suppose I'll have to be satisfied … oh, hullo. What's this?"

The two hadn't traveled a dozen paces, and ahead a figure passed on a side street in the faint light of a city lantern. Deirdre could just make out the form of a man, his coat pulled up around his face for the chill. There was nothing odd or suspicious about the fellow beyond his general seediness. But in that part of the city, such a shabby appearance was not unusual or even worthy of note.

"What are the chances?" whispered the fake child. "Ah ... what are the chances!?"

"What?"

"Pardon me for a moment, Tuppence."

"What? … Do you know that man?"

"Oy!" shouted the sham youngster beside her. "We're over here!"

Deirdre had imagined that her arrival had convinced the Fiend to forswear dining on the local miscreant population, at least for the evening. Now her assumption appeared untrue, and she gave an annoyed groan.

"Steady on, Tuppence. Here it comes."

"Must you really…?"

"Shh … child," the Fiend whispered. His tiny feminine hand went briefly to Deirdre's shoulder. "It's not as it appears. Stay here."

"What…?"

By that time, the stranger had turned, briefly regarded her and the Fiend, and moved in their direction in a gait that was uneven and, at first, cautious.

"What?" she again whispered.

The Fiend, who had moved forward, glanced back and mouthed an almost imperceptible, "*Dragur.*"

The hairs on the back of Deirdre's neck shot up.

The Fiend, apparently sensing her continued uncertainty, whispered, "*Wampeer*," before skipping off toward the approaching figure.

At that point, the newcomer who moved toward them was close enough that even in the half-light Deirdre could see a face that was not … well, it wasn't right. It was a twisted visage that was more animal than human, just a faint bit of pallid skin drawn carelessly over vacant eyes and wicked fangs.

In spite of herself, she let out a shriek at the same moment the Fiend's tiny form catapulted across the dozen paces that separated him from the coming *wampeer*—what her one slim bestiary called *homo vampyrus sanguinarius*, the Common Vampire.

That moment of terror wasn't the least bit necessary. The Fiend struck the creature in the middle of its narrow chest and sunk his fangs into the side of the vampire's neck. There was an explosion of wailing and screeching, like a pack of feral cats fighting in an alley, as the vampire spun and jerked in a vain attempt to disengage from the smaller monster that clung to it. A few moments of blurred motion followed before the two collapsed to the ground near a pair of thick wooden bollards. The sound of hissing and growling continued amidst the gruesome noises of rending and tearing flesh, sinew, and viscera.

Deirdre almost instantly found herself bored with the affair, an episode that was all too familiar in recent months. She'd seen the Fiend feast before, and from her book she knew that vampires were solitary hunters. So it was unlikely another would be lurking about. What was it to her that the Fiend had found its snack? At least it wasn't some unfortunate longshoreman or a wandering and homesick inebriate.

Of course, had the Fiend crossed paths with some prowling pederast, which seemed to be the prey for which the creature had been angling, would it have been such a great loss to humanity?

Quite idly, she found herself examining some stone pillars across the way from where the Fiend dined. Vicar Edgemont had mentioned several times the remains of an ancient heathen temple at the docks, and this appeared to be the place. The light still was dreadful, but with the faint glimmer of the distant lantern and what little there was of starlight, she was able to find a series of finely etched lines along the nearest stone column. It wasn't much, but with her fingers as an aid, she was able to make out a few glyphs and sigils. She didn't really understand ancient Trucian, but the Fiend insisted it was a language every learned soul should understand. So, she'd cracked the books, conjugating verbs, practicing syntax, and memorizing those words necessary to make herself competent in the stuff.

In the murk, she only was able to make out a few words here and there, but the exercise so thoroughly engrossed her that time flew past.

The moon was beginning to rise when she was brought back to herself by the sound of smacking lips. She realized a tiny female form was standing beside her and regarding with care the same images as she was.

"We could come back when the light is better," said the miniature Fiend.

"Let's do. How was dinner?"

Several more smacking noises. "Better than I remembered. A faint bit musty, but not the least unpalatable. It's a marvel how one's tastes change over time."

"I've never seen one before."

"A vampire? That's a surprise. They're not quite as common as tax collectors, but nearly so."

"—and I never guessed it was part of your diet."

"Yes. From time to time, I'll have a nibble. And, on reflection, I suppose it's no surprise you haven't seen one. Contrary to what storybooks tell, such creatures have a great deal of trouble passing for human—which is the real reason they seldom are seen during daylight. And 'tis the reason they mostly dwell in the countryside and along the outskirts of small villages."

While the creature talked, the pair had turned their backs on the ruins and had begun their leisurely return through the city, back toward the vicarage that was their temporary home.

In the first shadow through which they passed, the tenor of the Fiend's voice changed, and Deirdre sensed that she now walked beside a man of middling height. From the voice, it probably was Chance Medley, one of the Fiend's regulars. She honestly wasn't certain whether the creature was male or female, or whether such a distinction existed among his kind, but he usually presented himself as a man, and it was as a male that she usually thought of him.

But wait? What had the Fiend said?

"How come I never saw any such vampires in Edwin Township when I was growing up?" she asked. There were few places more rural than Deirdre's home township in the County of Blenheim.

"Of course. Your lovely home's proximity to my barrow," was his reply. "The beasts learned to stay shy of the area."

Well, being neighbors with the Devil had some small benefits after all. That thought led to another. It dawned on Deirdre that in his tussle with the *wampeer* the Fiend had been the first to attack. Devil though he was, the creature was forbidden, by a powerful enchantment, from attacking humans or from otherwise meddling in their affairs—or so he'd told her. It was all part of some ancient arrangement that she scarcely understood.

"I presume vampires don't fall within the bounds of that *gesh* of yours?" she asked.

"Ah! Very astute. You are correct. None of the, um … well, such creatures are not forbidden to me under that compact."

"Creatures? You mean fay folk?"

"That's not a word I've ever used. I'm not even perfectly certain what it means. Let's just say the rule applies only to humans. I cannot raise my hand against a person unless that person first seeks to harm me. But creatures that merely look human? No, that's another story.

Deirdre had known a great many people in her life that wouldn't pass muster as human, but she didn't dwell on that point. Instead, she wordlessly thanked the Fiend for restricting his appetites when he did indulge his penchant for human flesh to those random miscreants and murderers who he managed to gull into attacking him. If the trash needed to be taken out, or so she supposed, one should start with the worst of it.

Truth be told, the Devil wasn't such a bad fellow. There was no doubt about it, many of the softer edges the creature displayed were there for the sole purpose of shielding Deirdre's finer sensibilities. But it wasn't all pretense and mummery. He was especially nice to the weak and to the helpless. He'd never once, in all the time she'd known him, inflicted himself on anyone down on their luck, and he was the kind of fellow who often had a generous word and a farthing or two for those in need.

Hadn't she heard that somewhere before? Some old aphorism? Don't measure your friends on how they treat you—most people are nice to their friends by definition. Measure their worth on how they treat strangers, especially those weaker than themselves.

She sat that thought aside and enjoyed the rest of the stroll.

The creature was a great talker most of the time, and she listened to him natter on until sometime later they finally reached the vicarage and let themselves in through the garden door. It was a pleasant enough walk on an evening that otherwise was fair and balmy. Outside the docks and wharves, the area around Westport was pleasant.

They found Vicar Edgemont asleep in his easy chair when they returned, a book still open across his elderly paunch. Like many geezers Deirdre had known, the old cleric kept an odd schedule and slept like a cat, usually in fits and starts, whenever the spirit moved him. Of course, it was well after dark at that moment, a perfectly reasonable time to be asleep and, more important, to be abed.

Deirdre helped the Fiend, who now bore his more usual guise of the Right Reverend Moorcroft Ainsley, get the dozy septuagenarian to his bed. It took but a few minutes, after which the Fiend went about closing up the vicarage for the night, and Deirdre made sure nothing was left out in the library or the kitchen that might attract vermin.

They met in the vicar's small study, located just off of the library. It still was too early for Deirdre to retire, and the Fiend only feigned sleep from time to time to keep up his disguises. Mostly at night, he kept his own company in the library, reading old books, sipping old madeira, and nibbling on spiced dried peas, his greatest gustatory weakness.

As they often did in the evening, she and the creature chatted some. Deirdre began by reading a letter she'd received earlier in the day from their friend Lady Isabel, who after the campaign season had remained in Mont Clair with part of the royal army.

Isabel was a strange and beautiful woman, a lost traveler from another world, a fact Isabel thought no one knew. But odd duck though the woman was, she was Deirdre's closest and truest human friend, someone who she very much looked forward to seeing in the coming weeks.

The letter mostly was about the comings and goings of the castle. Mont Clair was the family seat of the de Vere clan, one of the most influential families in Albion, one to which the Fiend (or, rather, one of his many guises) claimed relation.

The creature was its usual attentive self when she read aloud of the happenings, general gossip, and personal chatter that Isabel had shared in her missive. It was all very warm and pleasant, which only went to underscore what the Fiend next said when he spoke from out of the blue.

"There's something afoot, Tuppence." The long face of Reverend Ainsley was impassive, with only a slight twist to his lips that sometimes appeared when he was deep in thought. "I've felt it for some time. But now I'm certain of it."

"What?"

He seemed not to notice her words. "It's a feeling that I've had for a while, something in my bones. But the wind has been … fickle of late. And I didn't want to mention anything until I was certain."

"Was it something in the letter?" she asked, picking the thing up and placing it on the table in front of them, as if it now had fangs.

The monster looked at her now as if first seeing her, and a faint smile formed on his lips.

"No, child. Not the letter per se. Just words … hints. It's sometimes difficult to see things without turning them around several times and giving them a nice twist. There's something between the lines when Lady Isabel writes, a subtle something I can't quite grasp."

"What do you think it is?"

"I don't know. But I've heard things on the wind."

The creature spoke sometimes of the wind in that way. Deirdre long before had determined that he didn't mean the breeze, at least not exclusively. When the Fiend spoke of the wind, he spoke of knowing things about which he should not have been able to know.

But was it magic of which the creature spoke?

"There's a reek in the air," the Fiend said when he continued speaking, "a stench I've smelt before." The beast's eyes had again lost focus, and he rose and began pacing slowly about the study as he sometimes did when in thought. "I think there's an Inquisition nigh."

What a terrible, terrible sound that was. Deirdre had heard the word Inquisition before, but she wasn't completely sure what it was. She'd learned a great deal during her months with the Fiend, but every day brought new puzzles. And each moment brought new questions to the things she once thought she knew.

"I'm not perfectly certain," her companion said before she could ask a question. "But from what I've gathered from the wind, and from good common sense, I realize that I erred last year, when I fetched you up your vengeance, at least in the way I went about it. I'd imagined that this Walking God of yours was too lazy and too feckless to take much mind of what I was doing here in faraway Albion. I begin to think I was wrong."

It was yet another issue on which Deirdre could not decide. The previous summer, the creature somehow had managed to gull, trick, and inveigle the entire country into a civil war. The beast had done so (at least ostensibly) on Deirdre's behalf by inducing a half dozen men into attacking him and … well ... bloody carnage followed. But it all seemed so unlikely, the timing and coincidence just too improbable.

She'd several times seen the Fiend do remarkable things, and she'd once even imagined that he'd somehow magicked on her when first they'd met, that in some way she was pivotal to all that had transpired during that time. Now she wasn't sure. It all seemed so distant now.

But the whole idea that someone was upset at the deaths of a handful of Gheet officials? That didn't trouble Deirdre at all. On the contrary, the bloodstained conflict that had erupted afterward was a salve to her soul, if only a tiny one. But the future? What might yet come to pass because of the Fiend's intemperate actions was important.

First things first. She needed to know more.

"What is a...?" she began. "I mean ... I've heard the word before. Is it like the Witchfinders?" In truth, that was another word of which she wasn't perfectly sure of the meaning, but she had to start somewhere.

"Inquisitors and Witchfinders are two sides of the same coin, lass. They both seek to squelch that which is different, one within the church and the other without. They are cruelty incarnate, things that reduce the individual to an object, an expendable afterthought. Either way, it doesn't matter. Inquisitor? Witchfinder? Such are no friends of ours."

2. On Topics Eldritch and Mundane

Such words ordinarily would have been the end of the conversation. Deirdre had learned to read the creature's moods, and she sensed now that he had nothing else to say for the moment on the subject of Inquisitors and Witchfinders.

But she'd also learned something of her own measure, especially when it came to navigating her companion's moods and eccentricities. Sometimes she just needed to push harder, and at other times she needed merely to shift the conversation to some topic close at hand before circling back around. Her direction now was simple. She asked questions.

"There are broad laws against the practice of magic in most every land," the Fiend said after a few minutes of her gentle pestering. It was the first time since she'd been acquainted with the monster that he'd spoken at all of things eldritch. "In theory, the Inquisition was formed to enforce the dogma of the broader Church, but in truth it concerns itself almost entirely with imposing the political authority of the Holy See in places outside Etruscia."

"And magic?" These were things about which Deirdre knew little or nothing, things often spoken of in her youth but never actually seen.

"Of course. There are rules on who may practice such arts, but those are roundly ignored. As long as one's politics are solid, and one has the right friends, casting a cantrip or two is nothing the clergy of any of the various denominations get in a tizzy about. It's accusations of witchcraft, the practice of magic outside the Church's control, that gets most folk to frothing … well, at least in theory."

"So, Witchfinders are worse?"

The creature nibbled a pea and gave her a sidelong glance. "Don't get me wrong. Inquisitions and witch hunts are terrible things, a bane that no sane monarch would ever allow in his demesne. They are each bad in their way, because neither truly seeks anything but senseless and continued extermination. Inquisitors seek heretics, and they always find them … even if they have to manufacture them. And Witchfinders? … Everyone has to justify their wages, Tuppence. A Witchfinder will always find a witch."

"Even if they have to make one up?"

The creature nodded in the affirmative. "A monarch or lord who thinks such things can be managed or controlled is a fool. They always outgrow their mandate, and they invariably seek power for power's sake, often turning on the monarch or the lord who first chartered them when they do. There hasn't been an Inquisitor or a Witchfinder General in Albion in many years. Let's hope it stays that way."

"But you don't think it will?"

"War does funny things. Often belligerents feel casting accusations of heresy or witchcraft will help their cause and weaken that of their enemies. And there is a great deal of pressure from the Holy See to extend their influence here. I know Albion is a land that now follows the New Rite, but that was not always so, and it need not always be so in the future. The Primate in Etruscia has great power … as does his Lord and Master."

The Walking God, she knew the creature to mean. That was another topic upon which Deirdre felt she knew less than she should. These past winter months, she'd been ensconced at the vicarage with the vicar and Reverend Ainsley. Two learned professors of religion, and neither of them had much to say about the Church, religion, doctrine, or scriptures. She'd spent most of her time learning her quadrivium, reading anything and everything she could find time to digest, from mathematics, to logic, to botany and chemistry.

But precious little religion. And positively no magic.

She reached her saturation point on such topics sometime later. The Fiend could shift from laconic to loquacious in a heartbeat, and he continued to gab on about subjects that grew more subtle and esoteric. The end result was that the Church was no friend of theirs. She traveled with the Devil, and it wouldn't matter in the least who caught them. If they were found out, that was that.

Still, she tried her best to remember what he said, so she could think about it and ask more questions later. Knowledge was a gift, as the vicar was fond of saying.

But she soon found herself yawning.

Before she knew it, the Fiend was off in the library sipping madeira and perusing books and she was smacking her lips and opening her eyes on the settee upon which she'd fallen asleep. It was late, and by reflex she muttered the Fiend a goodnight and headed up the stairs to her small chambers. There'd be time enough for Inquisitors and Witchfinders later. Now, sleep. Even she needed it, whether she cared to admit it or not.

As she usually did, she thought about her day as she prepared for slumber. It had been very much a typical day for her, at least typical for the past few months.

After the fight at the Moot the previous summer, she'd spent time with the royal army as it warred against a group of rebel barons led by Etienne de Margot—she still fumed that the man yet drew breath. During that time, the Fiend, in the guise of Alexis de Vere, had been her guide and tutor. Between the skirmishes, battles, and maneuvers, she'd learned much.

Winter was a pause in the campaign season, when armies returned to their respective homes, rested, and healed. Rather than staying at Mont Clair with the de Vere family, she and Sir Alexis traveled west to the coast. The alleged reason for the journey was to deposit Deirdre with Right Reverend Moorcroft Ainsley, so the clergyman might continue the lass's education. But the reverend was just another of the Fiend's many guises— and he had so many.

They'd taken rooms at a local vicarage. According to the Fiend, the vicar there, an elderly member of the Reformed clergy named Baliol Edgemont, was a formidable scholar, a man of great breadth and learning, whose library of 2,000 volumes was one of the largest and best-appointed private holdings in Albion. Many of the manuscripts were rare, some were priceless, and others had been produced through a process the Fiend referred to as "printing," an art that apparently was frowned upon in many parts of the world. It was something of an open secret that the vicar stored an old "printing press"—whatever that was—unused in a shed on the vicarage property, a relic of the septuagenarian's bold and rebellious youth.

It was impossible for Deirdre to think of the vicar without a smile. He was a sweet old bugger, and the man always was eager to help Deirdre with her studies when Reverend Ainsley was unavailable. The two men were like bugs in a rug when together, more often than not, deep in discussion over some minute point of science or some arcane theory of philosophy.

And that was Deirdre's life at the vicarage. The original bargain she'd struck with the Fiend was that she would work as his servant, but the creature seemed indifferent to that service. She cleaned up after herself, of course, and she did for the vicar when she thought he needed it. But the bulk of her time was spent in her studies. It was the first time in her life that she'd had the opportunity to be a full-time student, and she quickly had finished her trivium and moved on to the quadrivium.

And there were other things, loads of other things.

The Fiend was convinced she needed to learn to defend herself. Naturally, she'd fought and wrestled with the other children all her life, and she was a decent mark with a short bow, but several times her mentor had insisted that dark times were coming. And he could not always be there. So, in one or the other of his various guises, he taught her to fight.

Each morning they were up before dawn for a run, followed by a dip in an icy stream—the latter was something she could have done without—and a half-bell of training. They started with the short stick, moved on to the thick leather cosh, and then the knife.

The going was tough at first. She wasn't afraid to throw a punch, but the Fiend insisted that she put her all into striking him with whatever weapon they used of a day. Her reluctance shortly gave way—the Fiend seemed indestructible—and soon she was striking, cutting, stabbing, and coshing him with her every fiber. He made himself an easy target at first, but afterward she needed greater skill and ingenuity to fetch him a successful blow.

But the mundane wasn't enough. The creature insisted that she devise new ways to kill him each day. "A clever mind will always find a way," he would say, "often a new and ingenious one, when it comes to extinguishing others."

To that end, she'd thrown herself into botany. It was part of her quadrivium, and the Fiend earlier in the summer had gifted her a splendid volume of herbalism, *Flora Albionis*, that soon had become her prized possession. The thick codex now was carefully marked and annotated by her own hand and gave the taxonomy of every important plant in Albion, including its uses and indications.

Truth be told, under the Fiend's guidance her volume was as much a poisoner's handbook as it was an apothecary's manual. The Fiend seemed keen that she learn the compounding and uses of poisons.

"You don't have the hands of a strangler," he'd told her more than once, "so poisons might suit you fine." The difference between a panacea and a poison, after all, was just a matter of degree.

Her life very quickly had become a life of the mind. But what was she to expect? Even before they'd arrived at the vicarage, the Fiend forever was taking her about and showing her things. They'd once spent nearly 10 days encamped near a recent battlefield, and the creature each day had returned with her to the same corpse in order for her to get a sense how flesh rotted and decomposed over time.

"Putrefaction and decay are part of life, Tuppence," he often reminded her during that period.

Even now, she and the Fiend regularly would take breaks from their studies to go into the fields and woods surrounding the vicarage and examine this, that, or the other.

Such excursions had seemed without merit at first, but she soon found herself adding notes to her various journals after the outings. She once had thought she knew the plants, animals, and oddities of the outdoors as well as any crofter might, but in the company of the Fiend, a whole new world was open before her. Who would have guessed the maggots that infested the corpse of a horse dead for three days could clean a wound, but those found on the same horse on the fifth day could not? And that the tree moss found on an oak had a different effect on fever than did the precise same moss found on a poplar?

It almost made life pleasant. And from time to time, the busy mental life she led with the reverend and the vicar helped her to forget her pain. But it was always there, waiting for her, loitering in the shadows, especially when she slept. Her nights were weary and uneasy, filled with unpleasant things. But the days at the vicarage started early, and she never was one to sleep much.

Would it never end? Was this to be her lot forevermore? From time-to-time bits of happiness would steal into her life, and a sudden rush of guilt would assail her because of it. She didn't have the right to be happy when those she loved and cherished most were cold in the earth.

No, the torment didn't end. There always seemed to be something new on the horizon.

As the Fiend had foretold, the chaos that erupted at the Moot on the previous summer had ushered in changes. Some of them were good. There was a time not long past when the Surrey folk of many counties were not allowed even to bear arms, lest they face the wrath of their Gheet neighbors. But a product of the war was that the king had called up the levies of every community to defend the crown. Now Surrey infantry and archers marched beside Gheet cavalry in service to the realm.

Two months into the campaign season, a group of Surrey archers had marched past the squadron with which she traveled. Foremost among the bowmen was Deirdre's own father, a man who she had cursed when she'd last seen him. There was no question he saw her, dressed in the fashion of a Gheet lady, riding a fine palfrey amid a knot of Gheet knights and nobles.

The man said not a word to her, didn't even acknowledge her existence. He marched by with his company. It thereafter had been many days before Deirdre again could....

She stopped and took a seat on her bed. It was a few moments before she steadied herself. Even after six months, it was too painful to recall.

Time for bed.

3. The Inquisitors

Deirdre's best friend since her arrival in Westport was a half-Gheet girl named Vivian Story, a small, sweet, and animated being with a wicked sense of humor that she kept carefully concealed behind a pair of large and innocent eyes. The kid was a living delight, the only person she'd met in many months who could draw Deirdre from her shell.

On the day following their most recent chat, the Fiend declared a study holiday. He did that once every 10 days or so, claiming that socializing was the key to perfectly balanced humors. On such days, Deirdre could do as she wished, but he forbade her from lurking about the library, at least during daylight time.

As always, she'd opted to seek out Vivian. And, as often was the case, the kid was free to spend her day idling with Deirdre. The youngster's parents owned a dry goods store in Westport frequented by most every ship that made its way into the port. Vivian was still young enough to merit playtime, and Deirdre being under the charge of a clergyman, Vivian's folks saw her as suitable company for their darling daughter.

But gawd, the things she and Vivian said to one another.

Deirdre didn't fault Vivian for having a Gheet mother. It was the way of things in the city, as it was throughout much of the north. In the south of Albion, those peoples were like two armed camps. But elsewhere, Surrey folk and Gheet intermarried freely and had done so since … well, even Vicar Edgemont had a Gheet grandfather, and he was a man in his 70s.

Here in the city, folk even looked different. She'd never seen so many blue and grey eyes. And folk there weren't so dark as the Gheet, nor so ruddy as the Surrey. The vicar said the place had been a port from before the coming of the Gelts or the invasion of the Etruscians, even before people had begun to write. Deirdre had seen some incredibly old books in the vicarage library, so that must have been an awfully long time ago.

The result was that folks had traveled to Westport from all over the world, and they'd brought their seed with them and left it when they departed. And what a place it was. She'd never imagined a place so big and crowded. It was like a dense mountain forest of buildings and people. And the smell … whew. Not so bad as the docks, but the waterline wasn't so far away that they didn't occasionally get a whiff of that. She hadn't imagined anything could smell worse than a fresh cowpie, or a rotting corpse.

The Fiend had her on a generous allowance, so she and Vivian whiled away the early morning browsing and nibbling along the shops and stalls of the Grand Market, the busiest spot in the city, just off the Postern Gates that led to the mudflats north of the outer walls. There always was a chance of cutpurses and snatchers, of course, but during the daytime that part of the city was passably safe for two young girls to amble alone.

As they walked, they talked. Vivian didn't think she'd ever be big enough to have children. The lass was 18 months Deirdre's junior, but barely reached the top of her shoulder. The subject of marriage and mothering came up time and again with the two, as it would. Deirdre was past the age when her parents would have begun to explore paring her off. And Vivian was not far behind.

But such a thing now?

No. Now the subject made her sad. She'd never doubted she would marry and have children. It was the way of things. But now? No, probably not. In fact, the thought of children frightened her to such a degree that she couldn't even properly think about the subject.

But she went along with Vivian out of politeness. Besides, the kid was funny. Much of their chatter concerned, "the milch cow," as Vivian had nicknamed her older sister. At age 19, the elder Story daughter already had four children and one on the way. All of the children were alive and healthy—a minor miracle that—so it was a subject suitable for mirth. Good fortune was to be met with good humor.

"You don't have the hips for it," Vivian told her as they nibbled on cinnamon cakes near the silver merchants' stalls.

"I doubt your sister did before she went heavy the first time. They have a way of spreading."

The kid made one of her many faces. "Mm … I don't remember that far back."

"It was only five years." Deirdre had seen the Fiend change the subject so often that now it was second nature for her. "Besides, I don't need hips. I've decided on a life of the mind."

"Of the what of the what?"

"Reverend Ainsley says I'll make a great scholar one day if I apply myself." It was true. Women scholars were few, but neither were they uncommon. She liked the idea of, "a life of the mind," as she several times had heard the vicar and the Fiend refer to scholarly pursuits. It suited her.

"Ugh. Mother Story has nearly given up teaching me my numbers. But she says it's all that small people are good for, bookkeeping."

"I think she's just teasing you. You're not that small."

"Are you suggesting I merely use my size as an excuse to get out of work?"

"Yes."

"Fair enough."

None of that was true, of course. All of Vivian's brothers had apprenticed with shipmasters, and her older sister had scant interest in the business. Their mother and father still were young and healthy, but like as not Vivian one day would run the family enterprise. And if the kid's gift for haggling in the market was any indication, she had an exceptionally good head for numbers.

"Is the preacher your father?" asked Vivian from the blue.

"Reverend Ainsley?" She nearly laughed at the thought. "Heavens no."

"Hope you don't mind me asking … but you know, preachers and all. They do have a reputation."

"Not this one." She realized Vivian was waiting for her to say more. "He's, um … a friend of my father." More silence. Deirdre opted to ride it out. It was a wonder the subject hadn't come up over the past few months.

"So, what does your father do?" Vivian asked at last.

"He's a … well, he isn't *really* my father. After I lost my family, he took me in. He's like a father."

"And what does this like a father do?"

"He's a knight."

A sharp intake of breath. There it was. The distinction between the gentry and the common wasn't so great in the city as it was in the countryside where Deirdre was raised, but that difference still existed in the city. Educated and prosperous though they may be, the Story family were commoners. It was odd. In the many months she'd known the Fiend and travelled with his alter ego, Alexis de Vere, this was the first time the distinction had become an issue.

Of course, there was nothing gentrified in Deirdre's manners. Perhaps that was the reason for the sidelong and somewhat comical look Vivian gave her now.

"What's your father's name?" Vivian asked in all innocence.

"Sir Alexis." The mild way in which Vivian looked heavenward as she listened told Deirdre there would be no putting her off further. She had to clear her throat before she spoke. "Sir Alexis de Vere."

The younger girl let out a short and sharp shriek, as if a mouse had just leapt on her foot.

"It's OK," Deirdre reassured her.

"*You're a de Vere?*" her friend whispered.

"Well … yes. But I didn't mean to."

How had it not occurred to Deirdre that she one day would have this conversation? And yet, the whole thing was as much a surprise for her as it was for Vivian. Baron William de Vere, Sir Alexis's ersatz cousin, was the paramount lord in this part of western Albion and one of the most influential men in the land. It never before had dawned on Deirdre that when the baron had pronounced her to be part of his family … well, that was it. She was from that moment forward a de Vere.

"So …," began Vivian.

"Sir Alexis and the baron are cousins." Actually, they weren't, she wanted to say. But the Fiend and his machinations. She definitely didn't feel baronial, and she didn't understand Gheet custom well enough to explain the proper legalities of her supposed familial situation.

Happily, her companion's face lit up at the realization she wasn't dealing with a direct heir to the title, and she gave a wicked smile. "So, you're not going to have my head off for failing to curtsey?"

"I'm not even sure I'd know how to curtsey."

Those few moments of awkwardness passed in but a moment. Such was Vivian's nature. She was a sweet and lighthearted thing that didn't seem suited for the coarse and gritty world in which they lived.

As they went about their gamboling, Deirdre wondered if this conversation was something she should mention to the Fiend. He'd never told her to veil her identity, but it was part of the creature's personality to hide and to disguise his ways. No. He'd never expressly told Deirdre anything, but maybe she shouldn't have mentioned the de Vere name, even to a friend.

Her thoughts were interrupted by a short scream not too far distant. That cry was followed by another. Down near the Small Gate, several armored men emerged on horseback, and soon people were running. She grabbed Vivian by the hand and by reflex pulled her close.

In mere moments, more troops arrived, each draped in a livery unlike any she'd ever seen. And they were grabbing people. From the look of it, young women and girls.

She turned to run and dragged Vivian with her when she did. Her friend didn't resist, and soon both were dashing at best speed back toward the Sunder Gate, the portal that led through the tradesmen's alleys back to the Main Gate and thence down the High Road to the vicarage.

But they traveled fewer than 30 paces when more men emerged from the Sunder Gate, blocking their way. These soldiers seemed to be everywhere, and they were not the men of the watch, who seemed curiously absent. She felt a hard pull against her right hand and heard a distant voice—Vivian's voice—pleading with her to follow.

The place was complete pandemonium.

When they headed toward Farriers' Lane, ducking and dodging fleeing townsfolk, the two nearly collided with a small group of mounted men, forcing her and Vivian to stop and very nearly causing them to fall to the ground in the process.

She got but a glimpse, but this group was different. Rather than armor and tabards, this lot wore flat grey robes that she'd come to associate with clergymen of the Old Rite. The wrinkled faces and shaved pates told her she was correct. One of the aged crew, the one farthest forward, fastened a cruel gaze on her and hollered toward a knot of nearby soldiers in a language she did not understand.

She was off in a flash, and soon was running nearly even with Vivian. Heyman House, she thought. That must be Vivian's destination. The abandoned home was a place her friend had shown her. The broken windows and half-finished outdoor staircase made easy climbing, and local youth used it to scramble onto the high rooftops. The alley to the place was a dead end, so no soldiers blocked their way, but from behind them she caught the sound of rattling tack and clinking armor.

"Hurry!" she screamed with all the voice she was able.

"I ... I ...," was Vivian's breathless reply.

Something swiped at her hair, and the sound of an armored man cursing and falling pushed her onward. By then, her legs were numb and her lungs straining. Somehow, tiny Vivian managed to stay ahead of her, no doubt egged on by her terror.

Another hand grabbed at Deirdre's shoulder, and she stopped, pivoted, and drove her thumb into the nearest man's eye, before slipping from his fumbling grasp and continuing her course. Ahead, Heyman House was just around the corner.

She rounded the bend at a dead run, only to see Vivian leaping vainly to grab the nearest handhold. The kid was too short to make the first part of the climb on her own, so Deirdre grabbed her without preamble and lifted and shoved her toward the stairway ledge before scampering up after.

Deirdre was halfway up when a hand grabbed her right ankle. She lashed out with her left leg as hard as she was able, catching something soft on her heel, but she managed to scurry only another few feet before more hands clutched her legs and hauled her back. Above, she saw Vivian slip onto the nearest rooftop, and when she felt herself dragged back down to street level, her hand shot into her left sleeve and yanked out her cosh. With her trusty weapon, she began to flail at everything around her.

4. A Maiden of Mont Clair

It was yet another morning that Isabel had to force herself out of bed. It wasn't that she didn't look forward to the day. Even her morning kitchen chores were pleasant, and a day spent reading in the baron's library had come to mean a great deal to her.

She simply hadn't been feeling well, an ongoing malaise that first had settled on her in the late fall, about the time she last had seen Lady Dierdre and Sir Alexis. There was no symptom on which she could lay a finger beyond her blasé feeling and an omnipresent achiness and weariness, but it wouldn't let her go. Since her inexplicable arrival in Albion two years before, she several times had been ill, violently so more than once, but this bout of frail health just lingered.

It so far wasn't a thing that would justify loafing about. So, she did her morning preparations, dressed herself, and began her day.

Everyone who resided at the castle worked, from the meekest to the mightiest, but nothing she'd so far been asked to do had been onerous. She originally had remained at Mont Clair to help tend to those injured during the war, however, all but a few chronic cases had recovered and moved on. Now she tended to her chores at the castle and took her leisure with family and guests.

It had occurred to her that, for all their cultural shortcomings, the Gheet were serious about adoption and did not distinguish between children of blood and children by oath. Children were children, and even if the baron scarcely was 10 years her senior, she was his daughter in the eyes of the law. In this land, she was Isabel Castellan no longer, but Isabel de Vere. Albion was a brutal and a violent land, but she felt at home and safe with the de Vere family, a people who treated her as one of their own.

She needed that. Her first year in Albion had been a terror, and she'd spent so much time struggling with her new situation that it was possible to forget about ever again seeing her former home and her old friends. Her previous life in Savannah, Georgia, was gone, and she likely never would get it back.

But God, how she missed her mom, ever more with the passing of time. And what must her mother be enduring back home? These last months, as Isabel's fears for her own safety slowly had abated, the thoughts of the worry and the anguish felt by those she'd left behind had begun to pain her. The new friends and adopted family she'd found in Albion helped sooth that ache, even if just a little.

Her greatest pleasure, though, she found in the solitary pursuit of reading. But even that wasn't as it seemed in Albion, where reading often was treated as a collective pursuit. Many was the evening she'd spent in the family apartments at the castle listening to others read aloud from letters and books, or sometimes reading aloud herself to the gentle corrections and stifled chuckles of family members. She wasn't from this world, and the glyphs that formed the writing system of the common language sometimes escaped her. Even after nearly two years in this land, simple pronunciations occasionally felt like tongue twisters to her.

But it was good practice, and with every passing day she felt more at home. The baron was generous with his library, and the hours she spent reading alone there had helped her learn more about the land in which she lived. Knowing her a stranger—she told any who asked that she was from the distant country of Evaria—members of the baron's small staff had guided her toward the most informative books on the subject of Albion and its people. The variety and depth of some of the manuscripts she'd read simply was remarkable.

Her latest mania, though, had little to do with books, at least not directly. She'd begun to hear talk a few weeks before about a search of some sort, a hunt for something precious and long lost. It took some time for it to become clear that there was some sort of Holy Quest afoot.

Really? That was her first thought. *Really?*

There was nothing fairytale or enchanted about Albion. It was a hard, brutal, and coarse land, full of rough and often violent people. Never would she think of this benighted place in such romantic and glamorous terms.

Yet something in that talk seized her thoughts and quickened her imagination. A Holy Quest. Once it became clear that such a thing was being spoken of, she began to ask questions, tentatively at first. She honestly didn't know much about religion in this place, and her first thought was that she might have a chance to see Reverend Ainsley when Deirdre returned from Westport in a few weeks. He was a wonderful and learned man, and a great guide. Barring that, she hoped Sir Alexis might be a source of wisdom. Soldier though he was, he was thoughtful and had spent many years in the Holy Land.

Until such a time, she often spoke with the young cleric who tended the castle chapel, a strange fellow named Emmet Naseby, a friar of some sort. The young man had led her to a number of texts on religion and faith in

Albion, and in recent weeks she'd begun to challenge herself to understand them. It was a rough start, but she was determined to keep trying.

But duty called, and she made her way down the tower to the castle kitchens to get to her chores. The whole affair was quite nice. The kitchens were far tidier and more hygienic than she would have imagined, and the staff was pleasant and kind.

In fact, the community that comprised those who lived in Mont Clair was nothing at all as she would have imagined. She'd been to a number of manor houses and strongholds since her arrival in Albion, including the sturdy blockhouse of her first protector, a landed knight named Sir Utrecht Simon. But Mont Clair was enormous, a broad and lofty stone fortress set upon a single stone promontory in the midst of a vast fertile valley. Her first sight of the place, months before, nearly had taken her breath away.

And the people? She'd expected a greater distinction between noble and common, as she had seen in other parts of the country. At Mont Clair, everyone worked side by side. True, the baron and his wife spent far more time working at their books than as field hands, but everyone, including the baron himself, did some type of manual labor. And everyone worked hard, without being told to do so.

The upshot was that the distinction between the gentry and the commonfolk at the castle was much less than one would have expected. The nobles lived better lives, but even the castle servants ate, dressed, and lived well. The apartments in which the baron and his family resided were pleasant and comfortable, but not significantly finer than those of a scullery maid or a stableman.

Everyone there seemed happy.

True, Baroness Elise sometimes was short with servants in a way that made Isabel cringe, but the woman was far more tolerant and liberal than most nobles she'd observed, and it was the usual custom for the baroness to give orders through two senior servants, Sylvie, the Mistress of the Keys, or Ballard, the Chamberlain.

And the castle and its estates were the domain of the baroness. As near as Isabel could tell, the baron had little to do with the running of the property. The baroness made the decisions, kept the books, and allocated all resources. In hindsight, that seemed to be the case for other, smaller estates that Isabel had visited. It was another of the many interesting and unexpected notions she'd encountered in this land.

Making her way into the kitchen now, Isabel began her chores without a word from Maude, the head cook. The woman was hard, lean, and wrinkled, somewhere between 40 and 90 years of age. Isabel several times had observed Maude scolding the baron's children as if they were her own.

The daughters of the family might be a scant bit haughty, and the sons a skosh too cocky, but no one in the de Vere family was spoiled.

"Are you not with the sisters today?" asked Emelie, one of the apprentice cooks, as Isabel took a seat on a bench next to her and began shelling peas.

"Tomorrow. It's only once a week now."

"That's good news," the cook said, knocking the table thrice with a single knuckle. "Our brave boys."

For the first month of the winter, Isabel's daily chores were at St. Elmira, a small convent located at the foot of the mount. It was there that the most seriously injured knights and men-at-arms had received their treatment. Isabel was proud of her work there. A knowledge of basic hygiene went a long way, and the time she spent working with the crofters near Sir Utrecht's stronghold had taught her something about local herbs and medicines. She had learned much since.

And her stomach for bloodshed was much greater than it had been. After more than five months of campaigning, she had seen and treated all manner of ghastly wounds. Blood no longer troubled her as once it had. And she also was proud to say that the lads in her ward had survived and thrived, all save a few whose wounds likely could not have been treated with success in even the best hospital. Only a small handful now remained at the convent under the care of the sisters, and none needed her regular attention.

Her careful and compassionate treatment of the wounded had earned her much attention from the knights and men in service to the baron. She felt herself blush at the thought of it, and a smile crept onto her face as she worked. There was little vanity in her. She now was the legal daughter of a great lord and was unmarried. No doubt, many of her admirers saw her as a fine prospective partner for that reason alone.

Foremost among her admirers, though, was one knight whose ardor she was certain was sincere. Isabel and Deirdre had saved the life of Sir Armand de Bois-Guilbert during the battle at the Moot eight months earlier, and the man had since recovered and taken a place as a household knight with Baron William. Sir Armand now saw himself as her protector.

At first, Isabel wasn't certain what to make of any of it, neither the attention nor the many small gifts she received from former patients and others. Eventually, she sought the guidance of Baroness Elise. The woman could be aloof, but there also was a great common sense in her, and it was widely known Isabel was not from Albion. The baroness was a pureblood Gheet from Ghitland, and she understood the way of things.

"Among our people," the baroness told her, "men give women gifts all the time. You owe them nothing in return, not even a smile. It's our way." The aristocrat afterward broke into a gentle laugh when Isabel broached the subject of Sir Armand. "He's a good man, but a poor match for any woman. A great soldier, one of the most fearsome in Albion, but far too kindhearted."

Isabel still wasn't sure she understood any of that. Why was kindheartedness a shortcoming? If it was, what was she to do about it? Armand was a good fellow, and he wasn't bad looking when he cleaned himself up a bit. He just wasn't for her.

The fact she did not feel compelled to find a suitor was a cause of great relief in itself. Not only did accepting gifts not oblige her to anyone, but it was a further boon to find that the Gheet did not go for arranged marriages as the Surrey folk often did, not even among the gentry. Certainly, parents took a hand in such decisions, and the baroness had even suggested a few likely matches, but there was no pressure that she select any specific person or, for that matter, that she marry at all.

She felt herself blushing again and looked around to be sure no one had noticed. OK. She had to be honest with herself. She spent far more time than was healthy thinking about Alexis de Vere, her friend and protector. There was something just so good, decent, and honest about the man. He wasn't pretty, but there was a rugged beauty to his ugly face. With Alexis de Vere, you knew what you were getting.

OK, back to the peas.

———

Her work of the morning didn't take a great deal of time, and by 9:30 or so Isabel was back at her books. There were a few more things with which she would need to help in the afternoon, but for now she was on her own. She stopped first and said hello to Birdy, a servant who Sir Alexis had left behind to be at her disposal, and gave him a few errands to run. Afterward, she passed by the baron's study and collected a book upon which she'd been practicing.

It was, as near as she could tell, a book of prophecy. She wasn't completely convinced she believed in such things, but, what the hell, this was Albion. And despite some early setbacks, it wasn't a terribly hard read.

The language in which the tome was written was an archaic form of the common tongue of Albion, which meant that it was somewhat like

English. Better still, the script in which the thing was written, much to her delight, looked very much like the Latin Alphabet. Several letters were different, and several more, if Friar Emmet was to be believed, were pronounced in ways peculiar to that language. Much like English, enunciation often was based on context within a phrase or a sentence.

Occasionally she was at a complete loss and had adopted a few tricks to aid in her understanding. The most important was simply to read passages aloud, as the friar frequently had urged her to do. Such reading was so common in Albion that she'd noticed that native speakers moved their lips even when they read silently. It couldn't hurt.

She spent the rest of the morning next to a narrow window in the library, reading aloud those passages that she already had fully figured out. Oddly enough, it seemed to help, and over the course of the early afternoon she pushed through five more pages of the finely penned manuscript. She didn't comprehend all of it, but it was a huge breakthrough. She wanted to understand how such things worked, or at least how they were purported to work.

And such reading was a great help in allowing her to figure out the Quest.

It wasn't easy to get the story straight, but the idea of a Quest appeared to have been born some months earlier at a place called the Priory of Saint Lucien. She had to ask a few questions to discover what an anchorite was, but it appeared that a young cleric who had walled himself into the tomb of some long-dead saint had begun to have visions of a weapon that could destroy evil. Isabel didn't get paid to understand such things, but a number of clerics at the priory affirmed through diligent archival research that such a thing jibed with earlier prophecies, some dating back a thousand or more years.

Was any of that to be believed? The clergy appeared to think so, though when they brought the issue to the baron, he was skeptical. In fact, Isabel very nearly thought she saw the man roll his eyes at one point when the subject was broached before him. Of course—well, it wouldn't be fair to say the baron had strained relations with the local bishop of the Reformed Church, but to her eye their interactions were terse and polite. The baron was a practical man.

But the story of the Quest had a life of its own. In recent weeks, the idea entered into every conversation to which Isabel had been privy. People spoke of a great weapon, a Glaive, they called it, that could slay the Other One. That was another point at which things got fuzzy for her.

She knew something of the Walking God, a being to whom Reverend Ainsley first had introduced her in a concise way. The Deity of this world was very much like a great mischievous Santa Claus, a being who traveled throughout the land, incognito, doing good deeds, spreading justice, and chastening malefactors.

The Other One, now, that was different. People didn't use the name Devil to describe the Other One—at least they hadn't done so in Isabel's presence. But the name "Devil" often was used in common parlance. "Devil take it," or "Devil's own luck," or "the Devil only knows," were phrases she'd often heard muttered when people were especially irritated.

No, she'd never heard that name applied to the Other One. But she knew she'd hit paydirt when once, in a moment of curiosity, she asked Friar Emmet if the Devil and the Other One were the same creature. The startled cleric waved her to silence, and they never spoke of the subject again.

Well now.

She hoped the local superstitions weren't rubbing off on her. There was no question that beliefs, like panic, were contagious. When everyone around you believes something to their core, when even a learned cleric is too frightened of the boogeyman to speak its name aloud, it was awfully hard not to get caught up in the collective anxiety.

Indeed, a few things had occurred lately, things that left her feeling anxious and a scant bit worried. The most profound was the sense she'd had over recent weeks that she was being watched.

Of course, she had her admirers, some of whom didn't even try to hide the fact that they were pretending not to watch her. Lord, it was like junior high school.

No, it wasn't that.

It began with a simple feeling, that sensation a person gets when they feel that eyes are upon them. And then on several occasions she thought she saw someone. But she could never explain that sensation, not even to herself. After living in the castle for almost three months, she knew by sight most everyone who had business there. The figure she'd glimpsed always was elusive, and she couldn't describe the person beyond the sense that he, or she, was clad in grey robes like those worn by mendicant friars.

She was half convinced that she was just imagining things. Her reasoning mind told her a mysterious figure was just the manifestation of her anxiety and of the general sense of illness and malaise that had beset her of late.

But the other part of her? ... Well, no. She wouldn't indulge her unreasoning mind.

Perhaps it was just a stray friar she'd glimpsed on those occasions. After all, there were a great many mendicant friars in Albion from any number of sects, orders, and chapterhouses. The land seemed positively infested by them, and they forever were coming and going, as one would expect mendicants to do.

She'd come to discover, in fact, that such widescale peregrinations were a central element of religion in Albion. Pilgrimage routes were everywhere—and that was quite literally *everywhere*. Routes great and small crisscrossed both the countryside and the cities.

But what was one to expect from a religion whose central character was a Walking God? Pious folk of Albion, Gheet and Surrey alike, were perpetually walking places. Some pilgrimage routes were short, the type that might be traversed in a number of minutes. Others required the devotion of many weeks. And they were all over the place, especially along lakes, roads, rivers, and dells. One had a hard time going anywhere in the country without inadvertently following the "Way" of Saint Such and Such, or the "Path" of Saint What's Her Name, or the "Trace" of the Blessed Whazzit.

Small wonder that shoes, stockings, and walking sticks were considered especially auspicious gifts, and the only tradespeople seen as fit company for the gentry were cobblers. To that end, she had acquired several pair of remarkably good shoes and boots of late from her various admirers.

No, it probably was just some itinerant friar that she'd glimpsed, if she indeed had glimpsed anyone at all.

It was a strange world she'd landed in. Quite a bit like her own world in ways, but it was filled with odd ideas and peculiar notions. It would be nice to see her closest friends again.

5. In Durance Vile

Her nose got the worst of it, an affront she might have endured were it not for the laughter.

The first blow Deirdre delivered with her cosh took the three men who'd grabbed her completely by surprise, but as hard as she'd delivered that swing, it only caught the shortest of the three soldiers on the cheek rather than on his temple as she'd intended. The fellow staggered back for a moment, but he soon rejoined his friends in subduing her, and the remainder of her blows fell on the helmets and armor of the laughing and taunting soldiers.

They were not gentle with her even after she'd been disarmed, and the result was that she had a bloody nose and no doubt a fair number of bruises on her face and body. She'd check on that later, but she didn't know when. The men had wasted no time in hustling her from the area around the market and throwing her into a high cell with 20 or so other young women, all of whom looked to be between the ages of 12 and 25.

My heavens, she was angry, spitting angry, cursing angry. It was all she could do to keep from biting one of her cellmates.

Her ill humor drew the unpleasant glances of her fellow prisoners. No surprise that. She'd seen fear in people many times before, and nothing makes a person so angry as seeing a fellow victim who doesn't share that fear. Not that Deirdre wasn't afraid. She was terrified. But she wasn't about to share that fact. Because she wasn't without hope.

First, she kept her wits about her. She'd seen too much in the last year to allow a few thugs to throw her from her game. As near as she could tell, they'd imprisoned her and the others at an abandoned monastery not too far from the Postern Gates. She was close to the vicarage, and if she had even half a chance, she still might win her freedom.

Second, she had the Fiend. The creature wasn't any sort of augury, but events in the city had been complete and utter turmoil. Such chaos could not have escaped the monster's attention. He would come for her. Of that she was certain. But when would that be? And what would be done to her until then?

She refused to bleat and to cry like the other sobbing prisoners. But there wasn't much else she could think to do. She tested the bars of the cell door, explored the various corners of their high and narrow prison, and even shimmied up the wall to peek out the window slit. There was nothing to see, and some of her fellows hissed at her to stop, worried that it would anger the guards.

Small chance of that. Several times, passing guards had bawled at them in heavy accents to keep the noise down, but Deirdre and the others mostly were ignored. Why would the guards trouble themselves? They had the lasses where they wanted them, behind sturdy bars. No need to do anything further.

It was only after she'd examined and rejected her various options for escape that Deirdre began to ponder. What was all this about? Were they being abducted by slavers? Had the troops of Etienne de Margot sacked the city? Had the war come to Westport at last?

None of that seemed right. The men were soldiers, not pirates. Worse, they weren't even soldiers from Albion. The armor wasn't right, and she'd never seen such livery. More to the point, she hadn't understood a word the men had said. The Gheet, even those from Ghitland, spoke the same basic language as the Surrey. Their accents sometimes were heavy, and they occasionally said strange things, but Deirdre understood them for the most part.

And the men in grey! That should have been her first warning. Reformed preachers, monks, and friars sometimes dressed funny, but an Unreformed preacher dressed much like anyone else, save in more somber tones. The men she'd seen in the square were priests of the Old Rite. She remembered the hideous face of the man who led them, a cruel face that seemed half again too large for his body.

Were these the troops of the Inquisition? Given the creature's talk from the previous evening, it seemed likely they were. Of course, the Fiend had seemed uncertain whether an Inquisition or anything like it might come to pass. What had he said? The wind was being fickle? It wasn't clear what that meant.

Without question, the creature knew things he should not. But neither was he all-seeing.

Well, she hoped he was able to see where she was at that moment and was willing to do something about it. Unless, of course, he'd fallen victim to the Inquisitors as well? She long before had reasoned out that the Fiend wasn't indestructible; he'd even alluded to his mortality at times. Elsewise, he wouldn't need to depend on secrecy and subterfuge as he so often did.

No. Fear of something kept him on his toes. Was the Inquisition that thing he feared?

Was her so-called friend and protector even at that moment astride a fast horse pointed south? Heading for balmier climes and safer pastures? He was the Devil, after all. Could such a creature truly ever be trusted?

She continued to pace and to ponder that issue, but less than a quarter bell after the last of the prisoners had been placed in the cell, the guards came and began to take the first of the young ladies away. They appeared to grab them in no particular order, and not long afterward the screaming began.

And those shrieks were not the mere unhappy bleating of the frightened. The wails that erupted in the distance were the bloodcurdling screeches of those truly and deeply in pain. Was this not the thing for which the Inquisition was famous?

The guards came several times more, and, to their credit, some of the young women—Deirdre among them—attempted to fight back and to prevent their comrades from being dragged away. But they were met again with the blows and curses of the guards. The men showed no mercy, only sneering cruelty.

This wretched state of affairs went on for nearly a full bell, with the guards occasionally returning to drag off another victim or two. It soon became evident that Deirdre and the others who first had fought back against the guards were being left for last, a kind of macabre cruelty in itself.

She was terrified. Her nose hurt, her body ached, and she found herself trembling as if from the cold. This was not how things were going to end for her. She needed to reach down deep and to find the resolve to escape this nightmare. Her only reprieve came at about midday, when the screaming subsided, and the guards stopped coming.

There was a moment of silence when she sniffed the air. The fools had stopped whatever barbaric madness they were conducting in order to....

"What in the...!?" she nearly screamed when the realization came to her. They were having their bloody supper!

That's when she saw the girl on the other side of the bars. Was this lass one of their number come back to tell them it all was a lark? That it was all just a huge joke? ... Then she looked closer. The young woman outside the cell was fiddling with the door. The newcomer looked very much like Deirdre's dead sister Fiona, so tall and so pretty, and a lump rose in Deirdre's throat at the thought that someone she so loved was there for her in her final moments. Her heart wept with pain and joy.

"I own myself an ass, Tuppence," said her sister's doppelgänger. "What sort of teacher doesn't instruct a prized pupil on how to pick a simple lock?"

The door swung open, and Deirdre realized that it wasn't Fiona she was facing, but her own double. The young creature before her resembled Deirdre in every way, even down to the clothes she was wearing.

"Get on with it, child," the Fiend told her, before pointing to the other two girls who remained in the cell. "And take your new friends with you. Up the hall, down the stairs, and out the kitchen door."

"Wh … what?" said Deirdre, still confused.

"Go!" he hissed, again in a young woman's voice. "Stay out of sight and meet me at our spot. Whatever you do, don't go back to the vicarage. I'll be along. Now go!"

Without thinking, Deirdre grabbed the hands of the two remaining prisoners and half dragged them out the cell door. Soon the three were hurtling up the hall and down the stairs. They only paused long enough to allow a few workers to pass before bolting out the rear door to the kitchen and off the loading dock. It took less time than it did to count 30 for them to make it out an open side gate and out onto the flats beyond the outer wall.

Deirdre turned north and ran faster than she'd ever run in her life.

———

She lost track of her two companions soon after reaching the cover of the first trees. The lasses were free, so it was up to them to find their ways home. But a heaving and exhausted Deirdre slackened her pace thereafter.

She knew the spot to which the Fiend had referred. They kept their horses stabled in an out-of-the-way building not far from the beach, amid the salt marshes. It was a hard place to find for anyone who didn't know the paths. And it was far enough from the vicarage that no one would associate the place with them. The Fiend was cunning. He always had a plan to get out of trouble, sometimes two or three.

But it took some time for her to make her way to her goal. Several times she was forced to stop and to go to ground for fear of being seen. It wasn't soldiers that she'd spied, but there was no need for passing strangers to gab about the fleeing girl they'd seen. That was how trouble started.

It was well into midafternoon when, finally, she reached her destination, and her first action was to check on the horses, after which she took a long draw of wine from the supply that they kept there and cleaned herself up a mite. Their getaway gear did not consist of much, just a change of clothes, their horses, saddles and tack, and enough water and rations to last them a week or so on the road. Of course, there was some wine. One could never depend on finding good water.

After a short break, she began to prepare the animals and to pack their equipment. The food they stored in several large amphorae seemed to be in good shape, and nothing had gotten into it. The animals appeared sassy and healthy. The only trouble was the Fiend's mount, which always looked at Deirdre as if she were a passing vagrant. Her own gentle palfrey was as amiable as always.

There was no doubt they were departing. The Fiend would not have sent her to their place otherwise. But it was still several weeks before they'd planned on returning to Mont Clair to rejoin the army. Had the creature developed other plans? How much had this attack thrown things into disarray?

She couldn't lie to herself. She still was frightened. But the longer she waited for the creature, the more her fear shifted to annoyance and then again to outright anger. Who were these people, these foreigners, who thought they could come to her home and abduct and abuse people?

For the first time, she thought of sweet Vivian and prayed desperately to a god who did not exist that her friend had made it to safety.

There wasn't any great worry. The rooftops were tough going for anyone not as nimble footed as a child. Certainly, no soldiers in heavy armor could have followed the gentle kid onto the highest peaks of the city. But the very idea of her sweet friend being harassed or harmed in some way set an ugly fire to burning in Deirdre's belly.

She hoped very much to see Vivian again one day, but at that moment she would have settled for knowing the little kid was safe … and for skinning some Inquisitors.

Blah, she thought after another bout of pacing. She should have left something to read with their saddlebags. That would take her mind off things.

Evening rapidly was approaching when the Fiend again made his appearance. He no longer was Deirdre's twin, but now sported the familiar form of Chance Medley, the rambling reprobate and conman the Fiend used to teach her the skills any hustler or cheat needed to know.

Despite the ill timing of things, the creature appeared to be in high spirits, which she took to mean that he'd dined on one or more of her captors. She didn't ask, but she'd seen the signs before. It appeared more than half obvious that the Fiend supped on the chitlins of his enemies less for sustenance and more for the way such a diet elevated his mood. Such a repast seemed merely a type of intoxicant for him.

No matter that now. She was feeling more her normal self, still sore but less anxious.

"Is it time for a class in lock picking, then?" she called out.

The Fiend laughed. "I'll rectify that shortcoming in the curriculum soon enough, but we need to away first. Have you seen anyone?"

"Some passersby on my way here."

"But no one since?"

"No."

"Good. We can wait till dark then."

"What's happened?" she asked. This time she wouldn't let him slip away or change the subject as he often did.

"As I feared. Though I must admit, I can lay no claim to the timing. It shocked me as much as it did you that the Holy See acted when it did, and in broad daylight too. It was a bold move, one of which I hadn't imagined them capable."

"What did you do after … um?"

"Don't worry about what I did. Are you well?"

"I'm fine. Frightened, angry, but …," she began. "Wait! Will the vicar be OK after we're gone?"

"I think so." The Fiend took a seat on an old stump. "As near as I can tell, they weren't looking for you and me. At least … not us per se."

"What does that mean?"

"Have a seat and take another sip of wine. We've a bit of time to kill."

She obliged him, but asked again, "What does that mean?"

"Did you see any clergymen during your time at the monastery?"

"No … but there were some at the market, I think."

"They would've been the authors of this whole mess. But none were about when their guards came to take poor Deirdre to her inquisition."

"You mean me?" She fought to hide a smile.

"No, me. And it didn't end well for them. Alas, the guards and soldiers at the monastery didn't know anything. Their masters were far too clever to share too much. And there was blood being spilt. Men giving the orders often have soft resolve and even softer stomachs."

"So, we don't know?"

"Not perfectly. But the torturers did ask some questions. It seemed they were seeking a man travelling in the company of a young woman. They had little beyond that."

"I'm not sure what that means. They were looking for us?"

"That was never in any doubt. But they didn't seem to know precisely who or what they sought."

"But …." She chewed on his words for a moment. "But how did they know what they knew?"

"Good question. And I wish I had a clear answer. The Inquisitors have great resources and even some powerful magics. But even the best magics have their limits. No doubt they cast some scrying spell, and that trifling description, *a man traveling in the company of a young woman*, is what they found."

There was something else. She'd learned to read the Fiend. He was cunning, but even he had his tells. What she said next was just a guess. "What if it wasn't magic?"

"You really are clever," he said. "It may not have been magic. I was careless last summer when I fetched you up your vengeance. I thought I was shrewd and that the creature in Etruscia was too feckless and lazy to mind what I did. As I said last night, it seems I was wrong. He was watching, and carefully. It's very possible that his agents have been on the ground in Albion and looking around these many months."

"They know about Reverend Ainsley?"

"Ah. That, I don't know. It may well be that the good reverend has run his course. In any event, he last was seen earlier today heading south out of the city by several people well known to him. Hopefully, anyone seeking him will follow in that direction."

"But the vicar?" she said, returning to her original worry.

Deirdre had great concern for the old man. She hadn't yet forgotten the fate of the haberdashers the year before, when the Fiend first had supped on men and left their remains in public. It was only natural folks would wrongly presume a lycanthrope was to blame for the slew of savaged corpses. But who would have thought that so many people in Albion associated lycanthropy with haberdashery? According to what she later heard, the pogroms that had followed in Portsmouth and New Gate likely set back the sartorial arts in the kingdom many years.

"Tuppence, I cannot, for the life of me, imagine Vicar Edgemont is in any peril. Despite his doddering appearance, he's a great scholar and an important man in the Reform Church, well loved and respected. The Holy See wouldn't endanger a possible alliance with the Reformists by harming him. Besides, he's the vicar of this parish. It's his duty to play host to visiting clergymen like Reverend Ainsley. None will question that."

The creature's words assuaged her worry for the vicar's safety somewhat. But she would miss Reverend Ainsley, if this were to be the last that she would see of him. The Fiend had many guises. The reverend was one of those that filled her with the greatest comfort.

The creature seemed to read her mood and plucked a number of items from a small pack he carried with him and handed those to her. "I did swing by the vicarage and picked up a few things."

It was a small stack of books, including her copy of *Flora Albionis*, her beloved book of herbalism, and a book on mathematics that she'd been reading. (The Fiend could be irksome at times, but he also was blinking thoughtful.) Besides those were a few toiletries and, much to her surprise, her cosh. The thing had some brown stains on it, the provenance of which were in little doubt.

It was a weapon, after all.

6. The Flight from Westport

Deirdre and her fiendish companion set out the moment it was full dark. The creature had uncanny nighttime vision and knew the paths through the saltmarsh well. Still, they proceeded slowly and quietly on the off chance that those hunting them still were on their trail. She'd made a point earlier of grabbing some sleep just for this purpose. There was no telling when they again might rest.

She hadn't pressed him on what precisely had transpired at the old monastery at which she'd been imprisoned. She thought she knew, an impulse that was confirmed sometime later when they crested the first hill past the saltmarsh. Behind her, in the direction that she imagined the monastery would have been located, the light of a fire caused the heavens to glow, even after a full bell or more. It must have been an unholy conflagration.

Throughout the course of the night, she could tell that they threaded their way east. There were long periods of slow movement interspersed with short bursts of speed and frequent periods to stop, look, and listen, but ever onward they travelled. They continued moving even when the sun came up.

Deirdre was accustomed to hard travel, and she stayed in the saddle like a trooper. Their course kept them from the High Road, and they skulked and remained out of sight whenever possible. Such lurking usually was a thing against which the Fiend railed, but it was important now. They kept to back roads, game trails, and open country.

And they avoided other parties. As Deirdre had observed on her flight from the monastery, even the innocent eyes of a passing stranger might be a thing their enemies could use against them. In any event, it wasn't easy to know at a distance who was friend and who was foe. It was a time of danger. The area around Westport hardly was touched by the war, but many travelers in Albion now went about armed and asked questions only after the fighting was done.

When they finally did alight, she and the creature made a cold camp for the first several nights. It was the very end of winter, and the nights still were brisk. During the day, their mounts kept them warm. And the food they'd prepared for their departure was the type that could be eaten on the run. It was harsh travel but not unendurable. There was little time for talk or discussion beyond the necessities.

On the good side, Sir Alexis had returned at some point during their first night of travel. She always found the reverend comforting, but the knight buoyed her confidence in ways she could not explain. She knew they were the same creature, but there was something bracing about Sir Alexis.

And there was no way to avoid noticing that the creature was in top form. It was her first time seeing the knight since their last departure from Mont Clair, but a wicked wound across the faux knight's jaw, one that he'd taken the previous summer while shielding the baron's eldest son from a spear thrust, was perfectly aged and had mellowed into a convincing scar. The old scamp had skills. It could not be denied.

On the morning of their fourth day of travel, the Fiend let her sleep late, and Deirdre awoke to her first breakfast fire since their departure from Westport. After stuffing her face with warm bacon and biscuits, she asked the creature what their next moves should be.

"I thought we might take a little exercise before getting on our way," replied the knight as he toed a small branch into the fire.

"In the middle of our flight?"

"I think our enemies are well behind us now, Tuppence."

"What of all the creeping about on back roads?"

"Just an overabundance of caution. I let these rascals catch me with my britches down once. My vanity may not survive a second humiliation."

"What's to stop them from casting another … what was it you called it? A scrying?"

"They might, but such magics are unpredictable. In any event, I've come to think that you might be right. Our enemies may have arrived at Westport by using far more mundane tools."

"Spies?"

"A spy is just someone who looks around and asks questions, but yes. And the information they needed may simply have come to them through gossip. People talk."

That did make a certain sense, Dierdre had to admit. But there was something more. And it had been bothering her. "If they were looking for Reverend Ainsley," she asked, "how come they didn't begin rounding up clergymen?"

It was an uncomfortable few moments before the creature spoke. He again toed a branch into the flames.

"I don't think they were looking for you, and if they were they certainly didn't know who in particular they were seeking. They snuck a company of troops into the city, bullied the city watch into hiding in their barracks, and rounded up many scores of girls and young women. What person does such a thing, takes such risks, if they have a proper name or a reasonable description of who they seek?"

"So, again, why not start looking for a clergyman?"

Another few moments of silence. Despite the dire subject, she actually enjoyed seeing the creature near his wit's end.

"I can only imagine," he said at last, "that they know less about me than they do you. The Inquisitors sought a man traveling with a young woman. The man could have been any age, and perhaps they don't know they seek a clergyman."

"If they had their spies out, how could they not know something so crucial about Moorcroft Ainsley?"

"People are imperfect, child. Besides…."

"What?"

"I'll share something with you I've never told anyone else. I always know where my counterpart is. But he doesn't know where I am."

"Wait … your counterpart? The Walking God?"

"Yes."

"You always know where he is?"

"Every moment of every day."

"How…? By … some sort of scrying or augury?"

"No, no. I don't do magic in that way. My ability to divine his location is something that's natural to me. It's not a thing I could explain in just a few words."

"And he never knows where you are?"

"Not at all. I'm able to cloud his ability to see me, and the abilities of his followers. It's one of the few advantages I have over the shiftless rogue."

Something occurred to her. "What did you mean the other day when you said the wind was being fickle?"

An enormous smile split the face of Alexis de Vere. "I'm not teasing when I say you are clever. You truly are."

"What does it mean, then?"

"This Walking God of yours, and many of his followers, for that matter, have little tricks, ways of clouding my ability to read the wind. It isn't perfect, and they have to know with a certain particularity where I am for it to work."

"And they knew you were in Westport?"

"Almost certainly. Look, Tuppence, I don't say these things to give you a false sense of safety. You chose a dangerous path when you decided to stay with me. But that fickleness of which I spoke didn't begin until we reached Westport almost three months ago."

"When we *both* reached Westport."

"True, but you travelled openly alongside Sir Alexis for many months during the summer campaigns. The cloudiness, the fickleness, I felt in the wind didn't begin until after Reverend Ainsley reemerged a few months back. Our enemy may not have known precisely who they sought, and they no doubt have employed a combination of spies and magics in their search. And I did do a fair amount of coming and going during the winter, in various forms. Perhaps one of my alter egos did something or said something that tipped a hand to one of our enemy's spies. It wouldn't be without precedent."

His words gave her some comfort that she was not the specific target of an irate god. But otherwise, they left her with mixed emotions. It pleased something perverse in her to see that the Fiend did not always have the answers. He sometimes, like anyone else, was left puzzled. But that knowledge was discomforting as well. He spoke the truth. She had put herself in great danger by associating with him, and he did not know everything.

"How certain are you these people were from the Holy See?" she asked. "Are you sure they were Inquisitors?"

"Who else would it be?"

"My first thought was that the city was under attack, and that de Margot's troops had arrived. Why not him?"

A brief look of surprise lit the knight's face. "The troops were Etruscian, and the men you described sounded like priests of the Old Rite. I suppose...."

"How did they get to Westport?"

"From ... oh."

"They didn't come from the port." Etruscia, after all, was faraway overseas. "They first came to the market through the Postern Gates."

"Oh," the Fiend again whispered. "Tuppence, I'm not half so clever as I thought. They must have landed elsewhere. And to move so many troops undetected through open country would have required help from someone."

"De Margot?"

"Possibly. He has friends in this part of Albion, and a great deal of money to buy others. Even more, the war isn't going well for him."

She cleared her throat. "I ... um, only told one person ... and that was just that morning. Um...."

"Tuppence?"

"I may have mentioned the de Vere name."

"No reason you should not. In any event, it's highly unlikely de Margot sent these folks to snatch you away. Not that he's too squeamish to do something so dishonorable, no not at all. Etienne de Margot simply isn't that subtle."

"They would have sought me by name." That now seemed perfectly obvious, but a sense of relief assailed her all the same.

"Yes, precisely. But his helping the Holy See? That's very possible.

"Why would the…?"

"Why de Margot and the Holy See? It isn't so difficult to imagine now that you've pointed it out. Ghitland long has had good relations with Etruscia, and the Duke of Ghitland is a distant cousin of de Margot. I doubt the duke wants to get involved in a civil war in Albion … but, who knows? Perhaps he brokered something between de Margot and the Holy See. Such a thing wouldn't be a pleasant development for Cousin William at Mont Clair."

"Should we do something?"

"Warn the baron? Couriers already will have gone out to alert him to troubles in Westport. He's a clever man. If we've puzzled it out, so will he. Besides, how would we explain our thinking? The best bet is to stay out of sight for the time being, and to stick to our schedule. Events will sort themselves out."

Deirdre wasn't so confident as the Fiend that things would, "sort themselves out," but she listened as he continued to talk, going over various theories of events, and dispensing with them just as quickly. When the Fiend rattled on in that way, he had the appearance of a man juggling 10 balls at once and not knowing for certain how to stop.

But she wasn't worried, as odd as that sounded. True, the creature didn't seem convinced by any of his own arguments, and they were being hunted by the servants of an angry deity. But she again was traveling under the protection of Sir Alexis, a prominent and much feared knight. And they journeyed through the lands of her protector, William, the Baron of Flight and Inskeep.

Perhaps things *would* sort themselves out.

———

The traveling was lazy for the next few days. They weren't expected in Mont Clair for some weeks, so there was no reason to hurry. After a leisurely breakfast and some time spent in exercise, they travelled no more than seven leagues that first day.

The next day was even slower. After their physical activity, the Fiend took her to muddle about various sites in the countryside. Along with her companion, she dug for herbs, taking time to make some careful notes in her journal. Thereafter, they tracked a badger, examined some tree moss, and inspected a bunch of early flowers. As he often did, the Fiend quizzed her, not just on the plants' common and taxonomical names, but he expected her to identify them by touch and smell. That she likewise had to learn their uses and indications went without saying.

They didn't get on the road until midday, after which they made several stops to explore a pond, look for mushrooms along a hillside, study the consistency of mud in a wash, and catalog even more flowers.

By habit, she made notes throughout the day, often in her journal, but more interesting tidbits went straight into her book of herbalism. They barely made five leagues that day, with all the stopping and looking about.

In fact, over the next several days, she and the Fiend settled into their familiar rhythm, with the knight now her teacher rather than the reverend. The only thing that appeared to change was the intensity of their sparring. They were up early each morning, went for a run or a swim, and spent the better part of a bell fighting with short stick, cosh, or knife.

Her mentor in such instances usually was Jeb Fauquier, a stout yeoman who was one of the Fiend's regular alter egos. During that time, Jeb hammered home a number of refrains that he'd stated in the past.

"There's no such thing as honor, Tuppence," he said time and again. "Attack first, attack suddenly, attack through stealth, and attack to kill. You're not a warrior, and never will be. And your opponent will always be bigger, stronger, and quicker. If you must kill him, do so before he even realizes you're a threat."

The entire affair was harsh and unpleasant. Yet it wasn't a thing she minded doing. She'd never intended to be a soldier, and still did not. But despite her months of training with the Fiend, the walking apes of the Inquisition easily had taken her in hand. Her only solace from the episode was that it had allowed Vivian to make a getaway. She had no intention of again falling into such a situation.

No. Just fighting back wasn't enough. Winning was all that mattered. What was it the Fiend was always saying? "Your goal isn't to fight your opponent, Tuppence. It's to kill him."

So, she threw her every sinew into braining poor Jeb each and every time they met. There even was an opportunity to get some practice with Chance Medley, who taught her to do most everything by stealth—how to secret a weapon on the body, how to make a knife appear from nowhere, and how to cut or stick an unsuspecting victim so they'd bleed out quickly.

They even found time to practice picking locks with a rusty old padlock Chance fished from the knight's saddlebags.

What could she say? It wasn't a happy time, but it was a busy and a contented time. The nights were cooler as they moved away from the coast, but spring was right around the bend, and the days were tolerable. Best of all, she was able to scratch her itch to learn anytime she felt like it.

And soon they would reach Mont Clair. Much to her surprise, she'd grown fond of the de Vere family, and she greatly looked forward to seeing Lady Isabel. She even would be happy to see Birdy.

7. Wild Imaginings

Isabel had stayed in bed all the previous day. It wasn't a great sin at Mont Clair. The folk there were hardworking, but they also were sensitive to illness and disease. She'd seen no sign that anyone was a shirker. If folks there fell ill, they stayed in bed.

And there was no doubt she was ill. Her condition had been an ongoing source of comment for many weeks, and on the day that she decided to stay abed a number of people came by to see her to pass on their best wishes. The entire episode made her feel better, and she decided the next morning that she would try to get back to work. She hadn't been sneezing or coughing, and it seemed unlikely she had anything contagious. It was just....

Dammit. Her imagination was getting the better of her. She was convinced of it. Perhaps her fanciful thoughts were getting worse because of her worn and exhausted physical condition. It was difficult to say with any certainty.

She'd never had a vivid imagination, but in the early evening two days before, she became convinced that someone was following her while she walked alone on a stretch of pathway in the inner courtyard. Similar inklings had afflicted her in the recent past, but the sensation at that moment that someone was right behind her was so strong that she nearly broke into tears.

And yet when, finally, she'd found the courage to turn in order to confront the person, there was no one there. No one. Yet she was equally convinced that she sensed someone running the opposite direction.

She didn't know.

But she knew. There was an impression in her of someone, someone real. And the same impression came back to her of someone in grey robes, that same elusive figure who she'd sensed several times in the previous weeks.

Had someone truly been there, or was she just going bonkers?

The experience that day had so frightened her that she must have fainted, because her next recollection was of the stablemaster helping her to her feet and leading her to Sylvie, the Mistress of the Keys. The woman gave her some wine and put her straight to bed, where she passed a disturbed and fevered night. The entire next day she spent in bed.

And then, of course, there were the dreams, the other half of her tarnished coin. She'd never had vivid dreams in her life, but lately they'd been so damned lifelike, as if she'd been thrust into another reality.

But was that such a hard thing to imagine?

It wasn't even that the dreams were frightening. They were not. It was all just so … so real, vivid in a way she never imagined a dream could be. Worse, it was so incredibly familiar, as if she were replaying memories of places that she'd never been.

For a short time, she nearly succumbed to paranoia, thinking that Etienne de Margot had sent someone to spy on her—even to abduct her or to do her harm. Perhaps she was being poisoned? She knew the man loathed her, and de Margot was the type of man for whom hatred was an artform.

No. No one was coming to abduct her, and no one was coming to kill her. The castle was guarded and secure, and she ate the same food and drank the same drink as everyone else. There was no poison.

She was sick. Likely it was some ongoing flu bug or an infection of some type. There was no doubt she was running a mild fever and had been doing so for some time. What she wouldn't give for some antibiotics.

No. No, no.

What she needed was a little rest and some rehydration. As nice as it would be to see someone … well, she'd seen firsthand what passed for a doctor hereabouts. And none of the herbs she'd learned of in her time working in the hospital seemed appropriate for her symptoms. Perhaps she could talk to Sylvie and see if she had anything? These were a superstitious people, but simple herbalism certainly wouldn't lead to anything bad.

Until then, just getting out of bed that morning had been a chore. And walking down to the kitchen now was turning into a marathon. If she could just catch her balance.

OK, she at least knew she wouldn't faint again. Perhaps after kitchen duty she could stop by the chapel and do some reading with Emmet Naseby. She wasn't religious, and never intended to be, but reading aloud as she had been lately with the friar calmed her and made her feel better. The whole exercise was soothing.

And what would it hurt to read some more about prophecy and quests?

8. An Unfortunate Encounter

Deirdre lost track of the days while they traveled. On some, they saw hardly a soul. On others, their affairs were busy and of great interest. Just the previous day they'd done a dozen or more things. They'd picked early berries, helped a woodsman clear a culvert, repaired the railing of a rotted fence, examined the flora of a small pond, helped a lass search for a lost goat, arranged for the murder of a local miller, negotiated with two neighbors over the ownership of a duck, visited the market to buy some herbs, and shod a horse. In total, they'd traveled fewer than two leagues.

On a day preceding that, they'd traveled not at all. Early on that day, a frightened, but hopeful, young woman came to their small camp and asked for the help of the "brave knight," saying her brother was in an awfully bad way. Sir Alexis went with the young woman, only to return in the midafternoon. The lad, he said, merely had needed someone with whom to talk and to share his fears and worries. Deirdre didn't mind that the Fiend took his time with the youth. It was a day for her to rest her saddle-sore bottom and to catch up on her reading.

It must have been on their ninth or 10th day on the road that they happened upon a secluded inn and decided to stop. Traveling off the beaten path as they had, there were few places to stop and eat. And they'd grown weary of their own cooking.

The place in question was small but remarkably tidy, and the smell was magical, a combination of brisket and baked goods. She knew the Fiend at least feigned an interest in human food, but she was mesmerized, and they each had a tall ale as they awaited their meals.

"You're de Vere," said a man at the back of the common room after they'd been there a time. The fellow was a knight by the look of him, and the only other patron in the place.

"I am," was the Fiend's friendly response. "You have me at a disadvantage."

"Bouguer, Anton Bouguer," the fellow said. He was a thickset man and talked as if his name should be known to them. "I've met another de Vere, a baron."

"My cousin."

"So, you're the one who gave up his estates and became a hedge knight?"

"I am," was the Fiend's cordial reply.

Sir Anton barked a laugh. "What sort of person does that!? Gives up wealth and title?"

"The kind sitting right in front of you."

The man hadn't bothered to rise and join them, but the common room was small. He barely was a dozen paces away, so they could hear him easily.

"This is my daughter, Tuppence," the Fiend added.

"Ah! From her coloring, I took her for a Surrey tart. Shame. Thought you might let me have a throw. Last time was nearly two days ago. Minx wasn't the least bit grateful for my seed. They'll let anyone walk the High Road these days."

The man's wicked and vile words went on for some time, with the Fiend paying him scant mind, and Deirdre trying her best to ignore him all together. Sir Anton was a swine. Just when she'd begun to think better of Gheet nobility, such a creature had to slither into her line of sight. Without thinking, she felt her hand grip the cutting knife on the table in front of her.

The Fiend gave her a look, and she paused. Soon after, thankfully, their meal arrived. The savory dishes allowed her to ignore the scoundrel across the room.

But fate was not with them. No sooner than the odious knight had quieted down, and they'd begun to enjoy their food, than the sound of hoofbeats sounded outside. A party of riders dismounted in the place's tiny courtyard.

She found herself lifted from her chair, and it took some moments to realize that Sir Alexis was hustling her to the back of the place. She was unable to utter a word before his low and deep hushing.

"Out the back, child," he whispered.

She didn't protest, but cut a quickstep through the kitchen door and soon was dashing for the small lean-to at which they'd tethered their horses. Moments later, they were moving at a light canter through some sycamores and doing their best to be quiet about it.

The remainder of the day was much hard travel. They first slipped down a wash and followed a stream for some way. Several times they cut across the ribbon of water only to travel a ways and then cross that same stream yet again. For a short time, their course didn't seem to take them any particular direction, and on two separate occasions, once not long after they left the inn and another time later in the day, the Fiend drew up his mount and muttered some incomprehensible words before they again urged their mounts on.

It was hard riding, and there were only a few stretches where they followed sideroads and game trails. Most of their journey was across rough country, and several times she wanted to ask what was amiss. But staying in the saddle in that way took all her effort and concentration. There were several moments when she saw what looked like worry on the rugged face of Alexis de Vere, and she felt a tiny worm coil inside her at the thought.

They finally reined up and dismounted sometime after dark (near a swamp from the smell of it), and the Fiend bid her roll up in her cloak and get some rest. She didn't hesitate. It was their hardest day's journey yet, and there was nothing about it that she liked.

———

It was only the next morning that she was able to eke a few answers from her companion, none of them pleasant and few of them fully satisfactory.

They risked a small fire, and as the Fiend prepared their tired mounts and Deirdre made something to eat, she cast him a few queries. The first question was obvious.

"What was that all about?"

"Those riders who arrived as we departed."

"What of them?"

"They were from the Inquisition," was his flat reply.

The Fiend usually wasn't so terse, and she'd never known the creature to shy from anyone or anything. He was ferocious and could easily best a number of armed opponents. This didn't sound right, and she told him as much.

"My disguises are not foolproof," was his reply. "Usually, even the most diligent scrutiny won't show me to be anything other than human...."

"But?"

A look crossed her companion's face. It wasn't annoyance. Did she catch a flash of embarrassment in his eyes? Some moments passed before he replied.

"There was a magicker among them. I could nearly smell him, and I didn't want to risk a confrontation. There, no doubt, were more of them nearby."

Was the creature afraid? Of a magician? To her knowledge, Deirdre had never encountered any sort of sorcerer or wizard, but she would appease her curiosity on that point later. For now, it wasn't apparent what had gotten into the Fiend. She never before would have imagined him capable of fear. But ... no. It wasn't that.

"Are they searching for you, or for me?" she asked. A second look of embarrassment on the Fiend's face showed that her instinct had been correct. The poor thing wasn't exactly blushing, but she did for a moment feel bad for him. That moment passed, and she began to laugh.

"What's so funny?" he asked with the faintest hint of peevishness.

"You're embarrassed!"

"Mortified. But also, more than a touch worried. Our enemies should not have been able to follow us this far."

"And you think they're following me?"

"I ... I'm not sure. But it may well be." When he said those words, he seemed somewhat deflated.

"That's unfortunate," she said. Now that she knew, it didn't seem too bad. Why not be practical? "What are we going to do about it?"

"For now, keep moving. I sent out a few false trails when we departed the place. They won't fool anyone clever for long, but it will buy us some time. And we crossed over as much water as was available. That'll help. If we're lucky, that bunch just happened to be passing by and aren't looking for us. If not ... well, hopefully, they won't be able to pick up our trail again."

That sounded fair, she agreed, and the two soon were back in the saddle. The next few days would be challenging and exhausting.

———

The next two days indeed were draining, but on the morning of the third their pace eased. They did not straightaway go back to their regular schedule of exercise and lessons, but for the time they would adopt a sedate, albeit steady pace. The horses needed the rest, as did Deirdre.

The Fiend resumed his usual tranquil demeanor, and the young woman immediately fell in line. So, some danger might come their way? Witchfinders or Inquisitors beat the bushes looking for them? So what? This was the life she chose.

So, she relaxed and let the furlongs roll by.

The thought was long in coming, but it dawned on her during that first morning's sedate travel that the Fiend was rather lazy. True, the creature was capable of extraordinary energy and astonishing vigor at times. She had seen those qualities in him on many occasions. But often he just lolled around, and as much as he declared that he had no need for sleep, from time to time he even appeared to doze in the saddle.

At such moments, the Fiend's horse, sensing an indifferent hand at the reins, would amble from the road and begin to graze, forcing Deirdre to give the beast a swat to get it moving again. For the horse, the Fiend was an easy mark, but the animal often would give her a look like that of an unfriendly storekeeper eyeing a customer who'd loitered too long without buying.

And it wasn't only the Fiend's indifference at the reins. The creature didn't exactly snore as he rode, but his head on occasion would sway or bob, and he once nearly choked on a spiced pea when he dozed off mid-nibble.

He seemed to enjoy taking life easy. His natural pace, all other things considered, was a languid saunter.

While they rode now, his mount several times glanced back at her, as if calculating the odds on whether it should risk a snack. She pretended not to see it, and she paid no mind to the napping creature who rode beside her.

Instead, her head was filled with other things. She was thinking about magic. It wasn't something that had nagged at her—there was always so much more to study and to learn—but several times her curiosity about it had been piqued. On more than one occasion lately she'd wanted to ask him about it, but, honestly, she hadn't been certain how to start such a conversation.

Now, it couldn't be put off.

"I think I'd like to see magic," she declared in a loud voice.

The Fiend sputtered several times and then hemmed and hawed a few incoherent words as if to prove he hadn't been sleeping.

"Magic's a hard thing to see in this world," he said at last.

"How so?"

"It's been gelded from its genuine form—at least that's true of the magic one is most likely to encounter nowadays."

"I don't understand that."

"No, I suppose you wouldn't," he said. "The thing most folks intend when they talk about magic is much too potent and far too dangerous to be wielded by mere mortals. No ... only the Walking God's tribe can brandish such godawful stuff in its raw and untempered form. For it's a species of magic they once upon a time imported from beyond."

"From their world? You told me that once. Where are they from?"

"Another realm entirely. Don't ask me to be more precise. They're a tribe for whom the wielding of raw and tempestuous magics is as natural as drawing breath would be to one of your people. It's a terrible thing."

"Terrible how? ... I mean, that's not how they talk of it in books."

"Books? Bah. Stories for children. No human living has ever seen the nature of true magic. I swear, child … in all my living days. The magic of this Walking God of yours is a terror, a horror, the forging and the shredding of reality itself. True and proper magic of that kind … *oh*, to see it snaking and swirling across a battlefield like a maelstrom, wrenching apart the very fibers of creation…. In all my living days."

He glanced over, a strange look in his eye, and gave her a wink. "Such is the might of this Walking God and his folk."

"Can? … Could anyone…?"

"No, lass. Thankfully, such sights are no longer seen in these fair lands. Those days are long gone."

"Since the *gesh*?"

"Precisely. The type of magic you see now is but a remnant, muted, tamed, and harnessed. Bound in his mortal form, even the creature in Etruscia can only wield a fragment of what was once his to command. Though he still is a powerful, powerful being."

"And magic now is safe to look at?"

"Nowadays it's much like watered-down ale … well, far more water than ale. If you can see it at all, it's something you might glimpse from the corner of your eye. A person could blink and miss it."

That part didn't sound right to her. The few times that she'd seen the Fiend take on a new form had sometimes been hard to follow, true. But it wasn't always so. There was something else. "Wait," she said. "Only the Walking God can wield magic?"

"No, not at all. Some humans have the knack to master it in its diminished form, and the sorcerers of old could harness even more. It's not an easy skill to grasp, but with determination and the proper training a very few can wield it with success."

"Could you teach me?"

"Eh? … Source magic? I'm not sure I could."

"But don't you know magic?"

"There are different types, Tuppence. My species wields a kind of magic altogether different. Something of a lesser sort, if I'm being perfectly honest. I couldn't master Source magic if I tried. Nor could one of his people wield mine."

"Could you teach me yours?"

"Not a whiff of it," was his reply. "The magic of my kind is inherent in what we are. You'd have to be like me to control it."

"But I could learn the other kind? What did you call it? 'Source' magic?"

"Yes, but you'd need a proper teacher. And even if you did, not everyone has the knack."

Damn. Double damn, she wanted to say. There was no telling if she had this knack, but she certainly didn't have a proper teacher. Well, damn.

"What if I could find a teacher?"

"You might be able. But even for those who have the aptitude, it's exceedingly difficult to learn. And that's no accident."

"What do you mean?"

"Such magics grant the wielder immense power, so the Walking God and his tribe long have striven to limit access to it. Even their most faithful servants, including men and women upon whom they bestowed vast power in the ages before the *gesh*, have their abilities fettered. To wit, in order to master Source magic, one must learn a great many silly and often arbitrary things—tongue twisting incantations, mind-numbing rituals, precise invocations—all designed to make the acquisition of Source magic as daunting as possible."

Triple damn, she nearly said. It wasn't that she wanted to learn magic, but neither did she like knowing there were things she couldn't have.

"There is a shortcut," said the Fiend.

Hullo! "Shortcut?"

"Artefacts," he said, as if that word explained everything.

She said nothing in reply.

"Ages back, child, when the sorcerers of old wanted to wield more magic than their bodies would allow, they hit upon a trick. They used mundane items of great durability to channel magic."

"How does that help ... er, someone who wanted to wield magic now?"

"Source magic has a number of peculiar qualities in this world, Tuppence. It tends to strengthen things it comes into long contact with, to imbue them with more of what they are."

"Are you...? Are you talking about ... magic wands?"

"I've never known of anyone using a wand per se. But ancient sorcerers often would use simple items to channel Source magic. The more a thing is used to channel such magic, the more suitable it becomes for that task. The more suitable it becomes for the task, the more people will want to use the item for that purpose. Ancient artefacts that have passed through the hands of many users are powerful tools, especially if those previous users were unusually gifted sorcerers."

"And you don't need to have studied magic to use them?"

"It isn't quite that simple. A person wielding an artefact still would need to have a certain knack for it, but all that other mumbo-jumbo—the waving of hands, the utterance of tongue twisting incantations—all of that gibberish can be dispensed with."

Bother. She didn't have an artefact. But why would she need one? Never mind that.

"You called it Source magic. What does that mean?"

"It's just a name some people use to describe that type of magic. It's because the core power comes from a distant source."

"The Walking God's world."

"Exactly."

"Is…?"

"Go on."

She thought for a moment. "If that type of magic comes from the Walking God, is it … you know, safe to use?"

"That's a good question. The Walking God tries to control Source magic in this world, but the *gesh* prevents him from doing so perfectly. And he can't sever the flow entirely. As long as even one of his kind remains in this realm, some of his magic seeps through. In any event, so much Source magic already has spilled over into this world during the ages, it's impossible to control it all. Not even for him."

"What's your magic called? The magic of your people?"

"It doesn't have a proper name."

"You must call it something."

"Tuppence, don't get caught up in words. Many people use many words for many things, almost all of them contradictory."

"What do *you* call it?"

"Conjury is as good a word as any. Some people call it Deviltry, others Necromancy, others still Thaumaturgy. But those are just names."

"What does Conjury do?"

"Precious little, if truth be told."

"Really?"

"Indeed. The ability of my tribe to work magic is paltry compared to the might of the Walking God and his folk."

"Stop it. I've seen you do things."

"True. But many of the things I do aren't magic, not properly speaking."

"I don't believe you."

"Child, trust me. I am a third-rate practitioner of a second-rate art."

"Then name me one thing you do that isn't proper magic," she demanded.

"Taking on the forms of others."

"That's not magic?"

"Well … not truly. Though most might view it as such. My kind aren't tied to a single form. Changing shape for us is natural. Though, all modesty aside, I am unusually good at it."

"I should say you are!"

"You mustn't feed my vanity, child."

"OK, then. What magic can you do?"

"I was always a queer student of such things," he admitted. "A great many simple conjurings I was never able to wrap myself around. But several of the more complex notions came to me without the least effort."

"I want to see one."

He gave her a long look, as if this were a thing done under protest. Then he stretched out his right arm, palm downward. With a florid roll, he twisted his hand down, back, and around until it was facing skyward. When he did, a large purse was in his hand. She didn't see from where it came. It was just there, as if she'd blinked and missed it.

He passed the item to her. It was heavy, very heavy, and when she drew back the strings … oh, my. The purse was filled with gold. And not the flimsy gold coins one but rarely saw in Albion, but thick gold marks, each one heavy enough to stun a grown man if thrown properly. There had to have been 100 such coins inside, more than enough to buy a large farm and to stock it fully.

She wanted to let out a cry but was unable.

"How…?" she began. She couldn't finish.

"I've always been good at that trick. Few of my kind can conjure from nothing in that way." He gave her another long look before saying, "Now stash your new fortune out of sight, else the smell of it attract a swarm of taxmen."

She nodded and voiced a half-coherent, "Thank you."

There were other things she wanted to ask, a great many, but she rode on in silence instead, thoroughly dumbfounded by her new wealth.

9. The Tipping of Men

Deirdre managed to go some days without again asking about magic. The vicar always said to think before you ask a question, and you might come up with the answer on your own. Either way, you'll be the richer for the effort.

So, she thought about it, rolled things around in her head, and tried to remember everything the Fiend had told her on the subject. She didn't feel richer. Well, except for the gold marks, which she'd stowed away with her other belongings. Money couldn't buy happiness, but it could free up your time to concentrate on those things that could.

They'd gotten an early start that morning, but as noontime approached, the Fiend called a halt to their travels. They set up their small camp at a secluded glade near an old well, and the creature shrugged off his chainmail and suggested there might be time for a spot of exercise before they took their supper.

On such occasions, the Fiend insisted Deirdre take every opportunity to attack him, whether he appeared prepared for the combat or not.

"You'll never be a warrior," he often repeated—rather too often, she thought. "So, sudden and ruthless action can be the difference between life and death."

And learning new skills, he insisted, was never a bad thing. At that moment, the Fiend got it into his head that it might be a useful skill to practice tipping men into wells, which he declared, "Is a first-rate way to do away with someone without drawing attention."

At first, Deirdre was surprised at the notion. It seemed a ludicrous way to spend an afternoon, but on reflection it seemed no more or less so than many of the other ways he tutored her to dispose of an adversary. And he gave a rather intelligent explanation of the thing.

"I've pondered this for some time, Tuppence. Wells built along the style customary in Albion are death traps. Low railings, clay and brick stonework within, poor footing without. And the well itself is narrow. It may seem ridiculous, but you'd be surprised how frequently in this land that men get drunk and stumble headfirst into wells, where, if the fall doesn't kill them, they drown in waist-deep water at the bottom. Even if they manage to right themselves, the walls are too slick to climb, and hypothermia finishes them in no time."

"Very dangerous," she agreed, peering down the old well in question. "Especially if they have a little nudge."

"You catch my point."

He spent just a moment instructing her on the right approach, the where, when, and how of bumping a larger opponent so that his leg caught on the railing, and he went headfirst into the narrow opening. As she predicted, her first attempt was successful. With a comic scream, Sir Alexis virtually threw himself into the well mouth.

The Fiend was a nimble creature and emerged moments later, ready for another try, and, as she'd come to expect, each additional attempt was successively more difficult than the last. She soon needed to apply herself to tip the Fiend into the well successfully.

It wasn't monotonous. After the first few dozen practices, the Fiend took to emerging from the well in a new guise. First, Chance Medley, then Jeb Fauquier, and afterward many she'd never before seen. Each represented a different body type, tall, short, heavy, thin.

Even Reverend Ainsley made an appearance. "Show evil no mercy, my child," he intoned in mock piety before the first of five trips down the well.

Once she got the hang of it, the whole operation wasn't especially hard. The Fiend was right. The dimensions of the average well worked in her favor, and he already had given her much training on how to use an opponent's size and weight to an advantage. For want of a better word, it was fiendishly easy to knock a man over into a well, and to do so in a way that any passing witness would see as an accident.

When it appeared that she'd gotten the hang of it, the Fiend, now again in the guise of Sir Alexis, suggested they return to camp for her supper. It was only when they reached camp that Deirdre realized that the Fiend hadn't formally declared an end to their training.

Without even thinking, she snatched the cosh from her sleeve, spun, and threw all her sinews into a blow aimed at the Fiend's chin. The powerful strike, the best she'd ever thrown, caught the creature right on the button, sending him staggering back a half dozen paces. A look of absolute surprise and joy crossed the face of Alexis, but before he could utter a word, Deirdre stepped forward, and her backswing contacted the other side of his chin, sending him flying into the campfire.

The creature, still smoking, leapt from the flames and backed away with both hands held out in a sign of peace. He began to laugh. "You win, Tuppence. Training is over."

Deirdre didn't know whether to laugh or to cry. In all the months she'd sparred with the Fiend, she'd landed a few good blows. It wasn't uncommon. But this was the first time she'd caught the creature completely unawares, and she'd done so twice. It was thrilling.

Her teacher stepped over and gave her hair an affectionate toss. "I can see training is paying off. Keep that up, and we'll make a knight of you yet. Now … go down to the stream and clean up for supper. I'll have a surprise when you get back."

The stream was a good idea—that well was filthy—and she took some extra time for a much-needed and well-earned bath. It was cold but invigorating. And after a time dawdling and shaking her long hair dry, she meandered back to the camp. It was there she saw her surprise.

Sitting on a log by the fire was the Fiend in one of his many guises. If she were not mistaken, and it was clear that she wasn't, he'd taken the form of that swine of a knight they'd encountered at the inn some days before, Sir Anton Bouguer. Such a repellant slug of a man.

Besides her cosh, she carried just a small camp knife. The blade wasn't long, but it was sharp, and she pondered whether to slit Sir Anton's throat after she stole up behind him, or whether it would be best to stick him once hard in the kidney and watch him bleed out. Maybe the cosh? Once he was stunned…. A giggle almost escaped her as she took a grip on the camp knife and crept forward.

A strong hand took ahold of her knife arm, just above the elbow, and gently turned her about. There was a moment of confusion because she looked directly into the eyes of Sir Alexis. Wait … if this was Alexis, then….

No matter.

She turned to finish the deed. Few men she'd ever met needed killing as badly as this one, so if this were the real Sir Anton? All that much the better.

The Fiend pulled her back, his eyes wide as if he were trying to tell her something. Her eyes went wide in response. The two tussled for a silent moment before it became obvious that Sir Anton's gaze was on both of them.

"What's going on there, de Vere?" the brutish knight called out.

She felt the Fiend give her arm a faint squeeze, and she cast their new guest her oiliest smile before replying, "We're just arguing over who should have the honor of serving you your supper, sir knight."

"Well … just get on with it. A man could starve to death in your camp."

Those were the most pleasant words Sir Anton spoke all evening. He behaved as poorly as any guest Deirdre had ever beheld. Sir Alexis, on the contrary, was a gracious host. He always gave Sir Anton the first and best portions, and when time came for dessert, they both waited until the crude knight had finished his fill of the sweet pudding Sir Alexis had prepared before they had theirs.

The whole thing was appalling. Pudding, she supposed, was the actual surprise to which the Fiend had alluded. And Sir Anton Bouguer had finished all but a few spoons of it. Simply appalling.

And when Deirdre sweetly suggested that Sir Anton stop by the well for a cool drink following his after-dinner toilet? The Fiend had the nerve to insist on the stream instead. What was the Fiend's game? She was so angry she could have spit.

As evening turned into night, Sir Alexis took up his sword and sat on a stump near the fire. "Sir Anton, take your rest. I have the watch tonight."

The boorish knight grumbled an ingratitude under his breath and soon rolled over in his blankets to sleep. The Fiend looked at her and said not a word. On his lips played an inscrutable smile.

Was he up to something? If so, what? Just when she thought she had things figured out … bah. She closed her eyes and went to sleep.

10. A Series of Unsettling Events

Isabel had never intended to make Friar Emmet her confidante, but he was an intelligent young fellow and one of the few clergymen she'd met in Albion that didn't make the hairs on the back of her neck go up. For practical matters, the baroness gave wonderful counsel, but the friar was a convenient source for spiritual and intellectual knowledge.

It was something that had taken her a while to figure out, but everyone had their station in this world, from men like the baron all the way down to servants like Birdy. Each and every one was proud of their station and guarded the prerogatives they derived from it jealously, even the meekest. Class distinctions often were subtle, especially at the castle, but they were made of cast iron. It mattered not at all that she saw a person such as Birdy as an equal. He did not see her as such. His lifestyle depended on maintaining the status quo.

And few people had the pluck to stray from that path. The baroness was from Ghitland, a land wherein literacy among the commonfolk was discouraged. In other countries, Isabel had come to understand, it was outright illegal for a commoner to learn to read or to write.

In the baroness's world, Isabel slowly had come to find, literacy even had its limits among the aristocracy. A member of that class would be schooled in material trenchant to their status, military affairs and politics for young men and commerce and bookkeeping for young women. Everyone, of course, learned the basics of religion, but an aristocrat would no more inquire into an obscure tome of religion than he or she might pick up a book on smithing or carpentry.

It simply wasn't how things were done in most of the world, which was why the baroness had to force herself to tolerate the baron's bibliophilia. The people of Albion were infamous for their reading ways, and the baron, Gheet though he was, was a third-generation inhabitant of Albion. The man loved and admired books and would read anything on which he could lay his hands.

Isabel's time studying with the friar was a thing the baroness tolerated, but did not encourage. Was that why Isabel now was beginning to have mixed feelings about the pursuit of such knowledge?

It was difficult to say. Her thoughts had been so terribly muddled recently, part of her illness, or so she believed. And was it her imagination or had the friar been acting strangely in recent days?

Who could say? In any event, she was the last to point fingers. Her own behavior lately was nothing short of peculiar. In her more coherent moments, she felt herself slipping, knew that she needed to get a grip, but she didn't know how. She felt as if she were circling the drain and could do nothing to stop it.

Just the day before, she'd found herself on her knees in the chapel, praying fervently for some reprieve. She knew it was the illness acting out, but not just that. Somehow her dissipated state was making her fragile and emotional in ways she'd never been before. Three times that week alone she hadn't had the strength the get out of bed. And four days before she'd made the mistake of visiting the baroness in her chambers.

Lord, it was dreadful. Situated on the wall there was the only proper mirror in the castle. The reflection she saw of herself in the dim light of the chamber sent an arrow through her heart. She was scarcely 27 years old. The woman she saw looking back at her in the mirror appeared to be 50.

She'd never been so shaken.

Of course, she'd lost weight in recent months and hadn't felt herself, but the reflection she beheld looked so damned cadaverous and frayed. The realization was a shock to her system, and she found herself wondering if she was more ill than she'd imagined. There was a way the people of Albion treated those who were sick or injured in a bad way. It was an impulse that wasn't unheard of among the people of Earth. Some cultures simply refused to tell dreadfully ill people the full extent of their malady. Never give bad news about someone's health.

This was her second day in a row in bed. She had a few visitors, but not as many as the first. Perhaps that fact was just as well. One can accept only so many condolences.

The friar came by earlier, of course, and brought her some more things to read. He even stayed a while and listened to her recite, meticulously correcting her enunciation as he did. That part was beginning to be tedious. He was so damned insistent. But she didn't feel she was in any position to refuse him. When he departed, he left her some extra things to read. At least she wouldn't get bored.

And, of course, there were the dreams. Something inside her hoped they simply would go away, but of course they had not. They were worse. More vivid, more real. The experience no longer was surreal. It *was* real, so incredibly real.

And always the same. A Red Cobbled Square, a Mighty Stone Bridge, the Argent Shallows, a Dank and Dreary Gorge, and a handful of others. They always came to her in the same order, and she'd even come to think of them in the same terms, with the same names. Several were so strange that she simply couldn't figure them out. The dreams always ended with her arrival at an enormous cliffside into which had been hewn a wide opening.

Something within her had placed the name Eldritch Delve on the place.

Such a naming left her at a loss. She thought she knew what the word "eldritch" meant, but what in the living hell was a delve? And why the word "gorge"? It wasn't a word she usually would use, and why in her mind was that gorge always dank and dreary?

Her first thought was that perhaps she'd just read those names somewhere in one of the books the friar had left her. But she spent one of her sick days going over each passage she so far had read. They were fewer than 100 pages, and there was no use of any of those words in any of them.

The peculiar names were not as unnerving as the dreams themselves, but it was another thing to add to the pile of her anxieties. Friar Emmet was of little use when she'd broached the subject with him. He urged her to pray.

That was not what she needed to hear.

Thankfully, she no longer felt as if she were being watched. Then again, she'd spent much time in her chambers, and when she did have the strength to venture down and do some work, she went straight to the kitchen and back to her room afterward.

The de Vere family was good to her, and they treated her with much affection. Even the baroness had shown her tenderness of late. But Isabel couldn't escape the notion that the affection, real though it was, was driven more by duty than true sentiment.

She missed Deirdre, and not for the first time she wished she'd gone with the young woman to the coast. It would have been nice to spend time with her and to see the elusive Reverend Ainsley, such a complex and pious man.

Her somewhat unwholesome thoughts next turned to Sir Alexis when, much to her surprise, she thought she heard the man's voice. It was only when she paused to listen that it occurred to her that it was the baron's voice she heard. The two men resembled one another very much, and they even had the same way of speaking.

She tried not to listen, dreaded the idea of being an eavesdropper, but the baron's study was in the battlement opposite. She seldom was in her room at that hour, and this was the first time she realized how easily voices carried from the baron's desk. When he spoke now, it was louder than his usual.

"Miles, if they want war, they'll have war. They don't need our invitation to invade the country."

"My point being, milord, it would not hurt to reflect and, when the time comes, to show a prudent dram of cordiality."

"Miles, those fools can burn their own monasteries down whenever they like. But to send troops into one of my cities, abduct people from the streets, and assault members of the clergy ... *in my city?*"

"Milord ...."

"Am I then to play nice? To be cordial?"

"They are a delegation from the Holy See, and the Treaty of San ...."

"Where is Loyne?"

"Milord ...."

"I know he's your cousin, but I entrusted him with governorship of one of this kingdom's most valuable holdings. If he can't be bothered to come when recalled, I'll find someone better."

"He comes, milord. There was much to set right in Westport."

"And you told me not four days ago that it was a minor altercation, a few unruly guards. I want to hear from Loyne. And I want to hear news of Lady Deirdre there."

"It was far worse than I first was led to believe, milord."

"And what am I to tell the king when he arrives? That I did nothing? And that his majesty then should sit with this delegate and break bread? No. We both know the king wears his crown lightly, but even he would see this as an affront ... and I will not show weakness in that way."

"What would you have of me?"

"A plan. One that will please the king and that will send this jackass ... what was his name?"

"Krait, milord, Emil Krait."

"One that will send Delegate Krait back to his 'holy' master with his tail between his legs."

"Yes, milord."

"Anymore word from my cousin?"

"None, milord. His last missive was three weeks past to inform you he'd contracted the condottiere you sought."

"Right there is why we needn't worry about war with the Holy See."

"Milord?"

"Etruscia fields fewer than five thousand troops, most of which they need to secure their borders. Cousin Alexis has recruited the five best mercenary regiments available."

"It's a great deal of money."

"Worth every penny, Miles. I know you said we didn't need the additional troops, and we don't. We hired them to keep our enemies from contracting their services."

"Still, milord, a great deal of money."

"Worth every penny if it shortens this war by even a year. And it also is why we needn't worry about conflict with the Holy See. They can make things difficult for us in myriad ways, but they won't send troops against us."

"It seems, whatever he was doing, this delegate overplayed his hand in Westport."

"He did, Miles. Now come up with a plan that will teach him that lesson without making us look like bad hosts."

"I'll have something pristine, milord."

"Good. Walk with me down to the stables."

Isabel hated feeling like an eavesdropper, but what was she to make of that conversation? And where was Deirdre?

11. One's Authentic Self

They left a small pan of beans and biscuits on the coals for Sir Anton when he woke and made an early departure. The sky was overcast, and there was a faint drizzle, but the day otherwise had a pleasant feel about it, the way rainy days sometimes did.

As had been their habit, they set an easy pace and rode along some time in silence. The Fiend seemed in a cheerful mood, and Deirdre had gotten over her anger and her urge to kill the ugly knight from the night before. She still felt her feathers were somewhat ruffled, but she knew she'd get over it soon.

Unfortunately, her mouth didn't get that message, because after riding in the rain for some time it spoke up.

"Why didn't you let me kill him last night?"

"Kill who?"

"Who!? What do you mean who?" Those words no sooner left her lips than she realized the Fiend was having some fun at her expense. The nerve.

"Did you really want to?" the creature asked.

"What? Of course. Isn't that what you've been training me for?"

"True. I have been training you to kill, perhaps with somewhat too much zeal. Mostly, though, my interest has been to teach you to protect yourself, which often requires unscrupulous methods."

"I'll say," she said.

"I'm glad you agree. Self-defense is an important skill, and I won't always be ready at hand to come to your aid. And, more important, I savor certain … *unnatural* desires. I don't want my preferences to guide you."

The Fiend reined in his horse, and by habit her mount stopped as well. When it did, he reached across and placed an affectionate hand on her shoulder.

"Deirdre, I want you to find your authentic self, the true you, the person you are meant to be. You can do anything you want in this world, anything at all, achieve any goal or desire. If murder is a part of that, you need to decide that for yourself. Not because it's a thing I steered you toward, or because it was something you seized upon in a moment of anger or pique."

"And if I decide on murder?"

"Then I'll teach you everything you want to know."

"And if I want to become king of Albion?"

"There'd be a few obstacles to overcome first, but absolutely. There's nothing you cannot achieve."

By that time, their mounts had taken it upon themselves to continue along the road. Deirdre was deeply moved by the creature's words and tried hard not to show it, but she had to ask one additional question.

"But why did you have to give that ape Anton my surprise?"

"Surprise?"

"Stop having me on. He ate all the pudding last night."

"Child, I'll make you more pudding tonight, all you can eat." The ersatz knight turned in the saddle and began rummaging in a saddlebag. After some moments, he recovered a long object covered in cloth.

"What's that?"

"Your surprise. I meant to give it to you last night." He extended the package in her direction. "I gift this to you." When she reached for it, the knight added, "You have to say you accept it."

"Thank you. I accept your kind gift," she said, still not certain this wasn't another jest on his part. Like the gold he'd given her days before, this item was heavy. When she unfolded the oil cloth that bound it, she discovered a long-bladed weapon in a sheath. It wasn't so long as a sword, not even a short sword, but it was far longer than any dagger she'd ever held. When she drew it from its sheath, she discovered a thick fluted blade attached to its exceedingly long hilt. It wasn't fancy, just a plain steel blade, but it was a sturdy weapon.

"Be careful," he advised her. "It's incredibly sharp."

She gingerly returned the weapon to its sheath. "Thank you. But I don't understand. Am I to learn to use a sword?"

"If you like. But that's not what your new blade is for. It's extremely old, ancient even, and hasn't been used as a weapon for most of that time."

It took a few moments for his words to sink in before she understood. "It's an artefact?!"

"It is. I'm not sure you'll ever be able to channel Source magic with it. That's not a thing I could guide you in, and some people simply don't have the talent. But it is an exquisite item, and you'll be able to make good use of it as a weapon, if for nothing else."

She examined the thing and its sheath as they rode, several times pulling the blade partway out to look at it. "Where did you get it?"

"I've had it for ages. I couldn't even guess at its provenance, but it has a number of remarkable qualities."

"Like what?"

"You'll never have to worry about losing it."

"What's that mean?"

"The blade is infused with subtle and powerful magics. By some quirk, the thing will always find its true owner, which is you now, by the way. I've mislaid it several times and found it again. Once, in a moment of clumsiness, I even dropped it over the rail of a ship in the Southern Sea. Three days later, we made landfall, and I found the blade stuck in a piece of driftwood along the coast road."

"It came back to you?"

"It did, indirectly. I found out later that a fisherman had pulled it in with a haul and got so fed up with how often it cut and nicked him that he tossed it away. It landed where I found it."

"It's sharp?" she asked.

"Sharper than any razor you'll ever encounter. It'll cut through anything you're strong enough to force it through. And it never loses its edge. It will never dent, ding, break, or dull."

"It sounds too sharp," she said, now somewhat reluctant to bare the blade.

"That might be its most peculiar quality. It will never cut its true owner, not even a nick."

"Oh, tosh," she said.

"Give it a try."

With great reluctance, she unsheathed the blade and, after a few moments, gently drew the edge across the meat of her thumb. When she did, she jumped so suddenly she almost dropped the thing. It didn't exactly hurt, but a dreadful and an unnatural feeling raced through her hand and arm when she ran the naked blade against her skin. It was a ghastly sensation, but the weapon hadn't cut her skin in the least.

"And it will always find me?"

"Until you give it to another of your own free will, and that person freely accepts it."

"And I still get the pudding?"

"As much as you like, child."

———

The next few days' riding were easy and uneventful, and as they approached Mont Clair and saw more friendly and familiar faces, she and Sir Alexis resumed travelling on the High Road. They very nearly were at their destination.

It took a hard jolt for her to stop toying with her new knife. The keen edge of the weapon was a source of endless fascination, and she cut and sliced anything and everything that came within reach, including leather straps and pieces of tack and harness. When a careless swing of the blade nicked the withers of her sweet palfrey, she found herself landing heels over head in some roadside bushes for her trouble.

Thereafter she kept the blade carefully sheathed, but her mount joined the Fiend's mare in giving her unfriendly gazes. The Fiend said not a word in reproach.

They'd been on the road 18 or 20 days by her estimation when they finally reached the outer battlements of Mont Clair. She had to admit that it was an impressive fortress. Its heavy stone walls rose like a mountain above the valley that surrounded it. With all that, the place had a warm and congenial feel to it. To her surprise, the first person to greet them was a man she'd never before beheld who ran up and began kissing her left foot.

"The governor of Westport," the Fiend said after the man departed. "I imagine you being safe is a source of great solace for him at this moment."

To the sensibilities of a Surrey lass, their welcoming party was a peculiar affair. Among the Gheet, greetings were quick and informal for those returning from a long journey. Afterward, returned travelers were at their leisure to retire to their quarters and rest from the trip, for as long as three days by custom—the "traveler's grace" the Gheet called it—before they had to face a formal celebration of their return.

Greeting them now were the baroness, a few staff members, and two of the baron's children. Deirdre at first failed to recognize one of the women in their welcoming party. Her sweet and beautiful friend Lady Isabel was a worn and tattered shell of her former self, and Deirdre knew after her first glimpse of the woman that her friend was going to die.

12. Acacia Pandorus Majorem

The grippe was a wasting disease common to most parts of Albion, and there was to Deirdre's understanding no cure for it. It was why she nearly fell to tears when she saw Lady Isabel. The signs were obvious to anyone who'd seen the sickness, yellowed eyes, pale and drawn skin, and weight loss. In later stages, it wasn't uncommon for those afflicted to complain of stomach pains, bleeding gums, and tooth loss.

The course of the illness might take many months, even a year or two, but persons so afflicted just withered away to their graves.

It wasn't right for Deirdre to show her emotions in front of Isabel, but she scarcely could contain her worry and sorrow. And it was like ants were in her britches until she could steal away for a few whispers with Sir Alexis as their welcoming party departed and the servants took their effects to their chambers.

The Fiend clearly knew of what she spoke.

"I know of no magic to cure such an ailment," the fake knight said in response to her query. "It's a thing beyond me. Now, I need to speak with the baron. See to Lady Isabel. I'll return when I can."

She was furious when he strode away. What use was it to know magic if you couldn't help those dearest to you? Perhaps he was just a third-rate practitioner after all. It was difficult to keep the tears from her eyes, something it was obvious Isabel noticed.

"I'm just happy to see you," she told the woman, taking her into her arms. A few heavy tears seeped out before she stepped away. "Now, let's off to our chambers. I'm exhausted and want to hear of your winter's adventures."

"Where is Sir Alexis going?" Isabel asked.

"To see the baron. I imagine there're important affairs they need to discuss."

"What of you?" the woman asked. Isabel moved slowly, and the effort just to walk over to the staircase seemed much for her.

"Me? I'm fine."

"Even after the horrors in Westport? It's all people have spoken of at Mont Clair this last week."

"Oh, that!" Deirdre didn't know how the Fiend would paint the events at the city and wasn't certain what story she should give. The creature sometimes was not a keen planner. When in doubt, keep it vague and honest. "I had a few moments of fright, but Sir Alexis came early, and we made our departure."

"Everyone here was certain the baron would have the governor flogged when he arrived three days ago and couldn't give an accounting of your whereabouts."

"That wasn't his fault," said Deirdre. "The reverend thought we should keep ourselves to ourselves. I didn't often go into the city."

"Well, I'm glad you're safe. I worried for you when we first got news of troubles on the coast. Did you see any of the Etruscian soldiers?"

"Um…." This would require Deirdre to do a little dance. But why not continue with the truth? "I thought they might have been some of de Margot's scum at first. I wasn't certain what happened after that. Sir Alexis took me east, and the reverend left us soon after."

"How is he doing, by the way?"

"The reverend is his usual. I'm not sure the man ever sleeps. During the days, we were at lessons, and most nights he spent reading in the vicarage library, sometimes until dawn."

"It sounds like you had a wonderful winter." It was obvious the woman labored on the stairs, and with each flight she leaned more heavily on Deirdre.

"It was a pity you weren't there. You'd love Vicar Edgemont. Though I do worry about him. He's not young and only has a single servant who comes in once a week."

"That should be easy to solve," said Isabel. "We'll ask Sir Alexis to plant a bee in Sir Alfred Loyne's ear. I'm sure the governor will hasten to assign someone to look out for the vicar if doing so wins your favor."

The notion caused Deirdre to laugh. A Gheet noble worrying about what she thought? Hilarious. But then it came to her. From his name, Sir Alfred probably was a Surrey. If it was the same man who earlier had approached her on her mount, he certainly had that look. For the umpteenth time she had to remind herself that not everything was about the parochial conflict in Edwin Township.

By the time that thought occurred to her, she and Isabel had arrived at the tiny chambers the two briefly had shared the previous autumn. The place was cozy, and Isabel didn't seem to notice the smell of illness in the air. It still was early, but Deirdre went about getting Isabel ready for bed. The woman didn't protest, but instead made small talk of the various people in the castle, most of whom Deirdre knew only passingly.

When they'd finished Isabel's washing up, a smile spread across the woman's face, and she soon after began to cry.

"I'm really sick, aren't I?" There was a tone of self-pity in those words for which Deirdre refused to fault her friend. We all deserve to feel bad for ourselves sometimes.

"You'll be fine," she assured her.

"Would you tell me if I was?"

Deirdre slid into the bed beside Isabel and pulled her friend close. "Yes," she whispered, "it's bad. But Sir Alexis will sort it out. He knows all manner of things. And if it comes to it, he knows how to contact Reverend Ainsley. There's nothing the two of them can't fix."

Tears continued to flow, but Deirdre's words seemed to have set Isabel's heart at ease somewhat. If only Deirdre's confidence in Sir Alexis was as solid as she'd painted it.

No. Deirdre refused to slip into that type of despair. Her travelling companion was a monster, but he'd never once let her down on anything important. And Isabel's life was important to her, maybe as important as anything in the world. She'd lost too much, too many friends, too many family members. She refused to give up on her friend now. No one survived the grippe, but the Fiend would find a way if she had to set his tail on fire to make it happen.

After a long time had passed, she checked Isabel to assure that the woman was comfortable and truly sleeping. Then she slipped out of their chambers and went looking for the creature.

———

She had to search the castle both high and low, and she finally found her quarry long after sunset rattling through the castle's deep kitchen pantry. It seemed a strange spot, one of the last places she'd imagine the creature to be, but there he was, poking around in the near dark, a single meager candle ignored on the shelf nearby.

"The cooks soon will be here to start the morning meal," he said aloud before she'd even announced her presence. He was always doing that. "So, grab that box of things there on the floor."

"Whatever you're doing, stop it. We need to help Lady Isabel. There isn't time for any of your goosing about."

"Tuppence! Could you imagine in a thousand lifetimes I'd be up to anything else at this dreadful time of night?"

"The last I saw you, you said there was nothing to be done and scurried off to see the baron."

"The baron expected Sir Alexis, and I didn't say there was nothing to be done." He lowered his voice. "I said that I knew of no magics. That doesn't mean there aren't things we can do." He toed the box toward her with a single foot and shooed her along. "What we need to do needs be done under cover of darkness. Let's not waste time."

He hustled her through the kitchen, along the servants' hallway, and to the laundry, where they recovered an armful of sheets and towels. Then the two hurried across the training yard, into the residential tower, and up several long flights of stairs to her and Isabel's chambers in the family apartments. Several times, the Fiend bid her be silent. They spoke only after they were inside the chambers and the Fiend had checked to see that Isabel was sleeping.

"What are we to do?" she asked at last. "And why the secrecy?"

"The pantry doubles as an apothecary. I found all the items we need save one, and that one thing I'll have to conjure."

"Is it that easy?" she whispered.

"No. It's very difficult, and such things are dangerous to do in the castle." As he spoke, the Fiend organized bottles and vials on a small writing desk near the window. There was a brass apothecary's cup there as well.

"I don't …."

"Believe it or not, child, it's easier to conjure a hundred gold marks than it is to create a few grams of tree bark—and much less noisy. Now, mix a few drams from each of those bottles in the pestle there. It doesn't have to be perfect, just close. And make not a peep. I need to concentrate to make this as quiet as possible."

She did as she was asked, and a handful of moments later the Fiend lay a tiny sliver of what looked like tree bark on the table and sat back in a chair with an exhale of breath.

"My heavens," he whispered.

"Is it done?"

"It's done."

"What was that all about? You said there was no magic to help Isabel."

"True. No magic I know of. I just needed to conjure that one ingredient, the bark of an acacia tree that doesn't grow in these parts."

"Was it a spell you could cast only at night?"

He produced a small file and began to grind bits of the root into the pestle. "It's nothing like that, Tuppence. Conjuring things can be complicated, but not in that way. Like any such transaction, it requires a great deal of energy. Someone who is attuned to magic can sense such transactions."

"And they'll know someone has cast a spell?"

"Yes. But if they're asleep …."

"It's less likely someone will have noticed?"

"Yes, again," he said with a nod. "But this is just the first step. Do you know what the grippe is?"

"I only know it's a sickness."

"It is, a horrific one. But more specifically, it's a type of parasite, a living being that infects a person. It starts in the stomach and often quite swiftly invades the entire body, sapping a person's life."

"Like a leech?"

"Something like that, yes. This potion I'm preparing is a poison that either will kill the parasite or drive it from her body. But the potion is noxious to people as well. Over the next bell or two, your friend will grow deathly ill. If she survives that time, she should make a full recovery."

"How likely…? I mean, what are the chances it will work?"

"It definitely will rid her of the parasite. And Isabel is young and otherwise quite healthy. I think she'll be fine if we move now. But tonight will be very unpleasant, very embarrassing … and quite messy."

"Messy?"

"There's only one way for the parasite to leave her body."

"Oh … oh!"

"She'll need your help and comfort. Are you ready?"

It took only a short time for them to wake Isabel and to make the necessary preparations. After Sir Alexis explained what it was that they had in mind, the frightened and groggy woman agreed with a short nod.

The completed potion had no smell that Dierdre could detect, but it must have tasted awful, because it took Isabel several choking gulps to imbibe the entire draught. The reaction was almost immediate. The woman began coughing and groaning, and her body twisted and contorted several different ways.

It was a complete and utter surprise to Deirdre when sometime later the faux knight unceremoniously rolled Isabel over, bared her bottom, and reached between her legs. Even more shocking was the sight of what he pulled from inside her, long sickening threads of what looked like worms, all of which he deposited into a bucket he'd brought along. Isabel was beside herself with fear and pain. And all Deirdre could do was hold and console her friend.

The whole affair could not have taken more than a quarter bell, but it was simply horrendous. It was perhaps another full bell before Isabel no longer needed the chamber pot, and afterward, after Deirdre changed the woman's nightshirt and cleaned up the mess, she put her friend to bed.

Isabel was exhausted and asleep by the time the watch called dawn bell in the distance.

Soon afterwards, the Fiend returned with the chamber pot he'd gone to empty. The pot and his hands appeared freshly scrubbed. The room still needed a good airing and some more cleaning, but for now Deirdre was satisfied to sit by the desk for a few moments of rest.

The creature stepped over to the sleeping woman, smiled, and gently waved two fingers over her face. Almost as an afterthought, he touched Isabel's lip just once. When he did the same to Deirdre a few moments later, a surge of energy shot through her.

"What was that?" she whispered.

"Something I should have done before. Just a little cantrip to keep unclean food and water from doing you harm."

"Really?" It took her a moment to realize that she'd just been magicked upon. It wasn't at all what she'd imagined. It dawned on her further that perhaps this was the first time he'd done such a thing to her. She couldn't rightly say.

"Mm-hm," the Fiend said. "Such spells are simple and hard to detect. It won't protect you from poisons, but it's proof against most bad things you might ingest."

"Including parasites?"

"It should do so. Lady Isabel likely ingested a parasite seed in her water or through some bad piece of beef. She needn't worry about that again."

"Thank heavens." It truly was a relief. Perhaps magic wasn't that bad. "She'll get better now?"

"I think so. I checked her teeth. That's usually the sign there's been irreversible harm. Hers look fine."

"I have to ask," she said. "How are we going to explain this?"

"Ah … bother." The creature gave a weary look. "Let's keep the servants out for now, give the place a good cleaning. If anyone asks, we'll just say Sir Alexis had a pinch of acacia bark left over from his time in the Holy Land. That type of tree actually grows not too far from there."

"Have you really been to the Holy Land?"

"Many times over the ages. Though it isn't particularly holy."

"What do you mean, not 'holy'?"

"This Walking God is a powerful being, child. But he's no god, not truly. The power that people feel in the traces and pilgrimage routes of the Holy Land predates him by many ages."

"Wait. If it doesn't come from the Walking God, what kind of power are you talking about?"

"There are several routes in that part of the world. None have any deep power, but several are real … unlike the fake nonsense the church in its various denominations usually peddles as authentic."

"You've never shared any of this before."

"It never occurred to me. Your trivium and quadrivium seemed important to you, so it's on those we've focused your studies."

"I'd like to know about the Holy Land."

"Of course, but wouldn't you rather sleep first?"

"I'll sleep when I know Isabel is out of danger. Until then, I want to know more."

13. Walking the Ways

Keep one thing in mind, Tuppence. Whenever a tyrant wishes to dominate a people, that tyrant needs to win the cooperation of at least some of them."

"The vicar said something like that," she replied. "But he was talking about the Gheet invasion of Albion."

"That isn't exactly what I had in mind, but it's close. People crave dependability and continuity, especially in times of trouble. When the Gheet first invaded Albion, ages back, they adopted the existing land tenure rules they found here. So the Surrey gentry and free farmers who fell under the authority of Gheet barons knew with a certain degree of confidence that their laws of inheritance would be respected."

"That was smart of them."

"It was."

"Until the Gheet started murdering people and stealing their land."

"Child, that didn't happen everywhere in Albion. But let's not stray from the topic. Ages ago, in a time before my tribe came to this world, before the Walking God's tribe arrived, there was a way of doing things here."

"And that way of doing things involved pilgrimage routes?"

"After a fashion, yes. Folks didn't call them pilgrimage routes in those days. In ancient times, walking particular paths in a specific manner was a way that people had of expanding and nurturing their spiritual existence."

"That's simple," she said. "Follow the path of a saint, and you will be touched by the things the saint touched and share in his or her passion."

"Bah. Liturgical babble."

"What?"

"Tuppence, people in olden times walked specific routes not because of some silly saint, but because magic isn't evenly spread throughout the world. For that very purpose, ancient philosophers and magical adepts spent a great deal of time and energy mapping and studying the spread of eldritch power throughout their world. Once discovered, walking those mystical ways helped people cultivate their connection with the Earth and allowed them to develop a better and deeper sense of the power that flowed from it."

"Wait … you said this was before the coming of your two tribes?"

"Yes."

"There was magic in our world before the coming of your people and the Walking God's tribe?"

"Oh my, yes. There still is such native magic, great gobs of it in fact. This world of yours is awash with the stuff." The creature made a gesture as if shooing away gnats. "It's hard to see for all the magic sometimes."

"But not *just* Source magic?"

"No, of course not. There are hampers full of that stuff, true. But this world is practically soddened in its own brand of magic."

"How...?" Deirdre didn't know what to think. "... how would a person use it?"

"Almost no one does."

"No one?" she asked.

"Very few. There are a few practitioners of Earth magic here and there, witches and hexers who live along the fringes of civilization. But there hasn't been a proper wizard on this world in many ages."

"None?"

"Not a one."

"Where did they go?"

"It's not a pleasant story, Tuppence." The creature looked her square in the eye, a candid look on his face. "My tribe had as much to do with it as the other did. It took many hundreds of years, but we eradicated the native magic users of the world, tried our level best to stamp out their various cults and societies."

"But why?"

"The eternal reasons, child. Greed. Cupidity. Avarice. Both tribes wanted this beautiful world as their own, and both sought to wipe out any who stood in their way. The Walking God's tribe, though, those rascals were shrewd about it. They eventually usurped the system of routes and traces they found here, began calling them by new names after the various false gods they claimed to be. And then, over time, they slowly shifted those same cults to begin observing pilgrimages in new locations, along routes with no real power."

"And the real routes of power? What became of them?"

"They simply were forgotten. At least most of them were. The sundry branches of the Church still use a few of the true routes, but only minor ones."

"Like those in the Holy Land."

"The very ones."

"What sort of powers are we talking about? I mean … what does walking such a path do?"

"It varies. No two routes are exactly the same, and every person, who walks a route, experiences it with subtle differences. Some ways promote great physical strength or endurance, others great intellectual gifts, and others still help successful travelers understand magic and how to wield it. The routes the Church still uses tend to promote less-volatile things, obedience and complacency and the like. Ghastly notions, really. And an exceedingly small number promote healing."

"How would someone find one of these routes? You know, the forgotten ones?"

"That's something I might be able to help you with. Most ancient ways aren't terribly hard to find for someone willing to read some old books and who has even a skosh of natural ability, which most folks of this world do. With a little help and some practice, you should at least be able to learn to sense the presence of such power." The creature seemed to perk up. "And there are some obvious and natural places to look."

Something dawned on her, a connection between things she'd seen and others that she'd read in the past. "Waterways. Magic tends to follow waterways. That was why you ran us across streams and through swamps so many times when we fled the inn."

The creature smiled. "That is the precise reason."

"It should have occurred to me then," she said. "I don't recall exactly where I read that, but I should have put two and two together."

"Most scrying and spells of divination are very weak. Run through a stream or across a river, and it sometimes clouds someone's ability to see you or to anticipate your actions. Standing water is good, too. But it has to be old."

"Like a swamp, or a moat?"

"It's one of the reasons castles often are surrounded by water."

There were other things that influence magic, Deirdre was fairly certain. It probably was not something she'd read at the vicarage, but wherever she'd read such a thing, part of it stuck in her mind. Mountains sometimes caused magic to pool. And some minerals in the soil did as well. She would have to make that part of her lessons when she and the Fiend recommenced them.

"I'd definitely like to find some of these ancient routes," she said with greater confidence.

"That part shouldn't be a problem. The ways sometimes shift and change over time as the world around them changes, but only slowly over long periods. The hard part is knowing what to do once you get there."

"How so?"

"Some of the ways merely need to be walked. Others, especially the more powerful ones, often require something more."

"Like some sort of ritual?"

"I never conducted a detailed study of the subject, Tuppence. So I'm not sure. I think some of the things one needs to do to access the power of such ways are intuitive. And as you say, others may require some sort of ritual. Learning the finer details will require study … if such knowledge still exists. The Church long has sought to purge books that describe such things."

"Purge how? They burned them?"

"Sometimes."

"The bastards."

"True. But at times censors haven't even needed to exert that much effort. Many ancient books just died from neglect, either because the people who spoke the language in which they were written disappeared or simply because no one bothered to read them. It's an ignominious end, but books sometimes rot and molder on shelves because no one reads them or troubles to make new copies. Sad, so unspeakably sad."

"When can we do this? … Continue our lessons?"

"Not whilst we're at Mont Clair. People are going to make demands on our time for a while." He pointed to the young woman sleeping a few paces away. "And you have a patient to care for, at least for a week or two."

"I guess it can wait that long. When do we rejoin the army? We always had time for lessons last summer."

"Soon. Within the month is my guess. But I have some bad news."

Something cold climbed up her spine. "How bad?"

"Sometime within the next week, the king will meet with the delegate from the Holy See."

"The same fellows who we met at Westport?

"Yes, I think so."

"That's bad, but not that bad."

"They meet at Mont Clair."

She swore under her breath.

"Tuppence, we don't have to follow this path. I know you've become attached to Isabel, and in no small way to the de Vere family. But we could up and away and pursue our interests elsewhere."

"You are the sweetest monster," she said, a sudden hint of emotion in her voice. "The sweetest monster ever. I know our being here isn't all about me. You always have your plots and schemes at work, and I know being near the baron in this way suits your purposes."

"I can work those levers from anywhere."

"It's still a sweet offer on your part. But this place just so happens to be the safest spot in Albion right now. Have you forgotten our enemies know who I am? Or so we both suspect. And I can't change my face whenever it appeals to me."

"I just thought I'd broach the subject. Keep it in mind and let me know if you decide otherwise. Oh … one other thing."

"What?"

"William wants to grant Sir Alexis a small plot of land to cover his expenses. It's just a manor house with a few fields around it, not even a proper fief. But it might suit our purposes."

"How so?"

"A place other than Mont Clair to hang our hats. Perhaps, when Isabel is better, we can take a look. It's only a short ride away."

"Having that place won't interfere with all the lever pulling?"

"It has a property manager and a small staff. I'd only need to show up from time to time to make sure they aren't stealing the doornails."

"You couldn't say no to such a thing, I'd wager."

"No. And I think William has ulterior motives. His eldest is taking a stronghold up the river from there. I imagine the baron likes the idea of picking his son's neighbors for him."

"It doesn't hurt to have his uncle around." It was a strange Gheet custom, one she hadn't figured out, but the baron's children all called Sir Alexis, "Uncle," even though they were cousins.

"True … but speaking with the baron upon our arrival was a good thing. It's had me to thinking of our enemies. He's a clever man, William de Vere. He's under the impression that this delegation has come all this way to ask the king to appoint a Witchfinder General."

"That's what you first told me. Why is it a surprise?"

"It isn't really, except there's a degree of cunning I wasn't counting on. I thought, at first, that the Holy See might seek to invoke an Inquisition in Albion. It's the kind of thing someone does in war, calls the other side heretics."

"Why would they want a Witchfinder? Don't Witchfinders chase after those people you talked about who live on the edge of things, witches and hexers?"

"That's why a Witchfinder General would seem more palatable. Who doesn't like burning witches? The baron seems to think a Witchfinder is just a backdoor Inquisition. Only a few steps separate one from the other, and once one is invoked … boom. Too late to call it off, especially if the Holy See convinces the king himself to do the appointing."

"Why would the king do either?"

"Mm … it's more about politics than religion. The Holy See could appoint an Inquisition on its own authority, but such things haven't gone well for them in the past. They have other intentions in Albion, intentions I can't quite ferret out."

"Is it the Walking God's doing?"

"Perhaps. There's something I'm missing."

Deirdre couldn't suppress a yawn.

"I'm going to the kitchen to fetch some breakfast," said the Fiend. "You lie down next to Lady Isabel. She'll wake you if she needs anything."

To a suddenly sleepy Deirdre, that seemed like an awfully good idea.

14. The Traveler's Grace

The first thing Isabel sensed was someone in the room with her. It took some moments for her to realize it was Sir Alexis, on his hands and knees in his shirt sleeves, with a brush and bucket, scrubbing the flagstone floors near her bed.

"What…?"

"Good morning," he said. He tossed the brush in the bucket and came to his feet. "How are you feeling?"

It was only then that she remembered the events of the night before. Her head was still foggy, but clearer than it had been for some time. The whole episode was … whew. Words simply couldn't describe it, and she felt herself blushing.

"How…?" She had to clear her throat several times. "What happened?"

He sat on the bed next to her and gently checked her eyes. "I gave you a potion. Do you remember?"

"Last night … yes."

"The angels must love you, milady. The potion required an extremely rare ingredient, which I just happened to have a smidge of." He helped her sit up.

"Otherwise, I'd be in a lot of trouble, I think."

"The grippe is not an ailment to take lightly, but I have confidence you'll be fine now."

"How did you know?"

"About the grippe? It was something I discovered in the Holy Land. The folk there don't seem afflicted by it, and then I learned about a potion they make."

"And here in Albion?"

"Lady Isabel, our physicians try their best. It's something else I learned in my travels, always be candid with people about their condition."

She again saw the cleaning bucket. The room smelled fresher and cleaner.

"Certainly, there are servants for that?" she said to the knight. It was such an endearing thing about Alexis de Vere. He never hesitated to do for himself, or for others. It was so uplifting.

"Tuppence and I thought you'd like your privacy for a time, and it seemed appropriate. We both agreed we needed to do some small penance for having neglected you for so long."

"Don't be silly! Sir Alexis, you have been the best possible friend from the first day I met you."

"Be that as it may, we felt the urge to look after you ourselves. We hope you'll indulge us this tiny whim."

"Of course. Where is Deirdre?"

"Down at the kitchens fetching us up a supper. She'll be happy to see you awake. You gave her a worry." He lifted his hand when she moved to rise. "No, please. You'll need to rest for a few days."

"I still feel … oh, not as bad, but…."

"The nausea will pass. We have a libation we drink at such times, a mix of water and vinegar. I hope you'll sip as much as you can."

How could it have gone any other way? Of course, Sir Alexis was there in her hour of need. It was his nature, and for the first time, perhaps in forever, she felt especially blessed. He was such a good man, positively saintly. If he were any more wholesome and decent his feet wouldn't touch the ground when he walked. What woman wouldn't fall in love with him?

Where had that thought come from?

At that moment, the door chose to open, and Lady Deirdre entered with a heavy tray of food and drink. The young woman's face lit up and she rushed to deposit the tray on the desk and to climb into bed beside her.

"You look well," the youngster said.

"And you look taller. I didn't notice it yesterday."

The three of them visited for what must have been 30 minutes or so, after which Sir Alexis begged their pardon and, bucket in hand, left to attend to some affairs.

"You must have things to do as well," she told Deirdre.

The young woman, who had stretched out in the bed next to her, her head practically in Isabel's lap, replied in the negative.

"I'm sure the family will want to have time with you."

"We have the traveler's grace."

That's right, Isabel reminded herself. Those returning from a long journey had no social obligations for…?

"How long is it?"

"The grace? Until people start nagging us about being unsociable. Usually about three days."

"Sir Alexis says you're to be my servant for the time. But that doesn't sound fair."

"I bet you the great oaf claimed credit for that idea, too," said Deirdre as she rose from the bed to fetch the supper tray.

Isabel had to squelch a laugh. Sir Alexis showered Deirdre with affection, but Isabel so often saw the Surrey lass pummel the knight with abuse, even going so far as to refer to the man in her less guarded moments as a creature and a fiend. It first had startled Isabel to hear such words. Now she saw them for what they were, just part of the warp and woof of the love between them.

"He didn't claim credit. But you don't have to be my servant."

"I want to do it," said Deirdre, "at least until you're feeling better. And if you think you'll be a burden, don't. I put some blue carraway root in your stew."

"To help me sleep?"

"How did you know that?"

"We use it down at the convent."

"Ah, of course you do. Sir Alexis says you'll be sleeping a lot the next few days anyway. This'll make sure you sleep easier."

"I hope so," said Isabel. "I've been having the worst dreams lately. It will be wonderful if they're gone now."

The first spoon of the stew Deirdre fed her was lukewarm but delightful. She'd never been spoon fed before and felt a little silly for it.

"What kind of dreams?" the lass asked.

"Strange ones. Dreams so vivid it was like they were real, and the same ones over and over. They frightened me."

"Monsters and boogeymen?"

"No, nothing like that. They weren't nightmares. I don't know how to explain it."

"I always heard there was truth in dreams. I'm not sure now."

"I'll be happy to be rid of these." Isabel felt a little silly for saying it, but added, "I talked to Friar Emmet about them. He said I should pray."

"That's a friar's answer to most everything. That and urging folks to put money in the collection box."

"He's a nice fellow."

"I've found most friars to be halfwits or lechers."

"Well … I don't…." Isabel gave up her defense of the minor clergy. "I did find myself several times wishing I could talk to Reverend Ainsley about it."

This time, Deirdre gave a wholehearted nod. "Yup. He has his faults, but there aren't too many things the reverend doesn't know about. You might try talking to Sir Alexis in a pinch. He isn't as thick as he looks."

Isabel couldn't resist a laugh. Deirdre could be cranky and short-tempered, but she had a way of cutting straight to it and saying what was on her mind. It was refreshing in a way. There was no guile in the young woman, nor any real malice that Isabel could sense. And the youngster really had gotten taller and looked so fit she practically glowed. The coast had agreed with her.

And the blue carraway root appeared to agree with Isabel. She'd felt tired throughout her chat with Deirdre and the knight, but after having her supper a sleepiness came over her. She was having a difficult time keeping her head up. But Deirdre opted not to abandon her. The woman-child put away the tray and resumed her place on the bed next to Isabel, and the two talked for some time more.

———

Deirdre was still under the grace and spent the balance of her time during the next two days loafing around the castle's kitchens. Several times a day, she would stop by their chambers and check on her sleeping friend. Even in sleep, the woman looked better, and only once did Deirdre enter their chamber and find Isabel in an uneasy slumber. She did what her mother always had done. She kissed the woman's forehead once and rolled her into a new position. It seemed to do the trick.

Early on the second day, she was in the kitchen working away at a large slice of pecan pie when someone sat across from her at the table.

"Enjoying your grace?" It was the baron, a steaming mug of something in one hand and a stack of documents in the other.

"I am, milord."

"And how is your sister? Better I hope."

"Much better and sleeping away the rest of what ails her. She soon will be fit for visitors, I think."

"That's wonderful to hear. I knew something good would come of Alexis's many travels. We despaired for Lady Isabel's health until the two of you arrived."

"A minor miracle, baron." He was a nice man, she thought, a genuinely nice man, and his ways were very much like those of Sir Alexis. But Deirdre still wasn't perfectly certain how to speak with a nobleman. Should she have stood and curtsied?

"I'm happy Alexis has you in your books." He motioned to the closed volume on the table beside her. "What are you reading now."

"Oh … *Simonton on Algebraic Geometry.*"

"An old friend. Which edition?"

"I ... I'm not sure."

"May I?" asked the baron as he reached for the item.

"Please, milord."

The nobleman picked up and leafed through the slim volume like it were a lover, finally settling on a page near the front. A great smile cracked his face.

"The third edition," he said. "The very best."

Deirdre hesitated only a moment. "I'm not sure of.... What's an edition?"

"What? ... I guess someone your age wouldn't know. Some years back, folks tried their hands at making books through a process called printing. It's done through applying ink and paper to etched and raised letters on a metal plate. It's very efficient and makes books that are virtually identical to one another. Each time a set of the same book is produced in that way, that set is called an edition. The third of Simonton is the best, beautifully done and wholly free of errors. A masterpiece."

"They're all the same?"

"Indeed. If you find another copy of the third edition, there will be wear and tear on one that isn't on the others, but the two copies will read exactly the same."

"How clever! You said they used to do this?" Deirdre found herself trying to square such an exquisite notion as editions with the cobweb-festooned contraption she'd once stolen a peek at in the vicarage shed.

"Ah, well. Printing isn't exactly illegal, at least not in Albion, but it would be if the copyist guild and scrivener's union had anything to say about it. They make their bread and beans with quill and parchment. The parchment-makers didn't much favor printing either, come to think of it. Paper is far more suitable for printing. That lot wields great influence at court, as does the Church."

"The Church doesn't like printing?"

"That's a deep river to ford. Let's just say the last thing the high clergy want are cheap and easily available books. Such a state might lead too many people to thinking, and to asking too many uncomfortable questions."

"Is it ... would it be rude to ask how you come to know all this?"

"The same way you do, lass. I've read most of it in books. If you're of a mind, stop by my study and see Miles Lightfoot. He'll loan you a manuscript by a chap named Fester on the complete history of printing.

"A manuscript?"

"Ha! Irony of ironies, Deirdre. The finest history of printing in the land isn't available as a printed book."

Something completely unrelated to geometry and printing entered her mind. It was a thing she'd been gnawing on for many days, and the baron was a wise and well-read man.

"Milord, what does it mean to be one's authentic self?"

"One's authentic self? I'm not sure I know. Where'd you pick up such a notion?"

"It was … um ... something Reverend Ainsley said to me. He said I should strive to be my authentic self. I thought about it a lot, but now I'm not sure what it means."

"Ah, the elusive Reverend Ainsley. From what Alexis and Lady Isabel have told me of him, he sounds like the ideal clergyman, a man who is very much a scholar and a philosopher."

"He is many, many things, milord."

"Well, I'm sure the reverend has told you what the Church has to say about fate and our lot in life."

"We are each born to tread our own path, each one known only to the Divine," said Deirdre, quoting scripture to the best of her recollection.

"Exactly. I haven't seen anything in my studies or elsewhere that undermines that idea. On the contrary, many philosophers teach something similar. They don't use the same words as a theologian. Instead of the Divine, a philosopher would say we all have a part that the Universe has assigned us. Fate is fate, I suppose, no matter how it's worded."

"So we have no choice in selecting our authentic self?"

"That's what scripture teaches us, and it's hard to argue against. A man is a farmer because his father is a farmer, and his father before him. Isn't that just part of the natural order?"

"And someone can't be something else?"

"They can within reason, I imagine. The head of the tanner's guild in Westport once mentioned to me that he'd apprenticed one of his sons to a mason. The young man didn't follow in the footsteps of his father, but, in the end, he is still a tradesman."

There was something to what the baron said, but it didn't feel as if that's what the Fiend had in mind. She'd always grown up believing as the baron did. We are allotted our fate. It's why the commoners were the commoners, the gentry were the gentry, and the king was the king.

But was all of that simple destiny? Or was it just the nature of the world in which they lived? A man's lot in life could make him a farmer, but was it predestined that he be kicked to death by a mule at age 41? Or murdered by a covetous Gheet neighbor at 16? Was Lady Isabel destined to die of the grippe before she was 30?

Was that what the Fiend meant? It didn't seem so. He had, in fact, insisted that Deirdre could be and do whatever she wished. Perhaps he was talking about character? Was Deirdre, or anyone else, free to be a good person or a bad? Or was that predetermined too? If you believed the Church, it was. The clergy forever were talking about virtue and station. Why else were the gentry known as the "nobles"? And the Walking God always knew your heart, even before you were born.

But that couldn't be right. If a person walks a path that they were destined to walk, even before they were born, how could it be said they had any choice in the path or in the walking of it?

She smiled and thanked the baron for his counsel.

"No. Thank you, Deirdre." He came to his feet. "Now I'll have something interesting to speak about with the delegate of the Holy See when he arrives. Enjoy your grace."

She rose and did her best to curtsy, and then went back to her pie and her book.

15. A Day in the Sun

It was the first genuinely warm day they'd enjoyed since leaving the coast. Westport never felt the true bite of winter, and spring there came much earlier than it did elsewhere in Albion. But it was balmy that day at Mont Clair, and the Fiend somehow had coaxed Deirdre out to the pond that members of the family and staff used for their spring and summer leisure.

To her surprise, it was a delight. But she kept her clothes on. The Gheet were queer folk in so many ways, and it never ceased to amaze her the frequency with which they allowed their clothes to slip from their bodies. Not everyone bared themselves in that way. Usually it was just the boys, and several times in the past she'd walked through the common areas of the family apartments and found one or the other of the de Vere kin as naked as the day they were born.

That morning at the pond, about half the people were skinny-dipping, and the others lounged about in various stages of deshabille. It wasn't often that the baroness gave license to such wholesale frolicking, so folks were soaking it in.

As warm as the sun was, the water at the pond was cold. A scantily clad Deirdre made several bold sorties into ankle-deep water before beating a hasty retreat to warm and dry land. It was only after a smidgen of badgering from Sir Alexis and two of the baron's children, twin girls of about Deirdre's age, that the Surrey lass finally plunged in and splashed about breathlessly until her body grew accustomed to the chill of the water.

It wasn't that the cold water was a stranger to her. She swam in the cold often, but never for her leisure. And yet, it wasn't so bad, and for a time she lost herself. The worries, doubts, fears, and pain of the last year slipped away as she splashed about, played games with the youth, and even allowed the Fiend to take her up on his shoulders for a time as they tilted with other teams in a mock tournament. It was splendid.

After a time, as often was the case with such things, her body grew so accustomed to the water that she didn't want to get out, and she and Sir Alexis lounged in the deep water near some reeds. They talked of various things as the others present drifted back to work. It was the last day of their grace, and tonight there was to be a banquet celebrating their return. She wasn't sure what to expect.

"Will it be like a birthday party?" she asked the creature. It couldn't be too bad; the Fiend didn't seem the least bit vexed by the attention.

"Nothing at all like a birthday party. It'll be much like any other dinner, but with a bit finer fare. The baron and baroness will say a few words— all pro forma, of course—and you might be asked to dance."

"I don't know how to dance." A sudden fear crawled up inside her.

"You'll be fine. No one is likely to ask you to disrobe."

Not long before, it would have taken her some time to realize the Fiend was teasing her. She still needed to remind herself occasionally that she always should presume that he was.

"Stop it," she said. "I don't have to dance."

"Not unless you want to. As I said, it's just like any dinner."

"Mm … the Gheet do sometimes dance at dinner."

"Sometimes, but not often. And it's never mandatory. But, fair warning, the festival for the king, when he arrives, will be far more lavish. Young men likely will ask you to dance."

"Can I say no?"

"Of course, you can."

"Then I will."

"Do you have a sweetheart yet?"

"No, I don't have a sweetheart." She felt her hackles rise. "You're not marrying me off to anyone!"

"Tuppence, of course not. I'd never. Besides, it's not the Gheet way."

"You're not a Gheet."

"No, but Sir Alexis is. He is among the most Gheet-like of Gheets. And another warning. If the baroness hasn't already, she's likely to sit you down for a talk. With the arrival of the king and the gathering of the army, Mont Clair will be awash with eligible young nobles. Baroness Elise takes a well-deserved pride in her skills as a matchmaker. Don't be surprised at the young swains she steers your way."

"Yuck."

"I wouldn't say 'yuck' to the baroness. And don't close the door on it. I know the more delicate mercies of life are not something you need or want right now, but they are among the sweetest things this world has to offer."

"What would you know of it?"

"I had a sweetheart once."

"Oh, bollocks."

"Tuppence, I lie not. Many ages ago, I was curious about some doings of the Church and inserted myself as a young child at one of their more prestigious schools. Despite my considerable efforts to avoid such codswallop, several of my fellow students insisted on making me their friend. Among them was a young girl."

"And she was your sweetheart?"

"Not until much later. She was the beloved of a friend of ours, someone very dear to both of us. But after he died, she and I became close. Grief has a way of doing that. We ended up being incredibly happy together, she and I, and after our time at the school had passed, I stayed with her to her dying day."

"You had a wife?"

"I did. More important, I had a sweetheart. Her passing caused me great pain, it's true. But I wouldn't trade that time for anything. Don't ever be afraid of happiness, Deirdre."

The Fiend's tender story struck something deep in her heart, and she found herself looking up to the narrow window of the tower where her chamber was located and thought again of Lady Isabel. The young woman was doing much better, but declined their invitation to lounge by the pond. Deirdre smiled and waved when she thought she saw the foreign beauty watching them from the window.

"Do you imagine Lady Isabel will ever marry?" she asked the creature.

"I think in her own way she is as put off by romance as you are. It's understandable."

The woman was an eccentric being, Deirdre had to agree. Isabel was from another world, and their ways in Albion must have been a frightening mystery for her. But the young woman said such odd things.

"Lady Isabel once told me that if one plots revenge, one should dig two graves."

"Two?" said the Fiend. "I should think that wouldn't be nearly enough."

"I told her the same thing," said Deirdre with a laugh.

"A few thousand probably wouldn't suffice. What's the point in revenging yourself against someone if you leave any of his male relatives alive to seek retribution?"

Deirdre began laughing aloud, as did the Fiend. "Again, my words exactly. She didn't seem to understand."

A sudden shiver hit her, and, as she rose from the water, she became fully aware that the skimpy undergarments in which she'd been bathing were all but see-through. Her arms half draped across her in a pointless attempt to shield her modesty, the lass bounded for her clothes some paces distant, only to feel a wave of icy cold water strike the back of her neck.

The Fiend, bucket in hand, soon was hot on her trail, and Deirdre ran screaming toward the castle walls.

———

Isabel sometimes felt a knot rise in her throat when she watched Alexis and Deirdre together. As she observed the two now, she wished for a moment that she'd joined them at the pond. It looked wonderful.

But she still wasn't feeling quite herself. Nausea came and went, she still couldn't be too far from a chamber pot, and she trembled somewhat when she walked. But otherwise, she felt as if she was on the mend. Most important of all, her head had cleared, and her thinking was back to normal.

Lordy, it was as if she was emerging from a fog, one that had beset her for many weeks.

Sadly, the dreams were still there, but the intense realism of the images didn't disturb her as they had. The experience now was more focused and organized. She saw the same sequence of places, all brought to her with astonishing clarity, but it was less haunting. In fact, for the first time, just last night, there'd been something almost captivating about it.

It wasn't at all clear what she should do. She'd briefly mentioned the episodes to Deirdre, but in hindsight perhaps she shouldn't have. The young woman had been beset herself by uneasy sleep and disturbing dreams for as long as Isabel had known her. Perhaps they were kindred spirits, but until Deirdre opened up about what so troubled her, Isabel didn't feel it was her place to stir up ugly memories.

It did her heart good to watch the young woman from the window, basking and playing in the sundrenched pond below. My, how she and Alexis were a pair, so solemn and yet so goofy in turns. Even as she had that thought, Deirdre looked up from the pond and waved. There must have been a hilarious joke between her and Sir Alexis, because the two soon were nearly doubled over in laughter.

It was surprising to see this carefree side of her friend. Deirdre usually was conservative and fastidious in her personal habits. Seeing her young friend running now, scantily clad and screaming like a banshee, reminded her that Deirdre was just a kid. Back home, the youngster barely would have been old enough to drive a car.

She'd decided to talk with Sir Alexis. Deirdre was right. The man was no kind of Moorcroft Ainsley—they certainly broke the mold on that one—but it was without a doubt that the knight was wise and well learned. And she trusted him without hesitation. She several times had pondered opening up to the baron. He too was smart and well read, but there was always something on his plate. And she wasn't certain that anything she told him might not be taken the wrong way. Like most politicians, the baron was always juggling a dozen things. She was half suspicious he merely would refer her to one of his aids, Miles or … heaven forbid ... Friar Emmet.

"Go pray on it, my child," she whispered.

No. There was no guile, no ulterior motives with Alexis de Vere. The man had given up status and wealth to help others. A person knew with Sir Alexis that anything he did for them he did for them alone.

She made a resolve. No doubt the knight was busy, but she felt the need to share her dreams with him, and she'd very much these last weeks wondered what his thoughts might be on the quest. She had not stopped thinking about that.

Moving back over to her bed was easy, easier than it had been just a few hours before, and she leaned back on a pillow to do some recitations of one of the tomes Friar Emmet had lent her. She fully intended to attend the banquet that night celebrating the return of her friends, and she would need her rest.

16. An Outcome both Just and Wise

A little bit of knowledge is a dangerous thing." Those were the only words Sir Alexis spoke on the previous evening that Isabel hadn't perfectly understood.

The banquet could not have gone better. It was a fun and lighthearted gathering, with much food, drink, and dance. As she so often was, Deirdre was happy and forlorn in turns, but had put on a good face, even when a great many young men had come to ask her to dance.

The first contingents of the royal army had begun to arrive, mostly the soldiers of the baron's nearest vassals, and there were a great many faces at the fete that Isabel hadn't recognized. But it still had the feeling of a comfortable and intimate affair.

Afterward, Alexis carried Deirdre up to their chambers—the lass had imbibed far more than a few too many—and after Isabel put her roommate to bed, she recounted recent events to the knight.

Much to her relief, he hadn't poopooed away her worries. Rather, he'd taken them quite seriously.

In hindsight, his advice made a great deal of sense. It was normal for those afflicted by the grippe to run a fever, he'd told her, and such things often led to unusual thoughts and perceptions. The fact that those images were still with her? Perhaps she wasn't yet perfectly healed, and, in such an event, the dreams might stay with her for some time. Powerful memories often were like that. And what precisely was it that Isabel feared? Merely the unknown? There was nothing overtly frightening in her dreams, so why be frightened of them?

The knight had seemed irked only once, and that was when she'd mentioned her conversations with Friar Emmet. Alexis refused to naysay the clergyman expressly, but it now seemed to Isabel that he thought what the friar had to say on the subject was piffle. A little bit of knowledge....

She felt so good the morning after their talk that she decided to take a walk around the castle. Not too far, of course. Just down to the kitchen, and perhaps out to the stables. Not wanting to overtax herself, she gave herself as much time as necessary to rest along the way.

Happily, the walk down to the kitchen took no longer than usual. Although she was somewhat out of breath at the end of it, her spirits were bolstered by the warm reception she got there from family and staff. It was remarkable what a few kind words could do.

She dallied for a time, chatting and regaining her strength, before making the trek out to the stables. When she'd last seen Deirdre in the early hours, the youngster had been in her working clothes and was headed in that direction to help muck, curry, and make room for some new mounts the baron had obtained from a place called Eran. That land was famous for its warhorses and the hundred or so new beasts were the first in a large number coming to support the army.

By the time she excused herself and headed out the broad double doors to the courtyard, she again was feeling more herself. She was tired, but it was not the worn-down type of exhaustion to which she'd so recently become accustomed.

It was another balmy day, and a moment of embarrassment seized her when she saw a throng of people ahead at the stables. She thought it was another welcoming party. But no. There was something afoot near the south stables, and within a few minutes the crowd parted, and three burly guardsmen half dragged a young man toward the central keep. The lad looked both bloodied and muddy, but the cut of his clothing and his otherwise put-upon demeanor said he was a noble of some type.

Behind him, from the press, Lady Deirdre rushed up, murder in her eyes, and took a swing at the lad with something heavy in her hand. A fourth guardsman, an older man whose name Isabel couldn't recall, inserted himself between Deirdre and her target and, in tones that were surprisingly gentle, urged her to forgo further violence.

"He goes to his lordship for judgement, young miss. Be a fine young lady and leave off now."

The commoners, Isabel had found, had a way of gently managing the gentry, and that especially was true of the older generation of soldiers and servants. To Isabel's surprise, Deirdre did leave off, and soon was standing near the old soldier trembling. It wasn't clear if it was anger or fear that Isabel's friend suppressed. She didn't ask, but rushed up and put her arms around the youngster.

"There-there, now," were the old soldier's gruff but gentle words, "the young lady has you in hand now."

What in the Hell had that been all about?

———

It wasn't uncommon for local reeves and bailiffs to bring accused malefactors before the baron for judgment. Adjudicating in that way was not the central focus of the baron's duties as liege, but it was something that took up a certain amount of his time.

Such affairs were swift, but not hasty. Usually, judgement was put off for a number of days in order for witnesses to be found and brought to the castle. In the interim, those standing accused of minor infractions, or those against whom evidence was scanty, often would be released on their own parole, or after having paid a small surety. Those accused of more serious crimes might expect to endure days or weeks in the dungeon beneath the castle while awaiting his lordship's judgment.

Laying hands upon the daughter of the lord of the castle? That appeared to be one of those crimes that assured a defendant immediate justice, one way or the other.

Deirdre at first was too agitated to speak, so it took some time for Isabel to puzzle out the entire story, and much of what she learned was revealed during the course of the short trial later that day. A young aristocrat, the third son of a landed knight in the baron's service, had stolen up behind Deirdre as she worked in the stables and, no doubt presuming her nothing but a serving girl, had reached around and sampled the feel of the young woman's breast.

Those present at the trial were aghast at the testimony, as one of the young man's own companions had described the circumstances. "It was just a lark," the thickset young man said after giving those details. "We'd no idea she was...."

From time to time, Isabel had seen Baron William annoyed, several times even angry. But she never had beheld the man as he was now. His self-control was remarkable. His face gave not a hint of what he was thinking, but the man positively blanched as the testimony was given. The son of one of his vassals had laid hands upon one of his daughters. The baron hid his outrage well, but the gasps and pregnant silences as person after person came forward to testify to events was telling.

No one ever had seen anything quite like it. The most startling testimony regarded Deirdre's reaction to the assault. She'd spun around, snatched up something heavy, and cold-cocked the young man. The fellow then dropped face-first into a horse patty, whereupon Deirdre jumped onto the scalawag's back and began to pummel him further. Only the timely arrival of the sergeant of the watch had saved the young aristocrat from a further hiding.

His beating and humiliation at the hands of his victim wouldn't save him from judgement, however. The lad simply had grabbed the wrong young woman's breast.

The exact nature of her and Deirdre's status in the de Vere family continued to perplex Isabel. Technically, she and Deirdre were the wards of Sir Alexis, but adoption into the baron's family made both young women the baron's children in the eyes of the law. It was another of the many peculiar customs of Gheet society.

The assailant's father, Sir Elliot Coetzee, a burly old knight who stood beside his son Gerhardt in the docks, was the only person more mortified than the baron. The man was stone-faced and rigid throughout the proceedings. On any number of occasions, the baron gave the man an opportunity to ask questions of witnesses. The fellow always declined. And, when at the end of testimony, he was afforded the right to call witnesses on the behalf of his son, the knight called none.

It seemed rather open and shut, but to Isabel's surprise the baron didn't render a verdict after hearing testimony. He instead charged three knights among the large company present—all of whom were in full armor, fresh from the tilting grounds—to step into the next room and decide whether the lad was guilty of having assaulted a woman of the baron's family.

Deliberations were brief. A scant 15 minutes after having been charged, the three knights returned and said, yes, the young man had broken both law and custom. But to Isabel's further surprise, the baron turned to the guilty young man's father and instructed him to name a suitable punishment.

The knight promptly declared his son outlaw, and within mere moments of the verdict, young Gerhardt Coetzee fled Mont Clair with nothing but the clothes on his back.

What was she to make of such a thing? Isabel had watched proceedings of this kind a few times in the past year. The baron could be harsh, even cruel by the standards of Isabel's old world. Once, during the previous summer's campaigns, he'd ordered more than a dozen men hanged for assaulting a woman at a convent near an enemy stronghold. Among that number was the men's officer, who hadn't been present at the crime, but who shared their punishment, because he'd failed to keep his men in line.

The peculiar thing was that rape didn't seem to be a crime in and of itself. It all was tied to the status of the victim and to that of the perpetrator, and the location and circumstances of the offense seemed to matter. It wasn't the most inexplicable element of local custom, but it was frustrating.

Deirdre's reaction to the day's events seemed no less baffling. At first angry, the lass was sporting and joking with Sir Armand within minutes of the end of the proceedings. It was awfully bizarre, so she cozied up to Sir Alexis to seek his guidance again. Like the other soldiers who were present, the knight was in full battle array and smelled of sweat, horse, and turf. But his advice was no less solid.

"I know our ways are different," said the knight. "To be honest, we don't always understand them ourselves. But you are quite right, noble and commons are judged differently. The baron usually has the authority to pass judgment himself, but the member of any noble house can demand a verdict by impartial jury."

"But Sir Elliot didn't demand it."

"The baron granted it anyway. All could tell William was indignant, and he didn't want there to be any question that he was a biased judge."

"It still isn't clear to me," she said. "The baron gave the man's own father the right to name his punishment. I've never seen that."

The knight shrugged his heavily armored shoulders. "You may never see it again. That was my cousin being a wise and clever man."

"Wise in what way? He didn't want anyone thinking he was being biased? Couldn't he have asked the jury to decide?"

"He could have done that," answered the knight. "Or he could have decided himself. In Albion, Lady Isabel, laying hands on the daughter of your liege is a crime punishable by death. By allowing Sir Elliot to name the punishment, William was being merciful. But he also was testing the loyalty and good judgement of a vassal."

"Do you think the punishment was too harsh?" Isabel couldn't decide. Banishment seemed like a light sentence for a crime that could fetch a person death. But it seemed overly harsh for grabbing a young woman's breast. Sir Elliot's son was an outcast now, a man who was forbidden food, drink, and shelter anywhere within the baron's domains. And Baron William's domains stretched many, many days travel in every direction.

"That is a difficult question," Alexis said. "For some, banishment, declaring someone outlaw, is a fate worse than death. Others find it preferable to the headsman's axe."

"What if ... what if Deirdre wasn't the daughter of a baron?"

"You know the answer to that, Isabel. That young man and I would have settled the issue in an open field."

Isabel had seen the fighting skill of Alexis de Vere firsthand. Such a match would not have been any sort of contest.

"But what of people who don't have a great knight as a protector?"

"I wish I had a good answer for you," the knight said after a solemn nod. "The genteel response would be to say that a true knight defends the weak and protects the helpless, whoever they are and wherever he finds them. But that isn't always the case. It's a simple fact that in this land the lives of commoners and the virtue of their women are valued less than the lives and chastity of those of noble blood."

Those were the most honest and candid words Isabel had heard in Albion.

17. An Unexpected Caller

The day after her groping was a day like any other for Deirdre. Rather, it was like any other day until a group of riders arrived in the midmorning. According to those with whom she'd spoken, the delegation of the Holy See was not due to reach Mont Clair for nearly a week, a full three days after the arrival of the king and his party.

But the riders, clad in the red livery of the so-called Bishop of Etruscia, were no advance party of scouts, nor were they a group of servants sent forward to ready the quarters of the delegation. The captain of the group declared that His Eminence the Delegate would be arriving in the early afternoon. Deirdre promptly dropped what she was doing and went to investigate.

She found Sir Alexis leaving the baron's study and was able to maneuver the fake knight into the stairwell for a quick chat.

"What of it?" she demanded.

"Tuppence, you'll have to be…."

"They're here already."

"Oh, that. Yes, the baron received news of the delegate's early arrival late last evening."

"And you didn't think to…."

"Does it really matter?" asked the creature.

"Haven't I been caught unawares enough lately?" she nearly shouted. The truth was that being groped the previous day hadn't shaken her terribly, and she'd taken a certain delight in coshing the young noble in question, but enough was enough. She wanted to be kept informed of what transpired around her. No more surprises!

"Darling Tuppence," said the pretend nobleman, "you're quite right. I'll do my absolute best not to surprise you in the future. But, for now, the delegation soon arrives. I'll do everything within my power to shelter you, but breathe easy. You are under the protection of the most powerful lord in the land, and anyone who seeks to do you harm already has stirred that lord's wrath. You are a friend in these walls. These newcomers are not."

It made sense, and Deirdre went back about her business. If the Fiend had taught her nothing else in their time together, he'd taught her the great utility of blending in and pretending nothing was amiss. People who acted suspiciously soon had suspicious eyes cast upon them.

And she enjoyed working in the stables. Horses were good company, and even the high-spirited war mounts of Mont Clair had a certain charm she liked. They were a far cry from the plough horses with which she'd grown up, but it was pleasant work. After finishing her mucking, she curried a few mounts, helped mend two harnesses, and aided the blacksmith in shoeing a beast.

To her great delight, she more or less forgot about the arrival of the delegation from the Holy See until a great commotion and a sounding of horns announced their arrival as she and Isabel were finishing lunch in their chambers. The window there was narrow, but it provided an excellent view of the arriving clerics as they and their entourage approached the outer wall and the first of them wended their way up to the main castle.

The fanfare was to be expected. She'd always heard about the great pageantry of the Old Rite Church, even though that denomination now had few adherents in Albion. Nowadays most everyone in Albion followed the New Rite, in its Unreformed and Reformed flavors, though all denominations—and this was the hitch Deirdre never understood—labored under the belief that they remained a single Church.

It was odd, but one should expect little more from the clergy.

This particular body of Old Rite clergymen, the ones sent from the Holy See in Etruscia, she recognized from having seen them before in Westport. But she would have recognized their kind anyway. Unlike the Unreformed clergy, who dressed in a style somewhat similar to regular folk, Old Rite priests always were bedecked as if they were on their way to the bath. Great woolen robes, bared ankles, and simple sandals were typical. True, one sometimes saw Reformed Church monks and friars clad in such ridiculous fashions, especially those who were on pilgrimage. But Reformed clergy like Vicar Edgemont most always wore stiff-collared shirts and long frockcoats or cassocks. And they always wore trousers.

The bare-ankle group who arrived now were all in grey robes, and they alighted from their handsome mounts a furlong or so outside the perimeter gate. From there, they began to walk the last stretch to the castle proper. It was such a ridiculous affectation, one for which clergy of all stripes were notorious. Humble men walked, in the fashion of the Walking God, but many were the religious minded who kept a handsome stable and who never went farther than the lane's end without a saddle stitched to their backsides.

The cleric in the lead wasn't the ugliest man she'd ever seen, but there was something unpleasant and unseemly about his appearance. He didn't move like a pious man, and his face just seemed too large for his body. It was the very face she'd seen in Westport, the one who had sicced the guards on her and sweet Vivian.

Hate was an irrational emotion, she knew, but she hated this man. This was the kind of person for whom hate was the only proper reaction.

"I'm still not quite certain what they're here for," said Isabel. The woman watched through the narrow window, her head just below Deirdre's chin.

Deirdre gave Isabel's shoulders a light squeeze. How to respond to that? There was an exceptionally good chance that the men were at Mont Clair searching for Deirdre, but that wasn't something she intended to share, even with her closest intimate.

"Sir Alexis says there's some sort of politics behind it. I'm not sure either. They probably will offer to help negotiate a peace with de Margot and his trash. But Sir Alexis thinks they might want an Inquisition in exchange."

"An Inquisition? That doesn't sound good."

"I don't think it is," said Deirdre. "And I don't think the baron's going to encourage the king to negotiate."

"Why not?"

"Because kings don't negotiate with traitors. They hang them."

"Ugh. But de Margot is such a frightening man."

"He won't look so frightening on the gibbet," replied Deirdre. "Besides, the king's armies are winning."

The idea of being frightened by Etienne de Margot didn't appeal to Deirdre. The man did frighten her somewhat, but the idea of it? No, fear was not a sentiment she intended to harbor. That was no way to live.

She really should stay in her chambers and remain out of sight as much as possible while the delegation was there, but the idea of fearing the man with the large face was no more enticing to her than fearing de Margot. Besides, there was a strong likelihood her absence would be noticed. She had no intention of acting suspiciously, so after she put Lady Isabel to bed for her afternoon nap, she went back about her affairs.

The rest of the day was uneventful. There was a certain amount of chatter and a fair degree of gawking at the presence of so many foreigners, and several times the stablemaster had to crack a quite literal whip to get folks back to work. Deirdre paid the fuss no mind.

Most of the delegate's entourage was camped outside the castle proper, but a good host could not refuse to grant those so encamped the run of the place. The whole party could not have numbered more than 100, but the outsiders made pests of themselves. She couldn't understand a word of their language, but the soldiers of the Holy See had sneering and smirking to a high artform.

The Fiend once, many months before, had warned her about the sense of superiority held by many who inhabited lands closer to the Southern Sea. To such folk, their sunny homes were the center of the world, and anyplace that didn't have year-round spring was inhabited by people who were little more than cattle. She saw that in the sneering and condescending folk who now swaggered and loafed around the castle yard.

As near as she could tell, no one from Etruscia had anything to feel superior about. As a group, they neither were tall nor especially strong looking. And there wasn't a decent moustache or beard among them. With strong chins and heavy brows, they weren't a misshapen people, but neither were they so comely as the least favored Gheet.

And there was something else about them.

In that part of the world, or so she'd heard, farmers were tied to the land, not quite slaves but not fully free. Such an arrangement wasn't unheard of in Albion, but what sort of people allowed themselves to live in that way? Even her people, the Surrey of Edwin Township, at least owned their land and could come and go as they pleased.

She decided she didn't like any of these Etruscian people. Who were they to look down on anyone?

Still, though their unpleasant stares spoke volumes, none of the delegate's servants or soldiers said or did anything that a reasonable person could interpret as an affront. They had that much sense at least, especially given the large number of troops loyal to the baron that now camped outside the castle.

The rest of the day was uneventful. The foreigners had waived the traveler's grace, which meant there would be festivities that evening at which she would be expected. She would try hard not to say anything inappropriate and would refrain from over imbibing.

She wondered what the Fiend was up to.

——

The banquet that evening was not as unpleasant as she'd feared, nor as delightful as she might have dreamed. The man with the large face, Monsignor Emil Krait, several times had locked his gaze on her from down the table, as if attempting to study her countenance. The first time she'd observed him regarding her so, she'd felt uncomfortable. Afterward, she did her best to ignore the man and to immerse herself in the conversation around her.

It was the only real unpleasantness that she sensed during the feast. Was the man attempting to recollect her from Westport? Possibly. She certainly remembered him, but he was a mounted outsider with a face that was hard to forget. She was just one of many hundreds of people in the market that dreadful day.

Was the man's memory that good? Were his powers of observation that sharp? Could anyone have remembered her from all of the people in the press that day? It seemed unlikely, human memory being what it was.

But not impossible.

The Fiend could have done so. His was an uncanny memory for everything, including faces. And he had warned her that there were magickers among the delegate and his party, almost certainly more than one of them. Could magic improve a person's memory? And assuming the man Krait could recall her, would it be too much of a coincidence if he saw her both in Westport and here at Mont Clair?

Perhaps. But unlike the creature, she could not change her face, and there was no real way that she could conceal herself while residing at the castle. For a few moments that evening, she'd pondered what the Fiend had said about simply getting up and leaving and putting Mont Clair and the de Vere family behind them. Perhaps go back to Edwin Township?

No. The past for her was a closed door. And she did feel safe at the castle.

For now, she decided, she would do as she had been doing and continue to live her life in plain view. The creature could be inexplicable, and he several times had been at a loss for answers lately, but she'd come to trust his shrewdness and his cunning. She had a sneaking suspicion that having the delegate here at Mont Clair was part of some plan he had concocted. Naturally, the idea of being his bait was not the least bit attractive, but he'd never allowed any harm to come to her before. She didn't think he would now.

And affairs abruptly had changed at the castle. Just now, on her way back to their chambers with Lady Isabel, Deirdre couldn't help but notice more guards were about, many of them standing vigil at posts they never had before. The baron was taking no chances with this most recent visitor.

Preparing for bed that evening was a pleasant affair. Isabel had a glow about her that she hadn't had since their return, and for all the talk of bad dreams, the woman was out like a light the moment her head hit the pillow. It was the first time all day that Deirdre was able to let down her guard, and she took somewhat longer than usual cleaning herself and settling into sleep.

What a day it had been. The very idea of playing nice with a group of people who so recently had caused her harm, who had deprived her of liberty and threatened her life. It was horrendous.

——

It was Deirdre's own fitful sleep that alerted her to the danger. She seldom slept well, and often was up three or more times a night. After the first of her returns to wakefulness that night, something gripped her insides as she again began to doze off. Isabel was warm and real in the bed beside her. So, who was it that cast a faint shadow near the window as Deirdre again began to close her eyes?

For the thinnest of moments, she didn't stir, uncertain whether she'd in fact seen anything. Perhaps she was still dreaming? And then a shadow deeper than it should have been slipped past the bed. There was not a murmur to be heard, but the tiniest whisp of air touched her cheek, telling her that she wasn't mistaken and that she was not dreaming.

Someone was in their chambers.

She exploded from the bed, snatching the nearest thing from the nightstand as a weapon. Her first wild swing caught some resistance, confirming her worst fears, but her second blow caught pure air. The third found even more vapor, and the momentum of the blow sent her spinning to the ground. As she rose from the floor, humiliation nearly outstripped her fear, and she took a firm grip on the candlestick with both hands. Should she...? And then the thought occurred to her that her hidden opponent might have a knife.

Ah. … Double damn. She took a proper footing, as the Fiend had taught, lashed out in every direction with the candlestick in her hand, and let out a powerful scream to summon the guards.

Hiding in the shadows no longer was an option for the intruder, and a dark form erupted from the corner nearest the door and flew toward her at waist level. She swung with all her might, felt her weapon bite hard into something solid, and soon found herself weightless. Hitting the ground wasn't the greatest pain she'd ever experienced, but it drove the wind from her, and it took her a moment to find her feet. She did so just as the door flew open.

It was Sir Guillaume, the baron's eldest, a candle in one hand and a sword in the other. Behind him was Sir Alexis. A number of others followed.

"What's happened?" someone asked. It wasn't apparent who.

Deirdre went to speak, but nothing came out. A painful few moments followed, and she found herself back on her knees. She couldn't breathe, but felt her head cradled in soft arms. Lady Isabel was speaking to her in low and comforting tones.

"I had a nightmare," she said when her breath finally returned to her. She wasn't sure why she told that lie, but it appeared from the chatter that Isabel had been unaware that someone had been in the room with them. And that person now was gone, probably out the window. "I'm sorry. I didn't mean to alarm everyone."

Much to her surprise, no one was angry. Those who had responded to her cry treated the episode as a sweet misunderstanding, and soon she, Isabel, and Sir Alexis were the only ones left in the room. The knight volunteered to stay behind until both young women had gotten off to sleep.

After a short time, Isabel again was slumbering, and the Fiend spoke.

"Did you get a look at this person at all?" he said in a voice set just above a whisper.

"No," was her whispered reply. She knew better than to ask how the creature knew. A trace of blood on the candlestick, the drapes half pulled from the window, perhaps a smell in the air others couldn't detect. "I don't know how anyone got in and out of such a narrow window, though. I doubt I could manage it."

The fake knight rose and began to inspect the narrow windowsill. It took but a moment.

"And how indeed did anyone climb this high?" It didn't sound as if the creature expected an answer. "Whoever it was, the person wasn't here to harm you."

"Then why?"

"Look at Isabel's effects," he said, motioning toward her small table. "Is anything absent from there?"

At first, there appeared to be a hairbrush missing, but Deirdre found the thing knocked behind a wooden chest. The Fiend gave her a long look.

"What?" she asked.

"Our enemies don't know who you are," was his reply. "At least, they aren't certain."

"How can you tell?"

"The most powerful spells of divination require an article intimate to the person against whom the spell is directed. Hair and fingernails are best."

"Someone wants to cast a spell on Lady Isabel?"

"Or on you. Any servant at Mont Clair could tell our clerical friends that the two of you share a sleeping chamber."

"And they'd need a lock of her hair for the spell."

"It certainly would help." The creature gave a quiet laugh. "I wonder what a divination would tell them about our friend from another world. It like as not would merely confuse them."

Something occurred to Deirdre, and she too laughed quietly. "We know the burglar was a man, if we didn't already."

"What?"

"Half the women at Mont Clair have used that brush at one time or another. Not something a man would ever consider."

"That's truly fortunate. And it also was fortunate you woke up when you did. Were you hurt?"

"No, not badly. Why?"

"There's a spot of blood on the floor, and a few more here on the sill. Not yours?"

"No."

The creature dabbed something on the ledge and touched it to his tongue. "I'll know this fellow if I taste him again."

"But you won't know until then?"

"Hmm … only that you're right. It's a man. And this was caused by a head wound. It bled too much for anything else. We'll keep an eye on those surrounding our new friend, Monsignor Krait. Perhaps one sports a new scratch or cut."

"How many magickers are with him?"

"Several. Why do you ask?"

She stood and joined him near the ledge and looked out to the ground far below. "Wouldn't it have taken magic to make this climb and then to beat such a hasty retreat?"

"True. People with the agility to perform such a feat are more than just rare, so some sort of magic might have been at work. But the delegate and his people haven't been obvious about their spell casting. And they won't. There are too many people around the baron who could sense such things."

"Who?" She'd wanted to ask that before.

"It's difficult to say. Such things give off an odor, but it isn't always easy to tell from where that odor originates. If my guess is correct, his man Miles is one. And that idiot friar probably knows more of such things than he should. There no doubt are others, but honestly it isn't something I've troubled myself with."

"Will this person return?"

"I doubt it. But I'll be close, just in case."

"Thank you. But do you think everyone believed my story about having had a nightmare?"

"I imagine they did," he replied. "Young Guillaume was nearby, and no one left your chambers before he arrived. What else could it have been but a dream?"

"One person knows that I lied."

"Your burglar? Yes. He'll likely just think you were confused by the moment. If he and his master suspect anything, though, I might be able to use that to our advantage. Either way, I'm glad you're unhurt."

"As am I."

18. Of Kings and Prophets

The three days following Lady Deirdre's "nightmare" were happy and relaxed. Since that event, Isabel and her friend rose early each day, took some exercise, and then had their breakfast. From there, Deirdre went off to her chores, while Isabel returned to their chambers for a short rest before attending to some reading and recitations with Friar Emmet. With each passing day—no, with each passing hour—Isabel felt more her old self.

Deirdre had made no effort to discuss the specters that beset her at night, and Isabel never pushed the issue. When the young woman was ready, she would be ready. For her part, Isabel no longer feared her own dreams, but instead she heeded the wisdom of Sir Alexis and endeavored to learn as much as she could of them. While sleeping, she paid careful attention, marking every detail, and upon waking wrote down her recollections at her earliest opportunity.

The two women saw little of Alexis during that time. Aside from occasional short visits during meals, he was locked away with the baron, either in meetings with the delegate or discussing other issues of importance. The baron, having no brothers, relied a great deal on his cousin, and she understood the need for the knight's absences.

On the morning of the fourth day, she and Lady Deirdre were just finishing their regular walk when something unpleasant occurred. They were passing along the milking sheds on their way to the lower gardens when they rounded a bend and found their way blocked by several men standing athwart the pathway. One of them was Monsignor Krait, the delegate from the Holy See. The men made no effort to pardon themselves or to clear the path, and though Krait did not pay them any mind, there was something in his bearing that led Isabel, for just a moment, to think that he was waiting for them.

But how unlikely would that be?

Still, it forced the women to announce themselves. Isabel cleared her voice, but to no effect. The delegate and one of the men with him continued to speak in a casual tone in their own tongue, which sounded to her ear like a cross between Spanish and Italian. The man's three guards merely stood by with sullen looks on their faces, and when Isabel attempted to get their attention with a further polite, "Ahem," the guards exchanged sneers, and one uttered a phrase that even Isabel's limited Spanish told her was a horrid insult.

"Oy!" Deirdre shouted.

"In my country, women know their place," the delegate said in the common tongue. "We'll clear the path when we're finished." The man went back to his conversation.

Two of the guards sauntered in their direction, and for a moment she thought they might be allowed to pass. But as the men went by, she felt a sharp pain and heard Deirdre cry out. The man had yanked sharply at her hair!

Before Isabel could cry out in protest, Deirdre kicked the soldier nearest her hard in the ankle and delivered a strike at the man's eyes. The fellow drew back, as if to strike the young woman, but before he did, the delegate snapped an order, and the soldier stayed his hand.

Without further word, the delegate and his small party departed, brushing past Isabel and Deirdre as if they weren't even there. The men jostled the two women so severely that they very nearly knocked them to the ground.

It was the most shockingly rude behavior she'd yet beheld in Albion. Even the Gheet gentry, for all their brutality and senseless violence, were polite to a fault. She hadn't the foggiest idea what to make of it. Glancing over at her companion, Isabel was surprised at the look she saw in the eyes of the young Surrey girl. Rather than the fury she'd expected to see, there was something else. Was it glee?

No, it couldn't have been that, because Deirdre's expression suddenly became serious.

"Think nothing of that, Lady Isabel," she said. "I'll talk to Sir Alexis. This won't happen again. I promise."

And they continued on their walk.

———

Isabel tried hard to put the ugly episode out of her mind, and by lunchtime had managed to do so. There was so much else to do and to see. This was the day the King of Albion, Sebastian II, was to arrive. And despite herself, she was excited at the prospect of meeting royalty.

The royal arrival, it seemed, was a daylong affair. The night before, a few servants had arrived to prepare the king's chambers in the north tower, that very morning a series of heralds came with further messages, and just before noon several bodies of soldiers arrived. The bulk of the king's entourage would stay in pavilions outside the castle complex, but the king, his advisors, and his bodyguard would stay within.

She'd never seen the castle so busy and decided it was time for her to pitch in and help. Most of the morning was spent working in the kitchen, with only a few small breaks to rest and to catch her breath. At just before noon, she went with Sylvie and some of the men servants to arrange a few things in the great hall. The place, she'd observed, could comfortably seat about 200 people for dinner, but half again that many places had been prepared.

It was another peculiarity of local culture that the king did not observe the traveler's grace, under the notion that everyplace in the kingdom was the monarch's home, and there was to be a great banquet that would begin the moment the king arrived, a gala that would last for several days. She'd seen lavish affairs in Albion, but this celebration looked to be the most resplendent. There were even professional performers, as well as barkers, vendors, and tradesfolk of all kinds.

She was feeling somewhat winded by early afternoon when a great hubbub erupted on the far side of the great hall. She very nearly thought she would have to scold some of the lads for their continued antics, when she realized that the baron was moving toward her at the head of a large group of men and women. Among them was Sir Alexis, but to the baron's left was a thin and somewhat scraggly man of about 35 years. He was one of those fellows who didn't wear his clothes well, and whose fine blond hair already had begun to thin.

There'd been no horns or trumpets, not the least fanfare, but it dawned on her that this was the king. She made a swift and somewhat awkward curtsy.

"So, who's this, then?" said the monarch in a voice so deep it sounded like it should belong to a larger man.

"Milord," said the baron, "this is my cousin's ward and my daughter by law, Lady Isabel."

"Ah!" the king nearly shouted. "Very good to meet you. What a great addition to your household, de Vere. My congratulations."

She wasn't sure whether to shake the hand the monarch raised toward her, or to kiss it. Instead, she merely touched his hand and curtsied again. It seemed to be the right thing, because the man blessed her with another quite sincere smile and moved on.

"So, what do you think of our king?" she heard someone say after the man had passed.

It took her a moment to realize Sir Alexis was standing beside her.

"He seems very nice."

"An odd quality in a sovereign, I must admit. But yes. Sebastian is among the most amiable of men."

"It took me by surprise," she admitted. "I didn't hear him arrive."

"He was following his hounds and arrived ahead of the royal entourage. Festivities can begin all the sooner, eh?"

"I hope so, but I've been busy here and in the kitchen."

"Put that aside, Lady Isabel." He took her arm in his. "Come along. I'm sure the king would be delighted with your company for lunch."

"Are you…?"

"Quite certain. The more the merrier."

"Well, in that case." She walked with the knight toward the main table.

"Tuppence told me of the morning's unpleasantness," the knight said, his voice somewhat lower. "It's also come to the baron's attention."

"I … I didn't want there to be any fuss. It was such a trifle."

"Your concerns are honest ones. William can be … *sensitive* when it comes to his family. I promise you he won't overreact."

"Oh, thank you," she whispered.

She took a seat at the main table between Alexis and a handsome Gheet knight whom she'd never before met. After a short time, people began to filter into the room, and the food they'd been preparing in the kitchens that morning arrived in great heaping platters. It was extraordinarily pleasant and thoroughly informal.

The king ate, talked, and laughed with everyone like they were old friends or close family. She hadn't eaten since breakfast, and enjoyed the repast with far more relish than was her usual. Several times, she caught the king giving her a boyish smile.

"I admire a woman who enjoys her vittles," he observed at one point.

She wasn't certain whether such comments were his attempt at being flirtatious, but something in her said they were not. That he loved to eat and to drink was without doubt—it was a wonder the man was so thin— but after several hours a new group arrived. Among them was an ample woman about the king's age. The woman unceremoniously plopped herself in the king's lap with a weary sigh and, after a short kiss, began picking from his plate and drinking from his goblet.

The rumor was that the king kept several mistresses—or, rather, that they kept him—but that he still was smitten by Queen Kristjan after nearly 20 years of marriage. That appeared to be the case.

Isabel ate and drank far more than was usual for her, and somehow the time flew by. When next she checked, platters of dinner food were being brought out. She needed to take a break and to relieve herself. As she'd seen many do before her, she merely rose and curtsied to the king. He gave her a friendly wave to acknowledge that she was free to depart his presence.

There was a magic in that day and in those hours. It wasn't something she, so far, had discerned in Albion. That land was nothing like a storybook kingdom, no Avalon or Camelot. Heavens no. This world was far too smelly, raw, and unpleasant for that. They never talked about that in storybooks, how wretched things could smell, and how a simple bout of dysentery could wreck a person's entire life. There was plenty of that in Albion.

There was little doubt her sudden change in health and the return of her friends played a role in her improved spirits—that and a few goblets of unusually good wine. But this place was feeling far more like a storybook than she ever imagined that it could, and she was excited by the notion. Something seized her, and she wanted to laugh.

It wasn't clear to where Sir Alexis had made his way, but after a short trip to powder her nose and to catch a breath of air, Isabel found Deirdre on a bench with some of the de Vere children. She scootched in beside the lass, and soon was again sipping at the excellent vintage that was the night's libation.

Not even the appearance of Monsignor Krait clouded what promised to be a stellar evening. She spied the unsightly creature with several of his robed brethren at a table near the king just as dinner was being served. The gluttonous clerics seemed to enjoy their food and drink, and one of them— from the look of him, the fellow who'd been chatting with Krait early that morning—suffered his overindulgence poorly. The man stood, coughed, clutched his shoulder, and keeled over into a passing platter of pork. How suitable.

None present seemed overly concerned when the cleric's servants carried him off, though Deirdre did volunteer to inquire about the man's wellbeing. Isabel almost told the lass not to go. People in Albion were forever staggering drunk and passing out at banquets. Sweet and generous Deirdre.

While her friend went off on that errand, Isabel chatted with family and guests and enjoyed the spectacle of the whole thing.

There were a number of peculiar customs in this land, far more than she could count. Among them was an expectation that a person could importune a lord when that lord was in good spirits. It wasn't at all uncommon, nor was it considered untoward, for folks to engage in rather transparent types of flattery to get that lord into such a mood.

A common occasion for such fawning was the period right after dinner. In fact, in most great halls, no matter how crowded, there always was an open area between the main table and the hall's entrance for just that purpose. People lined up, the great and the small, to ask minor boons and favors of the lord or king.

It seemed strange, but it was tradition. Who was Isabel to say otherwise?

The custom after formal meals at Mont Clair was for the baron to see a few petitioners. On this evening, though, all were there to lobby the king, the paramount lord of the land. How long before such a chance again would present itself? And the pleas were as anyone would expect.

One man wished for his son to have a place in the royal guard. Another desired a pension for the war wounds suffered fighting under the king's grandfather. Another still sought a pardon for a nephew wrongly convicted. A young woman wished release from a convent, a man complained rebels had ruined his crops, a girl wished to marry someone outside her station, a guildsman pleaded to be absolved from an unfair fine, and on, and on, and on....

To Isabel's great surprise, the king took it all seriously. The man had been drinking since noon and had a reputation of being a monarch more interested in hawking than in statecraft. And though he at times pounded on the table and harangued people to get to the point, he gave each petitioner his undivided attention while they spoke, and he always begged their pardon when he took a drink or had a bite during their presentation.

True, not everyone got what they wanted, and a few he sent away with a short scolding. But most left with something, whether it was a promise to look into the issue or a document hastily drafted by a royal scribe and marked with the king's seal. Everyone, great and small, got a fair hearing.

It was only after some time had passed, and scores of petitioners had been heard, that Isabel recognized someone she knew in line. Two people, in fact. One was an older cleric who worked for the local bishop, a Pastor Something. And the other was Friar Emmet Naseby.

What could that man possibly want from the king? She found out soon enough.

When the two clerics were before the king, and after both had sung high praises for the monarch's wisdom and liberality, the pastor began a swift and breathless recitation about the Walking God and the gift of prophecy, which the Deity bestowed on His closest followers, those most dear to His Divine presence.

It sounded very much like a catechism, and the thing went on for more than a minute. Finally, a look of annoyance grew on the king's face, and he pulled off his shoe and began banging it on the banquet table in front of him.

"What do you want?" he asked in loud and precise words.

"A *quest!*" cried the friar in a voice that was almost musical.

Lord, part of her wanted to say, what silliness. But it had an effect. The word echoed through the room, flying from lip to lip like a wave. And even though Isabel didn't believe in such things, that mood swept her up. She suddenly was on her feet, as were many others. Most conversations in the hall stopped, and all eyes fell on the friar who stood before the king. The king, for his part, appeared both surprised and amused by the cleric's words.

"A quest," the friar repeated, "for the Glaive, a hallowed and sacred weapon forged for but one purpose, the death of Evil, the slaying of The Other!"

They want to kill the Devil? Isabel thought.

For a moment, her credulity slipped. If she were not mistaken, she'd seen a flash of exasperation on Baron William's face when Emmet had spoken. The nobleman had declared the idea of a quest quackery from the beginning. A swift search of the room found Sir Alexis standing against a wall not far from the king. His face was a mask. She wondered what the knight thought of all this, and what Reverend Ainsley would say.

"What in blazes are you talking about?" asked the king.

"There is a prophet among us, milord!"

"A prophet?"

"These months past, a holy anchorite at the Priory of Saint Lucien foretold the presence of a sacred weapon, one that in the hands of a true friend of the Walking God will slay Evil itself."

"If I'm not mistaken, milord," interjected the baron, "the young friar omits a tiny detail. The anchorite in question did speak of a weapon, but could give no hint as to its nature or its location. This is naught but pious flummery."

"Proxima Thule!" were the friar's next words.

"Pardon?" said the king after another sip of wine.

"Proxima Thule, milord. The Glaive awaits us in the hidden depths of a cavern in that distant land, along a long and tortuous path known only to one."

"This anchorite of which you speak?"

"No, milord. Tis the prophet of whom I've come to tell you."

"If not the anchorite, then who?"

Friar Emmet turned and looked directly at her.

"The Lady Isabel de Vere," he said.

19. The Knowing of Things

I fault myself for not having seen it sooner and for not having done something about it. But what's done is done."

The creature never ceased to amaze her. Deirdre had expected him to be in a great furor over the events earlier in the evening and had presumed he'd called her aside to give her a good scolding. But there was none of that. Of course, the Fiend was good at shielding his feelings.

"So, you're not angry?" she asked.

"Angry?" A faint smile flitted across the lips of the false knight. "Of course, I'm angry. I'm furious. But not at you."

"At who? Not at Lady Isabel!"

"At myself. At that half-witted friar. At anyone in holy orders. But not at Isabel. She's the victim in this farce."

"I don't understand any of it," said Deirdre. She checked her voice and looked around. They were alone on the battlements, but it never hurt to be cautious. "But Isabel isn't a prophet of any kind."

"No, of course not. There's no such thing, at least not as the Church teaches it. The moment she told Sir Alexis that she was having peculiar dreams, I knew something was amiss. But I hadn't imagined that friar clever enough to pull something like this off, or stupid enough to try it."

"He's cast a spell on her, hasn't he?"

"A spell?" The Fiend paced in silence for a few moments. "Yes, I suppose after a fashion that's what it is. Look … do you remember what I told you about the mumbo jumbo that practitioners of Source magic must learn to cast a spell?"

"Something about folks having to wave their hands and do tongue twisters."

"In a few words, yes. There was a technique magickers used in days past when they wanted to deliver information secretly. They'd write a mundane message with quill and ink, and then imbue those letters with power. Any stranger reading the missive would think it a simple piece of correspondence, but the proper recipient knew to recite it aloud, in a particular way, pausing in odd places, enunciating words in a particular fashion. And that act would complete the spell."

"And do what?"

"It might do any number of things. Generally, they were used to transmit secret information, often in the form of dreams and visions."

"So, this reading and reciting Isabel has been doing with Friar Emmet … her dreams, the things she experienced, couldn't have come about by an accident?"

"No. He somehow knew the proper technique and guided her through it. The dreams simply were a manifestation of the spell."

"What's the purpose?" she asked. "If the friar wanted to find a path to this Glaive, why didn't he just recite this thing himself?"

"That part isn't clear. Perhaps he wasn't sure of what he had or didn't trust its source."

"He was afraid reciting it might turn him into a toad?"

"That's anyone's guess. I wish I had the answers."

"Hasn't the wind told you anything?"

"Hmm … that. Not as much as I'd like. Our enemies in the Church have little tricks to throw me off. The wind's subtle whispers have been capricious things of late."

"What's the point in having magic if it lets you down?"

"Magic? You mean the wind?"

She gave him a nod.

"Tuppence, listening to the wind isn't magic. Listening to the wind is nothing more than the knowing of things."

"The knowing of things? What things?"

"Everything. The people of my tribe have very keen senses, and we have dreadfully clever minds. When I say I'm listening to the wind, it means I'm sensing things and sorting them out. Sometimes that's a rational process, sometimes an intuitive one."

"OK…?"

The smile the creature gave her was sweet and indulgent. "I can smell a forest fire burning on the far side of the world, I can see colors no human has ever imagined, and my sense of taste is so acute that I can detect every ingredient in every food I've ever tasted, down to the least little mustard seed."

She needed a moment to think about that. What did it mean to have such keen senses? The vicar would have known. What would he have said?

"The more information you have, the easier it is to make informed decisions."

The creature nodded. "The vicar is a good teacher."

"So, you just know lots?"

"Yes. I have access to a great deal of information. Much of it I've sensed myself, some of it I've read in books, and all of it I tuck away and think about in the greatest detail. That's what listening to the wind is. It's that special place where cognition and intuition meet to make something grand."

"Could you teach me to do that?"

"Tuppence! What do you think we've been doing the last nine months? The greatest gift a person has is the ability to know the world around them."

"OK," she said, trying not to show her delight at his words. "But if listening to the wind is not magic, how do our enemies make it hard for you to hear it?"

"The typical ways. Something as simple as casting a spell to change the direction of the breeze can throw a kink in my thinking. And the Holy See has far greater resources than that."

"What are we to do then?" she asked. "Do you intend to kill off Monsignor Krait's companions one at a time?"

"I don't know what you're speaking of."

"I had a look at the cadaver after that fat old monk dropped dead at the banquet."

"Brother Bernard?"

"The one with Krait this morning, yes. And it looked very much like vitriol poisoning to me."

"Tuppence, you've been keeping up with your studies! It gladdens my heart."

"The symptoms were obvious. And please don't try and tell me that wasn't you."

"As a matter of fact, the poisoner was one of the man's servants, a handsome young fellow upon whom Brother Bernard had been forcing himself for many months."

"Acting on his own, or with a little nudge from you?"

"Sir Alexis simply helped the young man find the courage to fight back against his tormentor.'"

"The courage?"

"Courage is a virtue, child. And I always strive to inspire virtue in others."

"Be serious. We can't count on angry servants to poison our way out of this. Do you have a plan?"

"True, and I apologize for the levity."

"And I apologize for ... I truly hope you're not angry with me."

"Why would I be angry?"

"For agreeing to go with Isabel on this silly quest."

"As I recall, you didn't agree. You insisted. And I'm not the least angry. Your love for your friend does you great credit. It's one of your finest qualities."

"You're going with us, aren't you?" she asked.

"No, but this whole thing could work to our advantage. I've thought it over. I don't think this quest is part of a scheme by the Holy See. It's likely something cooked up by that idiot friar and his nitwitted bishop. To what end? I'm not sure. Either way, the king has spoken. There'll be trouble if you and Isabel don't go."

"You said such things always end badly, with members of the party turning on one another."

"Yes, these so-called quests never end the way they do in storybooks. But you'll have Sir Armand with you. The fellow is fond of both you and Isabel, and he's a juggernaut in a melee. And there's a man I sometimes use, a wily and ruthless fighter, who just happens to be in the area. I've already sent for him. You'll be well looked after."

"But what about you?"

"Deirdre, it was a bad sign that Krait had the nerve to confront the two of you on the castle grounds this morning. For the life of me, I have no idea what he was thinking—or even if he's the one truly pulling the strings in the Holy See's delegation. At the end of the day, though, he and his people aren't searching for you. They're looking for me. No doubt there are some risks for you and Isabel in going on this meaningless quest, but getting you out of his line of sight for a moment or two is important. Once you've gone, I'll head out in another direction, making a bit of noise and leaving a trail that'll be easy for his magickers to follow."

"I don't like the sound of that."

"Tosh. They don't truly know who they're looking for, and once I've lured them away from you, I'll be able to evade them with no trouble. The moment the coast is clear, and Sir Alexis has finished up a few little errands for Baron William, I'll swing back and rejoin the two of you."

The plan he sketched out still sounded dreadful, but she decided she needed to trust the Fiend. The creature didn't know everything, but he was far more cunning than any person.

And she found her anger growing at the way lovely Isabel had been manipulated in this affair. Someone needed to pay the price for that. She generally took no pleasure in the suffering of others, but Deirdre felt herself soften on that issue from time to time. Friar Emmet was a tedious little man, but until that evening, she'd felt no real dislike for him. Now the idea of the man being snacked on by some hellish demon didn't seem so bad.

And the clergyman was coming with them on the quest.

She wanted to learn more about the whole thing. The more information you have, the easier it is to make an informed decision. There were three days before the departure of their small party northward toward … what was the place called? Proxima Thule, where Isabel was supposed to guide them to a weapon that may or may not exist. Maybe being out of sight for a month or two wasn't such a bad idea. But she wanted to know for certain, so Deirdre began thinking of ways better to inform herself.

20. The Road from Mont Clair

The following days were busy and eventful, which left Isabel little time to think of what had transpired. The only thing that lent her the courage to keep moving forward was that her friend Deirdre had insisted on going with her. Brave, sweet, steadfast Deirdre.

The whole affair was a muddle now, but somehow on the evening of the king's banquet, she'd been swept up in an incredible moment and had agreed to join a quest for an ancient relic, the Glaive. What had she been thinking? She didn't have the foggiest notion of what she was doing now. She hadn't the faintest idea of where they were going, even though she purportedly was to be the party's guide.

Part of her wanted to head to the main gate, start running, and not turn back. The only comfort she took beyond Deirdre's presence was knowing that brave Sir Armand would be with them. True, she felt awkward knowing the man held such unrequited ardor for her, but he was an honest and true gentleman, and by all accounts a gifted soldier.

The one man who she wanted to travel with them, the one person whose presence would have set her heart and mind at rest, needed to stay with the army. Sir Alexis de Vere was indispensable to the baron and to the war effort. So the day she and Deirdre were to set off north on their venture, Sir Alexis would set out with a party of riders to begin reconnaissance of the eastern districts in order to gain information on de Margot and his rebels.

She knew the whole affair had angered Baron William, especially her and Deirdre's participation. To her great relief, he blamed them for none of it. The king decided, and that was the end of it. For a moment though, she was convinced William might find some excuse to skin Friar Emmet for his role in events.

On this, the morning of their departure, her focus was on making sure she left nothing behind that she might need. But even that chore wasn't a daunting one. She had few possessions, most of which easily fit within the saddlebags of her mount. Only a few things, some spare cloaks and a few changes of clothing, would go onto the pack animals.

It annoyed her only briefly that she would be losing Birdy, who had been her servant throughout the winter. Sir Alexis needed him for other things, so Isabel and Deirdre would have to rely on themselves for personal issues, and upon a fellow Sir Alexis had recruited, a chap named Deckard, for help with their mounts and with things around camp.

The truth was that Birdy had grown rather lazy over the winter. She'd seldom demanded much of the young man, and … well, he also had gotten somewhat fat and a tiny bit surly. This Deckard fellow, of whom she'd gotten only a few glimpses, would have to do. He had a rough and unhewn look about him, more soldier than servant if her guess was correct, but she supposed that fact might work out for the best.

The reaction of the family to her departure surprised her. The baroness grew misty eyed as the servants moved Isabel's belongings down to the courtyard, and the usually dispassionate woman pulled Isabel into a loving embrace before releasing her without speaking a word.

The faces of the children held looks that reflected a range of emotions, from worry to envy. How could it be any different? This was a land in which people courted danger and death with every day, eager to place their lives on the line for the glory that it might bring them.

That facet was one of the things she'd noticed even about children in this world, a tiny component of family life that she'd come to love. There was none of the pointless teenage angst that was the usual in her old world. Every child from the moment they were old enough to walk wanted nothing more than to be an adult, to be taken seriously, and to find a place by the sides of their elders where they might be held in esteem.

Her brothers and sisters in the de Vere clan, from tall Sir Guillaume down to tiny young Lady Natalie, worried for her, but they also envied her this adventure. Their confidence in her made her final descent from the family apartments easier than she had imagined.

The members of the quest were to be a small party, but it wasn't until Isabel reached the courtyard and found the commotion there that she realized it was not so small as she'd imagined. Originally, the king had claimed a dozen knights would escort her and the friar northward to their final destination, wherever that might be. But she hadn't counted on the supporting cast.

Just a short survey of the yard told her each knight brought along a small retinue, and each new member would require mounts and provisions. There were servants, grooms, and armed retainers. From the sound of it, at least one minstrel was present. It was anyone's guess whether that boded well or ill.

Amidst the crowd of people and animals, it took her a short time to spy Lady Deirdre and even more to make her way to the young woman. Deirdre had been her usual self lately, shifting between sweet and sad.

Two days before, news had come from Westport that the elderly vicar with whom she'd lodged over the winter had succumbed to injuries he'd suffered in an accident several weeks before. The news left the young woman shaken, and for a time Isabel thought Deirdre might forego the trip north. But that wasn't to be. Her young comrade seemed even more determined to accompany Isabel on the journey.

By the time Isabel reached her, Deirdre already had her gear stowed and seemed ready to depart. The only thing with which she busied herself was her mount, who she was grooming lazily when Isabel arrived.

"Do you have everything?" Deirdre asked her.

"I think so. There isn't much to bring beyond clothes and personal effects. Sir Armand has taken care of everything we'll need for the road."

She couldn't help but notice Deirdre's mode of dress, which was somewhat tomboyish. The youngster's hair was pulled in a single thick braid behind her head, and she wore a mid-length dress with short britches underneath, as Surrey lasses often did. In a lanyard over her shoulder, Deirdre had slung a long dagger that Isabel had never seen before. The only other item she wore was a short leather jacket against the cool morning air.

Isabel couldn't repress a surge of envy. Back home in Savannah, she'd owned only a handful of dresses for church and what not. It now was all she wore. Perhaps on the road she could adopt a more practical style of attire? The dress she wore that day was the sturdiest one she owned. It was rather restricting, but for now it would have to do.

"Did you bring something to read?" asked Deirdre with a hopeful smile. The kid forever was with a book.

"Just a couple of storybooks." Isabel was finished with books on religion, and anything else serious—and she probably would be for some time. This whole adventure…. "Will we have time to read?"

"I should think nothing else when we're riding. And the boat ride north will be many days."

Talk of their travels left Isabel's stomach churning in an unpleasant way. She had no sense of where they were going and felt very much like a passenger on this journey. But according to Friar Emmet, the party needed to travel to a town called Musette along the River Ransome in far northwestern Albion, a journey of several weeks.

It was in that city that the cleric's research indicated they would find the Red Cobbled Square of Isabel's dreams. It wasn't tremendously deep research, or so it seemed. The city was famous for that particular feature after all. Beyond that single destination? The friar's reasoning was muddled. He appeared convinced, with little real proof, that their quest would take them from Musette across the Ransome into a wild and unclaimed region known locally as Transom, but marked on old maps as Proxima Thule. Where precisely would their path take them in Proxima Thule? Apparently, that was for Isabel to tell them. She wasn't optimistic.

Neither was she happy with Friar Emmet.

If the man had suspected that she was the repository of some special knowledge, why hadn't he shared that information with her before blurting it out in front of the king and half the nobility of Albion? The nerve of the man. It wasn't like she felt she ever could've said no to this trip. One didn't say no to royalty in such a land. But at least she would have been able to prepare herself. Was that all the clergyman's silly affectations and acts of solicitude had been about? Getting something from her?

She decided not to think about that, and she'd interact with the friar no more than was necessary on this trip. Though she did wonder whether she should warn anyone else about the man's duplicitous nature.

Before it was possible for her to decide, she felt a hand on her shoulder and turned to find Sir Alexis smiling down at her. For a moment, speech eluded her.

"Do you have everything you need, Lady Isabel?"

"Uh … yes."

"Good. If you have any troubles at all, ask Deckard. The man looks a roughneck, but he'll help you in any way. And I've left some coin with Tuppence. You should be able to purchase anything you need before departing north from Musette."

"Are you sure you can't come?" she blurted out.

"Alas," he replied with a smile. "It's a terrible mountain of responsibility being torn between competing duties. The royal army marches soon. They'll need eyes and ears, as well as other things. But be at ease. Armand is a great soldier and, if I'm not mistaken, is devoted to you. I've known few better fighters than Deckard. I trust those two with your safety as much as I'd trust myself."

She almost asked him whether she should go on this journey, but then thought better of it. No one in this land was their own master. Why put a wonderful man like Alexis on the spot by asking him to second guess the king? No doubt, he'd only give her some sweet yet enigmatic reply.

"Do you think you can do without Lady Deirdre for a few months?" she asked instead.

"Milady, angels willing, it'll be no time 'til we all are together again."

She hoped that was the case, but until then, they still had their goodbyes. Before she was able to share her final farewell with the knight, a newcomer arrived. Baron William joined them.

"Cousin," the nobleman said, a faint smile flitting across his lips, "they found him."

"The delegate?"

"The one and the same."

"No doubt holed up with some young serving…," Alexis began to say before glancing at Isabel, "… at his prayers, no doubt."

"Nothing quite so sacred. There's been a mishap. His servants found him in the south wellhead."

"What?" said Isabel.

"Apologies, Lady Isabel. It appears Monsignor Krait took a fall sometime last night and went headfirst down a well. A dreadful affair, such a calamity." The baron again was very obviously trying to hide a smile when he spoke. "His servants found him just moments ago."

Lady Deirdre let out a shriek at the news, and Isabel was certain Sir Alexis squelched a laugh. There obviously was no love for the delegate among the nobles of Albion.

"Absolutely horrible," the knight said instead, his face straight and sober. Alexis was a gentleman in every way. "I'll say a few prayers for the man."

"As will I," echoed Deirdre.

Isabel merely gave a solemn nod.

"You are all far more generous than I," said the baron. "I'm embarrassed at my own sentiments."

"The man rubbed each of us in different ways," said Sir Alexis. "No use holding grudges after he's gone."

"True." William nodded. "Age has given you wisdom, cousin."

At that point, Sir Lucas, the leader of the expedition, gave a marshalling call, and the baron went forward to give the man some last-minute instructions. Sir Alexis helped Isabel onto her mount before being attacked by Deirdre, who threw the knight into such a powerful hug that Isabel thought she'd break the man's back.

"I'll see you soon," the knight whispered when the lass released her grip and went to mount her horse.

"Sod off," was her reply.

Minutes later, their goodbyes complete, the party left on its quest.

———

The Fiend always had all the fun. How dare that scoundrel pitch Monsignor Krait down a well without telling her?

Well, the creature wouldn't have done it himself, of course. No. He would've enticed a resentful servant or inveigled some other poor soul into acting as his murderous cat's paw. And as much as she wanted to be angry with the oaf for leaving her out of the scheme, it was all she could do to stop from laughing aloud at the thought of the vile cleric's final moments. A person can indulge only so many emotions at once.

Still, Deirdre was under no illusions. Krait's band of Inquisitors remained a danger to them, even without their odious leader. She'd have to stay alert on the road ahead. The thought of what lay in front of them was irksome, but she found herself humming and smiling as their small party left the main gate of Mont Clair and got on the road to Musette and points beyond.

It was her first time being separated from the creature in nearly a year, but she wasn't worried. She'd even managed to pin the old blighter down and eke some instructions out of him. For all his talk of being a great planner, the Fiend very much resembled someone who took each problem as they came up, often resolving difficulties by the skin of his teeth.

Exemplar number one. When she'd voiced her worries about Deckard, their new hired man, the creature at first looked as if he'd wave away her concerns before responding, "Oh … well, if he gets out of line, just drop the name Beazley. That'll set him right."

She heard herself make a disgusted sound at the memory of it. OK, "Beazley," it would be. Part of her knew she should feel flattered that her mentor trusted her to handle affairs on her own. Part of her knew it was just him being lazy.

No, she shouldn't be angry with the monster. He'd shown her unusual kindness when breaking the news about the death of Vicar Edgemont. Her first reaction had been unalloyed outrage, but the Fiend had convinced her the man's passing wasn't a thing for which they could blame the Holy See, as much as they both might want to do so. The cleric was nearly 80 years old and took a minor fall on the day of the attack, one from which he wasn't able to recover. Such things happened.

The creature probably was right, but that knowledge didn't salve the pain and sorrow of yet another loss, not completely. So, she added it to the list of wrongs she held against the universe. She'd calculate that tab later.

Her parting with the Fiend otherwise had been uneventful. He'd given her a purse of silver and copper coins for expenses, urged her to keep her own fortune out of sight except for emergencies, and reminded her to always be pleasant … until she could no longer be pleasant, and then to strike to kill.

"Keep Armand and Deckard close at hand, but use your own wits," were his final words on the issue.

He did give her one gift as they parted, an unusually sentimental one. It was a slim volume of philosophy, entitled merely *Ruminations*, by a fellow named Sopwith. He told her that she might find it enlightening.

She'd stowed the thing with the other books in her small library. There were a few books on mathematics and geometry, some storybooks, and of course her slim volume on herbalism, but most of the things she brought along were histories and geographies of northern Albion and the uncharted regions to the north and west of the country. She even had a few rough maps of the area on the south bank of the River Ransome.

None of it inspired confidence. The area on the far bank of the river, a place the locals called Transom, quite literally was uncharted. Accounts told of dense and dark forests, the shattered remains of what in times past might have been villages and roads, and farther north were some high mountains. Few people ventured there, and fewer still troubled themselves to write about it afterward.

That didn't seem right to Deirdre. Land was precious in Albion, and the idea that there might be unclaimed acreage a mere boat ride away didn't feel proper.

When she'd asked him about it, Baron William had a reasonable explanation. In the far north of Albion, land was easier to be had, and many of the lords in that part of the country were indifferent to free farmers settling where they liked, as long as those farmers paid a reasonable tax. Such lords were far more concerned with battling occasional raiding bands from Cambria to the northeast, or from Wols to the west. According to William, the barons and earls in the north had their hands full just holding onto what they had. There were neither the resources nor the inclination to claim woodlands across a river that posed them no substantial threat.

In that light, it did make more sense.

And, of course, there were stories. Crofters sometimes crossed the Ransome and foraged for what the woodlands might provide. Hunters even ventured north of the river on occasion. But few dared tarry there long enough to exploit the land's great timbers. Loggers who spent more than a few days there had a way simply of vanishing.

A collection of letters she found in the baron's storage room talked of highwaymen and brigands who made the far bank of the Ransome a hideaway and from it staged raids across the river into settled lands.

None of that sounded good. Deirdre didn't like the idea of venturing into a land about which none in their party knew the slightest thing. And their only guide? Lovely Isabel, a young woman whose knowledge of the place was the product of some sort of ensorcellment.

The Fiend had been no help at all. He'd announced that it had been ages since last he'd ventured into the north of Albion. His only contribution was the certain knowledge that strange and unnatural things sometimes congregated where people did not.

Brilliant.

Still, she'd always been curious about foreign lands, even if she'd never before given serious thought to visiting any. Perhaps this would unfold as the Fiend had predicted. With the Holy See and their Inquisitors looking the other direction for a time, they might just forget about her and Isabel. And it perhaps would be a pleasant trip after all.

Perhaps.

21. Huntington and the River Silk

The party didn't move so slowly as she and the Fiend had while on the road from Westport, but Deirdre observed that the first leg of the journey toward Musette was an exercise in unplanned lethargy. The party started late each day, stopped early, and engaged in a great deal of gaming and carousing. It seemed as if they stopped for meals, drinks, and sport at every town along the way that had anything loosely resembling an inn or a tavern.

The upshot was that the jaunt from Mont Clair to the river port of Huntington-on-Silk, a ride that should have taken three days, took them nearly a week. One entire day of that was lost when a member of the party, Sir Bertrand Parfitt, came up missing. The fellow's servant claimed to know nothing of his master's whereabouts, and the other knights of the party restricted their search for the missing man to the same tavern at which they had made merry the previous evening. The bottom of each ale tankard carefully was inspected, but alas no Sir Bertrand was to be found.

The errant knight only reappeared after Deirdre finally managed to goad Deckard into prying his backside from the barstool to which it had become attached and to go looking for the misplaced man. A quarter bell later, Deckard found the knight in the cottage of a buxom serving lass not far from the tavern in question, still drunk from the previous night's revels.

Sir Lucas declared the day too far gone to get started and suggested an early departure the next day. They were on the road before noontime the following day, a small victory of sorts.

This simply wouldn't do. Deirdre didn't expect to increase the dawdling pace of travel while the party actually was riding. There simply were too many people and too much baggage for that. But stopping at every town and village and carousing half the day away? That would have to stop.

More to the point, Deckard already had become an annoyance. The fellow clearly was a fighting man and not accustomed to taking orders from a young woman, but though he always was polite and cheerful, the man had a way of plodding and dragging his feet when responding to her orders. That was another thing that was going to stop.

Not that she minded having the extra time to read. That was forever welcome. And she and Isabel both found things to keep them occupied. There always was something interesting to look for in the forest, she kept up her notetaking on herbs and plants that she found of interest, and the women had a bit of coin to spend. Isabel decided she wanted to know more of pharmacology, so the two spent time building her a small apothecary bag.

But Deirdre had no intention of wasting the next three years rambling through the countryside on some aristocratic bender. Their pace needed to increase. To that end, she had a conversation with Friar Emmet. It wasn't quite a scolding, but she laid down the law to the otherwise soft-spoken man and recruited him to join her in speaking with Sir Lucas.

A year before, the idea of Deirdre confronting a Gheet nobleman on any issue, let alone giving the man ultimatums, would have been ludicrous. After nine months with the creature, though, it was just another tedious chore to get done. As with Friar Emmet, she tried not to sound scolding, but she informed the knight on how it needed to be.

"Sir Lucas, I've spent my entire life around fighting men," she lied. "I understand that recreations are a necessary reward for their courage."

The knight nodded approvingly.

"But the pace we're making is trifling," she added. "This is a holy quest, and I'm sure the good friar will tell you it is not a thing that can be delayed. Evil never sleeps."

"Evil never sleeps!" the friar echoed.

The knight interrupted the holy man. "Milady, we will endeavor to strike a faster pace."

It wasn't quite that easy, but their pace did increase for two days, which was sufficient to get them to Huntington-on-Silk. Once there, more delays ensued.

She hadn't really counted on so many people being with the party. If truth be told, she hadn't concerned herself in the least with the planning of this journey. But she'd travelled the previous campaign season with the army led by William de Vere. She'd taken careful notice of what they did and why, and the Fiend, in the guise of Sir Alexis, had answered her every question about travel and supplies. The creature truly was a bottomless font of knowledge.

There really was no reason they shouldn't be moving faster, but who would have imagined so many people would be needed to go in search of one item?

There were a dozen knights, each knight had at least one servant or retainer (one knight had five), the friar and his assistant (a skinny deacon of some sort), and a handful of men to manage horses that hauled what seemed an inordinate number of bags and boxes. There were in excess of 50 people in the party, and more than twice that many animals. Oh, and one minstrel.

Theirs was a veritable tiny army, which would require a fair number of large flatbottom boats to move them along the river. That number of craft would take time to find and to prepare. Consequently, more damned dawdling. But as two days turned into three, and three days into four, Deirdre found her patience wearing thin.

It wasn't that she needed anything in particular. As a matter of fact, the very notion of having a servant was a thing that Deirdre didn't find appealing or necessary. But Deckard was along primarily as a bodyguard, not as a body servant. And the fellow was never where she needed him to be.

It was something impossible to explain to anyone in the party, but Deirdre had not forgotten that she had enemies, powerful enemies, who might still be on her trail. On more than one occasion, she felt as if she was being watched. And even while on the road, an uneasiness sometimes would settle on her. She hoped those feelings were just her imaginings, but she wasn't convinced they were.

So, she kept a careful lookout and was always vigilant when she went to-and-fro. But it didn't help that since reaching Huntington that Deckard spent more time looking after the local barmaids than he did looking out for Deirdre and Isabel.

Things came to a head on the afternoon of their fourth day spent idling at a local inn in Huntington, a place near the main gate called the Peartree House. Against Deirdre's instructions, Deckard had absented himself from the inn, no doubt seeking a watering hole not under the gaze of his employer.

The affair was of no great import until just past dinner, when she and Isabel were set to retire for the evening. The habitués of the inn's main room were not the most unsavory characters her imagination could have conjured, but neither were they the type with whom she most would want to be alone. Had she not been so watchful, she would not have noticed someone follow her and Isabel up the stairs to their room after dinner. As it was, the man's presence very nearly took her by surprise. Her cosh was out, and within moments their pursuer dove out a second-floor window, no doubt more frightened by the sound of Sir Armand bounding up the stairs in response to Isabel's screams and Deirdre's curses than he was dissuaded by Deirdre's pummeling.

It was never clear whether the man in question was anything more than a common thief or a rapist. No one had gotten a clear look at the fellow before he fled. But the affair gave Deirdre a fright and left Isabel shaken.

Deckard reappeared late the following morning, smelling of whiskey and whatnot. When the man took the news of an intruder with a light heart, Deirdre had reached her limit and berated the fellow for his absence, but to a degree that she thought more generous than he deserved.

His reaction to her scolding was his typical. He didn't even have the decency to act surly, but replied to her admonishment with his usual patronizing, "Yes, young miss," "Of course, young miss," "You're quite right, young miss" … ad infinitum.

He was a rough looking fellow, with thinning blond hair and a pockmarked face. Not so large as Sir Armand, Deckard still was big and to anyone else might have been intimidating. So, Deirdre did as the Fiend had suggested.

"Mr. Deckard, how am I going to explain your behavior to my Uncle Beazley?" She'd added the "uncle" part on the spur of the moment, but it had an effect.

At the mere mention of that name, it was as if she'd struck Deckard hard across the face with her cosh. His head shot back, and he turned white more quickly than she'd ever seen a face drain of its color. The man went to speak, but no words came out. And a wetness appeared in his eyes.

"Now, young miss," the soldier said in a raspy voice after clearing his throat several times, "there's … there's no need to go using that kind of language. I'm your man. N … no … no need to trouble your good uncle with anything, nothing at all."

Deirdre had never seen a grown man behave in such a way. Big and strong fighting man though he was, the mention of a single name very nearly had the fellow soiling himself. Who in the blazes was this Beazley? … As if there were any doubt.

"My uncle has arranged for Sir Alexis to pay you a pretty penny to do little more than keep a wary eye out for Lady Isabel and me. You can't very well do that from the bottom of a whiskey glass. Am I mistaken?"

"You are quite right," the man said with a newfound sincerity. "I am your man to the bone. Point me in a direction, and I'll be there."

"That's easy enough," she said. "Just be handy and keep your eyes open for any danger."

"It's done and done, young miss."

———

Isabel couldn't help but notice a tension had grown between Deirdre and the new hired man, Deckard. But after an attempted robbery at their inn two evenings before they boarded their boats north, the two seemed to come to some amity. From that point forward, Mr. Deckard was a new man, somber and cooperative in ways he had not been before.

The rest of their party? Somewhat less so. The dreamy veils of this so-called quest slowly had fallen from her eyes. She still felt it was an important undertaking, but the jaded feelings that so often had beset her regarding Albion and its people had begun to reassert themselves. This was a raw and brutal world, even if from time to time it enjoyed flashes of something magical.

During the journey, she'd so far managed to avoid interacting with Friar Emmet, and she was glad for the fact. There was little doubt she at least should cooperate with him, but something in her wouldn't allow her ever again to trust the man. And she also felt a smidge of guilt over the role she so far had taken in this quest—or not taken. Deirdre, a young woman 10 years or more her junior, seemed to be the person most responsible for the party moving forward at a pace greater than a crawl.

She hated thinking it—Sir Lucas seemed like a decent and pious man, and she had deep respect for Armand—but the knights of this quest were hardly ideal specimens of nobility. They spent far more time swilling spirits and filling their bellies than they did performing gallant acts.

If she thought those unknightly impulses would diminish once they boarded the riverboats north, she was sorely disappointed. The debauchery merely became maritime. The boats stopped each evening, and often several times per day, so that those onboard might stretch their legs and indulge in other pursuits. And if a single town or village was bypassed, it was a cause of great grousing and complaint.

She'd been under the illusion that travel by boat would hasten the pace of their journey, but it wasn't so. They traveled upriver, against the current, hauled by great teams of horses that plodded along towpaths on the bank. And gentle though it was, the current tugged at the wide bottomed vessels incessantly. The party made even slower time than they had when mounted. What was even the point?

River travel was more comfortable. That probably was its only recommendation. She and Deirdre shared a small aft cabin on the lead boat, and most of their companions made do sleeping under canvas canopies stretched over the middeck. There was a single deckhand on each vessel whose job it was to keep tiny braziers safely burning when the nights and mornings were cool, and the meals onboard were more than just palatable.

Members of the party outwardly were pleasant, and she couldn't fault anyone for that. Still, they were men and knights out on a jag, and she felt the occasional awkward moment before and after pulling up along the riverbank. Boys would be boys.

Around Deirdre, though, there always seemed to be something interesting to do. The youngster was fascinated with the world in ways Isabel never had been at that age. The lass took every opportunity to examine the universe around her, from the flora and fauna of the river valley to the construction and operation of the vessels on which they rode. It was in those moments when she was asking questions and hectoring the deckhands for knowledge, or when she was wading in the shallows looking for aquatic odds and ends, that the youngster's sadness lifted, and there revealed was the sweet and charming young woman beneath.

And who would have thought the lass would know so much about botany and chemistry? It was astounding the kid's depth of knowledge on a variety of subjects. Deirdre was a much better tutor than Brother Emmet ever had been, especially on the simple things. So Isabel's reading and writing improved as days passed.

The party had its first calamity five days out, halfway between Huntington and East Portage. A fellow by the name of Quackenbush, a minstrel who was accompanying several of the knights, fell overboard at some point during the morning's travel, and no one at first noticed his absence. It was on a rather narrow stretch of river, where the current had picked up, and Sir Lucas dismissed out of hand the idea of mounting a search.

"The man will be many leagues downstream by now," was the commander's reasoning. "And he isn't actually one of our number. We'll trust to the Walking God to guide his path home."

At least the knight hadn't made the lame excuse that a search would slow the party's progress, and all present were decent enough to lift a tankard in the man's memory. Quackenbush, who was a middling musician, but a gifted tenor, would be greatly missed. Isabel reminded herself to stay clear of the rails.

Their tedious progress continued for nearly another week, when the small flotilla at last came to a faint bend in the river at just past midday on their 11th day afloat. The master of the six vessels, a heavyset and balding man with skin like saddle leather, announced they would go no farther that day, and the boats soon were docked near what appeared to be a large manor house on the right bank.

By the reckoning of the map Deirdre had brought along, they were only a short way from East Portage, a stretch of river they probably could cover before dark. But the master refused to take them farther that day.

"The men and animals need their rest," he told her. "And it's our long custom to spend the night here before making an early start to the city. We'll have you to Portage by noontime a'morrow. Stay on the boats if you like, though they serve all types here."

The man's last words struck Isabel as somewhat peculiar. And then it occurred to her that the manor house in question wasn't an inn or a tavern. It was a rather swanky riverside brothel.

"Oh," she said. Small wonder the men in the party had begun dolling themselves up. None of the fighting men seemed to mind this particular delay. Nor would they, given what she'd seen of them.

"So, we're not moving on?" asked Deirdre, who up to that point had been buried in a book in their cabin.

"Um … maybe we should stay on the boat."

"Why are we stopping so early? We're almost to Portage." Deirdre took up the map and began to scrutinize it with care.

"The captain says the men and horses are exhausted."

"Oh, well. That seems odd. You'd think they'd be looking forward to being paid. Still, let's go and have a bite to eat."

"Uh … it's not an inn."

"What?"

"It's … um … a bordello." Isabel had no idea how to explain this to a child.

"A what?"

"A house of ill repute?"

"Isabel, you're not making any sense."

"It's for men only."

"Oh! A knocking shop," said Deirdre. The lass looked up from the map. "Mr. Deckard! … have the captain offload our mounts."

The bodyguard, who was just moving for the gangway, pulled up short. "Miss?"

"My family wouldn't approve of this place. We're going on to Portage by horse."

The man knuckled his forehead and ran down the plank bawling for the boat master.

"Is that wise?" Isabel asked her friend.

"We'll find perfectly good lodgings in the city."

"But is it safe?"

"The map says the High Road cuts through those hills, yonder. It's half the distance we'd travel if we followed the towpath along the river. We could be in the city in no time."

To be candid, waiting in the boat outside a whorehouse didn't appeal to Isabel any more than it did to Deirdre. But they were no longer in Baron William's domains, and Deckard was just one man. She would feel more comfortable with more hands.

"I'll fetch Sir Armand," she said.

22. The High Road to East Portage

To Deirdre's surprise, Sir Bertrand joined them along with Armand. The two men often were to be seen in one another's company, and she'd presumed them to be close friends. Despite the episode with the serving lass, Bertrand actually seemed like a decent fellow, though perhaps Deirdre was swayed by the fact the man came from a prominent Surrey family in the east. She often reminded herself that not all knights were Gheets, even though that people had brought knightly customs with them to Albion many years before.

When they set out along the road to East Portage, all were mounted, and the men armored and well-armed. A somewhat sheepish Sir Lucas made a few halfhearted statements about the entire party staying together. One could not shake the notion that the allure of music and laughter within the bawdy house influenced his judgement and curtailed his attention span.

And the two clergymen of the party weren't to be seen anywhere. No doubt, the duo was off praying for the souls of the sinners indoors, it being unlikely such a high-end establishment offered a clerical discount. But one could always hope.

So, Deirdre, Isabel, Armand, Bertrand, and Deckard slipped away, and made a course for the High Road. It took longer than they'd imagined. The area was heavily forested, and the High Road this far north was not the broad lane it was in most places in the south. They passed over it once, thinking it was a farm trace, before doubling back and striking a path northward along the thin artery. They soon settled into a comfortable trot, with Deckard taking the lead and the two knights riding near the women.

"Have you come this way before, Sir Armand?" Deirdre asked the enormous knight. The man was a Gheet, but she found it impossible not to like him.

"This way, Lady Deirdre? No. But I have been several times to Cambria. The land there is mountainous, and even along the coast it is not so heavily wooded as here."

It occurred to her that they hadn't seen a farm all morning, and she mentioned that fact now.

"The lands hereabouts aren't so peaceful, milady," volunteered Sir Bertrand. "We'll surely see farms closer to the city."

"Are the lands that dangerous?" asked Isabel.

"Warfare is something of a sport here in the far north," said Armand. "Cambria isn't quite an enemy, but border lords have great fun slipping into their neighbor's lands and making off with a milk cow or a few head of sheep."

"Don't worry, milady," added Bertrand. "A small party like ours, with three well-armed men, would mean more trouble than it's worth to any would-be raiders."

"Too many easy pickings elsewhere?" asked Deirdre.

"You have the rub of it, young miss," said Armand. The entire party had fallen into the habit of calling Isabel and Deirdre "miss" and "young miss," respectively. "It's a rough game, but it's seldom truly brutal. There's little burning or ruination."

"If you burn a man's house and kill him, you can't come back and rob him next year," said Deirdre. "Is that correct?"

The large knight began slapping his thigh and laughing, informing Deirdre that she indeed had the right of it.

The small party rode along in that way for some time, chatting and laughing about sundry things they saw or whatever happened to come to mind. Several times Deckard circled back to give them reports on what was ahead. They traveled nearly a quarter bell before they saw other travelers, a large group of merchants, a dozen wagons or more, with a heavily armed escort, journeying in the opposite direction.

It was the first tangible sign of any danger. Every merchant had guards in the south, but a train the size of the one they now passed never seemed to have more than a small handful. This group had an entire company of mounted soldiers.

After some discussion, they decided not to stop and eat. Deirdre had grabbed a bag of food on their way from the boat, but unless her map was lying to her, East Portage was less than a half bell's travel from where they'd encountered the merchant caravan.

They'd be hungry when they reached the city, but why tempt fate? No doubt, Sir Bertrand was correct. A small and heavily armed party wouldn't be worth the trouble of raiders accustomed to stealing pigs, but Deirdre felt a nagging something.

Not long after, Deckard made another return to inform them of the road ahead.

"Someone cut the road a half league up," he told them.

"How many?" asked Armand.

"They were in file," was the scout's reply.

Both Armand and Bertrand secured their half helms and fitted them on their heads. Neither knight wore full plate, but they were wise enough to be in chainmail, with helm and shield handy.

"What?" asked Isabel.

"Men ride in file to mask their numbers," said Deckard. "Not something an honest man needs to do."

"Like as not they're tracking the merchant train we passed," said Armand, "but no use courting trouble. We should make haste and be prepared for a fight."

From that point on, Deckard rode ahead of them, but not so far as he had been, just in case of trouble, and the five riders moved at something greater than a trot. The pace they set was brisk, but it wasn't grueling. There was no telling if they might need the animals fresh for a short sprint.

Deirdre wasn't from horse folk, had never been on anything save a plow horse before meeting the Fiend, but she'd become an accomplished rider in the last year. Isabel was somewhat less comfortable on a mount, so Deirdre kept close to her friend.

By Deirdre's estimate, they were well over halfway to East Portage when the attack came.

All of a sudden, a group of riders exploded from a tree line 50 or so paces in front of them and came forward in a rush. The ambush spot the attackers had selected was near a faint bend in the road, so as further to obscure their presence, and the riders were upon Deckard in moments. To her surprise, the bodyguard spurred his horse straight into the side of the lead rider and began flailing about him with the spiked war hammer he usually carried cradled across his saddle.

Deirdre's instinct was to turn and run, but she instead goaded her own horse forward, reaching for the bridle of Isabel's mount as she did. Like Deckard, the two knights were not men easily daunted, and their battle cries split the air as they spurred their mounts into the fray.

It was instant mayhem.

She and Isabel were liabilities, she knew that much, so she raced her horse toward a gap in the line of men in front of them. At the same time, a sound behind them told her that more riders were attacking from the rear.

There was no need to hold the bridle of Isabel's horse for long, the animal was larger and faster than her palfrey, and soon both horses were racing free of the melee, heading north down the road in their original direction of travel. For a moment, she did nothing but ride, and it appeared that it was all Isabel could do to keep her saddle.

A quick glance behind them told her not to slacken their pace. The thick dust their racing steeds kicked up would not allow her to discern whether the riders behind them were friend or foe, and there was no time to stop and ask. But turning back around … double damn. In front of them, more riders appeared on the High Road a hundred or more paces distant.

There was no place to flee except into the forest. And the angels smiled on them for barely a moment. Isabel's mount slacked its pace just enough for Deirdre to bring her palfrey abreast, and in one swift move she urged her mount to crowd Isabel's animal from the road. Both horses hurtled into the early spring foliage, but the leap jostled Isabel from the saddle. The woman clung to saddle and pommel for a half dozen strides before she dropped to the forest floor and her mount dashed away.

As Deirdre reined her animal about to assist her fallen friend, two mounted figures streamed past from the rear. She was able to discern only that one was in brown leather, the other in chainmail. Deckard and one of the knights?

A shaken Isabel was able to rise from the ground without assistance, and by the time the young woman pulled herself astride the palfrey behind Deirdre, the sound of battle cries and the clashing of blades could be heard along the road to the north.

Deirdre had no idea where she was going at that point, but she rode hard for a time eastward, through the trees and underbrush, before turning the palfrey toward what she thought was north.

Her animal was small and nimble, and she knew enough of strategy to realize their attackers were at a disadvantage. What she so far had seen of the men was that they were armored and mounted on strong and tall coursers. Even with two riders, her smaller mount could move more easily among the dense trees and underbrush of the surrounding forest.

She just needed to keep moving and to keep away from any pursuers. If one or more of their companions survived this skirmish, she and Isabel would rejoin them along the High Road closer to the city. The continued cries of pain and defiance to their left was the only lodestone that guided their flight through the thick and rugged woods. To their left, or so she prayed, was the west and the High Road.

Without her even thinking it, her dagger was in her hand, and she used it to hack and cut away brush, limbs, and vines that threatened to unhorse them. The two women said not a word, save when Deirdre several times urged Isabel to silence. And they dismounted only once, to allow their horse to traverse a series of deadfalls and brambles.

It was slow going, and she wasn't sure whether it was a good sign or not that the sounds of fighting to the left slowly died away. Best to be cautious. The women remained quiet and vigilant, and after what Deirdre estimated to be a dozen furlongs or so, she headed the palfrey back toward the High Road. The underbrush had begun to thin at that point, and they reemerged from the forest along a straight downhill section of the High Road.

The first thing she saw was a rider headed toward them from the north, and she very nearly headed back into the woods until she heard his cry.

"Huzzah!" It was Sir Bertrand.

"Where are the others?" she cried out. This whole thing had become a mess. Not for the first time, she chided herself for not having stayed with the boat. She at least should have had the common sense to keep to the river path.

"Glad to see you well," the knight replied, an enormous smile on his face. "Great spot of fun, that."

"We were nearly killed," cried Isabel. "I fell off my horse."

"Couldn't have been more than a dozen of them. You ladies were quite right to absent yourselves while m'lads and I straightened things out."

"Where are the others?" asked Deirdre. The moment she spoke, the sound of hoofbeats drew her attention.

It was Deckard, arriving from the opposite direction. The man looked as if he'd just escaped the noose.

"Young miss, good to see the both of you healthy." There was a tense warble in the mercenary's voice. "We need to get on the move. We broke them up some, but most of those rascals are still about."

For the first time, she noticed an ugly gash in the bodyguard's leather armor, just below the shoulder. There was a great deal of what looked like blood on Sir Bertrand's mount and across the front of his tabard, but from the easy way the man sat the saddle, she surmised none of it was his.

"Where is Sir Armand?"

"He's coming along, young miss. We need to hasten."

Moments later, they were racing north at something short of a full gallop. Bertrand, in obvious high spirits, continued to regale them with the details of the skirmish and his role in it. Such was very much the normal for knights, Deirdre had found. What the men lacked in couth, they made up for in steel and courage.

They traveled at that brisk pace for no more than a league when, off to the west, the sound of shouts and the crash of mounts racing through the forest reached them. It was impossible to make out what was being said, but it sounded very much like mounted riders on the hunt. Deirdre's guess was proved correct when moments later a horse and rider careened down a steep rise onto the High Road in front of them.

It was Sir Armand. The weight of the great armored knight nearly caused his courser to lose its footing after its ungainly descent from the hillside, and it took a moment for the man to get the animal under control. There were several arrows protruding from his shield, and one from his saddle. Two additional arrows jutted from the hindquarters of the horse he was leading, Isabel's mount.

"I don't think we're welcome here," the huge knight called out. "Let's not dally."

It was a race to East Portage from that point onward. Fortunately, none of their pursuers had managed to get ahead of them, and even Deirdre knew that only the most gifted archer could fire a bow while at a gallop and have any hope of hitting a moving target. It took a stretch of rough, stomach-churning riding, and Isabel had to switch mounts and ride with Deckard to spare Deirdre's mount, but they managed to distance themselves from their pursuers and to reach East Portage, all of them alive.

Getting into the city was another matter.

Deirdre happily paid something called a travel tax to the officious little bureaucrat who seemed to be in charge at the city's main gate. And they endured a series of questions about their identity and their business in the city. It was a small price to get to the safety and comfort of an inn where they could treat the minor injuries that she knew the three men were hiding. Men always concealed such things.

Deirdre concealed her thoughts.

Hers was an uneasy heart. Sir Bertrand had pointed it out early in the day. Why would a band of armed and armored men concern themselves with such a small party? Deirdre and her companions did not reek of wealth. They were well mounted, true, and the men had weapons and armor, but pickings no doubt were easier elsewhere.

That uneasiness grew as she recollected the distant snippets of speech that she'd heard from the men who'd attacked them. She hadn't understood a word of it. Of course, the people of Wols were said to speak a language unlike that of Albion and Cambria. She'd never heard that tongue, and it may well have been the Wols language that the enemy had spoken. But the bits and pieces she'd heard sounded very much to her untrained ear like the language she'd heard spoken by the men of Etruscia at Mont Clair.

In the rush and chaos of events that day, she hadn't gotten a close look at any of their attackers. There was nothing in the way the assailants dressed that gave them away as such, but might those men have had the squared shoulders and slight stature of men from the Inquisition?

She didn't know. It may well have been she was conjuring fears from nothing, as the Fiend conjured gold. But something in her told her to be wary.

23. The Via Musette

I'm dreadfully sorry about your bay," Sir Armand told her. "It was a fine animal. But we should find something suitable here to replace her."

Isabel had accompanied the knight to a market on the outskirts of East Portage that dealt exclusively in horses. They'd had to put down her previous mount when it became obvious its injuries were too severe to treat, and both Armand and Bertrand had guaranteed her that none of the spare mounts with the party would suit her. All were far too large or too rambunctious for an inexperienced rider.

Fortunately, every town of any size in Albion had a market of this type, a kind of place that dealt in both draft and riding animals. Price really wasn't too much of an issue. The baroness had left her some coin before they'd departed, as had the baron. And the generosity of Alexis seemed without limit.

With the help of Armand, she spent some time looking at animals. The knight, whose injuries from the day before appeared to trouble him none at all, scrutinized each animal, pointing out the faults and flaws of each in turn. The man proved himself a veritable aficionado of horseflesh. Out of the hundred or so animals on sale that day, he swiftly narrowed her choice to three.

"The black is by far the best," he said. "She's the right size for you, but she has more spirit than you might like."

"You think I might not be able to handle her?"

"With practice, yes. But the chestnut over there is more like the mount you had. Good sides, long legs, and probably less than three years old. Smart and obedient for such a young animal."

"You say 'obedient' like it's bad?"

"A little wildness in a horse is good. It means it's headstrong and less likely to give up on you in a pinch. Most seasoned riders prefer their mounts a little wild."

"By 'wild,' you mean spirited?"

The man nodded.

"What about that one," she said, pointing to the smallest of the three animals before them. It was about the same height as Deirdre's palfrey, but seemed stockier. There was nothing pretty about it.

"That's a Gelt," he said.

"A gelding?"

"No. A type of mount, a Gelt they call it. They're almost more pony than horse. Not fast, but exceedingly surefooted, and stronger than a horse twice its size. A plains steed like that can run all day and half the night on a handful of grass."

"Spirited?"

"In a stubborn sort of way."

"Would I have trouble with him?"

"If you're patient, and you earn its trust, they're as loyal as any animal under the sun."

"He isn't very pretty."

"No, not at all. They're less than useless as war mounts, but my father favored Gelts for hunting. As small as they are, he wouldn't ride anything else to hounds."

"Is that why you pointed this one out?"

The knight smiled. "Maybe, just a little."

After a bit of riding, it was clear she couldn't leave the market without the Gelt. The black tried to murder her from the moment her bottom hit the saddle, and the chestnut was far too docile even for Isabel. The Gelt had a short stride that even at a canter felt remarkably smooth. He was smart and easy to manage.

And there was something about the creature. It exuded something, a sense that made her feel like she'd met a large dog rather than a horse. Armand didn't laugh when she mentioned the fact.

"My father used to say the same thing. They're not perfect mounts, but they are loyal and brave."

"Brave?"

"Not skittish like many horses. They run wild in parts of the continent, don't grow nervous at the smell of predators. A herd of wild Gelts will form a circle and protect the smaller animals."

"I understand now what your father saw in them."

"Aye, milady. He often would track bear on a Gelt. I think this one will do you fine."

The price the trader asked for the beast was so trifling that Armand took another careful look at the animal to ensure there were no defects that he'd not first noticed, and afterward he and Isabel left the market with her new mount in tow. After some adjustments, her previous saddle and tack fit the animal fine, and she spent the remains of the day under Sir Armand's careful eye putting the Gelt through its paces in a yard near the inn.

The animal suited her perfectly, and she spent the next two days working with it, feeding it by hand to earn its trust, and scratching various places on its head until she found a sweet spot behind the creature's right ear. Having grown up in the city, horses were a mystery to her. This was the first mount in Albion in which she felt true confidence.

On the morning of the third day, they took the ferry across the River Silk to pick up the road to Musette, which, according to the locals, was a mere three days distant. She hoped that was the case, and Deirdre assured her it probably would be so. There were precious few places to stop along the Musette Way, which meant there was scant opportunity for the men of the party to take their recreation.

In any event, the time at the riverside bawdy house seemed to have sated those impulses—and lightened a few purses. All appeared ready to get to Musette and to get on with their journey northward.

"Baroness Elise has arranged for a party of freighters to meet us at Musette," said Sir Lucas in reply to Deirdre's questions about provisioning. "We only carry enough food and fodder for three or four days. We may be many weeks in Proxima Thule and likely will be forced to provide for ourselves for that whole time."

More people? It had never occurred to Isabel what a feat such a journey would be. But it made sense. Each knight needed to eat, as did his servants and mounts. That meant bringing supply animals, which needed drovers, and all of those animals and drovers needed to eat, which would require even more provisions and more beasts of burden.

They already had taken on a half dozen new men at East Portage, as well as some more animals, and as added security Sir Lucas arranged for their party to travel with a small merchant caravan for the entire distance to Musette. She strongly suspected some money changed hands as a part of that agreement, but said nothing of it. Who was she to say if Sir Lucas pocketed a few coins?

The dreams hadn't abandoned her throughout the course of their journey, and she continued to examine them carefully and to take notes on what she experienced. But nothing new had been revealed to her in many weeks. Is this what it was to be a prophet? She was at a total loss to explain her continued visions. Had she been in the land of her birth, she would have sought out medical help. Now?

Well, this was a strange land. There had been much talk since her arrival about magical and mystical things, but she actually had seen none of it. A great many coincidences? Yes. In a sane world that's how she would explain many of the things she'd seen and experienced. Mere coincidence. But she hadn't seen anything of magic, and not even so much as a single werewolf, fairy, or elf. And she'd seen not a single whiff of this world's God or its Devil, both of whom were purported to walk the highways and byways of the land.

When pressed, even people she liked and admired would not admit to having seen anything truly magical. But it was an accepted part of life. Such things as vampires? Werewolves? Simple articles of faith. But how many had ever seen such a thing? Even her truest friend, charming Deirdre, admitted that she'd never seen a lycanthrope of any kind, though she was quick to accept that an unknown sound in the night might just be such a thing.

But were such things real?

Were these so-called visions Isabel experienced real? Or just vivid dreams that lingered on after her illness? In many ways, Alexis de Vere was the most grounded person she'd so far met in Albion. He never expressly denied the existence of visions, but he'd assured her the simplest answer almost always was the correct one. And even when people were whispering that her recovery from the grippe was a miracle, the knight assured her that the medication he provided was a simple potion of naturally occurring herbs.

As time passed, part of her became more convinced that these visions were mere dreams in which an overzealous, or possibly ill-intentioned, cleric had placed too much stock. And now, somehow, she was on a quest to distant and dangerous lands based on that feeble notion.

Part of her, though? Sometimes she believed, and sometimes she became totally wrapped up in believing. Being surrounded by people who trusted in such things, who extended that trust with a total lack of evidence, had an incredible influence on her. Popular opinion was a tug against which it was hard to resist. It was like fighting gravity.

What a mess.

On the good side, the ride on the first day to Musette was pleasant. It was sunny and warm, but not uncomfortably so. Several of the knights teased her over her new mount. He really was scruffy and stocky, not a proper show horse of any kind. But others spoke of their admiration of the breed.

Sir Lucas claimed his family always kept Gelts because of the calming effect they had on the more high-strung breeds. Another knight stated they were positive proof against snakes.

"Oh, milady, a Gelt will go right after a snake of any kind, hoof and tooth. I've even seen them chase off a stray wolf."

She said a little prayer that her new champion wouldn't be put to the test that day. There had been several trying episodes since her arrival in Albion, but the attack by brigands on their way to Portage truly was harrowing.

Deirdre, of course, had known exactly what to do. The kid was scrappy and savvy in ways that Isabel envied. Her friend had not lost her wits when bandits arrived, but instead leapt straight into action as the three soldiers accompanying them had done.

Isabel wanted to be like that. At least in a tiny part, wasn't that why she'd allowed herself to be roped into this adventure? She could have fought back, dug in her heels when Friar Emmet began his ramblings about prophecy.

True, part of her at the king's banquet had been frightened by the sudden attention, too stunned to resist. Part of her was fascinated by the notion of magic and prophecy. But yet another part of her was seized by the adventure of the whole thing, like something from the pages of a fairytale. Who could say no to high adventure?

One way or the other, she was on this quest. Was there an enchanted weapon at the end of it? She would begin to find that out in Musette. That was where this trail ended, but where a new one began. And it was up to her to play guide along the way.

It wasn't something to which she looked forward.

24. The Red Cobbled Square

espite her every effort, Deirdre hadn't been able to enjoy the last stretch of their journey to Musette. In recent days, the sense that eyes were on her had become overwhelming, and it was only in fits and starts that she was able to relax. Was it paranoia or was it the Fiend's unrelenting influence on her that had her watching every member of their party and taking a careful accounting of each and every one?

And why not? It wasn't like she had known her fellow travelers before they departed Mont Clair, at least not most of them. If someone were watching her—and she could not escape the feeling that someone was— why couldn't that watcher be a member of the party as much as a stranger? Even more, they recently took on several new servants at East Portage.

And was it her imagination, or were they missing people? After a short tally, she determined that one of the servants, a fellow named Westrick, hadn't returned with the party after their excursion to the disorderly house near East Portage. No one spoke of the man afterward, and there now was an obvious tension between several knights in the party, including Westrick's master, a knight named Johan Withers.

And now this.

When their party reached Musette a few days before, they were greeted by a veritable regiment of new servants, drovers, and skinners. There was even a blacksmith and a few huntsmen.

"Better to have it and not need it, than need it and not have it," was the reply that Sir Lucas gave to her enquiry about the more than doubling of their number. There now were more than a hundred in their party, and several hundred animals. Who could have thought this was a good idea? Wasn't there a war on? Was this supposed quest just a backdoor way for the scruffiest knights in Albion to avoid the battlefield?

She had to admit that she retained no expertise in such things. But didn't quests in storybooks consist of a small knot of doughty travelers? Fighting all odds? Surviving by the barest of chance?

Well, she knew what the Fiend would say. He'd laugh, and then he'd tell her it's never like the storybooks. She could almost hear his gloating at times.

But in the storybooks, at least, everyone knew one another. There was absolutely no one to vouch for these new tradesfolk. Sir Lucas knew none of them, and his only proof of their identity was a letter of engagement one of them produced, presumably from Baroness Elise or one of her representatives.

Deirdre wasn't convinced Sir Lucas could read, but she didn't belabor the point. What would such a proclamation gain her but the man's antagonism?

But the new people were a churlish lot. Nearly all of the new pack animals were mules, and most of the new retainers were muleskinners. Their leader, or so it appeared, was a vile creature by the somewhat laughable name Chastity Skinner.

Skinner was a harridan, a virago, and one of the foulest women upon whom Deirdre ever had laid eyes. The woman's first words when getting a look at Deirdre was to pronounce her a "sweet little pot of cunny," before suggesting that the youngster could "make a fortune" on such an expedition.

Who would have guessed there were female muleskinners? And that one could be such a terror? In the days during which the party made its final preparations to cross into Proxima Thule, the woman made a menace of herself, terrifying both man and beast with a short quirt and a sharp tongue.

Lordy.

Deirdre made it a point to steer clear of the woman, and she urged Isabel to do the same. And yet her friend had problems of her own. The days since reaching Musette had seen a decline in Isabel's good cheer. There was little question why. People on the expedition wanted to know where they were going. Isabel was supposed to tell them.

And yet the foreign beauty knew nothing.

Friar Emmet, who so far had been all but invisible on this journey, several times had come by their inn hoping to speak with Isabel. None of that went well. Deirdre could tell Isabel wanted to try, but the more it became obvious that she didn't have any answers, the more the woman's anger seemed to focus on the cleric. On his last such journey earlier that day, Deirdre had urged the man not to return.

"I've always found a nice walk helps clear the mind," she told Isabel after the two had their lunch that day. "And it's an unusual kind day, today."

To Deirdre's surprise, the woman agreed with little hesitation. Very soon, with Deckard watching their backs at a distance, the women were walking down the lane to the town's central square. At any other time, the stroll would have been a delight. The place was a picture of beauty. But this wasn't their first such walk. On their first day in Musette, Isabel wanted to see the famous Red Cobbled Square, hoping that the sight of the place might trigger something inside her.

But nothing.

Her friend said the place looked very much like it had in her dreams, but that was all. There was no special knowledge, no sudden new rush of inspiration at the sight of a place that was, or so they thought, the first step in a journey into the unknown.

On this walk, Deirdre didn't press the issue. She didn't broach the topic of prophecy or visions at all. The Surrey lass was just as tired of the whole thing as Isabel.

Rather, she focused her attention on her friend, the quality of the day, and the things they found in the market. Even this far north, spring was in full bloom, and it was an unimpeachable day. They even found some suitable riding attire for Isabel to add to a few items the woman had acquired in East Portage.

Soon, the two women were laughing at various things common to them, the de Vere children, their first meeting, Sir Alexis, Mont Clair, Reverend Ainsley, and a score of other people, places, and things. Very soon the subject of the harridan arose.

"I don't think she's nearly as old as she looks," said Isabel in reference to Chastity Skinner. "It's the teeth."

"She has no teeth."

"Exactly. It makes her look years older than she truly is."

"And the enormous tits!"

"How does she stand up straight? ... and my heavens those thighs."

"I saw Sir Custis turn and flee at the sight of her just this morning."

"Well, in his defense...."

"... yes, so do I. There's a rumor that she killed a drover in Kingstown and can't leave the north for the warrant against her there."

"That can't possibly be true."

"If ugly were a sin...."

"The way she swears ... would put a sailor to shame...."

"Only one eye seems to focus...."

"Such a stench...."

Their scholarly disquisition went on in that way for some time, until Deirdre happened to notice an evil eye on them from across the square. It was the harridan, leering in their general direction. Deirdre stifled a shriek, grabbed Isabel, and dragged the woman away at a pace somewhat slower than a true run.

"Damn," Deirdre whispered. Why was she suddenly sweating? "Double damn."

The area north of the main square of Musette was a warren of streets, alleys, and footpaths, and Deirdre paid not the least attention as she dragged her friend along a torturous route as fast as she could get the woman to move. The Devil only knew why Deirdre was so startled. After all she'd been through, why would one toothless old hag frighten her, let alone frighten her so deeply?

But she decided that she'd come too far to be murdered by a muleskinner, no matter how ugly. Perhaps she could get Sir Lucas to dispense with the woman's service. He'd been amenable to her goading in the past. But would such a request only make things worse?

Wait a moment, she nearly said aloud. Where was Deckard? What the hell was the man doing? And why wasn't he guarding their bodies? A wicked thought entered her mind. Perhaps she'd have this woman murdered. Would Deckard do it? No, better. As top heavy as the old crone was, though, she'd drop down a well nicely.

"Where are we going?" Isabel cried after a time.

Both women came to a halt when Isabel finally dug in her heels. From the look of it, they very nearly were to the edge of the city, where the city wall opened onto the south bank of the Ransome River.

The sudden sound of someone running caught Deirdre's attention, and she reached for the dagger in the sheath to her side. Deckard came running around the nearest corner, a panicked look on his face.

"Ah! Young miss," he nearly cried, "don't be running off like that. Your fine uncle would have my knucklebones for dice if anything were to befall you." The bodyguard was beet red and panting heavily, a naked dagger in his hand.

Deirdre let out a gasp and blurted a general apology to the two people with her. Lordy, the days since the bandit attack had left her coiled far, far too tightly. Whether she was imagining things or not, she needed to come back down to earth.

"Whew," she said after a moment. "I don't know what's gotten into me." She took a seat on some nearby stone blocks and tried to catch her wits again. "Double damn," she whispered.

Deckard, a great look of relief on his face, sheathed the dagger and leaned against a nearby stone wall. Isabel didn't seem to mind Deirdre's bizarre behavior at all—or she was pretending not to notice to save her friend's feelings.

Either way, the older woman strolled the last few paces down to the great river. The Ransome wasn't the longest or widest river in Albion, but it was wide and from recent rains had a heavy flow. The hum of the passing water was almost something Deirdre could feel. As she watched Isabel, the woman bent, recovered a few stones, and began tossing them into the stream.

Things were fine again.

Deirdre nearly was ready to get on with their day when Isabel pointed across the river and said, "That's it."

"What?"

She turned and looked at Deirdre before again pointing, this time her gesture obviously was to an outcropping of heavy stones on the far side of the river.

"That's it," she repeated. "That's where we're going next."

25. A Shattered Stone Bridge

It was a proper bridge in my visions," Isabel told her companions later that day.

"That must have been a sight to behold," said Sir Armand. The man had wanted to see the thing for himself. "The locals say there's never been a bridge over the river."

"Yet, there it is." Deckard pointed to the stone columns on the far side of the river that once must have been a bridge abutment.

"How long before we can get across?" asked Deirdre.

Isabel imagined her friend still was a trifle embarrassed from her small panic fit from earlier and simply wanted to get on with things. There was nothing of which to be ashamed. The sight of the felonious Chastity Skinner had caught Isabel unawares too. The hideous woman could put the shivers in someone.

Both she and Deirdre were a little edgy if she were being perfectly honest with herself. And the men of the party weren't in the best sorts either. It was natural that there might be troubles when groups of people traveled together. Not all of the men knew one another when the journey began, and that faint patina of cordiality that sometimes exists between recent acquaintances had begun to wear away. It was dangerous to lose sight of the fact that these were Gheet fighting men, a breed prone to see snubs and insults where there were none, and to react with violence at the least affront.

It was a wonder there already hadn't been trouble. Up until that point, the leadership of Sir Lucas had been to indulge the men their whims and caprices, plying them with drink and food. She'd thought that folly at first, but perhaps such pandering was the reason the party so far had been free of conflict.

If Isabel was not mistaken, there were no taverns or "knocking shops," north of the Ransome. A shiver passed through her at the thought of the road ahead. She wanted to be optimistic, but it was becoming harder and harder.

Deirdre was right. Just get on with things.

"Sir Lucas is with the ferrymen now," said Armand. "Given the country on the far bank, those chaps don't work every day."

"You'd think they'd be grateful for the work, then," replied Deirdre. The lass turned to leave. "Let's go pack up our things. Perhaps that will set events in the right direction."

They strolled back to their inn mostly in silence. Deckard and the knight appeared to keep a careful eye open, and Isabel knew Dierdre was deep in her thoughts. The kid had been even moodier than usual lately, which was why Isabel was grateful for her company. The main reason Deirdre came out of her shell was to cheer up Isabel.

Isabel still was processing something, a phenomenon that was rather disconcerting. Her dreams were not simply dreams. It might have been a fluke that she recognized the streets of Musette before they'd even arrived there. The city was famous for its red cobbled stone. It was very possible she'd overheard someone speaking of them. And the square she saw when they reached Musette a few days before was not *precisely* as it had been in her dreams. Why not then suppose the whole thing was a coincidence? Or a product of her imagination?

But the bridge, the damned bridge. Sir Armand was correct. The locals knew nothing of a bridge, claimed there'd never been one over the river. When she reached the banks of the Ransome and began to skip a few stones earlier that day, the thing nearly leapt out at her. There was no bridge, but the shape and size of the abutment on the far bank was unmistakable. Even the carving on some of the stonework, aged and weathered though it was, was familiar to her from her visions.

The full weight of her observation hadn't struck her at first. After a time though, it dawned on her that there was something more at play than vivid dreams. It took her breath away to think of it now. Her visions were something prophetic.

But how could it be that? Wasn't prophecy the foretelling of things yet to be? If she wasn't mistaken, the bridge in question hadn't stood for many hundreds of years, perhaps longer. Certainly, it was older than recent memory. That wasn't prophecy. That was something else … wasn't it?

Deirdre was a good and true friend, and she was wise and canny in ways Isabel never would be, but Isabel never before had wanted so much to speak with Reverend Ainsley. The truth was that she'd scarcely had a chance to get to know the man, but he'd made such a powerful impression on her with his learning and his decency. They needed such a robust intellect on this journey, this quest. But what did they have instead?

Friar Emmet.

She tried not to think ill of the man, but time and again a phrase her grandmother used to say came to her mind. The man was about as useful as tits on a boar hog. And now, no doubt, that same fellow would be congratulating himself for having found Isabel. The thought of him taking any credit at all left her grinding her teeth in a very unhealthy way.

———

They crossed over the River Ransome in the early morning of the following day, first Isabel, Deirdre, and the knights and clergymen, and then, over the course of the day, all of the servants and pack animals. It was an all-day affair.

Happily, there were no casualties during the crossing, despite the height and heavy flow of the river. One pack horse went over the side of the small ferry, but it managed to struggle to the far bank with its load more or less intact. The harridan cackled throughout the ordeal, cursing and chiding Sir Lucas for not having exchanged their pack horses for mules.

"Ye get what you pay for, sir knight!" The woman somehow managed to make every word sound like an insult or a profanity.

The evening before, Deirdre and Isabel had spoken to Lucas, asking that the woman not be allowed to accompany them. He politely declined. Chastity Skinner and her team had been engaged by Baroness Elise, not the knight. It was not a contract he had the authority to break.

And besides, neither Isabel nor Deirdre could come up with a single reason why the woman should be let go, beyond the fact that the hag made people uneasy. She was a muleskinner. Folks engaged in such a trade were not famous for their geniality.

During the crossing, Isabel was employed in a somewhat more practical concern. Where to go to from there? The ferry landing was upriver some way from where lay the bridge abutment, and it seemed an easy enough problem. If a bridge once had been situated on that spot, there must have been a road running from it. Was that not the path they should take?

As the others crossed, she and Sir Armand went along the riverside until they reached the abutment. There was nothing there that indicated what the next step in their journey should be, but facing away from the river she looked northward. It seemed right. It wasn't a part of her vision, but something in her told her that the way in front of her was the way to go. And why not? Perhaps something along the way would spark a thought.

To Isabel's great relief, a huntsmen named Spears, a local man the baroness had engaged via a hiring agent, confirmed that a faint trace did exist in that direction. It was one used by game and sometimes followed by the occasional hunter that ventured into that area. Though overgrown, the trace went northward for some 20 leagues, or around 30 or 35 miles if

Isabel understood the local measures, before the trail forked. The huntsman did not know what lay beyond that point.

"It seems as good a way as any," announced Sir Lucas that evening, and the party struck its course the following morning.

The going was somewhat difficult at first, but after a short time the trace turned into a proper path. It wasn't cared for in any way, but the hoofs of passing game over the years had kept the ground firm and somewhat even.

Fortunately, they'd had the common sense not to bring wagons or carts, and as much as it pained Isabel to admit the fact, the harridan was right. The mules kept to the trail very well, only somewhat less handsomely than did Isabel's agreeable Gelt. This kind of travelling seemed like mother's milk to the shaggy brute. Hers was the only mount that didn't occasionally balk at a root or a branch in the path. He simply glided over them like that was his business.

The path wasn't dreadful, but neither was it easy or swift travelling. By the end of the first day, they scarcely had traveled five leagues, a fraction of the distance they might have moved on a proper road. She supposed that situation was something to which they needed to accustom themselves, as were the days that they kept.

They weren't up terribly early that morning, but they did travel for most of the day, taking only a few stops along the way to eat. In the evening, the party settled with just enough time to pitch camp while it was light. Thereafter, there was the expected eating and drinking around the campfire, but most folk bedded down early.

The next morning gave Isabel a fright.

She awoke in the small tent she shared with Deirdre to the sight of a monstrous form hovering over her. She at first was too frightened to scream, and then she realized it was the enormous head of a horse. It took but a moment to realize that her Gelt had slipped its tether and wandered into camp to find her.

Neither she nor Deirdre were certain what to think of that. Why hadn't the guards noticed a horse sniffing from tent to tent? And what had gotten into the animal?

"As I said, milady," Armand told her when she broached the subject later on the trail, "they are a loyal breed. He probably just missed you."

"That's what I get for being too nice to you," she said, reaching up and rubbing the spot behind the creature's right ear.

The rest of the day was much the same as the first, as was the day after that. The party started their day soon after sunrise, rode most of the day, taking liberal breaks so as not to exhaust the humans and the animals, and they stopped before sunset to make camp and rest.

It was sometime in the middle of their third day of travel that it came to her attention that the harridan had been going from tent to tent at night and making a bit of extracurricular coin.

"It's enough to turn your stomach," Deirdre exclaimed after Isabel told her the news.

"Who would have such a woman?" she whispered.

"Lady Isabel, remember who it is we're traveling with. Like as not, this crone is the only thing protecting the virtue of the party's mules."

Isabel let out a peep, before whispering, "She does love those animals."

"Her single redeeming virtue."

It was ghastly, but Isabel couldn't help but continue her gossiping with Deirdre on the subject in hushed whispers for most of the rest of the day. The knights had their sport and entertainment, she reasoned, and Isabel and Deirdre had theirs. The two women giggled themselves to sleep that evening talking about it, and they passed a restful night.

In the morning, they awoke to shouts and screams. One of the guards had been murdered.

26. 'Twas No Bear

The body was barely 30 paces from where she and Isabel had slept, so Deirdre made a point of getting a good look at it. A bear, they said. She happily would admit she didn't know everything, but traveling with the Fiend had taught her much about the various arts of dismemberment. The badly torn and mangled body she viewed that morning didn't look at all like it had been attacked by a bear or by any other animal.

The remains of the knight, one Sir Edmund Manque, were scarcely recognizable. The fellow hadn't even been on guard, but had gone out to answer the call of nature. The carcass, which was discovered near the tree line, was terribly shredded, and there was a great deal of blood soaking the ground around it, but little of him looked to have been eaten. Strange animal attack that.

She brought that up with Sir Lucas.

"What else could it be, milady? No animal but a great brown bear could bite through the steel byrnie the man wore. I've hunted plenty in my life. No doubt the great beast was chased away before it could dine on the poor fellow."

"Frightened away by what?" she asked.

The party leader hemmed and hawed a moment, before giving her a short, "No doubt the guards startled it."

It occurred to her that speaking with the man further would profit her nothing, so she thanked him and went looking for another member of the party. She found Spears, the older of their two huntsmen, near a fire chewing on a rasher of bacon. She'd noticed the fellow before. He was quiet, patient, and thoughtful, qualities she'd observed in every hunter she'd ever met.

"Bear? No," the man said. "Bears don't kill then eat. A bear will eat a man alive and not be bothered with his hollers."

"So, it wasn't a bear?"

He gave her a faint smile. "If it was, it would've made a ruckus, and it would've left some sort of tracks behind. Anyhow, the horses would've let us know if a bear was about … if any wild animal was about."

"It was a man who did this?" she whispered.

"No." He gave a lazy look around. "As I told your Sir Lucas, there's a reason people don't often come here. I've been in these woods more than any man alive, and even I don't stay long."

It was another short conversation. The man was canny and certainly was being paid well for his time, so in all likelihood he would keep his thoughts to himself. Besides, perhaps he simply didn't know what it was that had killed poor Sir Edmund.

Poor? Had she really thought that? Well, it was bad manners to think ill of the dead, but Edmund Manque was a Gheet the world could do without. She didn't like the way the man spoke to her, or the way he looked at lovely Isabel, like a man who too long had gone hungry.

Good riddance.

But what were they to do? If there was a beast about, something unnatural and dangerous, shouldn't they do something? As the party struck camp and prepared for its daily march, it didn't appear that Sir Lucas was doing anything. True, a handsome grave was dug for the dead knight's remains, and Friar Emmet was organizing a short service. But there didn't seem to be anything else.

She'd speak with Sir Armand and ask the knight when next they camped to place his tent closer to the tent she and Isabel shared. Deckard already slept nearby and knew to be on his watch, but it didn't hurt to remind him. What else to do?

By the time she made it back to her tent, Deckard had struck the shelter and was packing it away. She'd see to her own saddle today. Her palfrey eventually had seen itself clear to forgive her for the tiny nick she'd given it on the road from Westport. There still was the occasional wary look, but they were back on speaking terms.

She envied Isabel her new mount. The Gelt was an ugly brute, but she liked the way it moved and how it responded to Isabel, novice rider though she was.

No. There was no envy, and if there were, she chose to banish it away. This was a peculiar and a dangerous land through which they rode, and she was happy that her best and most beloved friend was well mounted. In such a place, a strong and dependable steed could make all the difference.

She found herself thinking of the Fiend as she saddled the palfrey, and she wondered about his safety. He said he'd try to join them after evading the magickers of the Inquisition, and she very much had hoped to find him awaiting them in Musette. But there was no sign of him, not a scent.

Was there more going on than he'd told her? Had he sent her and Isabel away on this quest to put them in a place of safety while he dealt with a danger that he knew he could not overcome?

She didn't feel very safe. And over the past days she'd swung back and forth between being angry with the creature and swallowing tears over her worry for him. Tough and resilient though he was, the monster was by no means invulnerable.

Bury that away, she told herself.

Perhaps other affairs kept him away. Weren't there some errands he needed to do for the baron? There was never any doubt in her head that he had his own schemes and plots. Perhaps sending her and Isabel off was just a way to put the two of them out of sight while he plied his evil craft?

Bah! She chided herself again for worrying about it. She and Isabel were on their own. That was all there was to it. They'd need to come up with a plan, a way to figure out what kind of beast was out there and how to deal with it.

It would help set her mind at rest if they had any notion of where the party was going, or even how far. There was no telling if their ultimate destination was many hundreds of leagues distant, or whether it might be around the next bend in the forest path. She couldn't be angry at Isabel for that state of affairs, but perhaps she should sit the woman down with Spears and see if the huntsman recognized any of the locations that Isabel described.

"What's the next place we're supposed to see?" she asked her friend as soon as the party was back in the saddle and moving.

"If we reach them in order, there's supposed to be a river ford somewhere ahead of us."

Deirdre began looking around again for the huntsman. They were only able to travel two abreast along their narrow path, which meant the entire column straggled for many hundreds of paces behind them. And the huntsman was one of those fellows who often traveled on foot, making it hard to spot him among the mounted party.

She very nearly was prepared to send Deckard looking for the fellow when the huntsman came into view ahead, walking beside the mount of Sir Lucas.

"I don't know of any fords," the hunter said after she finally got his attention. "But there must be a river somewhere on the path ahead of us."

"How could you possibly know?" asked Isabel.

"Rivers don't spring from nothing, miss. We should reach a fork in this path sometime by the middle of the day. I don't know what lies beyond that—the fork is as far north as I've ever traveled—but I know that south and west of here is a river, a tributary of the Ransome. That river flows from the general direction to which we're traveling."

"So we'll cut the river at some point past the fork in the trail?"

"We will. We just need to find the right spot."

"Any suggestions, Mr. Spears?"

"My nephew and I travel ahead now to scout north of the fork," the man said as he turned to go. "We'll keep an eye out."

The moment the huntsman departed, Isabel spoke.

"Was it really a bear that killed Sir Edmund last night?" the woman asked her.

"What? … Why do you ask?"

"Nothing really. It's just a feeling."

"I don't know. One would have thought a bear would have caused some sort of commotion. And Mr. Spears said there was no sign of tracks."

"Definitely that," Isabel agreed. "But … just the way everyone behaved this morning. When poor Quackenbush went overboard, the reactions were … I don't know. Authentic?"

"Not so much this time?"

"I can't put my finger on it. There definitely is a tension now that wasn't there before. Maybe it's this place."

Deirdre agreed. There was something about the forest in which they found themselves, but also a subtle something had changed within the group. It was another thing that she could not fully sort out. She reminded herself again that, with the exception of a few, these people were all strangers to her, even after some weeks together on the road.

———

Deirdre spent the rest of the morning's ride thinking about the people in the party, which now had grown far too large for her to keep everyone straight in her head. She concentrated on the main players, the knights, the clerics, and those people who seemed to be the leaders among the retainers and servants.

She trusted Isabel and Armand without reservation. They were honest and true. And she'd come to think better of Sir Bertrand, but still harbored some doubts. People could be tricky. She didn't have great confidence in Deckard. The man was a killer and a scoundrel. But the Fiend wouldn't have placed the chap with her if there was any doubt about whether he could be trusted.

Sir Lucas, who she'd come to find wasn't a knight at all, had earned his honorific "sir" because he was a baronet, a type of minor nobleman. Though she sensed no true wickedness in the man, as a leader he was weak and sometimes could be petty and short tempered. The remainder of the knights were mostly Gheet, polite but with the various moral shortcomings common to their breed. Sir Custis was an ugly drunk, Sir Laird was said to cheat at cards, and all were lechers of various degrees of sinfulness.

The clergy were of no greater use to her. Emmet needed to be placed in a sack and thrown into the river. And the young deacon with him, Wentworth, was completely out of his element. She respected a creature who was at home in a library, but Wentworth had little else to recommend him. And being bookish didn't make a person honest or trustworthy.

Spears struck her as frank and straightforward. The small handful of locals in the party seemed to look to the man for guidance, and the remainder of the new hires, most of whom were muleskinners, had arrived from elsewhere and were under the employ of the harridan. All of them seemed obedient to her.

Perhaps "cowed" would be a better word to describe the attitude of the muleskinners to their boss. The woman already that morning had given one of her men a walloping for having not secured a bundle properly. There was no telling what the evening might bring.

She rolled all these characters over in her head, looking at them from various angles, as the vicar always had advised her to do. But nothing was readily forthcoming. People seemed to be, for better or worse, who they purported to be. Did any have a hidden agenda? Might one or more be a concealed agent of the Inquisition? Such was a thing she couldn't deduce.

She gave up for a time when the party reached a broad opening, a place where their single path forked into three trails. She and Isabel were in their usual place in the march, just behind Sir Lucas, the clerics, and a few knights.

It was when she looked up and saw Spears standing on a faint rise near one of the trails, and realized the man was hollering something, that the arrows started flying.

27. The Argent's Shallows

The first shaft took the knight in front of her through the neck, and Isabel felt the Gelt surge to life. Without her having done a thing, the animal was racing forward, past the other riders, and into the opening beyond.

Things hissed through the air around her like swarming hornets, things that a year before she never would have known were arrows. She pressed against the Gelt's neck and squeezed her knees tight against the saddle in the way Armand had tutored her to do. Soon after, came the battle cries and the sounds of metal on metal and the screaming of men and animals in pain.

Her fear of battle had in no way abated, but two years in this brutal land had taught her to marshal those fears. The first thing she needed to do was get out of the line of fighting, so she didn't resist when the horse carried her toward the high ground where first they'd seen the huntsman Spears.

The next thing? Stay out of sight, and don't become mobile plunder. Easier said than done. At that moment, the Gelt was racing her toward where Spears had stood, but the hunter now appeared to be in a brutal scrape with two other men, both of whom were armed. No sooner did she crest the high ground than a number of mounted riders shot past her from the rear. The small hilltop soon was thick with knots of fighting men, mounted and unmounted. The Gelt danced over at a sidestep—a move she'd never before seen him do—and settled to the ground out of sight behind a cropping of heavy stones.

What in the world?

Her mount was playing dead, and she soon followed his example, sliding free of the animal and tucking herself up against a thick tuft of grass amid the stones. Anyone passing who saw her hopefully would presume her among the fallen. But she did have a view of events on the hilltop and in the small meadow below.

The mounted knights and fighting men of her party soon had the hilltop under their control, but there were a number of fallen men and struggling and screaming mounts in the opening beyond. She had no hint where Deirdre might be and could only trust that Deckard was keeping her safe.

Arrows continued to zip past in a deadly hale from a line of trees 50 or so yards distant. It was unrelenting and only increased over the next minutes. Sir Armand, who she could see clearly not 10 yards distant, took his mount by the harness and led it to the ground, where the beast lay as if it were wounded or dead. Soon, all the mounts were on the ground, and the fighting men, bows in hand, took up positions amid the rocks and deadfalls of the hilltop.

This exchange of arrows lasted perhaps 10 minutes, but the stream of projectiles from the other side increased minute by minute, until it was all Armand and his men could do to peek up over the rocks shielding them.

That's when the attack came.

Isabel was dreadful at gauging such things, but there had to have been more than 100 fighters storming out of the tree line 50 or 60 yards away from where Armand and his 20 or 25 men crouched. The incoming rain of arrows slackened with the attack, but the enemy was on them before the defenders had a chance to let loose a single shaft.

There was no telling what direction the battle might take.

Their party was outnumbered, but one brutal lesson she'd learned from her time in Albion was that even unhorsed an armored knight was an incomparable killing machine. Armand and the others proved that now. The score or so knights and their men-at-arms leapt up and met the enemy at the crest of the hill, and it was bloody carnage.

She'd often heard of Armand's skill in battle—Alexis spoke of it with admiration—but she'd never before seen it up close. The knight truly was a thing to behold. And outnumbered though they were, he and the men of the party cut a bloody swath into the advancing enemy, an enemy whose attack faltered just below the crest of the hill.

And yet there were so many! The battle could have gone either way as the parties hacked and cut at one another on the hillside. But after more than 10 minutes of the brutal and gory stalemate, another wave of enemy exploded from the tree line, yelling and screaming as they ran. There had to have been 50 or more of them, and at their lead was Chastity Skinner!

Treason! Isabel wanted to yell.

But then this new wave of attackers fell upon their comrades from behind, and it dawned on Isabel. This new wave was the party's skinners, drovers, and remaining fighters come to their rescue. The harridan was in the thick of them, her weighted riding crop in one hand, and a cudgel in the other. With one she slapped at her men who moved too slow to the attack, and with the other she struck down any of the enemy foolish enough to come against her. The woman was a devil.

Under this onslaught from fore and aft, the enemy wavered and soon broke. Some few attempted a fighting retreat. Most merely ran for their lives.

There was no time wasted in victory celebrations. She heard the voice of Sir Lucas over the din.

"Sir Armand, to horse and get after them. Madam Skinner, get the party moving. We are away!"

———

It took Deirdre some time to sort out what had happened, most of which she did on the far side of the river after the fighting was done. She'd seldom been so mad in her life.

The moment after the first arrows began to fly, Deckard had her in hand and pulled to the ground. He then dragged her, fighting and struggling the whole way, to the safety of an upturned bole in the forest. It was only after the combat had died down that she managed to threaten and cajole the man into letting her go. The nerve, the bloody nerve. The two of them would have to have a long and serious talk about such behavior.

She and her overzealous bodyguard made it to the small hillock where the worst of the battle had raged at just about the time the enemy finally broke and took flight. In an uncharacteristic moment, Sir Lucas made two very sound decisions when the enemy quit the battlefield. He sent Sir Armand and some mounted men to harry the enemy as they fled, and he ordered the convoy to prepare to depart.

But then their leader vacillated. He didn't know which way they should turn. It was only after the earnest entreaties of a wounded Mr. Spears that a plan took shape. The huntsman urged the leader to move along the trail to the northwest. A league or less along that trail was a shallows across a river. If the enemy returned in greater numbers, better to have a river between us and them, the man claimed.

At first, Sir Lucas was uncertain, asking of the hunter whether it was not he who had led them into a trap. Why trust the huntsman a second time?

"Because it was Lady Isabel who foretold the presence of this river and a path across it," Deirdre told the stubborn baronet. "We have dead and many injured. I trust Mr. Spears. Trust me now."

Her words seemed to do the trick. Sir Lucas ordered their movement, and by midafternoon, the entire party had moved to a point where the trail met a broad river. The shallows over which they forded were thigh-deep to a walking man, but they were crossable. By late afternoon, the party was across the river and ensconced in a secure camp for the night.

There, they licked their wounds.

The party had lost seven dead and a score more had serious injuries, two of which were life-threatening. Most everyone had some sort of scrape or cut from the affray, and each tended to himself or to his neighbor. Isabel looked after the serious injuries with Deirdre's help.

It was during that time that she got the full story from the huntsman.

"Macargue and his band came across my nephew Latham and me late morning and held a knife to the boy's throat. Said if I didn't lead your party down a trail to the northeast, he'd bleed poor Latham right in front of me."

"Wait," said Deirdre. "Who are you talking about?"

"Macargue, miss. Gifford Macargue. He's been thieving in these parts since I was a lad. I told your Sir Lucas about him before we set out."

"And…?"

"There's no faulting Sir Lucas, young miss. Macargue's a cutthroat and a thief. Mostly he hides out here in Transom and plies his trade back across the river. I've never known him to range this far north. And he don't ever travel with more than 10 or 12 others like him. No one could have figured something like this."

"Then why now? … And why did he want you to lead the party northeast?"

"I don't know the why, miss. But they planned on a proper ambush farther up that trail. It was only when I got sight of you at the fork that I saw young Latham had slipped loose and was dashing through the woods. I'll not lie. I'm glad I didn't have to choose between you folks and my nephew. But I reckon Macargue knew the jig was up and attacked before you were in place."

"It didn't go as well as he hoped," said Deirdre.

"No, miss. If it had, you and me wouldn't be having this pleasant chat."

The man had a few wicked cuts that Isabel finished stitching up, and the two women were finished with their doctoring before night fell. It was only when they returned to the campfire near their tent that the day had its one last ugly episode to dish up.

The knights who had pursued and harried their attackers were back by then, and sentries had been set, but the harridan had pinned down Sir Lucas near his tent and was haranguing him over a change to their contract. There was, she said, nothing in their contract about fighting in battles. And the woman demanded extra compensation for the one skinner dead and those skinners injured. There also was a matter of some dead animals.

To Deirdre's ears, the woman's demands sounded ludicrous. She insisted on a doubling of their rates, and an immediate cash compensation for the dead and injured tradesmen. Payment for the dead mules could be made at the end of the journey. The hag tried to sound magnanimous when making the claims over the animals.

Sir Lucas's response merely was to scoff, and to inform the woman that Baroness Elise had made the contract, and only the baroness could alter it.

It was at that point that the harridan spied Isabel, and a wicked look flashed across the creature's face. She moved close, giving Isabel a long and appraising look from top to bottom.

"Fair enough," the hag said. "But in exchange, I've a monopoly on the peddling of all pussy for the duration of the journey. And no credit. I'll expect cash on the barrelhead for a throw with this exemplary young darling, here."

Isabel let out a cry of surprise. The Gelt, who Isabel had been leading back to picket near their tent, reacted by shooting out its head and biting the harridan hard on her enormous left breast.

The hag screeched in outrage, and Deirdre jumped between the two women, grabbing the arm in which the dreadful old woman had raised her quirt, before kicking the hag several times in the shins. It took nearly a dozen strong men to separate the two of them, and as some knights and retainers led Chastity Skinner back to her fire, Deirdre realized something important.

She was going to have to murder the harridan.

28. A Dark and Dreary Gorge

It wasn't something she could do straightaway. Were the crone suddenly to die so soon after a quarrel with Deirdre, even if the woman passed under the most natural of circumstances, it would be too obvious. So the youngster bided her time, schemed, and plotted.

The woman's death would have to be something stealthy—she'd seen how the old hag could fight—and then only after Deirdre had been seen to make some attempt at rapprochement. Yes, that would do it. Cozy up to the woman, say some kind things, maybe swallow her pride and make a public apology for kicking the woman in the shins. Put the crone off her guard and divert suspicion.

That would do it simply fine.

She allowed her mind to wander before she slept that night, just to give it a chance to sort through the various alternatives. A fall from a height? An accidental drowning? Any number of mishaps might be arranged.

Always use your imagination. Poison kept coming back to her thoughts. She had access to a dozen or more concoctions in her pack that would do for the woman without leaving a trace.

Deirdre had every intention of sleeping well that night. Her decision to plant the old creature had put her in good spirits, and any immediate danger of attack had appeared to pass. There were double guards and a hastily constructed barricade along much of their perimeter. Even more, Armand and Deckard were nearby. And the Gelt was picketed close at hand to act as a watchdog for the night.

But happy things were not to be.

Several times throughout the course of the night and into the early morning, movement along the camp perimeter roused the guards. The enemy had returned, but in larger numbers? No. It was something else. Perhaps it was just a predator rooting around at the smell of fresh blood or at the aroma of food in camp? Another bear? Well, definitely not that.

There was nothing overt, but the subtle noise and the occasional snapping of limbs, rustling of branches, and swishing of leaves kept everyone on edge throughout the night. By the dawn's first light, Deirdre had managed only snatches of sleep here and there.

And then they found the body.

No one knew at what point Sir Custis's squire disappeared, but as soon as the sun lighted the morning sky, guards found what was left of the young man near a cluster of oaks a few dozen paces from the trail. Unlike the body of Edmund Manque, young Squire Dietrich's remains had been thoroughly picked over, and several large parts of him were missing entirely. It was difficult to identify the lad at first.

"What could have done such a thing?" she asked Spears after the bodies of Dietrich and those killed during the previous day's battle had been interred. "And how could any creature have done such a mess so close to camp without anyone hearing?"

The man gave her a long and helpless look.

There certainly were monsters in the world. Deirdre had always known that. She'd have to figure out which kind of monster they now faced without the huntsman's help. Alas, she wasn't sure where to start. It simply hadn't been something she'd learned from the Fiend.

"Imagine that," she said aloud.

Of all the people to have as a teacher, she had the Devil. But all he wanted to teach her was math, chemistry, and biology. And it wasn't even biology of the obscure and esoteric variety. Was there even a single work of arcana, or more than a single slim bestiary, in the library at the vicarage at which she'd stayed that winter? She'd never felt so poorly equipped for any task.

By the time the party buried the last of its dead, had its breakfast, and again broke camp and hit the trail, she was in no better mood. And it was a spirit shared by everyone in the company. Armand and Deckard were as quiet as the grave, Isabel was of no mind to gossip, and there was none of the cheerful and teasing banter up and down the column as there had been in past days.

On the good side, there was only one trail for them to follow, and it was broader and clearer than their earlier trace. At most places, four riders could travel comfortably abreast. It was not so fine as the High Road, but it eased their travel, and they made tolerable time during the course of the day.

The party kept a careful guard and chose defensible camps each night, and for the next two nights there were no further attacks or unexpected deaths. That is to say, there were no dangers from without.

Several times over the next days, Sir Lucas stopped knights from coming to blows over some imagined personal slight, and a muleskinner that very evening had murdered a comrade over a game of chance and was, in turn, hanged for his troubles.

Tempers were wearing dreadfully thin.

The only person who seemed to be enjoying herself was the harridan, who took great glee in bullying and tormenting both man and beast.

Happily, a certain pattern in the crone's life appeared to Deirdre during that time. Even with the mysterious deaths the party had experienced, the despicable woman was in the habit of keeping her tent apart from the others. No doubt this was to facilitate her nocturnal activities, which continued unabated night after night.

And there were noticeable moods through which the harridan passed during the course of the day. Those changes seemed fueled by the large demijohn of malt whiskey that the woman kept slung from a strap on her saddle. The spiritous liquor, which she nipped at throughout the day, appeared to sharpen her tongue as, at the same time, it curbed her more violent impulses. And the woman was in the habit of sitting alone near her tent at the end of each day's travel, taking leisurely swigs of the stuff.

Always study your subject carefully before applying a solution, the vicar often said. May the angels bless that man.

That evening, Spears and his escort returned from scouting ahead to announce the next milestone in their journey, a dark and narrow gorge, was a brisk day's travel ahead. They would camp at the mouth of the gorge the next evening.

That was the very spot at which Deirdre would begin her own scouting mission. At end of march tomorrow, before the party retired for the night, she would approach the crone at her tent under the guise of seeking the old woman's pardon for any and all offenses. The visit would give Deirdre a chance to see the woman up close and to put her at her ease, all while looking for opportunities and weak points by which to end her miserable existence.

Deirdre went to bed that night nearly purring in anticipation, but the next morning gave her a few moments of hesitation on whether to follow through with her plan. During the night, something had dug up and savaged the bodies of the murdered muleskinner and his slayer, which had been laid to rest in a pair of graves well outside of camp. It was another grisly find, and the party departed the area with great haste. They didn't even bother to rebury what remained of the remains.

Events were coming in such rapid succession that for a time Deirdre nearly gave up on her plan. True, with all the bodies dropping, it would be far less likely that one more would be noticed. In fact, her earlier concerns on that score now seemed daft. The late Squire Dietrich had been well liked, and yet, beyond shoveling some dirt over the young man and mouthing a few pious words, few paid him much thought after his death. It was unlikely given the harridan's squalid character that anyone would trouble themselves even for a moment to ponder the circumstances of her demise.

But did the party need another death? Was the harridan's demise absolutely necessary?

It had been several days since Deirdre's altercation with the old battle-ax, and from that time the woman hadn't scowled or leered at her and Isabel any more than she had before. The old woman cast upon them the same covetous and wicked glares as she always had, muttered the same nigh indecipherable carnal profanities. And the party needed every able hand, if they were to survive this ill-conceived and ill-begotten quest. The thickset hag was a fighter, if she was nothing else.

No, Deirdre decided in the end, she still would go that evening and make a peaceful gesture to the woman. The visit would give her a chance to decide whether the crone intended her and Isabel actual harm. If not, that was the end of it.

But if Deirdre thought the woman a continued danger? That would be the final nail in the termagant's coffin.

That decision having been made. Deirdre tolerated the rest of the day as best as she was able. She informed Isabel of her decision to visit the Skinner woman, though of course did not inform her of the finer details of the plan. And she even took an opportunity during a meal break to have yet another careful talk with Deckard, informing the man that grabbing her and pulling her away from danger was a thing that she would not tolerate.

Both conversations appeared to be successful. Isabel was worried for her facing the demijohn-swigging crone alone, but Deirdre convinced her it would be safe. She would go full-armed.

And Deckard agreed to refrain from future manhandling, although the fellow did express a clumsy and candid worry about what would happen to him, if he allowed any harm to come to Deirdre. She did her best to placate the man's worries over the fate of his various body parts, but she refused to budge on his behavior.

In the end, the day went well. After the party pitched camp late that afternoon and the guard was set, she was ready to face the harridan.

———

Deirdre went to see the woman fully prepared for danger. Along with the cosh up her sleeve, she had the dagger tucked into her belt and a small bottle of essence of gilder root concealed in a small pocket on her jacket. The gilder root was a slow-acting poison, the bitter taste of which was concealed perfectly by powerful spirits, and the symptoms of which resembled a fatal apoplexy. She carried it just in case.

At just past dark, she pardoned herself and worked her way through the camp to the harridan's small fire. She found the old woman alone, as was her usual, meat on the fire and her great bottle on the ground between her feet. There was no one else close enough to hear.

"If it's whiskey you're after, ya little minx," the crone called out as Deirdre approached, "I ain't a tavern. Come back when you got something sweet to peddle."

The woman's words were harsh, but her tone was surprisingly friendly and playful. Still, the harridan was a fright to behold. There still were a few teeth left in her head, which was worse than none at all, and with her hair down and her jacket off to reveal her full figure, she looked like a witch from a storybook.

"I've come to make my apologies," she told the old woman.

"Fer what?"

"Kicking you in the shins."

The old witch cackled. "Don't ever apologize for standing up for yourself."

"You're not angry?"

"Maybe I was. But life's too short to hold grudges."

Without asking, Deirdre took a seat on a log near the fire just to the harridan's right. She tried to act as if she were relaxed, but she knew there was no fooling the woman.

"In that case, I'm sorry my friend's horse bit you on the boob. But you did take her by surprise."

"Shouldn't she be the one tendering apologies for that?"

"You frighten her." She found herself getting annoyed at the woman's pleasant tone. Enough with the congeniality. "She's not going to work for you in that way, or in any other way. And neither am I. If the so-called knights of this party don't have the spine to put you in your place, then I will!"

The crone howled with glee. "You saucy little tart. These so-called knights—and you're right to call them that—will tire of old Chassy's boney wares sooner rather than late and come looking for some sweeter honey. You mark my word, they will. I was just offering to negotiate the terms for you two little sweetmeats when the time comes. Sorta soften the blow, as it were."

Deirdre felt her hand inching toward the cosh up her sleeve and had to fight the temptation. It wasn't that the woman made any threats. The lass just didn't like her manner, didn't like being spoken to in that fashion. The old woman seemed to sense her anger.

"There, there now," the harridan said. She raised the whiskey bottle and placed it between the two of them. "I've gone and upset you. Here, take a little swig of my tonic. On the house, of course. It'll have you feeling yourself in a trice."

When the woman spoke, she turned her body and began to rummage about for something in the tent. The cap was off the demijohn. For the faintest of moments, the woman's attention averted, Deirdre saw an opportunity. It was like her hands had a mind of their own. In a single swift move, the gilder root poison was in the bottle and the empty vial returned to Deirdre's sleeve. She hadn't even thought to do it, and her own motion was so quick she wasn't even certain that she'd done it at all.

But she had. She'd dosed the bottle with sufficient poison to do for a dozen old crones.

When the old woman turned back around, she had a fork in her hand and several times used it to stab the slab of salted beef grilling over the fire.

"Not thirsty, are you?" the old woman asked.

"No. You go right ahead."

"Don't mind if I do." The harridan hooked the fingerhold of the bottle, shifting the weight of the thing to her elbow, and raised it as if to take a drink. But then she paused and lowered the bottle to the ground. "No. I can't stand the notion of drinking alone with such lovely company. Lemme see if I have some sweet wine in my kit."

"No! Don't trouble yourself."

The woman already was half-turned toward the tent. "Are you sure?"

"Positive. Bottoms up," she urged the harridan.

The bottle was again to the old woman's lips when she asked, "Can I get you anything at all? Some water? Some beans? A bit of beef?"

It wasn't that the old hag's friendly overtures had changed Deirdre's mind. She very much still wanted this woman numbered among the dead. But the creature's awkward kindness reminded her of something— something very, very important. She'd poisoned the whiskey bottle on a sudden impulse, in a moment of pure anger, and just as suddenly she changed course.

"I'll have the next drink of whiskey," she said, and then, upon taking the demijohn in hand, just as quickly dropped the large bottle onto a nearby rock in an act of feigned clumsiness. The bottle shattered into pieces.

"Oh! I'm so sorry!" she exclaimed.

"Think nothing of it, Tuppence," said the hag in a soothing voice. "It's just a little whiskey."

Deirdre stood to depart, apologizing profusely as she did. She'd handled this whole thing terribly, from start to finish. She was a failure as an assassin. She hadn't taken five steps when she came to a stop and looked back at the old crone.

"What did you just call me?"

29. The New and the Old

Y ou are a *monster*."

"Tuppence, you've known that from the first moment you met me."

"Don't you 'Tuppence' me! It's been you all along. You could've told me. Don't you trust me? Didn't you think I'd be worried when you didn't meet us in Musette?!"

"I apologize, if I've given you a scare. But things became complicated when I evaded the agents of the Inquisition."

"Complicated in what way?"

"For one, when finally I gave them the slip, they wasted not a second trying to pick up my trail again. They headed straight north."

"To Musette?"

"Like homing pigeons."

"That explains so much," she exclaimed. "I'm certain they've been following us."

"You have good instincts, T…, um, may I call you Tuppence again?"

She waved her hand. "Of course. … What's going on?"

"I'm not certain. Some of the Inquisitor's people may well have been following you and Isabel from the beginning. But after my pursuers abandoned the game, I followed them part of the way, even got a look at a few. I'm confident they've recruited at least one person in the party to act as their agent. Maybe more."

"How could you know that?"

"Because they tried to recruit me."

"You?"

"Chastity Skinner."

"The name alone should've given you away," she hissed. "*Chastity*."

"Believe it or not, child, that was the woman's true name. I fell in with a group of muleskinners on the road to Musette led by the scabrous old bird."

"Where is she now? Don't tell me … she thought to rob and murder you and now lies in a ditch somewhere. Then you took her place."

"In a few words, yes. When I reached Musette, some men with Etruscian accents made Chastity an offer."

"And they ended up in a roadside ditch as well, I'd wager."

"In the River Ransome. Sadly, though, they didn't provide much information, and something about the diet Etruscians enjoy doesn't agree with me."

"Are you the one that's been snatching people and digging up graves along the road?"

"No. The party's being stalked, by a jotun of some kind, if I'm not mistaken. But that's far from our greatest worry."

"Worse than a man-eating ogre?"

"Technically a jotun isn't…."

"How would I know that!? … Do you realize how frustrating this has been? Not knowing anything!?"

The faux hag took a long breath, and when she again spoke, she did so slowly. "I apologize. I didn't do nearly enough to prepare you for this journey. And I've miscalculated at every step of the way. The truth is that I'm not certain what our enemies are about, or what their plans are. I know they have at least one agent in the party, but I haven't been able to narrow down who it is."

"I could have helped you," she said.

"You are one of the cleverest people I know, child. But you are a poor actress. And whoever the spy is in our midst has been watching you and Isabel closely. I couldn't afford them knowing that I'm here."

"I get it … I get it." She patted the hag's leg. "Who do you think it is?"

"I *was* leaning toward Edmund Manque."

"But then the jotun killed him."

"Oh, no. That *was* me."

"What?"

"I had a long talk with the fellow on the night of his demise. He admitted to some terrible things before he passed on to his reward, but working for the Holy See wasn't one of them."

"How terrible?"

"The man was a usurer. He'd loaned money to half the men in the party, a great deal of it, at extortionate rates."

"Small wonder no one mourned his death."

"There was an enormous sigh of relief," agreed the creature. "He wasn't above a little blackmail, either. Sadly, though, I had to start from nothing after he didn't pan out. Who did you have in mind?"

"Deacon Wentworth," she said. The man hadn't been foremost in her thoughts. But some things had begun to fall into place.

"Why him?" the Fiend asked.

"To start with, I ruled out all the knights."

"How so?"

"I can't rule them out with perfect certainty, not all of them. But as a group they're simply too thick to do anything terribly clever and underhanded."

"That could be part of their disguise."

"The vicar always said it's just as hard for a clever man to pretend to be dull-witted as it is for dull-witted man to play at being smart. I've watched this bunch. They are dull. And several, including Sir Lucas, are nearly illiterate."

"Edmund Manque ran a rather sophisticated usury and blackmail scheme."

"He's dead. And isn't it you who's always saying that if a man does something wicked it's either for love or money?"

"True," said the Fiend, scratching at her fleshy chin.

"How many were in debt to Manque?"

"Half the knights in the party at least."

"Doesn't it seem unlikely that, if a knight were taking coin from the Inquisitors, they'd be borrowing money from a comrade as well?"

"Possibly. Let me ask you. If it *were* one of the knights, which would you choose?"

Deirdre thought for a moment. Eliminate the impossible, and then winnow away the improbable. "It's not Armand. You and I both know it's not in his nature."

"Agreed."

"It's not Sir Bertrand. When on the road to Portage, some men I suspect were from the Inquisition attacked, and he protected us. And if Lucas wished us ill, he could have led the party into that trap at the fork in the path. Edmund is dead, as are Sir Lowell, Sir Michel, and Sir Johan. Sir Custis is a mean drunk, but he's also a blabbermouth when he's into his cups. The same with Sir Coy. Neither can keep a secret.

"Which leaves who?"

"Laird Claes, Irwin Quarrels, and Jewel Renard, idiots all. It would have to be one of those three. Sir Laird is a card cheat, but a poor one so I've heard. Sir Irwin can barely write his name, and Sir Jewel seems one of the few honest ones among them."

The fake hag again scratched her chin and reached a lazy hand down to the broken whiskey jug. "Essence of gilder root," she said after raising a finger to her tongue. "Shrewd choice."

"To what end?" Deirdre asked.

"Pardon?"

"You say there's a spy among us. I've felt the same. But what's he spying for? What is it you fear he'll find out?"

"As we've discussed before. I fear they'll seek to harm you or Isabel to get at me. They seem dogged this time."

"This time? What do you mean?"

The hag gave her a sweet smile, as sweet as that toothless face could muster. "It's the *gesh*, child. It is a powerful, powerful force, a combining of the magic of the two tribes, his and mine."

"What does it do?"

"It binds us, prevents us from doing certain things."

"From interfering in the world?"

"In certain fashions, yes. It's even difficult for us to work against one another at times. The *gesh* is a subtle, powerful, living thing. It sometimes presses so hard that it feels like it might crush me. At other times, it's as light as the gauziest linen. Over the ages, I've learned much of its ebbs and flows, when I can cheat it and when I cannot."

"And the Walking God?" It had become difficult for her sometimes to use that name. "Does he know its ways?"

"I think not. Don't get me wrong. Even in his mortal form, his is a power that dwarfs mine. But being rendered so weak has made him lazy and complacent. He only works through others, and even then, only indirectly for fear of triggering the *gesh*."

"Then why now? What's happened that he's moved against you?"

The hag clucked several times. "It may not be him at all. Every few generations, someone in that infernal Church that he allows to linger around him gets it in their heads to hunt me down. Sodding true believers. It always ends badly for them, but…."

"But sometimes people get in the way."

"I'll not allow any harm to come to you or Isabel, but the party we travel with is followed by another party of men, scoundrels from the Inquisition."

"The ones that attacked us at the forest fork?"

"No. Those were just some hired men sent, I suspect, to cut away at our numbers. The others will catch up to us soon enough."

Something occurred to her. "They don't know whether you're traveling with us."

"Right you are. I think they suspect it, but they're being cautious."

Deirdre found herself laughing. "This may well end up being a quest to kill Evil after all."

"It certainly looks to be a true donnybrook," the hag added as she reached around and produced a new demijohn from the tent.

The first swallow of the caustic stuff caused Deirdre's lips to pucker, and a shudder ran through her. "One more, please."

"Tell me about this deacon," said the hag after plying Deirdre with more drink.

"Wentworth? He seemed hind-tit at first. Couldn't understand why he was with us. But since Isabel was avoiding Emmet, Wentworth came around from time to time with questions and what not."

"What was it about him?"

"He's bookish, which seemed promising. So I tried to be friendly. And then he said a few curious things."

"Such as?"

"He's one of those meek fellows who thinks too much of himself. Couldn't help but brag that he'd studied abroad, but avoided saying where. At first, I thought he was just having me on."

"What made you change your mind? Something he said?"

"It was more something Baron William said. His heart was all aflutter over my copy of *Simonton on Algebraic Geometry*. He told me all about printing and editions and all that, and then he lent me a book on the subject."

"Tuppence, I don't follow."

"I was reading Simonton one day when Wentworth came by, told him it was a rather famous edition, and offered to let him borrow it if he was interested. You'd thought I offered him a creek viper the way he reacted."

"Go on," said the hag, leaning closer.

"Then he let slip the word *odium*. According to the book the baron lent me, that's a word they use in Etruscia to name banned books."

"Indeed it is, especially printed books." The hag again ran her fingers and thumb across her heavy chin. "Young Wentworth wouldn't be the first Reform scholar brought over to the Old Rite after studying at a college of the Holy See."

"Is he our spy?"

"He may well be one of them. Alas, he hasn't invited sweet Chastity into his tent for recreations, so I'll have to find another way to get close enough to have a look at him."

"Is that what that's all about?"

"Pardon?"

"The fornicating?"

"There are various ways to get men to talk, child. A good and jolly rub is also an ideal pretext to have a look around a person's tent. Mostly, I'm just staying in character. Far too many people in this party knew the real Chastity Skinner. Thankfully, they knew her best for her promiscuity and her propensity to violence, so no one has asked any questions about her occasional lapse of memory of late."

"What should we do next?" asked Deirdre.

"Keep your eyes open, but don't be too obvious. I promise I'll keep you apprised of events as I'm able. But for now, you'll have to play act. Chastity is a grotesquely unpleasant woman. Do try and treat her as such."

"It won't be a problem. But are we to ignore the monster that's stalking our party? Couldn't you just …?"

"Contrary to the scriptures, Tuppence, I don't have dominion over the beasts of the Earth or lordship of the hosts of Hell. The jotun would gobble me up with the rest of you if he thought he could get by with it."

"What then?"

"For all their size and strength, they're timid hunters who attack by stealth. They'll dig up corpses or pick off the occasional stray, but none will attack the main party."

"Is that meant to reassure me?"

"We'll run across more such creatures the farther north we travel, but those people pursuing us march in smaller numbers, 20 or 30 by my estimate. They'll suffer more from the predation."

"But don't they have sorcerers with them?" she asked.

"Even the most powerful magics can do little against such creatures. Cold steel is always a better weapon. And, before you ask, the hired men they used to attack us before won't be so foolish as to travel north of the River Argent—as the river we forded after the battle once was called. When the Inquisitors come, they'll come alone."

30. Through a Forest Deep

Seeing a sudden improvement in Deirdre's mood couldn't help but elevate Isabel's spirits. These were among the most trying times she'd faced in Albion, including the time she'd spent with the army over the last year. Something—or some *things*—had been stalking them these last days, and there was no escaping that fact.

It often was difficult gauging her friend's moods. But the same quiet sense of dread that had fallen upon the party after the battle at the forest fork appeared to have settled on Deirdre. There were occasional quirks in her moods over the next days, moments where the youngster seemed to have shaken off the dark, but it wasn't until after her meeting with the odious Chastity Skinner that something in the young woman seemed to change.

It wasn't anything Isabel could put into words. Deirdre's spirits just seemed to lighten. She even heard the kid humming to herself from time to time as she occasionally did.

Apparently, the meeting with the crone had gone well. Upon Deirdre's return, she informed Isabel that, yes, the old woman was a monster, far eviler than even she had imagined. But she reassured Isabel that the woman posed them no threat and, in her own way, was trying to do them a kindness by demanding a stake in any proceeds from prostitution she and Deirdre might enjoy. The old woman essentially was setting herself up as their protector. Any man who approached either of the young women would first have to face Chastity Skinner.

In its own demented way, that notion was perfectly Albion.

Still, Deirdre had encouraged her that it might be best to steer as far from the woman as possible. "But if she gives you anymore guff, let me know. I'll set her straight again."

Her young friend had enough moxie for the two of them. But conditions around the party in no way improved.

The half-day it took them to pass through the gorge was harrowing, but otherwise harmless. The sides of the chasm were so high and steep that they allowed little light, and it was a somber and a stressful passage.

The two days travel since that time had been through a dense forest, the very forest that she recollected from her dreams, so she at least knew they were on the right path. Thankfully, the road remained relatively smooth and passable, but these were the densest and blackest woods she'd ever seen. There were long stretches where it would have been difficult even to leave the road for all the tightly packed trees and underbrush.

Two men had gone missing in that time. During a break on the first day in the woods, one of the drovers wandered off from the faint meadow at which they'd stopped, no doubt to relieve himself, and had not come back. The party tarried some time, hoping for his return, and a number of his comrades set to shouting aloud his name on the off chance he would hear them and return.

Sir Lucas would order no search, and few people seemed inclined to venture into the dark woods in pursuit of the missing man. The harridan finally volunteered to make no claim for damages at the young man's apparent death, if the party chose to move forward without him. It was a meaningless gesture, of course. The missing drover wasn't even part of the muleskinner contract, but the offer got the party moving again.

Just last night, Friar Emmet's assistant, Deacon Wentworth, went missing from his tent. The party was camped at another of the rare meadows the forest had to offer, and it seemed unlikely that the young man simply had wandered into the woods on the way to the privy. The surrounding forest simply was too dense.

What, then, might have become of the deacon? Rumors abounded. Monsters, bandits, the Other One himself. Isabel harbored an unpleasant thought. The man seemed fragile and bookish. Though none of his personal items were missing, Isabel was convinced the cleric simply had turned on the trail and headed back south, toward home. In all likelihood, it was a decision made in a moment of panic. She'd been seized by those feelings herself in recent days. Some people were too fragile for this world, including some of those who had been born into it. She hoped some passing predator hadn't gobbled up the young man, but she knew better.

In one single way, and in one way only, spirits had improved over recent days. There was great talk among the men of the party, rumors of a vast fortune to be had at the end of the journey. Some of the rationalizations she'd heard whispered over campfires and along the trail were astounding. Some of them even made sense.

Why, for example, had the king insisted Baron William mount this expedition in a time of war, if there wasn't some great treasure to be found at the end of it? There was talk of huge mountains of gems and gold. Perhaps a dragon's hoard? It was well known that trolls and ogres kept great heaps of valuables that they'd plundered from unwary victims over the ages.

"Well, I heard...."

"My cousin once knew a man...."

"In a barrow, so they said ... enough gold to break a wagon's axle."

"Why else would we go to all this trouble?"

And on, and on, and on.

Isabel had her doubts about treasure, but, honestly, as silly as it sounded, it wasn't a notion she could dismiss in its entirety. A number of people had importuned her in recent days, asking those very things. She was their guide after all, a prophet.

My, how she nearly blanched just thinking of such things. She was no kind of seer or prophet. And, yet.... She did have those dreams. And if she had those dreams, dreams that in succession had come true, then what? With each point on their journey, her certainty that *something* awaited them at the end of it grew and grew.

Well, she would see.

Until then, it was the morning of their fourth day since passing through the gorge, and there were no indications when the forest would come to an end. Mr. Spears, who each day went ahead with a party of armed men, returned each evening with the same news. More trees. And he assured her that it wasn't out of the question that the forest might stretch on for many weeks or months. These were unsettled lands, with not the faintest signs of human life. Without human hands to hew down trees and to clear fields, nature had a way of taking things back. It was a small miracle that the road on which they traveled, as rough and rutted as it was in places, was still intact and uninterrupted.

"What shall you do with your share of the treasure, Mr. Deckard?" she asked the man as they got underway. Against all rights, she suddenly was in a good mood.

"T'aint no treasure, miss."

"You seem confident."

"I've walked this world from north to south, and east to west, for nearly 50 years. All the talk I've ever heard of dragon hoards and dwarf treasure is long on talk and short on treasure."

"You don't believe in hidden treasure?"

"There's plenty to be had, miss. But it usually entails plundering another man's city or boarding another man's ship with a blade in your hand."

She admired the mercenary's certainty. He was a practical fellow, with great nerve and confidence. He'd even become an admirable traveling companion. Despite his early laxity, he'd grown vigilant of her and Dierdre's safety and, to no small extent, to their comfort. He went about his camp duties with no urging and no supervision. And if afterward he snuck a few snorts of whiskey, it never effected his duty.

Still, she needed occasionally to remind herself not to become sentimental about men like their bodyguard. The man was not a house pet. She'd met many like him in Albion, the type who would look down on the lifeless husk of a person with whom they recently drank ale, even upon the body of a close friend, and would think nothing of it, would even joke at the fact. Don't grow sentimental about those lacking in sentiment. Nothing good will come from it.

She urged the Gelt forward to take her place beside Deirdre in the order of march. From time to time, the lass would set aside her schoolbooks and read lighter fare, and most of the preceding day Isabel had spent in the saddle listening to her friend read aloud from a storybook, something about an enchanted forest—of all things. She looked forward to another day of stories.

———

Deirdre needed to find an excuse to speak with Chastity Skinner. But it wasn't evident how she should go about that. The Fiend's new persona made getting close an annoying inconvenience.

It was only moments before that the shouting and the howling had stopped. The day's march scarcely was done when someone found the dismembered body of Sir Custis Greaves half-eaten in a nearby stream.

There was no doubt in Deirdre's mind what had befallen the man.

Not a quarter bell before the discovery of the chap's corpse, Deirdre had been returning from the tent of Sir Lucas when she spied Lady Isabel walking down a faint trail toward the stream, her skirts gingerly raised against the muddy earth and a happy bounce in her stride. It was unusual for the woman to go anywhere in camp alone, but before Deirdre could ask, Isabel spoke.

"I shan't be a few moments, Tuppence. Do be a darling and wait for me back at the tent."

Deirdre did as she was bid. There were a few others about, and Isabel sometimes used Sir Alexis's pet name for her. So, Deirdre thought nothing of it until she got back to the tent.

And there was Isabel, sitting on a saddle by the fire, reading a book.

Her friend on the saddle was clad in a different dress, the very same dress she'd traveled in earlier in the day. And then Deirdre recalled that the Isabel who she'd seen on the trail to the stream had her hair swept up in a slightly different fashion, a style that was somewhat provocative.

From that moment, it was no time at all until the screams and howls began. Sir Custis had been foully murdered at the stream.

Deirdre spent most of the early evening fussing with Isabel over what might have happened to the knight. Truth be told, she nearly blurted the whole thing out to her. She didn't like keeping her friend in the dark.

But how to explain all of *that*?

At just past sunset, Deirdre ran out of patience. She excused herself to Isabel and headed to the harridan's campsite. If anyone inquired, she'd tell them that she wanted to speak to the old woman about a missing bag. But at that point, she didn't much care who saw her with the Fiend.

"Looking for another shot of Chassy's whiskey?" the crone called out before Deirdre had even entered the light of her fire.

Deirdre flopped down on the ground near the fire and took up the offered bottle. For a moment, she was satisfied just to sit and sulk. She had so many questions. After a time, and a few shots of whiskey, she managed to find again her good humor.

"So, what did Sir Custis do to spark your anger?" she asked after a great sigh.

"Alas, not what I'd hoped."

"Say again?"

"I rather thought he was one of the spies, was certain of it, in fact."

"You really are off your game," Deirdre said.

"Well … yes."

"Tell me about it."

"First off, you were quite right about the young deacon. The lad was an Inquisition spy up to his eyeballs. Huzzah to you."

"Did you learn anything helpful? Like who the other spies are?"

"Wentworth believed himself to be the only one, but I doubt that's true. And he knew only to watch you and Isabel and to report back with anything unusual."

"Wait. Report back to who? And how?"

"He said he didn't know who …."

"He didn't know who he was reporting to?"

"Child, that's not uncommon. A comrade of his from Etruscia visited some time back, taught him a simple cantrip, and told him to attach himself to this quest and who to watch. When he needed to send a message, he'd write a short note on a slip of parchment, enchant it with the charm he'd been taught, and then burn the slip. The message he'd written would arrive on a notepad owned by some unknown recipient."

"That can't actually work," she said.

"Indeed. It's not unlike a method I use to communicate with my own agents and factors."

"Damn it," she whispered. She really did want to focus, but she had to ask. "I've heard you mention agents before. Who are they?"

"Folks all throughout Albion, and many beyond." He gave her a wink. "Your friend Sir Alexis is one of them."

"What are you talking about?"

"Even now, Sir Alexis travels the midlands, scouting strongholds, taking notes, and referring those by messenger back to Baron William."

"Hogwash. You're right here."

"True," said the hag. "But Birdy is ensconced in a middling good inn upon the road to Portsmouth. Several times a day, he gets messages and refers those on to the baron in my name. Some of those messages Birdy gets are from me, through a system wherein I write notes on a simple pad, and those same notes arrive moments later in a box I entrusted to Birdy."

"It's magic?"

"Nothing but."

"And you can be two places at once … with Birdy's help."

"It's Birdy this time. It'll be another person another time. Now, don't you want to know about the deacon and Sir Custis?"

"Who's Beazley?"

The harridan let out a delightful cackle. "Just imagine the Prince of Hell had a drunken and wicked stepfather who beat him every single day as a boy, morning, noon, and night."

"Beazley sounds very much like you."

"I'm guessing from Deckard's behavior that you invoked that name in his presence."

Deirdre nodded. "I said he was my uncle."

The hag very nearly choked on the whiskey she was drinking. "Deckard has seen the wrong side of Beazley, but only once. I doubt he'll want to see it again. Shall we speak now of what you visited me to ask about?"

"The deacon," she said. "He had nothing to share?"

"Nothing of much import. And I was totally wrong about Custis." The hag took a swig of whiskey. "I was certain he was the one."

"Why him?" she asked.

"Events back at the camp we made after we forded the Argent. It didn't dawn on me at first, but it was peculiar that the jotun got ahold of young Squire Dietrich. Anyone staying close to camp should have been safe."

"You think he strayed away?"

"Yes, but I don't think it was an accident."

"Ah! He left camp to meet someone," she said. "One of our enemies?"

"I think so. Piecing the events of that evening together, it came to me that he was killed while coming back to camp from somewhere. But would a squire really do something like that of his own accord, or was he working for his master?"

"Sir Custis."

"But it wasn't Custis," said the hag. "Though don't feel pity for the man. He'd tried several times to bribe Chastity to arrange for him to get Isabel alone and having failed that he followed her down to the stream today with wicked intentions. I'm sure he thought Lady Luck had dropped your lovely friend in his lap." The creature began giggling in the mad way he sometimes did.

"But he didn't confess to working with the Inquisition?"

"No, not at all."

"It's Sir Laird," said Deirdre with conviction.

"Eh? Why him?"

"Laird's only recently gotten his spurs. Before that, he was a squire to Custis's brother. Laird was the only other person in the party Dietrich knew before the journey began. The two men were companions since boyhood."

The hag rose and began pacing about her small campsite. Several times she went to speak before finally spitting out, "Oh … bother."

"Such language," Deirdre said. "Am I right?"

"Yes," said the Fiend. "You certainly are."

"We need to be certain. We can't afford anymore dead knights, if we're to fight the Inquisitors when they finally arrive."

"I agree fully, Tuppence. And they're not far behind us now."

"How far?"

"A half-day, give or take. But they seem to be taking their time. They'll likely stay close until they see an opportunity."

"How will they know?"

"What?"

"How will they know when there's an opportunity? Would Sir Laird have a … what did you call it? A cantrip?"

"It's unlikely. It would require some knowledge of magic."

"And basic literacy," she said. "That rules out Laird. But would there be others? Among the knights and their people? Or among the drovers or muleskinners?"

"I'm confident Chastity was their only attempt to bribe anyone among the muleskinners. Might there be others? Perhaps, but I don't think so. Even if this Sir Laird is another agent, which he almost certainly is, I suspect the deacon was the single dependable window the Inquisitors had into this party. And even he didn't communicate with them on a daily basis."

"What will they do once they notice his silence?"

"That probably won't happen for a few days. Still, I felt the faintest hint of magics being cast in the distance late last evening. Those must have been powerful spells to detect from so far away. Likely they were attempting some sort of distant seeing. If that doesn't work, they'll resort to the old-fashioned way."

"More spies?"

"It's a tried-and-true method."

"But they'd have to find us," said Deirdre. "It's a shame there aren't any sideroads and that we don't have a map to speak of."

"We'll be out of the forest in a day and a half or two days. Once we're into the mountains, there'll be streams and a few ridgelines to follow. The terrain will muddle their ability to work any divination, and the road splits in a few places once we ascend to the high plateau. That should work to our advantage."

"Wait," she said. "You've been this way before?"

"I've traveled this road many times, child."

"Wait," she said again. "Wait…. You know where we're going, don't you?"

"Of course, I do. I've known from the moment Isabel first described her visions to Alexis."

Deirdre found herself growing angry again. She should have known. "Why…? What…?"

"Child, it doesn't matter. I've told you from the outset this whole quest is a farrago, complete humbuggery. There's nothing at the end of it. It's always the way with these things. Some gibbering old hermit or half-crazed anchorite mutters some words, words that might even have some feeble nibble of truth to them, and then ardent young clerics spend days, weeks, or months poring over ancient texts in chanceries and libraries looking for some flesh to slap on those bones. Any old facts will do, as long as it leads the questors to some ancient fortress, or dead city, or hidden catacombs, any old one that will fit the bill. Once there, Tuppence, what do you imagine happens?"

The girl took a drink of whiskey and shrugged, her ire for the moment suspended. The Fiend continued with her tirade.

"Those self-anointed adventurers go inside and battle monsters. Do they battle monsters because the monsters are guarding treasures or ancient relics? No. They battle monsters because monsters need someplace to live, and they get irate when armed intruders invade their homes. And these so-called adventurers *never* find what they're looking for. But they always find *something*. Tell me, Tuppence. What exactly is a glaive?"

After another drink of whiskey, she was feeling even less irate. So, she gave the Fiend another innocent shrug.

"Precisely! Glaive is an old-fashioned word that's been used at one time or another to describe most every type of weapon ever forged. The place we now travel to is an old, abandoned fortress. I guarantee you we will find an old weapon someone left there at some time in the past. And assuming the members of the party don't kill one another in a dispute over who deserves credit for the find, we'll take that *glaive* back as a holy relic, but only after rousting a few dozen innocent creatures and getting some of our comrades killed in the process."

Deirdre wiped her mouth and lay the demijohn in its place by the harridan's feet. "Do you have any of those spiced peas?"

"What?"

"The dried spiced peas, the ones Reverend Ainsley loves so much?"

"Oh." The harridan turned and rummaged among a few items in her tent before returning with a familiar looking pouch. "Here you are."

It was Deirdre's first try at the delicacy, and after the first one touched her tongue, she leapt to her feet, hopped up and down, and shook her hands like a mad woman. Her eyes watered until she could barely see, and she thought she would choke to death, so severely did the fiery spice that coated the pea constrict her airway.

"Ah," she said after much hopping about, a long drink of water, and another sip of the caustic whiskey. "I'll have another, please."

31. Mountains High and Crystal Clear

What lay before them when at last they cleared the dense weave of the forest didn't just take Isabel's breath away. It snatched her heart through her very throat.

Her first glimpse of it came from overhead through the branches of some tall trees. The thick woodland canopy over recent days had stolen from them all but rare glimpses of the open sky. When, for the first time in many days, it appeared that they would be blessed with sunlight, Isabel took a glance skyward. It was some moments for her to realize that what she saw above her was not blue skies and white clouds, but the snowcapped peak and blue ice flows of an immense massif, a mountain loftier and grander than any she'd ever beheld.

She'd visited Europe several times while still in college, and once had even spent a week backpacking with friends in the highest Alpine valleys of Switzerland. There simply was no comparison. This world's bitter and obstinate beauty sometimes left her speechless.

The mountain valley through which they rode when they fully emerged from the forest an hour or so later was about a mile wide and stretched upward toward the distant horizon as far as her eyes could see, with precipitous walls that rose so high that she needed to crane her neck to see the clifftops. The dozen or so ribbons of water that cascaded down the valley walls in the distance told her that this valley must be the foot of a higher place, one well above their view.

It was grand, simply grand.

"Does any of this look familiar?" asked Deirdre after they'd ridden up the winding valley trail for a time.

"In general, yes." It was difficult for her even to lend words to what surrounded them. "My vision was of a mountain lake, with a series of peaks in the distance. This all looks right, but I don't think we're there yet."

Their final days in the forest had not been without cost. Young Sir Laird had met a ghastly end one night along the edge of the camp, and a dozen or so horses and mules had either strayed or were snatched away. The crone Chastity Skinner had been beside herself, demanding immediate compensation for the loss. Sir Lucas, vacillating as always, made various statements about what they should do next. The man now seemed to be into his cups at all hours of the day.

Fortunately, Sir Armand had filled the gap. Those who had questions, doubts, or concerns about the march, or about the safety of the party, addressed them to him. Isabel liked the man, admired him in fact, but the fellow was no great thinker. But was a thinker what the party needed now? Or did it just need someone brave at the helm? If the latter was the case, Armand de Bois-Guilbert was the man.

The opening up of the country around them provided other good things. At just after noon, Mr. Spears returned to camp with the carcass of some sort of great sheep slung across the saddle of his horse, and for the first time in many days they had fresh meat.

These highland meadows provided much in the way of such delicacies. Deer, mountain goats, and rams abounded. And there were even several varieties of wild ox and cattle, the likes of which she'd never seen. If there were predators about, they saw none during the day, except for a pack of long and skinny wolves that they passed among some tumbled rocks later in the afternoon. The animals regarded the party with thorough indifference.

The mountains shouldn't have been a surprise. Travel the last few days in the forest had felt somewhat more labored, something at the time she'd put down to the exhaustion of both men and beasts. And it had begun to feel cooler, as if the spring were rolling back into its lair.

The weather overall in Albion was mild, with only scant snow in the winter and moderate waves of heat in the summer. She hoped that mildness would persist at elevation, since she'd brought little in the way of cold-weather clothing.

They would sort the logistics out somehow. What truly had begun to concern her was the near future. With each successive milestone in their trip, it had become clearer to her that they would reach their objective, this Delve of which she'd dreamt.

But what would they find there? That was a thing of which she hadn't a clue. But perhaps that was not her part in this journey.

Still, a faint worry had begun to grow in her. Over the past days, the men of the party began to look to her, often quite literally, for answers. What would happen, if they reached the end of the road, and these same men expected her to show them this Glaive foretold by the anchorite?

God, worse. What if they expected treasure, and there was none?

The day before, she finally expressed those worries to Deirdre. The kid was blasé. "Don't worry. Sometimes we just have to have faith."

"I'm having a little trouble with that right now."

"Lady Isabel, that's a common enough problem. We'll sort things out, one way or the other. I promise."

Sorting things out appeared to be Deirdre's strong suit, and the young woman's confidence in her was a source of constant strength.

They made their first mountain camp on a high point in the middle of the valley, a place that Armand announced once must have been a keep or a large watch post in times long past. The place now was fallen to ruins, but it provided a secure spot to sleep for the night, one that would require anyone seeking them harm to climb a steep embankment in full dark and then to overcome the place's walls. Ruined as they were, the walls still were chest high to a tall man. Save for the dozen or so men who watched the animals in the meadow below, all slept securely in the cool night air.

They were up early the next morning and on the trail quickly. No animals or people had gone missing while they'd slept, though the guards did report some sounds for which they could not account. Mr. Spears related finding tracks nearby that might have been those of men, but it was hard to say given their great size and strange shape.

The party pushed onward.

At just before midday, they reached what appeared to be the top of the valley. The air was thin, but it was a place of great beauty. Isabel spent some minutes pacing the Gelt up and down the south bank of the smooth and shining lake they found there before pronouncing it to be the right place. The lake was somewhat different from her dreams, but the mountains were nearly identical.

"We need to go that way," she said, pointing down the lakeside to the west. It wasn't something she thought to say. It just seemed the correct path, and folks accepted her instructions without protest. After taking a short time to prepare and to consume their noon meal, the party set out along the lakeside at a slow but steady pace.

Over the next few hours, they crested several slight rises, waded a series of streams that were scarcely more than trickles, and, as evening approached, they reached a crest along the faint trail. Below them was another valley, broader and deeper, but also interspersed with sections of woodlands. The vista before them ran on as far as the eye could see. They'd reached a plateau of some sort.

"If I'm not mistaken," Sir Armand called up to Lucas, "that ahead is another abandoned watch post. It might suit us nicely for the night."

With a nod from their leader, the party proceeded down the trail, and within an hour had begun to pitch camp for the evening. At that same time, Mr. Spears and his escort arrived from ahead.

"We are watched," the man said.

"Who? And how many?" asked Sir Armand.

"It's difficult to say who," replied the huntsman. "Men, not men."

"Speak plain."

"They move on two legs, but their spoor is … not that of men. And their numbers? We caught but glimpses. A few score perhaps."

"Enough to do mischief. We'll mount a heavy guard tonight."

The heavy guard appeared to be an unnecessary precaution. The area around their watchtower camp was open, and it was an unusually clear night with a starry sky and a full moon. Visibility was excellent.

It never failed to amaze Isabel how very much the moon of this world resembled the same satellite from the world of her birth. The constellations were nothing at all like she remembered them from home. The night sky of Albion, if anything, was clearer and heavier with stars, several of which were so bright that they often could be seen during daytime. But the moon? There were faint differences. It seemed somewhat larger, and it lacked the familiar face. But it otherwise was the same silver coin in the sky.

After a peaceful and clear night, the party started later than usual, and by midday they still were some way above the first trees that from the top of the valley had seemed remarkably close.

At that higher elevation, plant life was sparse. The only things of which they needed to be wary were occasional stone outcroppings and thickets of scrub and bush. These they steered clear of for fear of ambush and picked a careful way down the valley, occasionally straying from the road when necessity demanded. Out of caution, the party traveled more slowly than they had been, and kept themselves bunched, riding as many abreast as the trail safely would allow.

With their slow travel, occasional stops to scout ahead, and pauses to scan the area for dangers, Isabel estimated that they'd traveled less than 10 miles on their first full day moving down into the plateau. In fact, their travel was so slow that it could not properly be said that they even had emerged from the mountains, which still loomed over them.

They were in the mountains still when they reached a widening in the valley where mountain meadows gave way to the first thin and scruffy copses of trees. It was a place she recognized immediately. Ahead of them, the single trail upon which they were traveling diverged, and though she only could see three routes, she knew there was a fourth trail that wasn't fully visible in the trees somewhere ahead.

It didn't matter. The widest of the paths in front of them, a trail that appeared to take them due west into the heart of the valley, was the one they needed to follow. This was their final waymark prior to reaching their destination. Of that she was certain.

———

After some discussion with Sir Lucas, Armand decided it was best to camp there for the night. The day was early yet, but the party had suffered enough losses during the journey to warrant a little caution in proceeding.

As was their custom, she and Deirdre took their toilets together. When Isabel first had arrived in Albion, the hygiene standards had left her mortified. There was nothing to be found in the land similar to toilet paper, but toiletries were many and were varied based on class and locality. In the countryside, certain types of leaves were harvested for just such purposes, but among the gentry, a type of fine cloth affixed to a delicate wooden handle was used for cleaning one's privates after making stool. The thing had to be cleaned after each use, and it took a great deal of getting used to.

Fortunately, food and exercise kept the human digestive system remarkably regular. To her wonderment, the average person in this land made stool precisely twice per day, once in the morning and again in the evening. And unless one was ill, or had been imbibing quantities of alcohol, passing water was performed with equal regularity, morning, noon, and evening. Everything in this world, it seemed, had its own rhythm.

She and Deirdre had found theirs, powdering their noses together with regularity. Deckard always was close at hand, his eyes carefully averted, and since they'd crossed into Proxima Thule, the women had taken turns making waste. One kept watch while the other excreted.

Once an ungainly affair, such simple bodily functions had lost all of their awkwardness. At least they had … until on this particular instance, when Isabel discovered a strange man watching them from across the tiny creek at which they bathed.

Isabel let out a scream.

Her shout of fear and warning seemed to set something into motion. Without hesitation, the stranger on the other side of the stream lunged into the water and was very nearly on them in eight or 10 long strides. He was a hideous creature, hairy and bony in a way she never imagined a man could be. But she couldn't run, not with Deirdre in an awkward squat five feet away.

Deirdre pushed past her, and the man rushing toward her collapsed as something bright flashed in Deirdre's hand. Suddenly, there were forms everywhere, erupting from the water, crawling from beneath tufts of sod, and slipping to their feet from behind stones not large enough to conceal a squirrel. There were a dozen or more, and without hesitation, Deckard was among them swinging his spiked war hammer.

To Isabel's surprise, Deirdre pushed her to the ground. From her spot prone on the grass, she saw Sir Bertrand, in full armor, hacking at three assailants, and the harridan cracking skulls with no more effort than she would take to urge on a stubborn mule. At the same time, sounds of fighting erupted from all around.

Just as swiftly, the uproar ended. The affair was quicker by far than had been the battle at the forest fork, and she soon was being dragged by an arm across the mountain heath.

She fought for some seconds against the hand that dragged her before she realized it was the bearlike paw of Armand who half carried her from the site of the carnage. By that point, the sounds of fighting had died to nothing, and loud voices shouted orders and encouragement back and forth across their camp. She found herself hastily dumped with her kit near the center of camp, and Armand departed in a great rush. Deirdre soon joined her, a look of ... well ... she couldn't say what it was. But there was something else on the kid's face that seemed part fear and part glee.

It was a feature of her dear young friend that Isabel knew she would never understand, any more than she would ever truly understand this world. Such violence. It came so suddenly and just a swiftly was gone. Deirdre already was unpacking a few things, cleaning herself up. She said a few friendly words to Isabel that simply went right past her, and the next thing she knew Deirdre was brushing her teeth, all as if nothing had happened.

"You still need to make your evening soil," the kid said after spitting outside the circle of where Deckard would erect their tent.

An uncomfortable realization struck Isabel. "Oh, no. I'm afraid I don't."

32. An Unfriendly Trail Ahead

Attacking a person while they were taking an otherwise pleasant poop simply was too much. Deirdre had endured a great deal in her life, but this was a new low. It was her good fortune that she very nearly was finished with her evening relief when the enemy attacked, and she had enough wits about her to respond.

And my, what an enemy! She'd never before seen or imagined such a thing. There was no telling what her emotions should be, but thanks to the many days spent training to defend against such attacks, she and Isabel were alive and well.

Poor Isabel. In spite of plentiful experience, Deirdre had never developed the proper finesse when it came to comforting the woman. But after Sir Armand got the woman back to their gear, she helped Isabel clean herself and then put her to bed. It seemed she was forever putting the woman to bed. Things simply must be different in the land from which Isabel hailed.

After her friend had slipped off to sleep, Deirdre retrieved the Gelt from a string of horses picketed nearby. Sometimes the animal fought her, but this time it was docile when she staked it next to their tent. The beast seemed devoted to Isabel, and it had keen senses, should there be further intruders. Even absent additional danger, it would be comforting for the foreign woman to see a friendly face should she awake before Deirdre's return.

Deirdre quickly had grown passably fond of Chastity Skinner's whiskey, and that thirst was convenient. She no longer needed to fabricate an excuse to visit the woman. If anyone asked—not that anyone ever would—she simply would tell them she was stopping off for her evening swill.

"I thought you sorted things out with your friends," she said when she reached the harridan's campfire. Even with enemies about, the Fiend had pitched the muleskinner's tent out of easy earshot of anyone else in the party. People were too afraid of the crone to ask her to do otherwise.

"These are fractious beings," was the creature's response, "divided among many bands. In three or four weeks, I might be able to hammer them into submission. It was pure folly to think I could do it all just last night."

"So, we're to fight all the way to our destination? Am I to have a single peaceful squat anytime in the next week?"

"The place we seek isn't that far, Tuppence. A rider on a swift horse could reach the place by first light."

"How many days not on a swift horse, and having to fend off those things?"

"Two or three days. You needn't fret though. They're not bold fighters, and divided among many bands as they are, they don't pose a serious threat. Kill a few, let them snatch a mule or two, and they'll give us little real trouble."

"Are they … are they people?"

"Only if you don't look too hard. … It's not like you've killed your first man."

Deirdre felt herself color.

"Don't trouble yourself over it," continued the harridan. "These are the remnants of what a great army left behind when it departed this world. That and the offspring of some failed experiments. Their ancestors might have been human, but these benighted creatures are something else."

"Sir Bertrand calls them goblins."

The hag shrugged. "As good a name as any."

"Will they attack again tonight?"

"Unlikely." The hag took a drink and then passed Deirdre the demijohn, which never seemed to empty of its venomous fluid. "They'll have taken their dead with them, so their bellies won't be empty. Just in case, I dropped a few wards when I walked about camp. I'll know if they come again."

"Enough warning next time to pull my pants up would be nice." She took a sip of the bitter whiskey and made a face. Thoughts of magic brought something else to mind. "Do you think Isabel's horse is enchanted?"

"The Gelt? I can't imagine how. Why do you ask?"

"I left it with her when I came over just now. The thing is so bloody clever, and affectionate to her. I've never seen anything like it."

"Gelts are exceptional mounts, bred for intelligence and courage. Best war mounts ever."

"Armand told Isabel they're terrible for war."

"Pshaw. A ridiculous Gheet bias against anything that isn't heavy cavalry. For light cavalry and mounted archers, they are mounts without equal. This particular beast is especially clever and well trained."

"But not enchanted?"

"I should think not."

"Is it as smart as the creatures we just fought?"

"Hmm? … I'm not sure I could say. These ... um … goblins, as we're calling them, aren't terribly clever. But they are cunning and cruel, and the keenest of them are nearly as intelligent as a dull-witted man. They have a language of sorts, too, but not more than a few hundred words." The hag slapped her knee. "Reminds me of a debt collector I know from New Gate, a sadistic brute whose talents I sometimes make use of. Doesn't know more than 50 words, half of those curses, but he's the last man you'd want banging on your door in the wee morning and demanding payment. I'm sure he'd thrive here among our goblin friends."

"Maybe the Gelt isn't that smart," she agreed. "But I'm happy Isabel has something to look out for her. She's just in such need of…." A thought came to her that she should've had before. "Is there any way you could help her find her way home? She really wasn't meant for a world like ours."

"I've pondered the same thing a number of times," said the faux muleskinner. "In ages past, it would have been a simple thing for me to arrange for a passage between worlds. Alas, the *gesh* won't allow it."

"But she came through on her own, despite the *gesh*."

"The *gesh* doesn't constrain her, Tuppence. Any more than it constrains you. It's a thing to keep me and that other fellow in check."

"Then how did she get here?"

"As I told you when we first met Isabel, sometimes the barriers between worlds grow weak in places."

"And things just tumble through."

"Yes. With Isabel's help, I might be able to find that weak point again, that door through which she tumbled, but even under the best of circumstances such a search would take years. And there's no guarantee that door is still there. Even if it is, some doors swing only one way."

"But it's possible?"

"Tuppence, I'm very fond of our lovely friend, and her plight tugs at my heartstrings. I too am a stranger stranded in this land, a land not my own. But I can't drop everything to begin a search that would take years, even decades, with no guarantee of success. The only thing I can promise is to look out for her while she's here, and to do my best to return her home, if any opportunity arises."

"So, you haven't given up?"

"Of course not."

OK, in for a penny, she thought. "I don't feel like a very good friend to her."

"You are a wonderful friend and a good person."

"Do you think it would be safe to tell her our little secret?"

"Which secret? That you've become overly fond of whiskey?"

"No, everyone knows that." She slapped the harridan's knee. "You know what I'm talking about."

"I know something of the world from which Isabel comes, Tuppence. My kind have a worse reputation there than we do here. And you've seen how she is with the unknown. I think telling her would terrify her to no real profit."

"I know, but I feel terrible, like I'm keeping a secret from her."

"It's not your secret, child. It's mine. Try thinking of it that way."

"I don't...."

"Deirdre, you've shared thoughts and feelings with me that you've never shared with others, haven't you?"

She nodded her reply.

"It wouldn't be very fair of me to share those intimate details with others, would it?"

"No. I guess it wouldn't."

"Because those are your secrets to tell and not mine."

"Would you be angry, if I told her?"

"Not angry, just worried. I've been exposed before. It's a trifle for me. I just assume another form. But if it became widely known that Alexis or Moorcroft were not as they seem? Anyone close to them, including you, Isabel, the baron and his family...."

"I understand," she said. "We'd all be in danger."

"There are a great many things you can share with Isabel that I'm sure she would love to hear."

"For instance?"

"Child, I know you don't sleep well still. And drinking whiskey and ale of an evening will only keep that pain in check for so long. Isabel has a heart big enough for her worries and yours."

That was a subject Deirdre didn't think she'd have the strength to talk about, not anytime soon. But perhaps the creature was right. Telling Isabel the truth about all of it would terrify the woman, to what real benefit? So that Deirdre's conscience might feel a little lighter? That was being selfish in its own way.

"Did you ever tell your sweetheart?" she asked.

"About my true nature? No, never. She was called Bronwyn, and she loved a studious fellow named Abelard. He was her second choice, but he made her happy. What more did either of them need to know?"

"That she's married to the Devil? I assure you, it's the kind of thing a woman wants to know. … Though if Sir Alexis was to marry Isabel, certain facts needn't ever come up."

The crone cackled with glee. "Is that blackmail I smell?"

"I was taught a true blackmailer never uses that ugly word."

"Indeed. But sadly, there's a tiny dictate in Gheet custom that forbids a man from taking to wife any woman who's ever been his ward."

"Without his lord's approval," corrected Deirdre. "At least, that's what the baroness says."

A look something akin to shock flashed across the harridan's fleshy face, but the creature said nothing.

"It was Sir Alexis who pointed out the baroness's talent for making matches," Deirdre added. "Did he imagine that he was immune?" There was constant gossip among the women of the de Vere clan over who might marry whom, but Deirdre had never taken any of it seriously. She scarcely even had listened. And then something else came to mind. "Why do you think the baron insisted Alexis take that little plot of land to hold? So he'd have someplace to store his old suits of armor? Or is his lordship expecting more de Vere cousins?"

The old hag began to chuckle. "True … true. You may be onto something, Tuppence. Isabel is an unusually beautiful lass, with an angelic disposition. But I'd like to think she could find someone better for herself than a vagrant hedge knight. Perhaps a great nobleman, or even some foreign royal."

"I think she has her heart set on the hedge knight."

"Yes. Perhaps it's inevitable. The baroness is persuasive, and Isabel would make a fetching bride. But the hedge knight simply wouldn't feel it right to marry before finding an advantageous union for each of his wards."

"So, where are you off to tonight?" asked Deirdre, beating a hasty retreat from all talk matrimonial.

"I'm going to sit right here for a time," said the hag, "and watch to see if anyone leaves camp."

"You still think there might be another spy?"

There's probably not, but I've made too many miscalculations lately to be overly confident. Once I'm certain no one is leaving, and that our goblin friends won't return, I plan on slipping back the way we came and getting a look at our pursuers."

"Are they that close?"

"Right up the way," the hag said with a nod. "They could reach us in a half-bell of hard riding, if they were of a mind. Let me ask you. Didn't you tell me you and Isabel felt as if you were being watched?"

"The whole trip from Mont Clair to Musette. I felt like I had eyes on me."

"Did you ever see anyone?"

"I thought I did, just once, along the river. Isabel said she thought she saw someone watching several times in the weeks before we reached Mont Clair. It had her frightened."

"She may well have had a watcher. As did you."

"How?"

"There are magics that allow someone to mask their presence."

"Was it the same person in our chambers that night at Mont Clair? And there was someone at the inn at Huntington-on-Silk."

The creature nodded slowly. "It's very possible. I'll drop some extra wards before I depart tonight, just in case. And when I reach our pursuers from the Inquisition, I'll leave a few extra surprises for them."

She found herself suppressing a laugh. "What kind of surprises?"

"Something that will make them easier to track. I've felt their conjurings several times today. And on a number of other occasions, I looked to where they should have been on the valley trail behind us and didn't see anything."

"They're making themselves invisible?"

"Yes, after a fashion. The little gifts I'll leave for them will be like placing a bell on a cow."

"So you can find them more easily."

The creature began to laugh in earnest. "Yes. But not just me. It might make our passage through the plateau easier, if I give our goblin friends someone else to play with."

33. In a Great and Ferocious Rush

The next days were tedious and filled with danger.

The party continued to make slow progress, because each day they were met with a series of short and sudden attacks from the surrounding woods and fields. None of the assaults were serious—a man injured here, an animal gone missing there—but the attacks wore down the men and their patience, and the party's movement slowed to a crawl.

Each evening, they stopped early for the singular purpose of establishing a secure camp, and each night there were raids against the camp and its baggage. But, with all that, there was not a single death among members of the party during the next three days, and, as much as nerves were frayed, people simply endured.

Deirdre was convinced much of their success they owed to the Fiend, who continued to carry on as Chastity Skinner during the day. At night, the creature would slip out of camp to terrorize and to punish the local goblin bands, attempting to bend them to his will. He was only partly successful. As the Fiend had foretold, there simply were too many separate tribes for him to organize them in such a short time.

So busy were those days that she saw the creature only briefly here and there. On one such meeting, he admitted to her that he first hoped their party would abandon this misbegotten quest when Sir Lucas saw how great the hostility of the locals was. Ultimately, though, it again became clear that the party's continued survival was the main thing keeping her and Isabel safe from their clerical pursuers. They needed to keep going and to keep the party intact.

The Inquisitors remained on their trail, even drawing closer in recent days. There were no clues as to why their pursuers hadn't yet attacked. Deirdre was beginning to wonder whether the Fiend hadn't got it all wrong. Perhaps, despite his protestations, there was something worth having at the abandoned fortress to which they traveled, and the men of the Holy See were there to seize that thing from the party when they found it.

No. That didn't sound right. What seemed more reasonable was that the group following them simply were too few to stage a successful attack. They no doubt had suffered losses on the trail. And the party led by Sir

Lucas still was the larger body, even if it consisted largely of drovers, porters, and muleskinners.

Either way, they soon would find out. The huntsman and some men had ranged ahead and located their destination, the place Isabel called the "Eldritch Delve," on the previous day. At their current pace, the party should reach the site by midafternoon.

What awaited them there? Would they find what they sought? Or … well. The Fiend often was correct about such things. Perhaps this journey was all nonsense, "naught but pious flummery," as Baron William had called it. But Deirdre loved her storybooks, and there was a thin little slice of optimist in her that didn't want a disappointing ending.

They'd had their breakfast and had broken camp when the first murmurs of a commotion reached her and Isabel as they helped Deckard saddle the mounts for the day. The hubbub seemed to come from down the road, in the direction from which they'd traveled, and Deirdre excused herself to appease her curiosity.

When she reached the center of the commotion, near the end of the column, she saw several men gathered around someone sitting on the ground. She didn't get a good look at the fellow at first, but after pardoning and pushing her way past the assembled soldiers and porters, she saw someone on the ground who shouldn't have been there. Their eyes locked at the same moment, and the fellow let out a shriek somewhere between fear and anger. Deirdre commenced to kicking the man in the shins and ankles as hard as she was able.

"You sonofabitch," she screamed. "You miserable fondler!"

She didn't remember the scoundrel's name, wasn't sure she'd caught it in the first place, but on the ground before her, scrambling to avoid her kicks and curses, was the same fellow who many weeks back had groped her breast in the stables at Mont Clair! What was the cretin doing here? How had he gotten this far?

"Steady, young miss," said one of the soldiers, a retainer for dead Sir Custis.

"He's begging for his life, milady," said another in a shocked voice.

She realized the dagger was in her hand, the naked blade held ready at her side, and she returned it to its sheath. A shudder ran through her, and it took a moment to find her voice.

"Take him to Sir Lucas," she said before stomping off toward the head of the column.

———

Isabel was shocked to see the young man who staggered, broken and bedraggled, into their camp that morning. Would there be no end of the surprises? For the life of her, she couldn't remember the lad's name, Sir Elliot Coetzee's son. But even dirty and unkempt, she recognized the young man who had been outlawed back in Albion. Had the man followed them all this way? For what purpose? To exact revenge on Lady Deirdre for his expulsion? Had he been dogging their trail this entire time?

It seemed the only reasonable answer, but the young man told a different tale. Not long after fleeing Mont Clair, if the outlaw were to be believed, four men approached him and offered him a place in their party. He knew the men were breaking the law by offering him sanctuary, but they were foreigners. What would they know?

"I did my best to survive," the young man said. "None can fault me for that."

"That these men had something in mind for you is clear," said Armand. "But what brings you and them here, now?"

"I … wasn't sure at first. They asked nothing of me but to help around camp. And then one of them, a preacher, I think, began asking questions of me."

"About?"

The scruffy young man looked the other way and said in a weak voice, "First about Lady Deirdre and Lady Isabel. And then only about Lady Isabel."

"What kind of questions?"

"Stuff his head in a sack!" cried Chastity Skinner.

The woman appeared at each counsel Sir Lucas invoked whether invited or not. Other than the hag, it was only a few of the knights, Isabel and Deirdre, and the huntsman. All others continued preparation for the day's march.

The harridan continued to howl. "Stuff his ears with wax and stick his head in a sack!"

"Madam…," said Sir Lucas.

"He'll give us all the evil eye! There's nothing good to be got from this one. A cursed fellow if ever there was one, to be traveling alone in such a place."

"But … but I'm not alone," the young man cried. "I've tried to tell you. They made me a virtual prisoner in the end. It was only when I discovered there were others about, other people from home, that I found the means to escape. They mean to attack you!"

"A bunch of foreign men, you say?" asked Armand.

"I only learned some of their tongue. Etruscians they are, and they mean you no good. Believe me!"

"In this faraway land?" asked Lucas. "Lad, perhaps Goody Skinner has the right of it. You are either mad or cursed."

"'Twould be easy enough to see," said the huntsman in a calm voice. "We've been peering far to our front. Perhaps a quick look back down the trail would avail us somewhat."

"We are this close," said Sir Lucas with more resolve than Isabel had heard him muster in many days. "Let's push on, one final drive to our destination. We can sort this nonsense there."

"Wise words," agreed Armand.

The nods of those present showed others shared the large knight's view. Only the harridan, a look of anger and disgust on her broad face, seemed at odds, but for once the vicious shrew held her tongue.

Within 15 minutes, they were ahorse and moving. It was the best time they'd made on the entire journey, and it was some of the easiest movement. The road wasn't of the best quality, but their sudden brisk pace must have taken the bands of wretched and misshapen men who'd been attacking them by surprise. ("Goblins," Armand called the poor degenerate fellows. Who would imagine?)

There were a few rocks and spears thrown, and there was some angry chattering and running about of figures in the trees, but another 90 minutes hard riding found them near an open area that she recognized instantly. Against a far cliffside was a large hollow that she knew would give way to a high grotto beyond. And farther beyond that grotto? The opening into the Delve.

It was if she'd walked that path a thousand times before, though she'd never once been to this place in her life. True, there were a few things out of place. The trees didn't seem right, and the cliff face appeared more worn, with boulders and debris about that she'd not seen in her dreams. But it was the very place.

Mr. Spears, who it appeared had raced ahead of them, was guiding the first riders into a defensible rise when she pulled the Gelt to a halt near where Deirdre and Sir Armand stood holding their mounts. She joined them on the ground. The knight had an uncertain look on his face, as if something were amiss. He merely shook his head when she asked him what it was.

It was some time before the last of the party, the tail end of the mule train, lurched awkwardly into the meadow near their new camp. The harridan was the last one in. Isabel had never seen the creature so angry. Astride the swaybacked old beast she sometimes rode, the foul-mouthed virago slapped, whipped, cursed, and battered man and animal with wild abandon.

When it looked as if the slattern woman might stop to join them, Deirdre greeted the vicious creature with a stern, "Keep it moving, you old hag!"

Hag? It was hard not to think of the venomous woman in that way. She bore every bad moral quality Isabel had been taught to eschew. But truth be told, Chastity Skinner probably wasn't too much older than Isabel. With her rawboned frame and stooped shoulders, her toothless scowl, and skin worn to leather by long years in the sun, though, she was the very image of what most folks would imagine an old woman to be. Chastity probably was somewhere in her 30s.

Heavens, how this land could age a person.

It was only when Chastity began hollering aloud, demanding to know why the party had not yet pitched camp, that it occurred to Isabel just what had caught Armand's attention earlier. At least, she thought she did. There was something about this area, the sound of it. It wasn't like it was in her dreams. There was a silence there now, the type that one never truly heard in the forest, a hush that she'd come to associate with something bad in the offing.

One of the sentries cried out that riders approached.

It took a few minutes for the five men to come into view, riding at a light trot. The newcomers, three men in armor and two clad in the robes of Old Rite clergymen, came to a halt at the base of the rise where Sir Lucas and several of his men stepped forth to meet them.

"Oh, good," said one of the priests, without greeting or preamble, "you've found our runaway boy. Get over here, young man."

"Your spy, you mean." The voice was the harridan, who stood some paces behind Armand and Sir Lucas. The hag edged closer as she spoke and spat when none stood between her and the priest.

"Is this woman your leader?" the cleric asked of Sir Lucas.

Isabel didn't recognize the man speaking, nor had she before seen the men in armor. But the second cleric was familiar to her. The fellow had been among the party of Monsignor Krait at Mont Clair. His name was a mystery to her, but the man several times had cast her furtive glances in the moments since their arrival, stolen glimpses that led her to suspect he was trying not to stare.

"State your business," said Sir Lucas.

The Gheet generally were courteous to guests, but these circumstances seemed strange. Isabel didn't fault the baronet for his brusqueness. Something just wasn't right here.

The cleric's reaction was to let loose an angry sigh. In one fluid move he pulled a rolled parchment from his sleeve, flipped it open, and tossed it to the ground between them. The words that followed were annoyed and lazy. "I am Massimo Pietro-Victors, legate of the Holy See, and that document is a warrant duly signed by His Excellency, the Bishop of Etruscia, Dutiful the Fourth, for the immediate arrest of the heretic who travels under the name Isabel de Vere. I have 50 mounted knights to support my claim. … Is that enough?"

There was a faint moment of dead silence before a voice cried out from the ranks of the party.

"Over my dead body!"

She couldn't tell who it was who had shouted those words, probably one of the drovers. But other voices sounded out, all adding to what soon was a crescendo of defiance and common vulgarity.

"They want to take our prophetess!"

"I'll give you something to ride back home, you foreign...."

"... Devil take you...."

"... and with your whorish mother...."

"... good for nothing, donkey pleasing...."

The assembled members of the party, which numbered all those not on guard, surged toward the newcomers as one, causing the mounts of the men to begin edging away. Isabel wasn't certain what happened after that, not completely, but a sharp look was exchanged between the two clerics. The younger of the two, the one who was trying not to stare her way, produced something from his sleeve and hurled it at her.

The projectile, some sort of glass bottle, shattered at her feet, covering her boots in an odious liquid. It was dreadful, but not one sliver so dreadful as what happened next. In a spot, not 20 feet away from where Isabel then stood, suddenly appeared an immense creature, dark and wicked like something from a demon's nightmare.

And then came complete chaos.

34. Poor Tidings Indeed

It happened so swiftly that Deirdre missed it entirely. The Fiend was standing before her, but no longer in the ample flesh of Chastity Skinner. The creature situated near the base of the hill, towering over men and animals, wore the precise form the creature had when first they'd met nearly a year before.

That creature moved in a flash. Shooting out an enormous black and grey mottled arm, it grabbed the younger of the two clerics by the head and wrung his neck with the type of short twist a farmwife would use to slaughter a chicken.

And then from at least two directions at once arrows began to fly, and guards on every side of the camp let loose with cries of "Attack! Attack!"

Their newly established camp was under assault, and there was no time for her to dawdle about. A battlefield was a terrible place, one in which no woman was safe. The creature could take care of itself, so she needed to get her and Isabel out of sight while the fighting raged.

But when she turned to take the woman in hand, Deirdre saw that Isabel had vaulted into the saddle of the Gelt and was racing toward the cliffside a few hundred paces distant. Deirdre could do nothing but follow, and she flew into the saddle of the palfrey before Deckard could utter a word of protest.

To her amazement, Deirdre wasn't the only person following after Isabel. The drovers and muleskinners had dismounted, but hadn't yet begun to unburden their beasts, and the great baggage train and its handlers moved as one in the direction of the cliffside.

Perhaps the tradesmen sensed safety along the high rock walls, but Deirdre had no idea what animated Isabel, so she urged her mount on. Behind her, the sounds of battle cries and clanging weapons was joined by the wicked screeches of goblins. The death screams of horses were a piteous noise to which she never would become accustomed. In the blink of an eye, this had transformed from another bad day into a terrible day, a wicked and a foul day.

The Gelt was a sturdy mount, but it was not swift, and Deirdre overtook her friend as the two arrived at a pile of rocks near the base of the cliffside.

"Where are you going?" she cried when she pulled even with the woman.

"I...," Isabel turned in the saddle, and the pace of her horse slowed. "I don't know. Something...."

"We need to get to cover. The goblins have come. The whole day is a ruin."

"Follow me," said Isabel. The woman urged her mount forward toward a smooth stone platform that rose gently toward the cliffs.

The sounds of fighting were drawing closer, and Deirdre looked back several times as they rode. Deckard had reached them moments before, and, like her, his body pivoted in the saddle and his eyes shot left and right seeking potential dangers.

There was no telling who might be winning in the fracas behind them, but the Fiend was not to be seen. Perhaps he reverted to human form. She refused even to contemplate that he was dead. *You should be so lucky*, she nearly said aloud.

What had that buffoon gotten them into?

To Deirdre's surprise, the path on which Isabel led them went into the hollow in the cliffside, and then turned left through a short passage into another area, one that appeared to be a towering grotto, its ceiling partly open to the sky.

Isabel immediately called for those who'd followed them to hasten within, and then Deckard bellowed for each to return with their weapons to guard the cavern opening. It was a cascade of knees and elbows, of cantankerous animals and unfamiliar spaces, but in no time at all men began to return to the mouth of the cavern with their clubs, maces, hammers, and axes in hand.

The tradesmen formed up not a moment too soon. A wave of goblins erupted through the outer cavern opening, and after a moment to find their prey, the wretches charged against the line of men holding the inner cave mouth. It was anarchy as the short, squat, and ugly creatures threw their half-naked bodies and stone weapons against the ill-kempt and raggedly armed line of a score or so muleskinners.

Deirdre found herself behind the press, but soon she was sidestepping back and forth behind the line of men, razor-edged dagger in hand, stabbing and cutting at the occasional humanlike form that tried to slip between the legs or over the shoulders of the defenders. There was no telling what egged on their attackers, who in the past four days had not demonstrated such demonic zeal in their raids. The creatures attacked now like rabid animals.

In a short time, the last of the tradesmen settled their beasts and joined the fight with boxes and barrels to help block the 10-paces wide portal. But more and more goblins arrived. Even with that impromptu barricade, it soon was all the men could do to keep the creatures at bay.

Isabel helped as she could, dragging back men too injured to fight and staunching their bloody wounds, but wave after wave of the things came. Each attack was more frenzied than the one before. Deirdre finally stepped up into the press and began cutting and stabbing at the mass of filthy, shrieking, and writhing bodies beyond their barricade.

It was a bloody and grimy mess, and though there was not a warrior among them save Deckard, the tradesmen were hard and strong fellows, accustomed to the harsh and sometimes violent life of the road. Not a one of them broke or quailed from the fight, and soon the waves of attacks slowed.

When the last goblin attack finally faltered and collapsed, after what seemed forever, the first of the fighting men from their party already were visible near the outer entrance to the cave. Pressed between the drovers and muleskinners within and the soldiers without, the last of the goblins finally found their wits and ran.

The chaps manning the impromptu barricade were too exhausted to utter a single huzzah. They instead slumped to the ground where they stood. Deirdre joined them, but only for a moment. There was much to do. When at last she rose, it was to see Isabel lugging a demi-keg of rum, the favorite drink of the tradesmen, toward the exhausted men. Perhaps there was hope for the woman in Albion after all.

Dagger in hand, Deirdre slipped past a panting Deckard and over the barricade and began to pick her way through the piles of dead goblins toward the outer cave entrance. The ground was slick with blood, and she was cautious of any fallen enemy that yet lived.

There still were sounds of fighting outside, but most of those were calls back and forth between the soldiers, warning a comrade to be wary of one position, or ordering them to advance to another. She soon was able to pick out the voice of Sir Bertrand, and then that of stalwart Armand, and felt it safe to proceed.

Outside the cave was a mess. Most of the bodies that littered the ground were the bloody and bashed remains of goblins. Toward the bottom of the stone rise, she could see a number of cadavers in the armor and livery of the Holy See. An occasional arrow still flew from a distant thicket, so she stayed well out of sight. But it seemed at least for the moment that the fight was over.

She craned her head several ways to see what she could.

A squire below was sprinting about in an effort to gather loose horses, most of the score or so fighters still standing were firing arrows in various directions, and a handful of men were stretched out on a stone shelf to the right of the main cavern opening. At least two, including one she took to be Sir Lucas, lay unmoving, and the huntsman leaned against a boulder halfway down the rise, cradling the body of his nephew in his arms.

It was dreadful. And she nearly leapt when a form slipped past her. Isabel, head down and bent nearly double, scooted to where the injured men lay on the shelf. Deirdre scurried out to join her. The position to which they hurried was shielded by some high stones, and it was close to Sir Armand.

The man knelt before she even had a chance to speak.

"What of the party inside?"

"One dead," volunteered Isabel. "The rest badly used but alive. Mr. Deckard is putting them in order."

"Good," the knight said with a nod. "Some happy news is welcome."

Deirdre's eyes strayed to where three men lay dead, their bodies covered in cloaks.

"Sir Lucas died bravely," said Armand.

"The rest?" Deirdre asked. Truth be told, she was wondering what the knight thought of the sudden appearance of the Fiend in their midst, but she had no idea how to ask that question.

"Sir Coy and his man Ethan died well. A few porters didn't make it within. The huntsman's nephew died fighting alongside the blacksmith and Goody Skinner down in that thicket yonder. ... I swear...." The man shook his head. "I thought the Goody was the first to die, so near was she to where those scoundrels conjured that demon against us. But she showed them a thing or two before she fell."

It was the most Deirdre had ever heard the big knight speak in one breath. And she did not for a moment imagine that the Fiend was dead. It was just another of his tricks. Still.

"Reverend Ainsley says men who truck with demons are fools. They always turn on their masters." Deirdre couldn't recall where, but she knew she'd read that last tidbit somewhere.

The knight chuckled. "This one turned on them, as did their goblins. I don't know if that priest had half a hundred men as he claimed, but they were considerable in number. And much fewer now."

"Have they fled?" asked Isabel from where she tended to an injured squire.

"Most have, I think … at least for a time. When we regain enough mounts, I'll sweep the wood free of their archers. Then we can recover our dead and prepare for further assault."

"Will they attack again?" asked Isabel.

"If they don't, they've come a long way for nothing," said the knight. He gave Isabel a playful wink. "I didn't know you were in trouble with the law."

Isabel began to laugh. "I had no idea either."

———

It was late in the afternoon before the knights and men-at-arms were able to get the area under control. There was not a goblin to be seen alive, but it took some doing for Armand to kill or to drive off the archers the clerics of the Holy See had set to harass them.

The gathering of the bodies was a point of toil and sorrow. To Deirdre's great surprise, the corpse of the harridan was where Sir Armand said it would be, in a thicket near the remains of the blacksmith. Both bodies had grievous injuries. It took her some moments to compose herself at the sight.

And then she began to think.

The total count was tragic. Their party had lost 15 dead that day. Two were missing, including Friar Emmet, whose bloody and ripped cloak suggested goblins had made off with the silly clergyman. It was a great effort not to laugh at the idea.

They laid to rest the knights and their men, Chastity and a handful of tradesmen, and young Latham and the smith.

There were other problems in the meantime. The party was leaderless, and without the vicious swipes of Chastity Skinner, the muleskinners would be a handful to manage. But there were solutions for each issue.

The few remaining knights agreed Armand would lead. All were on good terms with the man, and he was a proven article. And Isabel coaxed the muleskinners and drovers into helping dispose of the enemy dead, lest their presence foment disease. The men at first growled that such labor was not part of their contract, but Isabel had an effect on them. It took no time at all for the fellows to fall in line and to assist with burning the bodies.

Then servants prepared food and drink, the animals were picketed close to the cave mouth to graze, and the party rested. Throughout, there was much talk of what had transpired. Their enemies had used dark magics against them. That much was clear. The priests of the Holy See already had a reputation for such foul intrigues. And there was little doubt as to why the scoundrels were there. They'd announced it in their own words. They'd come to take away the party's seer and to claim the Glaive for themselves.

What other answer could there be?

Deirdre kept her lips closed on that issue, lest someone recall her occasional nighttime visits to the harridan's fireside. Someone had to have noticed the crone's sudden transfiguration. But? Well, perhaps not. Hadn't the Fiend said magic was a thing one never truly saw?

But why the sudden interest in Isabel? Did the fools of the Inquisition imagine she was the Fiend's traveling companion? Fair enough. It simply wasn't something the young woman did knowingly.

When evening fell, they stabled the animals in the hollow of the cliffside and took shelter in the grotto. Armand and the remaining knights held counsel on what their next step should be. All pardoned Mr. Spears, who took the first watch outside. The fellow mourned the loss of his nephew, and the blacksmith had been a longtime friend.

Well, almost everyone pardoned the man. Deirdre slipped out later and found the fellow sitting some paces outside the cavern opening with his back against a boulder. She took a seat next to him.

"Funny thing that Chastity Skinner would die fighting next to Latham and the smith," she said.

"I didn't imagine anyone would notice that but you, Tuppence."

"How did you do it?"

"I've had plenty of time to learn the man's appearance, and Latham and Mr. Smith were the only ones who truly knew him. The rest was easy."

"That's not what I mean. I saw the body."

"Ah," said the ersatz huntsman. "Altering a body takes less skill and energy than conjuring one from nothing, and I didn't want the fellow's brave death to be for naught."

"Why not just let folks imagine the goblins dragged Chastity away?"

"Just hedging our bets. The human eye doesn't want to see certain things, so it's unlikely anyone truly saw Chastity's sudden transformation."

"But it's possible?"

"Some of those present might put the pieces together. Sorcerers schooled by the Holy See, in particular, are trained to observe such things. So why not let them have a body?"

"Will they believe such hokum? That they've somehow managed to kill you?"

"Don't ever underestimate the vanity of a sorcerer, child, or the self-righteousness of a highborn cleric. If nothing else, it'll keep them guessing for a while, which should give us some time to figure out their designs."

"Their designs?" She didn't enjoy being cruel, but certain words simply had to be said. "You haven't been right about anything so far, have you?"

"No," the faux huntsman said with a pitiful sigh.

"Why are the Inquisitors looking for Isabel? … And don't sulk."

"I, umm…."

"Really."

"I don't know … I…."

"You don't know!" She checked her voice before continuing in a lower tone. "How could you not know?"

"Tuppence, after having been scorned and pursued throughout the ages, I think I can be excused for assuming this was all about me."

"The Inquisitors aren't looking for you at all, are they?"

"I ... umm … I don't think so."

"OK," she said. "Let's start with what happened today. Where did all those Inquisition soldiers come from? When last we spoke, you said barely a dozen of them remained."

"They were clever," said the fake huntsman. "They traveled in two companies, one group so far back that it was beyond my ability to sense it. The second bunch only rushed forward when it was time to attack."

"Very clever," she agreed. "But why did you reveal yourself?"

"Ah! There was some sort of enchantment in that vial the lad tossed at Isabel. It was intended for her—why, I don't know—but I was close enough that it caused me to.... Well, I'm not sure of the right words. For a moment, I was forced to revert to my other form. It was a dreadful experience."

"What did it do to her!?"

"Nothing at all."

"Nothing? She began to act...."

"Tuppence, it was nothing. Such magic is intended to entangle something like me for a short time, to weaken or to render me powerless. It has no effect on humans. Isabel acted the way she did because I gave her a little push."

"You cast a spell on her."

"Yes, a minor one. It's hard to compel someone against their will, particularly when working on such short notice. All I did was urge her to do what she wanted to do already: To flee. The Gelt did the rest. It really is an exceptional animal."

"Wait … what became of the boy who found us this morning? I'd nearly forgotten him."

"The fondler?"

"Yes, that miserable…."

"If the goblins didn't get him, I'd imagine he's back with his masters."

"So, he was a spy?"

"Of course. Whether he was willing or being compelled, I don't know. But, no doubt, he was sent forward so his masters might peer through his eyes and see our numbers and location before they attacked."

"Little bastard," she hissed under her breath. "Is that why they dragged him all this way?"

"Mm-hmm. They likely needed to find someone on short notice who knew both you and Isabel by sight, someone who wouldn't be missed."

Something occurred to Deirdre, something that had been rattling in the back of her mind even before this conversation had started. She voiced it now.

"Did they think Isabel was you? Or did they think Isabel was something *like* you?"

For a moment, something like surprise crossed the huntsman's face. "Go ahead."

"It could be that simple, couldn't it? That scoundrel Krait had his men pluck some hair from Isabel and me. You said yourself the results of a divination spell of her would confuse them. If that spell told them that she was from another world…."

"Why not assume she was from my realm?"

"Why not?"

The faux huntsman let out a breath and reached across his body to scratch his shoulder for long moments. It was the exact gesture she'd seen the real huntsman make many times. The mimicry was astounding.

"It does make a certain amount of sense," the creature said after a time. "Except that the *gesh* binds all beings of my kind, so why would anyone…? Bah. I'll have to think on it for a time. And I do apologize. My thoughts have been muddled of late, and you've been put in far too many dangerous positions because of it."

"Are they still clouding your ability to listen to the wind?"

"Yes, they are. And it's gotten worse in the last week or so. Oh so subtly worse. Whoever is doing their castings has a graceful hand. The interference is so light at times that it's difficult even to detect it at all. It's exceptionally delicate and adept work."

"There couldn't be that many of the Inquisitors left after the walloping they got today. Perhaps that fellow is among the dead."

"I rather hoped it was the lad whose head I popped off this morning, but I can't imagine being that lucky. Whoever it was, it probably was the same magicker who infuriated the goblins I've been setting upon them these past days, turned them upon *us* instead … at least some of them. That was a clever and a powerful spell. Not one sorcerer in a thousand would even dream of attempting such a casting."

"You have a rival," she said with a laugh.

"Not for much longer," said the Fiend. "After my shift at guard, I'll slip off and find our friends from the Inquisition. There might be some fun to be had tonight."

"What should I do while you're whooping it up with the neighbors?"

"For now, make sure those foolish knights don't take you and Isabel any farther into the caves and tunnels of this place than they have already. I never thought this silly escapade would get this far, and there are things in the belly of this mountain that are much, much worse than goblins."

35. Into the Delve

Mister Spears returned after a day and a half, and it was a homecoming that lightened Isabel's heart. The man had sacrificed so much for the quest, including his only living relative. The idea that the hunter also might have been killed was much too much for her to stand.

Since that fight, the party had rested. Beyond those who were killed, none had suffered life-threatening injuries. There was no sign of the monster that abruptly had appeared among them and just as swiftly had vanished. No one was certain what had transpired, and no two people told the same story of that event. What a terror. A demon, Sir Armand had called it. Her heart skipped a beat every time she thought of it.

A demon. It would be some time for her fully to digest the very concept.

The huntsman brought harsh tidings and a dreadful message with his return. The soldiers of the foreign party that had attacked them two days before were still in the area and, according to the huntsman, in sufficient number to cause them great harm. The question from that moment was what next to do.

On a happy front, there seemed to be not a single goblin remaining in the area, an estimation confirmed by Mr. Spears on his long scouting of the area.

"I didn't mean to be gone so long," the man said soon after his return. "But I wanted to have a good and thorough look around. For many furlongs in any direction, there's naught but those foreign fellas. Not a single trace of those goblins that came with them."

"We couldn't have killed all of them," said Lady Deirdre.

"No, miss," said the huntsman, "but those that survived likely found the climate here no longer to their liking. It's those church fellas, the ones with the funny way of talking, are the real trouble."

"You said you spoke with them?" asked Isabel.

The man nodded as he often did. "Earlier today, I ran into a party of them near a stream somewhat east of here. They chased me around a mite, but before I could give them the slip, they called out that they wanted to talk."

"And did you?"

"At some remove. They said a thing or three, but I didn't give no reply."

"What did they have to add?" asked Armand, who had stood some time listening to the hunter's tale.

The scout gave Isabel a shy look. "Much the same as the last. The fella what did the talking said, if we turned over the miss—Lady Isabel, that is—well, the rest of us were free to go."

"That'll not happen." Armand looked grim and determined. "What did you make of them, Spears?"

"I reckon they still have 40 or 50 fighting men among them, at least half mounted, some injured. How many of them hexers they got with 'em? I couldn't say."

"Apparently, we didn't hurt them as badly as we thought," said Sir Bertrand. "Not enough of them to successfully attack us as we're encamped … at least not without deviltry. But more than enough to cause us trouble out in the open."

"You beat several times that many in the battle at the fork," said Isabel, wanting to sound optimistic.

"Those were ruffians and brigands, milady," replied Armand. "These men of Etruscia, for all their faults, are fighting men. Had the goblins two days ago not vexed them worse than they did us, we would have been hard pressed to stave them off."

"But we still outnumber them?"

"Aye, milady. And the tradesmen are doughty lads, but fighting isn't their stock-in-trade."

"True," said Mr. Granger, a muleskinner who since the death of Chastity Skinner had been standing in as the head of the tradesmen at war councils.

"I think I might have an idea," volunteered Mr. Spears in a quiet voice, "if you care to hear?"

"What do you have?" asked Armand.

"I didn't travel as far as I wanted, but I got a look at the country south of here from that ridge—way yonder." The man gave a lazy gesture to the southeast. "I reckon this whole area was one big fort in ages past. And, near as I can tell, this ain't the only way in and out of these caves. If we want to avoid further fracas with these folks, we might be able to pass through the caves and come out to the south of the mountain."

"What advantage would that give us?"

"Well, if they wanted to vex us anymore, they'd either have to follow us into the caves, or guess what we're doing and then race around the mountain and figure out where we're coming out."

Armand paid careful attention as the man spoke. "And how much time would that buy us?"

"How long would it take them to get around the mountain? Two or three days, if they know the way."

"What then?" asked Sir Bertrand.

The huntsman toed the ground in front of him as he sometimes did. "Well, as near as I can figure, we took the long way around getting to this spot. About five days due south of here at a steady pace lie the Wols marches, and Albion a few days past that."

"How do you know where we are?" asked Isabel. "I thought you'd never been here before."

"You learn to feel your way around, miss. From the ridge, there's a few peaks in the distance I've seen before. If I ain't mistaken, we'd have to cross through a stretch of country where the River Strand rises. I don't know that particular country firsthand, but I've heard tell of it. And I've been through the marches a time or two. I know the way back home from there."

"That's good information," said Armand. "But we still haven't finished our duty here. We need to search the caves. That was never in doubt. But do we really want to bring the entire mule train through the passages that lie beneath this place? We've only just started looking, but most don't seem wide enough to take a mule. ... Mr. Granger?"

"Aye, milord, they're wide enough ... if you don't mind loading and unloading six-score animals every time the passage narrows. It's not something I'd recommend."

"There's an easy answer, milord," said Mr. Spears.

"Which is?"

"Send the drovers and muleskinners ahead. If we're to believe these foreign fellas, they've no interest in them. Once the tradesmen reach the far side of the mountain, they can wait for us there. The rest of the party, miss included, can go through the caves."

"How certain are we that these caves all join at some point?" asked Isabel. "Or that we won't get lost once inside?"

"I have a keen sense of direction, miss," said the huntsman. "I always know true north. Though I can't say I'm eager for a few days spent under that mountain."

"But you are game?" asked Armand.

"You're paying my coin, milord."

There was some discussion more on the point, but it appeared that Sir Armand had decided to accept the huntsman's advice.

Part of her was horrified at the notion of descending into the tunnels beneath the mountain. What sort of madness was that? On her old world, such an experience would have been stressful enough, but in Albion? Who possibly could guess at what awaited them below ground?

What was she thinking? Could it be worse than what she'd already seen? She finally had witnessed firsthand a real monster, and that had been in broad daylight.

And they'd come all this way. For what? The item they sought had to be something of tremendous value. Isabel couldn't come up with any other reason why the foreigners were interested in her. Those men must imagine that she carried some special knowledge about what was to be found in the tunnels beneath them. And that thing, this Glaive they sought, must be of untold worth.

Alas, Isabel had no special knowledge of the thing, no knowledge at all. That was the rub.

Nothing in her dreams had even hinted at what might be found at the end of their journey. And now that they'd arrived, nothing new came to mind.

In fact, the memory of those dreams had begun to fade. She still could recall them, but the great vividness and sense of reality had begun to diminish. The dreams now felt like ordinary dreams, the finer details of which were harder for her to summon up.

It appeared that she was intended to guide the party to this spot, but then what? Was her role in the quest done?

Either way, she had no choice in the matter. It seemed that Armand had come to a decision. The tradesmen would travel ahead and await them on the far side of the mountain. No matter what dangers lay beneath them, she and Deirdre were safer with the knights than without them. She must travel downward.

———

To Deirdre's surprise, the Fiend's new foolishness actually made sense. Before his departure to scout the area the previous day, the ersatz huntsman had assured her that, for all its hidden dangers, the tunnels beneath the mountain were an ideal place to elude their pursuers. The base rock was formed of a type of iron ore that blunted magical scrutiny, an underground river ran beneath the area, and, though ancient, the fortress's wards and other magics still were quite potent.

If the Inquisitors wanted to find them within, they would need to come looking for them on foot. Their magic scries and divinations would be useless there.

And now it seemed Deirdre and the rest of the party would descend into the tunnels, whether she wanted to do so or not. All to look for something that … well ... wasn't there.

It would be a lie to say she looked forward to the trip. What person genuinely likes closed spaces? And as the Fiend had said, there was no telling what dark monsters might dwell beneath. She just needed to put her faith in the monster she called friend. That thought didn't stop her stomach from churning in dreadful anticipation.

The plan Sir Armand finally settled on was a simple one. At first light the following day, the drovers and muleskinners would make a great show of departing south, following a map that the huntsman had sketched out for them. Once they reached the south slope of the mountain, they would establish a secure camp and wait for the remainder of the party to rejoin them.

Isabel and Deirdre also would make a great show of seeing the men off. There no doubt were enemy scouts watching them, and they'd promised the tradesmen they wouldn't face any additional dangers in their departure. The foreigners wanted Isabel, and only Isabel.

Still, a number of the tradesfolk only agreed to depart after much argument and no small amount of persuading. Most had accustomed themselves to the idea of finding treasure at the end of the journey and were not ready to forsake that for a few promises that no such prize existed. And most had not foreseen so much bloodshed and felt themselves more deserving of reward for that extra burden.

In the end, Sir Armand, with Isabel's help, was able to convince the tradesmen to go along with the plan after the knight made a written promise that any treasure found within would be shared honestly among the party. The document seemed to do the trick.

After seeing off the tradesmen, the remainder of the party, fewer than 20 souls, would make their way down a set of stairs that adjoined the main cavern in which they had been resting since their arrival.

Sir Bertrand and some of his men already had taken a few short looks down the stairs. The steps descended for some length before intersecting a hallway that went left and right for a hundred or so short paces in either direction. That was all the farther the men had dared to venture. Everything beyond that point would be new territory.

The party would carry only the essentials, food, water, blankets, and torches and lanterns to light their way. The soldiers would leave their heavy plate armor with the baggage train, but would wear chainmail and carry every weapon they could shoulder. One never knew what one might need.

Beyond what they could carry on their backs, they would bring along the only two donkeys in the party. The animals were small and surefooted and were ostensibly to have served as mounts for the two clerics. The beasts largely had gone unused, the clergymen preferring to ride handsome palfreys instead. So bloody typical. It was nice to see the creatures' presence was not a waste.

Most of her effects were packed away to go with the tradesmen, but Deirdre kept one book with her, *The Tale of Emerald Sassafras*, which she spent the evening enjoying with Isabel by the fire. Both women were remarkably calm throughout the wait.

Morning came early.

There was something to be said for not needing to break camp and pack the animals. The departure of the tradesmen was actually quite casual. And in no time at all, Deirdre was heading down the first long flight of stairs with 18 other souls, including … well, she wasn't sure whether the Fiend counted as a soul, or even if he had one, but the party was nearly 20. Even with the donkeys, neither of whom counted as souls, they moved swiftly and quictly.

But how to begin searching?

That was the question the party had been asking itself. They could only speculate how many caves and tunnels were beneath them, and how far they went. If, as they feared, the caves and tunnels went on in an endless maze, how to find a single item?

It was a question Deirdre too had pondered, but from a different angle. How to find something that wasn't truly there? The answer seemed simple enough. The creature would lead them around for a time, making some great show of looking for the hidden Glaive, and then he'd conjure some weapon and claim he found it concealed somewhere among the midden. Quest fulfilled, time to leave.

She hoped it would be something like that.

It, so far, had been an assumption on her part that the Fiend knew his way around this darkened labyrinth. She hadn't had an opportunity to speak with him alone since he returned from scouting. There was little doubt in her mind that the fake huntsman had spent his days absent from the party rooting around in the dark, trying to find them an easy path through the mountain and on to the other side.

Perhaps that was being optimistic.

She didn't like this place very much. And it was more than just the dark. The first stretch of passage had left them in an inky blackness that was cut only by the few torches that burned among them. They might be down below many days, so only three of their wooden and pitch torches would burn at a time.

But the dank and damp smell that assaulted them when first they began their descent soon gave way to a musky stench. Animals dwelt there, and from the stink of it no animals with which she was familiar. Around that unpleasant aroma was the faint scent of feces and blood. It wasn't overwhelming, but the farther they walked the more pronounced it became.

Deirdre really didn't have anything else to do but observe their surroundings, as little as that was. Two of their party were tasked with taking a careful counting of their paces. Three men carried torches, and one man, a servant who now was attached to Sir Bertrand—the man originally was a retainer of Sir Michel Ferris—walked near the head of their tiny column with the fake huntsman and Sir Armand and sketched their path on a piece of parchment.

All others kept guard, except for Isabel and Deirdre.

Even in that faint light, her keen vision saw things. The stairs they descended clearly had been carved into the rocks by human hands, and though stretches of the path they followed seemed to be of natural stone, most sections of wall and flooring looked and felt to have been carved from the rock with the same degree of care and skill as had the stairs. Were it not for the thorough want of light, the path they followed would have resembled a passage through the dungeon level of a fortress, such as Mont Clair.

Were those faces that she saw carved into the stone? Or was it just her imagination? There seemed to be patterns at times, shapes of faces, bodies, and other forms etched into the walls. Perhaps the passing of time had left them to fade. It was only after having been at the cliffside for a full day that Deirdre had first discerned that there, too, were patterns along the cliffside that once may have been some type of carvings.

She knew from her reading that wind, water, and weather could do such damage, even to the hardest stone. Were those things once sculptures and statues like those she'd seen on the ramparts of Mont Clair and elsewhere? Perhaps the creature knew, but time hadn't allowed her to ask.

There was no way to tell time in the darkness, no way to track the passing of the sun. It felt like nearly a full bell had passed by the time the hallway in which they marched gave way to another series of rooms and passages. It seemed a good place to stop, eat, and rest. And Sir Armand thought it might be a good place to start looking around.

The knight's reasoning was sound. She'd never imagined the man a deep thinker, but he suggested that Isabel's visions must have brought them to that particular entrance—one of many to the fortress, it seemed—for a reason. Perhaps the Glaive was to be found close at hand? It wasn't a silly notion. In fact, the idea made a great deal of sense.

So, after resting and eating, the party broke up into groups of four and searched the area nearby, not straying farther than the light of their torch would carry, but carefully scrutinizing what they found. Along with Isabel, Deckard, and a retainer named Kittle, she looked through a pair of stone chambers. The smell told them that an animal once had dwelt there, but they found nothing beyond a few rusted bits of metal that might long ago have been door hinges.

The search soon was over, and the party moved on, striking a course that the counterfeit huntsman said was to the southwest. Their path stayed more or less level, until they reached an empty chamber. The only other exit went downward. So, they followed it to another level, one that they stayed upon for what felt like the rest of a day. It was hard to say how long precisely. Along the way, they stopped at likely places to rest, eat, and look about.

On the fourth such stop, Sir Armand took a quick count. One of their party was missing.

36. Something Nearby Lurks

From the moment Choate went missing, something changed within their party. Deirdre hadn't gotten to know the man well, at least no better than she had any of the other retainers. The fellow had begun the journey as a servant and man-at-arms for Sir Laird, but since that knight's death had attached himself to Sir Bertrand. And now the chap was gone, and where there had been dread before … now there was fear.

There wasn't much to do. The fellow had been bringing up the rear with two others, and since last anyone remembered seeing him, the party had passed no chambers nor encountered any forks in the path. The man somehow had disappeared somewhere along a long and straight passage.

Armand visibly swallowed his anger, but aside from calling out the man's name and pacing back down the corridor for a time, there was no search. Where would they look? There was no other path except for the one on which they then marched. The alternatives were limited. Either the man had turned and fled, had fallen down a hole no one else had seen, or something had stolen up behind the party in the darkness and snatched the man away without making a noise. Each option was equally ridiculous, though unequally frightening.

When they resumed their travel, Armand warned all to be vigilant and never to stray. Still, the party had begun to weary. Deirdre certainly felt tuckered. There was no way to keep time in the depths of the mountain, so any amount of time may have passed. On the off chance that Choate might yet catch up to them, they decided to bed down at the first intersection to which they came. It seemed the least they could do.

It was all very dismal and depressing. If Deirdre had not already learned the lesson, it occurred to her that there was nothing pleasant or romantic about adventures. Bah. The smell of the place alone would lead a dung fly to turn tail and shoo away.

When they reached the next intersection in the passage, a quick look told them there were a series of small and empty chambers there. After a short search and a longer time to scout past the intersection in each direction, the party bedded down in the largest of the chambers. The huntsman announced he would take first watch, and Deirdre hastened to volunteer as well. She hated always being in the dark—so to speak—and it was time for some answers.

But after making a short and awkward toilet behind a blanket held by Deckard, she returned to the passageway to find it empty. The pretend huntsman was not to be seen, nor was there a light of any kind. No … wait. There was the faintest glow just to her left, up the corridor in the direction they'd been traveling.

Perhaps the creature wanted to be out of earshot when they spoke. Sound possessed a peculiar quality in these austere stone corridors, carrying and distorting in ways she was not accustomed. But as she crept toward the distant glow, a voice deep within her screamed at her to halt. Something wasn't right. Something dearly was amiss, but she couldn't imagine what.

Her hand slid down to the dagger dangling at her side, and the thing slithered from its sheath. The weapon went to her side, blade up as she'd been trained. It never occurred to her to resume moving forward, but her free hand lightly brushed the wall on her left as she did, and she kept the center of her weight on her back leg as she moved.

It took her eyes many moments to adjust to the utter dark of the hallway, and she strained her ears to listen. Nothing.

Three more creeping steps forward, and she paused to listen. Nothing. Three more silent steps. Another pause. Nothing.

By that time, she was within 20 paces or so of the intersection. The faint light she followed seemed to emanate from around the nearest corner, and it cast a glow sufficient for her to make out the outline of the corners where the passages met. It was a light scant greater than a firefly might give off, but it was sufficient for her to see a dim shimmer in the shadow furthest from the light.

She dropped to one knee as she felt, rather than saw, a rush of movement to her right. She swung the lower edge of the dagger in a full arc, and raised her free arm, palm inward, to block a blow she somehow knew was coming. The knife was like a razor, nay, even sharper, and it met the faintest resistance. But something heavy and hard struck the meat of her forearm, driving her wrist back into the bridge of her nose, sending her sprawling.

The Fiend was virtually indestructible, so she felt not the least worry about inadvertently harming him, which left her free to cut and hew with all her might at the unknown form that had collided with her in the corridor. In moments, she was on her feet, her indestructible blade lacing wide arcs in front of her. She used it as a guide, and several times felt the blade bite into stone, steering her down the passage. Several times more, the blade slid through something softer and less resisting. At last, she was rewarded by a faint cry that only could have come from a human, and a man by the sound of it.

This entire flurry of cuts and hacks took but a few heartbeats, and then Deirdre again was sent sprawling when something thick and heavy struck her across the left shoulder. She again hit the ground, but, as the creature had trained her, she spread the force of the fall across her shoulders and upper arm.

Still, the wind was knocked from her for a short time, and her hand lost its grip on the dagger. For just a moment, she gasped pitifully for a breath as she groped about on the ground until the sickening sensation of the blade's razor edge caressed her fingers. When the weapon's hilt again was in her grasp, she heard a slight whisper.

"Tuppence, are you hurt?"

It was not clear what instinct or impulse had motivated her, but Deirdre so far had resisted the urge to cry out an alarm. Their scuffle appeared not to have alerted anyone sleeping in the chamber nearby. Now she replied to the creature's query in the same tiny murmur.

"I don't think so. ... Who was that?"

"Our little spy," the creature whispered in her ear. "Stay here. I'll return soon."

After she heard the creature depart, she wiped her dagger clean, sheathed it, and took a seat on the ground. Her right knee was throbbing and both elbows were skinned and burning. To her surprise, her left shoulder felt tender, but gave her no real pain. Her nose ... ouch. It was delicate to the touch, but it probably wasn't broken. Either way, she would be sore in the morning—whenever that came.

After a short time, she found her wind, rose, and hobbled to the spot around the corner where the Fiend had left the tiny lamp. The thing was precisely where she imagined it would be, its shade lowered so as to release the least amount of illumination. The creature no doubt had placed it there and skulked around in the dark searching for their intruder. "Our little spy?" she whispered. Was this the person who had been following and observing them all this time?

She took a few paces outside the glow of the lamp, crouched, and waited.

A bit of cheese and some decent bread would've been welcome right about then. It had only been a day, but the jerked beef and rock-hard trail bread they'd brought with them into the tunnels was not pulling its weight. Her stomach already was cursing her as a blackguard and a traitor.

The dark didn't frighten her. It seldom did. But on this occasion, as on most, she came to trust the creature. He would not have left her there alone if there were any dangers close at hand. And he always seemed to know when dangers lurked.

She allowed herself a few brief moments of thought. Time and again over recent days, her mind had turned to a book the Fiend had gifted her, *A Punter's Journey*, by a fellow named Burgoyne. It was one of those volumes she'd left in her packs with the muleskinners, but she'd read long bits of it during their journey north. Ostensibly a memoir of a lifelong gambler documenting the various games of chance, and how best to win at them, the book also was a thorough exposition on every imaginable scam, trick, and confidence game a person could think to run, as well as how not to fall for them.

The creature thought it profitable for a youngster to know such things, and she recognized in the thick volume a number of simple cheats and slights of hand that Chance Medley, one of the Fiend's seedier incarnations, had taught her. In a number of ways, Burgoyne's book summed up her companion perfectly.

If the creature was, as he had claimed, a third-rate practitioner of magic, he was a first-rate schemer, conniver, cheat, and scoundrel. To her knowledge, she was the only one with the privilege of peering behind the curtains of the monster's artful performances, and even for Deirdre it was difficult to keep an eye on the pea, to count the number of balls he was juggling, or to determine whether he had or had not palmed a card or dealt from the bottom of the deck.

Lord, it wasn't even easy to determine who the mark was in any of the many confidence schemes and swindles the creature was running, or whether there was a single mark and not two or three or 20.

A fine example, why were they in these caves? Was it just to muddle the ability of the Inquisitors to find them? Or was there something else at play? Some other mark that needed to be trimmed? It amused her to no end to see the creature sometimes at his wit's end, but she did not for a moment believe he was as flustered as he let on.

No. There was something else at play. He'd never lied to her, but neither was he always forthcoming with details. She just needed to figure out which questions to ask.

Moments later, a faint whisper, "Tuppence," heralded the creature's return.

It dawned on her that she very nearly had forgotten the tussle in which she'd just been engaged. Her body still trembled somewhat from the excitement of it all, but her mind had moved on. Such was her life now.

"Did you catch up to the fellow?" she asked as the Devil slid to the ground and took a seat beside her.

"He didn't make it far. One of your cuts split his hamstring to the bone, poor chap." The creature giggled in that familiar way, the way he did after a meal.

"Was it the same person?" she asked. "This spy?"

"From Mont Clair? Unless my sense of taste is deceiving me, yes."

"Yech. What did he have to say for himself?"

"Hmm … surprisingly little. Either someone compelled the fellow not to speak, or he has far greater courage and grit than most."

"Is that the doing of your mystery sorcerer?"

"It's a good guess. There's something about the flavor of the fellow … not the literal flavor. But something about the magics in which he was enveloped seems similar."

"So, the Inquisitors know where we are?"

"They no doubt have a better sense than I'd like. Their magics won't work well here, so I'd be surprised if this fellow wasn't tagging along and leaving breadcrumbs as he went."

"Should we wake the others?"

"No. Let them sleep. I'd know if our enemies were close."

"They're not clouding your senses anymore. Good."

"No. They're not, not as long as we're within this fortress. But we shouldn't tarry in this spot too long. You should go get some sleep."

"Why are we here?" she demanded. "Really."

"For the reasons I gave, child. I would have preferred not to venture along these paths. There was nothing to be gained from it. But with so many following us, it's our best chance to slip away without additional trouble."

"I'm not sure poor Choate would agree with you. … Was it the spy who took him?"

"Oh, no. We're near the lair of an especially unpleasant ogre. It's remarkable how stealthy such a large creature can be. They're like the jotun in that way."

"Shouldn't we...," she began to say.

"No need for that. Poor Choate, as you say, will keep the ogre sated until we've passed from her range."

"So, what's the plan?"

"Ah! There once was a large armory near the main entrance to this place. We should be able to make it there in no time at all."

"And then?"

A noise came from beside her, the creature again scratching his arm as the huntsman did.

"That's the muddle," said the Fiend. "We can't make it too easy, or no one in the party will believe it. If my senses don't deceive me, a young reiver makes its lair near the armory. Sir Armand and his warriors should be able to make short work of it. When they're busy with that, I'll slip ahead and plant a convincing weapon somewhere that will be easy for them to find."

"Ha! I knew it. How far to this arms room?"

"We could be there in no time. But I'll lead the party around a bit, just to make it seem more authentic. If we're lucky, we'll bump into some Inquisitors along the way. A nice little fight with those jackals will help sell the story."

Deirdre wanted to scream. "I thought we were trying to avoid the Inquisitors!" she hissed.

The creature had the nerve to giggle before replying. "Without their magics, and without a scout dropping them breadcrumbs to follow, those fools from the Holy See will have to search each new passage they come to."

"And they'll have to split up into smaller search parties to do so." It suddenly was clear to her.

"Exactly. We'll be long gone from this place by the time they realize what a waste of time it's been."

"Hold on," she said. Deirdre had some sense how the creature knew the things he did, so something here didn't make sense. "How do you know where there's an armory?"

"Tuppence, I've been here many, many times. In fact, for a rather long time this was my home."

"What?"

The huntsman let out a pleasant sigh. "Remember I told you of the great war? The one that raged between the Walking God's tribe and mine?"

"Of course."

"This place once was an important fortress near a major battlefield of that war. I was stationed here then."

"You were a soldier?"

"Oh, yes," he said. "A terrible one. Lazy, insubordinate, disobedient, you name it. In fact, off to your right about 10 furlongs and one level down is my old barracks. A bit beyond that is the brig."

"You've come home!"

"It was never much of a home. But there are some pleasant memories here."

"Why did you stay on our world?" she asked.

"You know the answer to that, child. It's part of the agreement that each tribe leaves a...."

"No. Why *you*? Was it a punishment?" The moment she said those words, she felt bad. But to her surprise, the creature began to laugh.

"Yes. Shiftless malcontents get the shit duty in every army." He chuckled some more. "And it is a terrible punishment, I have to admit. My kind are unusually gregarious. We enjoy the company of others of our kind, revel in it in fact."

"And you're alone now." For a moment, it felt like her heart skipped a beat. And something shifted inside her.

"It's not that bad," he assured her. "My fellow tribesman would laugh to hear me say it, but I've found some humans to be extraordinarily good company. And I have my barrow."

"But you're alone there."

"No. I chose that spot for a reason. It's one of those points where the walls between worlds are at their thinnest. I can't cross over there, but from time to time I'm able to hear voices from my world. It's quite comforting."

The creature took it all rather well, but she didn't want to risk hitting a tender spot. So she backed away and asked about a topic that, until that time, had been too uncomfortable for her to speak about. A lifetime of fear and reverence nearly caused her to hold her tongue, and she trembled inside when she spoke.

"Is the Walking God like you?" she asked.

"Do you mean is he a prisoner here?"

"I suppose that's what I'm asking."

"Mm.... That's an exceedingly difficult question."

"How so?"

"The members of that tribe aren't like us. ... And they're nothing at all like the folk of this world either."

She swallowed something down before saying in a weak voice, "I'd like to know."

"Well, where to start on that? ... Look, imagine it this way. The world in which you live, this mortal realm around us, is made up of matter and essence."

"Body and spirit?"

"Exactly. Just imagine a realm where there is little spirit, but where matter is much more matter-like. That's the realm from which I come. ... I know that doesn't make much sense, but some things belie easy explanation."

"Could I go and see it myself?"

"My realm?! That would be a terrible idea. No human could survive there, at least not for long, and only then with some special protections."

"And the Walking God and his people? What of them?"

"That lot? Their nature isn't any easier to explain. Look at it this way. … Imagine a realm that has little or no matter, but where most everything is composed of spirit."

"Like Heaven, in the scriptures?"

"Yes. Precisely. Perhaps explaining this isn't so hard after all."

"Could a human live there?"

"Oh, child, I'm not sure. I rather doubt a person such as you could survive for long in the Walking God's realm. One thing I do know for certain is that members of his tribe cannot survive long in this realm without special protections."

"What kind of protections?" Deirdre asked.

"There are two ways. In days of old, the Walking God and his people would place their spirits into artificial structures, special carapaces. Such things were enormously powerful, able to channel the spirit's magical energy with little limit."

"What did they look like? Those … corpuses?"

"Carapaces."

"Yes. Those."

"Most looked very much like human beings, except far larger and beautifully formed, like the comeliest of men and women … to awe the locals, I suppose."

"So they can take any form, like you do?"

"They can take on new forms," he replied. "But what they do isn't the same. For one of their kind to take a new form, they either must shift their essence to a new carapace … or they must inhabit a new human host."

His words took a short time to sink in, but when they did, she found herself gasping. "Wh… what do you mean 'human host'?"

"It's ever the way, Tuppence. Folks forever are conflating the ways of his tribe and mine. This Walking God that so many worship in this realm no longer resides in an artificial carapace. Those devices were forbidden under the terms of the peace between our two sides. To live in this realm, the Walking God must pass from one human host to the next, taking a new human body as his own with each transfer. His true essence would not survive in this realm without it."

"He possesses people?"

"Yes."

"So … when preachers speak of demonic possession in sermons, and what they say in psalms and in scriptures?"

"Child, I wouldn't have the foggiest idea about how to possess a person. None of my kind can do such things. It's the creatures of the other tribe, whether you care to call them gods or angels, who do such things. Well, now there's only one of them in this land that does it."

"The Walking God?"

"The very one."

37. A Wicked, Wicked Place

Late on the following day—for it did seem a full day had passed—the party found themselves on the edge of an enormous hall. It was the first time since entering the horrid place that they could dispense with torches. From somewhere high above, faint bits of light, gentle and diffuse, filtered in to allow for the least tiny smidgen of illumination. It was barely more than the torches provided, but it took Isabel a few moments of blinking to adjust her eyes to what seemed like a considerable glare.

Travel for the preceding day had been long and tiresome. The air was close and clammy, their path was dark and depressing, and on more than one occasion they'd discerned the distant cries of some sort of creatures and, much closer, the scurrying about of feet. Thankfully, they'd suffered no further losses.

Well, there was one tragedy. Deirdre took a tumble in the dark while the others last slept. The poor kid was bruised and scuffed up, but otherwise didn't seem the worse for it. She was a trooper and complained far less than any of the men, most of whom had taken to groaning and cursing under their breath.

In truth? The passageways hadn't been that bad. The conditions were terrible, but they so far had encountered no obstacles of which to speak. There were loose stones here and there for which one needed to watch, but the going was easy. It simply was depressing.

All seemed much relieved when Sir Armand called a halt. The party would rest in the great hall, a room so vast that it was difficult to see the other side. The air seemed a little fresher there too. No doubt they had some type of openings in the ceiling to thank for that. For the life of her, though, she couldn't make out from where the light or air came, but she was grateful for it all the same.

What she wouldn't give for a phone or a watch right then, something to help chart the passing of time. When she'd gone camping on that fateful day two years ago, she'd opted not to take any technology. She'd planned on being in the woods only for a few nights and thought it might be liberating to disconnect for a short time.

Having such an item in Albion would have helped her puzzle out the local method of charting time. It took her forever to sort that out, and, even then, imprecisely, largely because time periods in Albion were so absurdly flexible. They changed during the course of the year, and even over the course of a day.

There were six bells per day, but those bells didn't seem to be spaced evenly, and the duration between bells changed with the shortening or lengthening of daylight throughout the year. There were, by her calculation, fewer bells at night and more during the day. And as near as she could figure, a bell could be anywhere between two and a half and four hours.

There were no hours, minutes, or seconds. All other calculations of time were fractions of a bell. Folks thereabouts might speak in terms of a moment, or a trice, or a nonce, and other such expressions. But those words simply meant a short time, a period that could be as short as a heartbeat or as long as many minutes, depending on what the speaker had in mind.

Longer calculations of time were no less deceitful. Days in this world seemed to be about the same length as those at home, and the seasons broadly were the same, but months and years?

Oh, what a godawful mess.

Happily, the year was about the same length as back home, roughly 350 days, divided between 12 months of four weeks each. Hallelujah! But some dates were charted using a solar calendar, others a lunar calendar, and there were two other calendars for registering various religious observances and commercial transactions. One of those was a 10-month calendar, and the other she simply hadn't been able to understand at all, owing to the fact it was tied to the comings and goings of the tides. Worst of all, it wasn't always clear which calendar would apply to which observance, occasion, or transaction. Even the locals sometimes were left scratching their heads.

Weights and measures were fraught with equal chaos. Shots, fingers, spans, grosses, hogsheads, galleons, freights, slides, fathoms, rods, discuses, and a thousand other terms of measure were tossed around freely. Every craft, trade, and guild had its own fashion of weighing and measuring, as did the various localities. A span in King's Gate was not the same length as a span in Westport, a hogshead in the midlands was one-third less than the same in the southern counties, and each locality had its own estimation of what a rod should be. Even the supposed standard measures of guilds could vary from guildhall to guildhall.

It was unruly and frenetic, and it was a thing that every young woman of decent breeding was expected to learn as a child. The looks the baroness had given her when she discovered Isabel didn't know the simple weight-and sizing-tables any 10-year-old should know.

Heavens.

Isabel gave her head a shake. The silly things her mind turned to when she let it wander, especially without sweet Deirdre to keep her focused. The kid even now napped with her head across Isabel's lap, sore and exhausted from her tumble and from a rough night's sleep on the stone floor. She didn't fault the youngster at all. These tunnels were like a weight on all of them. The knights most of all carried it poorly. These were men accustomed to the open skies and fair fields of Albion. This dark and wicked delve was not a place for them.

It was barely three days, or was it four? What she would not give to see the sun, moon, and the stars again.

On that pleasant note, she decided to join Dierdre in slumber. Sir Armand had promised it would be a long break. The huntsman and some of the men would scout ahead, looking around some of the many passages that led from the enormous room in which they rested. And, of course, Deckard was nearby, mending some straps for one of the donkeys, and peering off into the gloom as if looking for the arrival of the Four Horsemen. She didn't feel bad at all when she allowed her eyes to droop and finally to close.

———

When she awoke, Isabel for a moment was surprised. She hadn't meant to go so thoroughly to sleep, and when she finally cracked an eye and looked around, there was just a moment when she thought she was alone in the great hall. Deirdre no longer was on the ground next to her, and Deckard was gone from the barrel on which he'd sat. Then she craned her neck and saw Deirdre standing 20 or so feet away. Had the youngster been any farther, Isabel wouldn't have been able to see her in the umber.

Was the kid talking to someone?

Before Isabel had a chance to ask, Deirdre turned and moved toward her at a run, her skirts flying and a look of determination on her face.

"We need to go now," the youngster said.

"What?"

"Don't worry about the donkeys. Just grab your pack and some water and let's go."

It dawned on Isabel that there were a handful of fighting men nearby preparing their gear. "What of the…? What's going on?"

"We've been discovered," was her friend's reply. "We go now to join Sir Armand and the men."

"What? … The Etruscians?"

"Sir Bertrand and his men were attacked by a small party of them. We gather now near a small cavern where dwells some type of creature. Sir Armand hopes to fight through. That path seems to be our only way out."

They had begun to move by then, going at a brisk walk. It was Isabel, Deirdre, and three fighting men who's faces she couldn't purely see in the dark, even with the help of two torches. Despite the nap, she soon was out of breath.

"What of the relic we seek?" she asked after some minutes rushing. "Aren't we to stay and look for it?"

"I don't know," said Deirdre. "For now, safety is our concern. The men have been scattered while looking. If those scoundrels from the Holy See find us while we're separated, they can kill us in ones and twos. … Hurry."

They soon were moving too swiftly to converse, and Isabel lost track of time as they progressed from one hallway to the next. She did have the reassurance of catching sight of Deckard not far behind her. Perhaps 30 minutes later, they joined another group from their party and after a few hushed whispers continued their pace. The air again grew close, and there was a stench around them as if some animal might have made its lair nearby.

At one point, a human scream ripped the air. It wasn't apparent whether the cry was from one of their comrades, or even whether it was a cry of pain or anger … or both. An unpleasant ripple ran through their small group, and for a moment they hesitated before hastening along at a greater pace.

They weren't exactly jogging at that point, but they moved at a rapid step with which Isabel found it difficult to keep up, even after some days growing accustomed to traveling in the dark. Several times she missed her footing, and one time she nearly fell to the ground before being grabbed up (by Deirdre, she thought) and pulled to her feet. It was hard to see anything even with the torches, and it was difficult to hear with her own heavy breathing filling her ears.

The more time that passed, the more anxiety she felt. The previous days had been careful and methodical. It now felt like they were flying along without plan or destination, and that notion filled her with dread.

That sensation fled her, if only for a moment, when they came to a high and broad juncture in the hallway where they met Sir Armand and some others. Her thoughts for just a moment hearkened back to the many times she'd heard Sir Alexis refer to Armand as an absolutely fine fellow. She'd begun to feel that in her bones over the course of their journey, and she felt herself gravitate toward where he stood speaking with one of the men-at-arms. Deirdre was beside her, and it took Isabel a moment to realize that the man who she thought was sleeping along one of the walls was not in fact sleeping. It took a moment more to distinguish the smell of blood and death from amid all the heavy and putrid smells in this part of the dungeon.

"It lies yonder," she heard Sir Armand say. The man was glancing between her and Deirdre and pointed a lazy thumb toward a broad passageway a dozen paces distant. "Spears found a plaque next level up with a map of the place. This seems to be the entry to the fortress's main armory."

"The thing we seek is here?" she found herself asking.

The knight nodded. "If not here, then the Glaive could be anywhere. Our enemies press us hard. They must know we're close to finding the relic. Else they would not be so bold."

"What are we to do?" asked Deirdre.

"The last of us are here. Some foul bugbear makes his lair in the chamber next, and beyond that we seek the Glaive. We first slay the beast. The huntsman will watch our rear. You ladies hang back, in between. Your man Deckard will mind your safety."

Without another word, the giant knight strode toward the hallway down which lay the beast, a knot of fighting men about him. A howl of a great and mighty monster echoed from beyond.

38. A Little Sleight of Hand

Giving Deckard the slip proved to be no problem. He was merely one man, and at the moment that one man was carefully attending to Lady Isabel, a young woman who looked to be at the end of her tether. So Deirdre simply pitter-pattered away in pursuit of the huntsman.

She'd only seen bits and bobs of the creature over the past day, but when last she'd pinned him down, earlier in the great hall, he'd informed her in the loosest terms of what his plans were. So when the men were engaged with the monster—a reiver the Fiend had called it—she managed to sneak off.

Afterward, it was no trouble at all to find the Fiend, even in the dark. He had told her the direction he intended to go once the party again began to move. She just kept the wall to her right until she heard his voice.

"I'm right here, Tuppence," was the huntsman's whisper.

"Were you waiting on me?"

"I knew you couldn't resist."

The curse of an infernal curiosity. She didn't want to miss anything, but she wasn't sure what she thought of how predictable she was to the creature.

Either way, the Fiend took her by the arm and led her down the hallway. His eyesight in the dark appeared nigh perfect as he guided her along the corridor, several times turning and moving up and down short flights of steps as they went, until after some short time the faintest hint of light could be perceived ahead.

"Where are we?" she asked.

"The armory proper. ... On the other side of the chamber where Armand and the others are fighting the reiver."

"Wait," she said. "They could have just walked around...?"

"Tuppence, we can't make it too easy for them. Otherwise, they won't buy into it. And we'll be stuck here forever, looking for something that isn't...."

"And there's always a monster guarding the hoard," she said, remembering every story of questing she'd ever heard.

"Exactly."

A thing occurred to her that she'd intended to ask sooner. "Aren't you supposed to be watching the party's rear? What happens if the troops of the Holy See come upon the others while they're fighting the Bugbear?"

"Armand dealt with their nearest scouts. The rest of those scoundrels are nowhere close. Come along, give me a hand."

The two of them were in a chamber that wasn't large, but was fairly deep. On the far end, another of the peculiar sconces they'd seen in the great hall was set into the ceiling. The device wasn't powerful enough to light the entire area, not fully, but it did illuminate the far section of the place with a powerful beam, one that provided enough light on the side of the chamber nearest Deirdre for her not to stumble when she walked.

Despite copious refuse and debris on the floors, there was little else in the armory. A series of high stone pedestals were arrayed throughout the center of the room, and many stone recesses were set into the walls.

"This was where the garrison stored it's most powerful weapons," said the Fiend, as if anticipating her next question. "I'd prefer not to conjure from nothing, and there should be something useful here. Lend a hand and start looking about."

"What am I looking for?" she asked, while toeing away what may once have been a wooden pallet of some sort. Most of the thing crumbled to her touch.

"Any old piece of swag that might pass for a Glaive," was his wearied reply. "And do let's hurry. The reiver won't keep our companions occupied long."

Over the next moments, she found several bent and rusted items that might once have been blades and spearpoints of some sort. The Fiend declared the damaged and abandoned pieces insufficient for their needs, and she tossed them aside in turn. It would help if she knew what a glaive was. And after some moments longer she dusted aside some nasty and smelly rubble near one of the pedestals to find an object like no other she'd ever seen.

What caught her attention was a narrow tube about as long as her forearm. The thing seemed solid but weighted little, and despite all the decay in the room around them the metal from which the thing was forged seemed only slightly corroded.

"What's this?" she asked the creature.

He looked once, did a quick double-take, and then moved in her direction. As he took the item from her grasp, he said, "Well, isn't that ironic."

"What?"

"It's a weapon."

"It doesn't.... What kind of weapon?" she asked, her curiosity again aroused.

"An immensely powerful one. A type of weapon that should not have been left on this world after my tribe departed from it."

"It doesn't look...," she began, poking the item several times before snatching away her hand. "Is it dangerous?"

"It once was." The creature scrutinized the weapon briefly. "But the working parts are missing or corroded to nothing. It's harmless now."

"It doesn't look...," she began again. "How does it...?"

"It's a device not unlike a powerful crossbow," he said as he bent and twisted the device double in his powerful hands before tossing the now ruined thing into a recess in the wall. "Save it casts a powerful bolt of energy, one sufficient to kill at a great distance."

"Sooo...," she said with great innocence, "a weapon sufficient to kill the Other One himself?"

"Yes, I rather think so. ... Ironic."

The Fiend then leaned over and recovered a thing from the floor near where Deirdre had found the strange weapon. It was a narrow blade of middling length. There was a great deal of corrosion on the metal, but it otherwise seemed serviceable. "This should do. Come help me move a few things."

On the far side of the chamber, Deirdre helped the creature shift one of the bulky pedestals to a position immediately beneath the beam of light that emanated from the chamber's ceiling. The thing was heavy, but it seemed designed for easy movement, and after they finished wrestling it into place, he bid her hurry and gather a pair of bricks.

She did not ask why, but when she returned with two square stones a few moments later, the Fiend was running a gentle finger up and down the side of the blade. There was a faint glow along the tip of his digit where it met the cutlass, and a pleasant smell, something akin to the scent of a fresh rain shower, rose above the stifling and wretched air of the dungeon. The blade now looked cleaner and newer, virtually flawless. Even a slight bend in the ancient weapon appeared to have been straightened.

"That should do it," the creature announced. "Set those two stones on the middle of the table, about three spans apart."

Deirdre needed to get on her toe tips to do as the creature asked, after which he gently placed the blade on top of the stones, so as to suspend it between them. He then led her back a few dozen paces to get a look at their handiwork. The ancient blade, made new, positively glowed white under the beam of light.

"There are no jewels or precious inlays," said the faux huntsman, "and I don't have time to replace the leather on the hilt, but not bad for a slapdash piece of work."

"It *looks* magical," she agreed.

"It'll have to … shh! Let's go. From the sound of it, the fighting has done, and our friends soon will be here."

The first voices were just discernible in the distance when the Fiend led her to a deep recess in the stone wall, one that opened into a small side-passage that paralleled the main entry into the chamber. By the time she and the creature emerged from the other end, their companions had passed in the opposite direction. Deirdre stole a glance out from where she and the fake huntsman secreted themselves and was rewarded with a glimpse of the party as they first caught sight of the Fiend's pseudo-Glaive on the pedestal within.

Of course, it was all mumbo-jumbo, more of the creature's smoke and mirrors, but for the merest moment she had to fight off a tear. The party had endured great hardship and suffered tremendous loss during the quest, and as they caught sight of the item that they thought to be the relic they sought, the party, Sir Armand in the lead, went to their knees as one and raised their hands in supplication. The brave knight shared with the empty room a short prayer of thanks from the Common Breviary.

The moment passed, and at the gentle urging of the Fiend, she emerged from their hiding place and quietly slipped again among their party. She soon was walking silently behind Lady Isabel as the young woman trod toward the makeshift altar. In the darkness and the hubbub of the battle with the reiver, no one seemed to have marked Deirdre's absence. And she fought the urge to look around to determine who may have fallen during the fight.

When they reached their destination, a pin drop in the distance would have sounded as a gong, so quietly did all in the party approach the object of their reverence. There was a moment's hesitation before Lady Isabel rose on the tips of her toes and took the shimmering blade from the pedestal, followed by a great gasp from all those present.

Deirdre felt another tear forming in her eye. It was all a sham. But the emotions that washed over her from her companions left her trembling. And when Isabel turned from the pedestal with the weapon in her arms, the look in her eyes was so joyous, so complete, that Deirdre knew she'd rather chew her own tongue from her head than ever to speak the truth of what had transpired there that day.

Lady Isabel had recovered the Glaive, the true and proper Glaive, and that's all there was to it.

———

"I'm not sure I see the irony," she said as she slid down the wall to take a seat beside the huntsman. The exhausted party was taking a rest near where they'd found the Glaive, and Deirdre had volunteered to bring the huntsman his dinner where he sat on watch. "Finding a weapon suitable to slay Evil was supposed to be our reason for coming here."

"True enough," replied the creature. "It just seemed unlikely. Prophecy is nonsense. I never said it was *absolute* nonsense."

The creature, in fact, had used those very words a number of times, but Deirdre opted not to raise that point. She focused instead on the present.

"How do you know the item we found in the armory, the one you tossed aside, wasn't the Glaive the party was intended to find?"

The creature didn't answer for a moment. "There is no such thing as destiny, child." Another pause. "We are not foreordained to do or to be anything. In sum, we set our own paths."

"What could that possibly have to do with finding the Glaive?" she asked. "We did find a powerful weapon here."

"Which is why I say prophecy is not absolute nonsense. Look, powerful magics can help a person divine the future. But even the best such magics are hit and miss. Prophecy portends *possible* futures, and even the most powerful magics can only predict *likely* outcomes. There is no force known that can predict distant events with perfect accuracy. *Because nothing in the future is set in stone.* That's the first way that prophecy can fail."

"There are others?"

"At least one other. Imagine that under the influence of some great magic, a person in the distant past predicts an event with perfect accuracy. As unlikely as that seems, what are the chances that folks nowadays, if that prophecy even survives to the present day, would understand the prophecy with perfect clarity?"

Deirdre gave a shrug and made a sound that signaled her uncertainty.

"Child, I've seen prophecies come, and I've seen them go. The most accurate foretelling is useless, if someone misreads or misunderstands it— which is often the case. And the fact that one prophecy proves to be right should be taken with a grain of salt, when many thousands turn out to be unfounded gibberish."

"But the weapon?"

"Tuppence, our friend Isabel led us to an ancient fortress, one of the most important in this world's history. That much is correct. Yet it was not Isabel who led us to the armory."

"That was you," she agreed.

"Indeed. And there, it's true, we found one broken-down old item, a device that once, when new, was a powerful weapon. But old fortresses often are strewn with ruined and shattered weapons."

Deirdre wasn't completely convinced, but the Fiend's words made a certain amount of sense. Albion was littered with barrows, battlefields, and ruined strongholds. Hardly a season went by in the County of Blenheim that some farmer or another didn't plow up a rusty old sword or the head of an antique battle-ax. Such things were abundant in a land of frequent strife and warfare.

"So, things are not destined to be?" she asked. It wasn't the first time she and the creature had spoken of such things. But it was something around which she was having a difficult time wrapping herself. Her befuddlement was about more than prophecy. Things either were meant to be, or they were not. The book he'd given her to read on the subject before she'd departed Mont Clair, a slim volume by a fellow named Sopwith, didn't seem to clarify much in her mind.

And what did it mean to be one's authentic self if there was no measuring stick by which to gauge that authenticity? That truth? No guiding principle of the universe? That thought kept coming back to her.

"What did you think of Sopwith's book?" he asked her.

"How did you know I was thinking about that?!"

"Not by prophecy. Just by the questions you've been asking, and the questions you've asked in the past."

"What does it all mean?"

"You tell me. ... You read the book?"

"Yes."

"What did it say?"

"I'm not sure I understood any of it. It seems to suggest that things are both destined to be and *not* destined to be."

"Well," agreed the creature, "that's one way a reader might interpret Sopwith. May I suggest another?"

"I insist."

"Sopwith picks up an argument that began many, many years ago with the Leveling school of philosophy. He doesn't do a good job of explaining his starting point...."

"I'll say."

"No, child. He doesn't. But what he's getting at is this. Virtually every school of theology argues that all things are predestined, and every person is bound to a path laid out for them by some Divine figure. That much you know."

She gave a nod to signify her agreement.

"But there also are some philosophers, men and women who study the physical world, who agree, for better or worse, that things are that way. If studying the physical world has taught such people nothing, it is argued, it has taught them that physical laws are immutable. And if physical laws are immutable, they can always be predicted."

"Always?"

"Always."

"That...," she began. She wanted to say that all of that made no sense. But it actually rather did. As she often did as such moments, she muttered under her breath.

"No," she said at last. "That doesn't make any sense. How could anyone predict what I'm going to have for breakfast on eventide morn three years hence?"

"That's easy," said the creature. "Sweet pudding, if we have any."

"Well ... OK. But not everything can be predicted."

"With the proper information, Tuppence, yes. Just take ... oh, imagine the sun. I know you can't see it now, but it burns hot, and it comes up every morning. One day it will burn its last."

"Pshaw!"

"Yes, it will be many ages from now, long past the time when even long-lived creatures like me have passed away, but it one day will end. A clever scientist, with the proper tools, can tell you the precise moment that will occur."

"But not what the sun will have for breakfast on that day," she said with a victorious smile.

"Perhaps not. But Sopwith's point is this. Imagine a world where everything is predestined, whether by the gods or by nature. How could such a universe be fair and just? In such a wretched place, we all would pay penalties for things that were perfectly out of our control."

"How so?"

"Well, Tuppence, think of it this way. If things are predestined, then we have no choice in whether they come to pass. If we have no choice in whether they come to pass, how can we be held morally responsible for their outcomes?"

"That doesn't sound very fair," she agreed. It didn't. If a thing were predictable, she had to agree, it was destined to be, even what she'd have for breakfast on a random day 10 years hence. … Or whether she stole a coin or took a life? If such a thing was destined to be, if her actions already were decided before she was born, what right did any god or any magistrate have punishing her for doing it?

"But what if that weren't the case?" the creature asked. "What if we lived in a universe where nothing was predestined? Would such a world be fairer?"

Deirdre sat a moment in thought. She tried to remember what Sopwith had said, and what someone like the vicar might have thought. The creature's question sounded like it was a trick, but it probably wasn't. He was never deceptive in that way.

"No," she said at last. What Sopwith said suddenly seemed clearer. "Because a universe without a notion of a guiding fate, a guiding principle, is a universe where everything is up for negotiation, where chaos reigns. It would be a place where words like 'just' and 'fair' have only the meaning we give them."

"So?"

"Well," she continued. "It's a choice between a universe where there is no justice and a universe where the word 'justice' has no meaning." It finally occurred to her what Sopwith had concluded. "You have to believe that both worlds exist at the same time. To live a healthy mental life, we have to believe in order and destiny. But we also have to believe that no destiny binds us, that we are free to chart our own paths."

The creature sat mute and idle.

"Is that what it means to be one's authentic self?" she asked.

"That's for you to decide."

39. A Day Both Fresh and Sharp

At that moment, the smell of fresh air was all that mattered to Isabel. What else could be more important?

If she'd assumed that finding the Glaive would be the end of their quest, she was far from correct on that note. After the survivors of the expedition discovered the gleaming blade, they spent what felt like a full day making their way through a series of corridors, stairs, and chambers in search of what Mr. Spears believed was a southern entrance to the fortress. It several times felt like they were wandering in circles, and they were forced more than once to halt or to change direction so as to avoid what sounded like enemy soldiers.

It was a long and strenuous escape from what had come to feel like a prison.

But at last, the scent of fresh and clean air hit her. Not long after, the faintest hint of light became clear in the passage ahead. It was all Isabel could do, trembling though she was with fatigue, not to dash forward into the daylight.

Happily, they'd avoided further bloodshed on their way to the exit, but Armand was convinced that they weren't yet out of danger. And though all present wanted to get free of these wretched tunnels, the great knight had bidden them to wait.

So they waited and continued to wait.

An hour or so earlier, Mr. Spears went ahead to have a look around. The huntsman was the only one who didn't seem bone wearied by the long and arduous trek beneath the mountain. The man never rested and seemed as lean and hard as his name. Even the knights, robust and stalwart though they were, seemed happy to take a rest while the hunter went forward and looked for hidden dangers.

When the huntsman finally returned, he had no good news to bear.

"It seems there are a good many of those church folks combing the woods to the south of here," the man said after taking a long drink of water and depositing himself on the ground.

"How many?" asked Armand.

"Difficult to say. Fewer than 50, I'd guess. But they're spread out in smaller parties."

"Mounted?"

"At least half. But that side of the mountain is broad and mostly heavy forest. It'll take them a time to assemble, if they must."

"But them mounted and us not," muttered the large knight. "What of the mule train and the tradesmen?"

"Some ways distant down the valley. I spied them from a rise. They seem to have followed your instructions, and threw up a wooden stockade along a stream. They don't look to have been harassed."

"But they are distant?"

"Not as the crow flies," said the huntsmen. "But it would take us some time to get to them."

"We didn't anticipate the enemy moving ahead of us," said Armand. "But it's good our friends are safe. We just need to make it to them. Together we can best these foreign rascals."

Deirdre produced a pencil and a sheet of parchment, and the knight encouraged the huntsman to sketch out a map of the southern slope of the mountain. The man did so swiftly, and with a remarkably skilled hand.

"There's no question," said the knight after scrutinizing the improvised map for a time and asking the huntsman a number of pointed questions, "we'll have to fight them at some point."

"But us just over a dozen fighting men," said Sir Bertrand, one of only three knights left alive other than Armand. The rest of their fighters were men-at-arms.

"How long to reach this stockade of which you spoke, Spears?"

"It's midmorning now, the frost just off the grass. If we set a brisk pace, we could be there just after the sun noons."

"And you say our enemies are spread over this side of the mountain?" asked the knight as he waved his hand over a portion of the map.

"It'll be some time for them all to gather together."

"We leave when the sun is highest in the sky and follow the woodlands along the east of the valley," their leader commanded. "They don't know where we are, so that gives us an advantage. We stay out of sight until they detect us, and then we run, fighting them as we must with arrow … and with sword only when we have no other choice. Once we engage, we keep moving to the stockade at every hazard."

"Until then, milord?" asked Bertrand.

"We rest, eat, and drink our fill of what remains of our water. When we depart here, we take only the things we need."

"And our enemy's magickers, sire?" asked another of the knights.

Armand made a blowing noise, as if at a loss for words or ideas, before saying simply, "Pray."

———

The party consumed its rations before leaving the caves behind several hours later. After quitting their camp at the great hall the day before, they'd carried little enough. Now the travelers abandoned cloaks, blankets, and lanterns and torches. The fighting men retained their many weapons, but left even their shields behind to travel with greater ease.

Stepping into the sunlight was glorious. Isabel knew that danger awaited, but she'd rather face a thousand enemy warriors at that point than to go back into those wretched halls and tunnels. There was no precise way of knowing how long they'd been underground. Three days? Four? Five? It was too many. She never intended to go below ground again.

The going for the first hour was easy. The gate through which they emerged was set among a copse of thick and high trees, and the ground was smooth, as if part of a park or a garden. Slowly, though, the terrain began to twist and to bend, and the undergrowth became thick and knotty. It wasn't terrible going, but it was slow going for a short way until the huntsman led them to a faint trace in the forest, a game trail of some sort.

The walk thereafter was easy. The calm and clear air, combined with the smooth and soft path down which they then walked, made the passage almost pleasant. Birds sang, and the occasional deer or bunny was startled by their presence. It was a lovely stretch of wild greenery, one that she would have enjoyed traversing in her hiking days. There even was a clean stream to refill their water skins.

On several instances, she needed to remind herself that there were men in these woods who meant her evil, who intended to murder her friends and snatch her away. The fear she'd endured, and the discomfort of the caves, hadn't allowed her the time or the resources to ponder that particular horror. This was Albion, and it was always something. That some distant pontiff now wanted her seized and slapped in chains? Or worse?

Perhaps she'd gone crazy, and all of this was some delusion she'd conjured from the warmth and safety of a bed at some loony bin her mother had placed her in? (God, how she missed her mom.) She'd cogitated such a possibility before, but she'd always dismissed the notion as too farfetched. Her imagination wasn't that good. But hadn't she imagined those dreams, dreams more vivid than any she possibly could have imagined, dreams so real that they were like reality?

But they weren't dreams, were they?

She felt herself beginning to chuckle, until she caught a cautionary glower from Deckard. Now, there was a man she didn't have the imagination to make up. No.

No. There simply was too much going on in this world for it to be a figment of her mind. The rough and earthy presence of Deckard, the wholesome support she felt from the de Vere clan, her love for sweet Deirdre, and … oy, she tried not to think of Sir Alexis.

He was a fellow she never would have looked at twice in her old life, not in a million years. Now? Oof. She spent far too much time thinking of him, wondering where he was and what he was doing, hoping against hope that he might at any moment sweep in and drive off her pursuers.

She forced herself to pay attention. Since her illness, her mind still wandered, often at the most damnable times. They were in the forest, being hunted, and she needed to stay focused.

She gave a quick look around.

To her surprise, Mr. Spears was not 10 feet away, walking apace with Deirdre. Deckard was close, Armand was at their lead with a pair of archers, and Bertrand was in the rear with another knight, Sir Jewel from the look of him. All were in chainmail and half helms, with their faces partly obscured.

She looked out farther, attempting to spy what might be immediately around them. When she glanced ahead, there was nothing. To the left, Deckard blocked her view of what lay beyond, and to the right … she thought she saw a figure move among the trees. Before she could even think to be afraid or cry a warning, the nauseating hiss of arrows sounded around them.

To her surprise, she didn't panic. But she very nearly dropped to the ground as she'd been instructed to do in the past. But that wasn't their plan now. An arrow ricocheted from the helmet of the man in front of her, and the party began to run. When they did, it was straight at the position from whence the missiles flew.

A shaft erupted from the arm of the soldier nearest her, but it wasn't the first time she'd seen such a thing, and she continued on. By impulse, she stole a peek to see if Deirdre was OK. Her glance came just in time to see the huntsman snatch the lass aside and take an arrow in the chest that was meant for her. Isabel let out a scream that rose in unison with the battle cry of those around her.

She was swept up in the rush, and there was nothing she could do to control the moment. All in the party ran through the underbrush at full tilt. Most of the fighting men were armed with short and heavy bows, and knocked arrows as they ran, pausing only a heartbeat to loose a shaft before speeding on.

By the time they reached the point in the bush from where their enemies had attacked, most enemy archers had fled. Isabel had to bound over one enemy body, and a second adversary was struck dead by a knight as he tried to struggle away.

The group soon was hurtling down a broad wash, one covered with leaves under which the stones proved to be treacherous footing. She nearly fell several times, and strong hands righted her before she crashed to the ground. It could be none other than Deckard, though she had not the time to look. There was a constant cursing and screaming around her until they came to a point where their course gave way to a flat woodland. Armand was there, urging them onward.

"Don't stop, don't stop," he hissed. "But for all that's holy, be quiet!"

They raced on. Speed and silence today were their friends.

It was only then, legs tired and lungs heaving, that she stole a look at Deckard. The man had a harried and frightened look on his face, but not out of fear of the enemy. Men like him weren't built that way. His head craned this way and that, a steady stream of whispered curses and imprecations ushering from his voice. He'd lost track of Deirdre and looked near panicked at the notion. She didn't want to feel sorry for the man, but she did worry that Deirdre had not yet rejoined them.

But there was little she could do about her young friend at that moment, so at their first short stop she made herself useful. The nearest soldier, a man-at-arms named Costars, had an arrow in his arm, a type of injury she'd treated many times. She probed the wound swiftly before grabbing the arrow and yanking it out. The missile wasn't lodged deep, and the point had no barbs so as to better penetrate chainmail. The chap squelched a shout of pain and thanked her as she knotted a bandage over the wound.

As they again began moving, Isabel took another quick look around. By her count, five people still were missing, and Deirdre was among them. When she cast Armand a look, he answered before she spoke.

"Your friend and the huntsman were still moving when last I saw them. If they live, none knows the way better than that man. We'll meet them ahead."

She moved to protest, certain she'd seen the huntsman fall.

"Lady Isabel," the knight whispered, "we cannot help them if we are dead, and you are captured. We *must keep moving*."

The party soon again was on the trail, no longer running, but moving at a pace far faster than the walk they first had taken. The enemy had detected them, and others soon would come. That much was obvious.

They again kept to the woods. Sometimes she caught the sound of horses running in the distance, but in the dense spring woodlands, a horse was of no great utility. The animals simply weren't nimble enough there. Their first attackers had abandoned their mounts, if they rode them at all, and assaulted them on foot. No doubt the others would realize the usefulness of the tactic, but for now Isabel and her comrades continued to move with only the occasional shout or sound of enemy activity in the distance.

That didn't last. About 20 minutes after their last stop, they beheld a handful of riders burst through the tree line near an open field Armand's party was skirting to the west. The enemy did not at first detect their presence, but Armand and his men let loose a volley of arrows, and the hunt was on.

As they wended their way south over the next 30 minutes or so, the party drew fire from enemy archers on four different occasions. Each time, they returned shafts, and beat a deeper path into the woods. On one other occasion, Sir Bertrand, who then was in the lead, rounded a bend along a hilly patch of trail and saw a half dozen enemy fighters creeping away from them, as if readying an ambush. Bertrand and the men fell on the enemy unaware. It was a bloodbath.

Their party took injuries, most of them minor, and on the last exchange of shafts Sir Irwin Quarrels took an arrow through the neck and died of blood loss in mere moments. It was terrible.

And yet, the terrain seemed to work to their favor in more ways than one. The enemy appeared somewhat less than entirely organized, and Isabel was convinced more than once that an enemy patrol near them was lured off by the sound of their own comrades in the distance.

No question about it, Armand's party was having the Devil's own luck. Numerous times during their breakneck journey through the forest, members of the party became separated after clashes with enemy archers and riders. But each time they managed to stumble back and meet up later. Beyond the five who'd gone missing when they first encountered the enemy, they'd only lost one, Sir Irwin. It was good fortune.

It often was difficult for her to estimate time, but they'd been on the move for more than three hours when Sir Armand bade them stop near a thicket of trees. There was a crisp stream nearby, from which they all drank deeply and refilled their waterskins before their leader spoke to them.

"It's my guess that the stockade the skinners and drovers erected is near at hand," he said, pointing south toward what appeared to be a break in the trees. "We are but few now, but we have the Glaive and Lady Isabel to protect. We shall creep to the woods' edge and, if all is clear, we shall make a rush. The stockade is no more than a furlong or two distant."

"Through the open?" asked one of the soldiers.

"Aye, lad. These men from Etruscia have proved themselves poor archers. To hit us in the middle of the vale, they'll need to get close and expose themselves as well."

"And their mounts?" asked Bertrand.

"We've seen no more than five mounted men together at a time. With sword, hammer, and axe we'll meet them. And once we're in the open, our friends within the stockade will rally to our aid."

Isabel wasn't sure about that last part. She so far hadn't seen proof to her satisfaction that the drovers and skinners still held the stockade. The hired men may already have quit the place, and she and her friends might be racing for nowhere.

But she held her tongue. Not out of any piety, mind. She simply was too exhausted to speak. A furlong or more, 200 or 300 yards by her guesstimate. Well, as exhausted as she was, she'd always been a good runner. And she wore her best and lightest pair of boots. It was the stockade or nothing.

Sir Armand next led them in a short prayer for success, a prayer in which Isabel joined earnestly, after which they prepared to move.

40. Bedlam!

Sir Armand had just finished their prayer. That's when all hell broke loose.

When the battle cries of the enemy erupted, it was as if the enemy host already was upon them, and a great thunder of hooves threatened to trample them into Hell. It mattered not that the first of their mounted attackers were many yards away, something overwhelming swept through Isabel. A great and insurmountable fear it was. She could do nothing but run.

And run she did.

The sound of combat was everywhere around her, and soon she had no clue where she was or to where her comrades had gotten. And it simply didn't matter, not one bit. For all the fear she'd faced in this cruel land, this was the first time she felt thoroughly and properly unhinged with terror. Even her sudden flight at the battle near the grotto had not been true fear, just an overwhelming impulse to flee.

Now?

Now her fear so overcame her that she couldn't think to plan even her next few strides. She ran, fell. Ran, fell. And ran again. Branches, limbs, and thorns whipped at her body, cutting, tugging, and tripping her. She ran.

And as she ran, she fell to the ground more times than she could count. Pain and fatigue meant nothing. Fear and fear alone allowed her numb and shuddering body to rise from each tumble, to move forward when she had not an ounce of energy to give.

She'd never known such horror.

And she ran.

She had no idea how long she ran, but when her pace finally slackened, she knew she'd traveled many miles and had crossed over at least one stream. And when the fear at long last unclenched its icy grip from around her heart, she fell to the ground in utter exhaustion and did not rise.

Did she lose consciousness then?

That was a thing she couldn't decide. But she lay where she fell for some time. How long? She couldn't say.

At one point, as evening approached, she found the strength to pull herself into a thicket and hide beneath some leaves. The only proof that God loved her at that moment was that she hadn't lost her waterskin, and she drank deep and long.

Once she drank her fill, she remembered hearing hoofbeats and thinking that enemy patrols again sought her. But what was she to do? She knew not where she was, knew only that she was separated from her friends and surrounded by enemies. Fatigue, lingering fear, and despair at her situation left her unable to think or to consider what to do next. She was too overwhelmed even to move.

But move she must. Something in her understood that. Like a child too frightened to look from beneath a blanket at night, she finally won the courage to peer from beneath her leaves. It would be dark soon. Not a sound occurred to her ears but the chirping of birds, rustling of the wind, and a faint babbling of a distant brook. She might have been the only human on the planet.

It was now or never. She crawled, rose to a crouch, and tried to remember what she knew of woodcraft. It took her a time to determine what she thought to be south, and she began to walk. No, rather she limped. She'd banged up her knees and elbows more than proper when she'd fled.

Her body ached and trembled, and she traveled barely 50 yards before she again collapsed from exhaustion. Her protracted illness, the long journey to the fortress, her time in the caverns, their hurried escape through the forest, and her terrified flight from the enemy all ganged up on her. She was as weak as a mouse.

After she knew not how long, she rose again. This time she traveled barely 20 paces before succumbing to fatigue and despair. She lay panting and exhausted.

Should she cry out? Even if only their enemies came, would a distant prison be worse than dying in the woods? Consumed by some savage beast or by a band of wretched cannibals? She had not forgotten where she was. Things creeped in the night here.

But she refrained.

In time, she again lifted herself and was proud that she made it 30 stuttering steps before crumpling to the ground. She repeated this, one, two, three times more.

It was unlikely that she'd covered even a hundred yards by that point, and her stomach howled with discontent. She had not a bite to eat, and the water in her skin soon would be gone. Should she make for the stream?

Wait.

Hadn't she been moving toward the sound of water? There wasn't the faintest clue of it now. What direction had she been traveling? Which way was south again? By then, it was full dark, and it had begun to grow cold. What did it matter which direction she moved? Like as not she merely would wander in circles in the dark.

"Oh, Lord," she whispered, her voice scratchy and weak.

This time she was certain she lost consciousness. Or did she just fall asleep? It was difficult to say. As she drifted in and out of awareness, something in her mind tried to convince her that her fever was back. It certainly felt that way. She was losing the ability to think straight, and there was little she could do about it.

When next she roused herself, it still was dark, but the night had grown so terribly cold. It felt like the ground was sapping what little strength she had left, and her body was terribly stiff and numb. Panic again nearly seized her when it took five minutes of constant effort just to rise to a sitting position. When she at last sat up, her arms were so numb that they did little more than rest on her lap.

It was then she realized she wasn't alone.

Something was creeping toward her through the dark woods. To her surprise, she not only lacked the ability to scream in fear, but the inclination. She'd reached the end of her strength. At long last, she could do no more.

The looming figure that came for her in the dark would be doing her a favor to snuff her out at that moment. Nothing remained in her with which to fight or to flee. And her body was so numb with cold and fatigue that she wouldn't feel a thing.

"OK," she whispered, more to herself than to the creature stalking toward her. She was so, so terribly cold. Time to go.

Except the villain that descended upon her didn't plunge its fangs into her flesh. Instead, it pressed a wet and sticky muzzle against her neck and began licking. Her fatigue-addled mind took a moment to inform her that she wasn't being consumed alive, and this was no villain.

It was her friend, the Gelt.

———

Isabel warmed herself against the animal for a time.

At first, she couldn't even lift her half-frozen arms to embrace the shaggy brute, and after the animal lay beside her, it took her even more time to realize the creature was attempting to coax her into climbing aboard. She just needed to warm herself against him first, to get the circulation back into her extremities.

When at last she finally threw an arm and a leg over the creature, taking a handful of his withers as firmly as possible, she nearly slipped from his back when he came to an abrupt rise. It thereafter required some strenuous wiggles and pulls to bring herself fully onto the beast's bare back.

Once her squirming ceased, the Gelt began a slow amble into the darkness.

Where was the beast taking her? How had it found her in the dark? How had the animal emancipated itself from the skinners and known to come looking for her? Now that Isabel no longer felt alone, something of her wits returned to her. She still was so cold and so exhausted that she barely could move, but at last she could think and to plan for when her strength returned.

Her first realization was how silently the animal moved. It was something that hadn't dawned on her before, but the creature scarcely gave off a whisper as it passed through the forest. Even the sound of its hoofs on the ground were little more than a faint murmur.

When thoughts of the creature's sedate and gentle passage occurred to her, it raised another thought. Was it moving with such care out of mere instinct, or was it conscious of her weakened state?

Had she found an enchanted horse? Did such things exist on this world? She'd seen her first monster. Why not other things?

At any other time, such questions would have been nothing short of ludicrous to her. She simply didn't believe in magic, or she hadn't. Now, well ... she'd seen so much, and in her current condition she would have believed almost anything.

She decided at the moment she needed to give the animal a name. Such wasn't the custom in Albion. Animals almost never were humanized in that way. But this was special. She'd talk with Deirdre about what was appropriate.

Deirdre!

Where was her friend? It shamed her that she'd thought only of herself these last hours. But now another panic nearly took her in its teeth. She had so few people in this world, and Deirdre was her most precious. The idea that the youngster might have been harmed, or that she might be a captive of these scoundrels, filled her with fear and rage. That notion, if nothing else, stoked her body with warmth, and she was able for the first time to raise herself somewhat and to look around.

There was little or nothing to see. They still were deep in the woods, and hints of light filtered in through the leaves from the moon and stars above. If her guess was correct, they were moving downhill, even if only slightly. That information told her little. People traveling in the woods tended to follow the course of least resistance, whether they meant to or not, and often that course would lead them gently downward. It was one of the first lessons she'd learned of land navigation.

This seemed more deliberate. Was the beast taking her to the stockade? It was possible. There was no guessing how far she'd run that afternoon, and she could have ended up anywhere. Was safety now down the valley, or up it?

The faintest of sounds caught her attention. Was that a human voice? She perked her ears and listened. At about the same time the chime of human voices became clear, the barest hint of a campfire came into view in the woods ahead. It was but a smudge of light, but even at a distance, it was enough to show her that the Gelt travelled along a narrow game trail, a mere trace in the woods that headed directly toward the campfire.

An impulse told her not to call out. It wasn't possible to make out the voices. The people might be friends. But even though her mount moved toward the tiny camp, it just didn't seem right.

Then the animal began to trot.

By the time she could make out the men around the fire, enemy soldiers each and every one, the Gelt had picked up his pace to a canter, and when the creature emerged from the darkness, it took the men totally by surprise. Her steed brushed the first two aside as if they weren't even there, after which it hopped the fire in a single graceful bound and went straight for where the men had picketed their horses on the other side of camp.

Isabel, who had taken a careful grip on her mount, was astounded by what came next. The Gelt threw itself into the picketed horses, biting the nearest one so hard that the entire string panicked and stampeded into the dark. Her mount made one more graceful hop, probably over a stray picket cord, and dashed off into the night.

Isabel held on for dear life.

It must have been a terrible surprise to the men at the fire, because it was some moments more before the shouting began. Soon, hollers and shouts of warning and anger echoed throughout the woods. Her enemies were all about her.

The Gelt broke into its fastest gallop. The creature's gait was smooth and easy, and it was as surefooted as a mountain goat, even in the dark of night. But for all her time astride a horse of late, Isabel was not a gifted rider, and she now was riding bareback, thoroughly and completely exhausted. It was all she could do to stay mounted as the Gelt led her on a helter-skelter chase through the dark mountain forest around them.

The sound of arrows hissed through the air, and once the steed veered so sharply to avoid something in the trail that it nearly unhorsed her. Soon, however, the weaving and dodging stopped, just in time for the true challenge to begin.

She sensed rather than saw riders behind them, and after nearly 10 minutes of grueling riding, the Gelt put on a burst of speed unlike any she so far had experienced. It was smooth, clean, effortless running for the animal, but the creature's heavily muscled frame arched and twisted with each gallop, and Isabel's grip on the racing mount loosened as her strength faded.

Unable to hold on any longer, she lost her grasp and toppled from her mount.

41. Nigh on Defenseless

Deirdre was the first person to Isabel's side when the foreign beauty slipped unconscious from her mount. It was a miracle, a true miracle of the angels, that the young woman again was among them. How had the Gelt escaped and found her? And how had the two of them managed to elude their pursuers and gain the safety of the stockade in the dark of night?

A great many well-wishers came to help at news of the young woman's return. Foremost among them was a grateful and teary-eyed Armand. As the knight and some men helped her carry Isabel to her tent, Deirdre faulted herself yet again for having lost touch with the woman.

When first they'd come under attack early that day, she sneaked off with the creature when the others bolted south. It was easy enough to do, the attack was total confusion. Nearly half of the party scattered to the wind among the trees, and afterward the bulk reformed under Sir Armand's leadership.

She and the creature spent the rest of the day shadowing the group still led by Armand as it wended its way through the forest. The large knight was a canny leader, and the party enjoyed good fortune and made great time toward the stockade. But on more than one occasion the Fiend intervened secretly and directly on their behalf, and on several occasions, Deirdre helped the monster steer enemy patrols in the opposite direction.

It all was organized chaos, of course. The recent trip the creature had made into the countryside as the huntsman was spent assessing the location of enemy patrols, as well as their numbers and equipment. With the help of the Fiend's considerable cunning, and just a hint of magic, he'd arranged things so that the party could win its way through to the stockade with minimal loss of life.

She and the creature even had time to loaf around during the day, stopping to pick berries and dallying to investigate some fallen logs, where they recovered some mushrooms that the Fiend assured her had remarkable qualities.

It wasn't a bad day, not bad at all. Until, that is, they reached the stockade not long after Sir Armand and his men had fought their way through and realized that they'd lost track of Isabel.

Deckard, the poor wretch. By that point, the soldier thought he'd lost both of his charges and very nearly crushed Deirdre in his embrace when she and the huntsman arrived looking worn and exhausted. (They were neither.)

All Deirdre could think about was Isabel, and after a short and heated discussion with Sir Armand, it was decided that a large search party would be purest folly. Mr. Spears and Mr. Deckard set out straight away in search of the woman. Deirdre practically had to order the huge knight to stay at the stockade, the only cross words she'd had with the man.

Only to have Isabel turn up in the middle of the night, pursued hot and heavy by their enemies, astride that ugly little horse of hers.

It was nothing short of a miracle, and Deirdre never looked a gift miracle in the mouth, especially one who had just saved the life of her dearest friend. It would be apples and carrots on demand for the rest of the Gelt's life.

Isabel was a mess, with cuts and scrapes along nearly every inch of her body. Her knees and elbows were heavily bruised and skinned, but there didn't appear to be anything even dimly life threatening. With her most tender hand, Deirdre changed the unconscious woman from her traveling clothes, cleaned up her scrapes and cuts, and left her to sleep.

A bloody miracle.

Her enormous sense of relief aside, Deirdre had other things about which she needed to worry. The enemy had been clever enough to feign interest in searching the forest near the fortress, but instead had raced most of its fighters to guard the area nearest the stockade at the first sign of Armand's party.

And there had been magics. According to the men with Armand, a great cacophony of noise, light, and … something else. The men were vague on what, the phenomenon had so unsettled them. But of the 15 or so people who had departed the fortress caves, only 10 made it through to the stockade. Isabel now was 11.

An absolute miracle. Deirdre's feeling of relief knew no bounds.

She decided she would let the Fiend deal with their enemies, especially with the sorcerer among them. The creature already was angry enough to burst because he again had been fooled, first that the enemy so swiftly had withdrawn and reformed their troops from the fortress, and second that the creature was lulled into a trap earlier that day, one that nearly had cost them sweet Isabel. When the creature got its fangs into the poor foreign magicker, it would be all the chap's life was worth.

No, Deirdre was far more worried about the skinners and the other tradesfolk.

When Armand and his team had returned from the caverns with little more than their weapons and chainmail, the tradesmen had been beside themselves. They'd said not a word, all smiles and gladhands, but the eyes of each and every one of them told stories. The tradesmen had been at the stockade for nearly a week, waiting and watching, enduring fear and threat from local wildlife and, more recently, from the soldiers of Etruscia, for what?

They expected treasure, mountains of treasure, riches beyond the dreams of avarice. Those were the stories they'd been telling one another for weeks, the frenzy that they'd stoked in one another even more in recent days. Now all they had was the Glaive, one slim and shiny blade. The story the Fiend had told her of parties tearing one another apart over ownership of the object of their quest now seemed far more believable.

Armand and Bertrand were the only remaining knights, and there were barely a handful of men-at-arms. All were worn from their recent trials. The tradesmen numbered more than 50, and, though not soldiers, they had proven themselves bold and tough. And they were rested.

The two groups certainly had needed one another to survive before, but what of the loyalty of the hired men now? Isabel had delivered no great treasure. Although she had never claimed that she would do so, what matter that today? A few bags of gold might buy the workers, and Etruscia was famous for the depths of its pockets when the clerics there wanted something.

What to do? What to do?

As night moved inexorably toward dawn, it was unlikely anyone would reach decisions about treason while still abed. Aside from the guards, only Armand was awake, mending his armor. Deckard and the creature still were away, and she was glad her and Isabel's tent was near those of the soldiers. It seemed safe to grab a few winks of sleep. She needn't worry about oversleeping. She seldom did.

———

She was up at first light, after barely having closed her eyes. The camp was awake, and there was the smell of food in the air. Deirdre very much wanted something of the bacon that she sensed, but the sound of men's voices, not raised in anger, but somewhat close to that, could be heard nearby. One of the men was Armand.

She checked on a still sleeping Isabel, pulled on her boots, and stepped outside the tent. A quick look around told her the creature had not returned.

As an afterthought, she recovered something from her pack and went in search of the voices.

Before she even reached the canopy that the tradesmen had established as their common area, the same old and tired refrains were clearly discernable above the normal noises of camp. The contract. It always was the contract with these men, and the fact that the tradesman had been required to engage in activity and to provide services not called for in the contract. For this, they expected compensation, and heavy compensation.

In the presence of the harridan, Mr. Granger, the new leader of the skinners, had been a meek and retiring man. At the moment Deirdre reached the meeting place, that man was pounding the makeshift table in front of him with a boney hand, demanding what he termed "fair compensation."

Deirdre listened a time more. There were, in total, about 30 other people present. Included were Mr. Granger and several other leaders of the skinners and drovers, a number of the rank and file, and Sir Armand and a few of his soldiers. Things did not appear to be going well.

Sir Armand nodded his understanding, a patient, but somewhat distracted, look on his face. Did the knight understand the potential peril they faced? Not all of the workers had joined them at Musette, and some were tied to Armand and the other knights by bonds of service and fealty. But how many of those servants would remain loyal now that their masters were dead?

She had no reason to believe that the men from Etruscia had approached the tradesman before Armand and the others returned from the fortress, but it would be foolish to dismiss the notion. The men of the Holy See had a reputation for duplicity and ruthlessness. Deirdre had seen that herself. Were these tradesmen already bought? Were they merely seeking from Armand a better offer without tipping their hands that they were?

Armand's only counter position was that there was no treasure. There never was a treasure. They'd come for the Glaive, a sacred and powerful weapon against evil, and they now had it. Was that not enough?

Without considering a moment longer, Deirdre stepped through the crowd, walked up to the makeshift table, and placed the purse containing her 100 gold marks on it. She didn't exactly throw the thing, but she let it drop from a height sufficient that the sound of its great weight resounded throughout the tent. As an afterthought, she pulled out her smaller purse, which contained the silver and copper that Sir Alexis had given her for expenses, and placed it alongside.

"There is no treasure," she said to the men in the kindest and most generous tone she could muster. "But your courage and loyalty will not go without reward."

"What's this, then, young miss?" asked Granger. The man didn't touch the leather purse before him, but it was clear his hands very much wanted to do so.

"My inheritance," she lied, "the legacy from my parents and their parents before them. A dowry meant to find me a well-born husband." With a single hand, she undid the purse and spilled the 100 large gold discs onto the table for all to see. "My entire fortune down to the last farthing."

The men were silent, and she gave her words a moment to sink in. This handsome pile of cash was not the vast mountain of coins of which the men had dreamed. But though a land rich in fields and farms, Albion was a country poor in coin. Most men didn't see a small handful of silver in a year, and some went an entire lifetime without seeing gold, not even the paltry gold coins the crown minted.

"Sir Armand is correct," she said. "There is no treasure. I give this to you all, to divide among you as you see fit, based on station and service, *not* as compensation, but as a gift from me to you, for your friendship and your loyalty. And I'll not take no for an answer."

It was an enormous amount of money. No one was more aware of that than a Surrey farmgirl. But ... Deirdre had a friend who could conjure the stuff from nothing. It stung a little to part with her coins, and she hoped that fact showed. She wasn't a good actress.

And the whole scheme seemed to work. Mr. Granger was struck mute, Armand rose as if the entire episode now was closed, and the assembled skinners and drovers doffed their caps and nodded their gratitude, looks of surprise and admiration on their faces. Several of the men paused to thank her in hushed tones. Even one such heavy gold mark could purchase a fair plot of good bottomland or buy an apprenticeship for one or more sons or daughters.

She felt as if she'd done something right, but soon excused herself to look after Isabel and to fetch something to eat. She hoped very much that her act of altruism put to rest any notions of changing sides for the tradesmen. Time would tell on that.

When some moments later, she returned to the tent, it was to see Mr. Spears standing before it with the tent flap open, staring within. It took her a dozen heartbeats to realize how grotesquely inappropriate that was. The real huntsman never would show such cheek, no hired man would, and the creature knew that.

When she reached him, it was to express a loud, "Oy!" in protest.

To her great astonishment, the creature turned, a blank and startled look on his face. The Fiend never broke character this way in public. Not ever. It took her a moment to realize his misstep was a pure and unplanned reaction to finding their friend alive.

"We have Isabel back, now," she told the faux huntsman when it appeared he'd composed himself. As an afterthought, she gave him a stern, "Steady on!"

"I apologize, young miss," said the creature in a voice loud enough for anyone nearby to hear. "I overstepped my mark."

"It's quite alright, Mr. Spears," she said in the same tone. "It's been a trying few days for us all."

"I really had thought I'd lost that child," the creature said in a voice just loud enough for Deirdre to hear. He cleared his throat. "Did a few things in reply I should not."

"Such as?"

"I'll tell you later. That's bacon I smell. Have you eaten?"

"Let me look in on Isabel."

When Deirdre reemerged from the tent a few moments later, she took a look around. "Where's Deckard?"

"He'll not be joining us."

"Not for breakfast...?" The bodyguard never dined with them. Then she noticed a peculiar look on the creature's face, not quite smug, but.... "*Did you eat him*?!" she whispered.

They'd begun strolling toward the main cooking fire by that point, and the creature tarried just a moment to reply. They now were well out of earshot, in the middle of the broad wooden stockade.

"In my defense, Tuppence, I don't often lose my temper."

"What did he say to anger you?"

"Nothing at all. He and I were on what seemed a promising trail, looking for Isabel. When that trace suddenly petered out, it was the bad fortune of an enemy squad that they crossed our paths, the poor bastards."

"Ah, the enemy killed him!"

"No."

"Argh … then what?"

"As I said, it was a moment of anger, and Deckard saw a side of me he should not."

"Oh! … Then you ate him?"

"Tuppence, men such as Deckard exist to be used and discarded when no longer necessary. I hadn't realized...."

"I'm not being sentimental," she insisted. "We still needed his sword."

"Yes, well. Our enemies are eight men the fewer after that particular fight. It was a fair trade."

"I'm more worried about the tradesmen at the moment. And, yes, I know you warned me about this."

"Angry about the lack of treasure, are they?"

She explained in brief words about the events of just that morning. "I think I bought us a reprieve, but I can't promise it will hold."

"It was very smart of you," said the Fiend. As always, he'd seemed to weigh her words carefully as she spoke. "Trust is a funny thing. I think your generosity may have a more profound effect than you imagine. It sounds very much like your act of selflessness won the trust of these men rather than purchased it."

"I hope so." The two already had spoken in hushed tones rather longer than they should have. She needed to hear the answer to one last question. "When will these foreign scoundrels come for us?"

"Soon," said the creature. "Their men are fewer than they were, and there is just as much discontent in their camp as in ours. If they don't move now, they may not be able." He pointed to the cook fire. "You have your breakfast. I need to speak with Armand."

The smell of fresh bread and bacon would not allow her to protest.

42. Into the Breach

The enemy no longer sought to conceal themselves. It was the first and most obvious sign that a fight was near at hand when a party of riders entered the northern edge of the vale upon which the stockade was situated and began to establish their own camp.

Over the course of the morning, and well into the afternoon, more people arrived. Horses were picketed, a number of tents were raised, and the enemy sent mounted patrols here and yon, but no attempt was made to build any sort of stockade or fortifications.

Were these foreign clerics that confident?

In between trips to check on Isabel, Deirdre spent most of her time at a small platform on the wall with Sir Armand. The Fiend had pronounced the knight to be a man with a keen eye for such things, and Armand spent the day watching and keeping tally on enemy activities.

"There aren't so many of them as they'd want us to believe," the knight said after a time.

"How so?" she asked.

"Well, milady, like us, they have a fair number of workers and tradesmen with them, men hired in Albion I should imagine. Whoever commands over there wants us to think some of their workers are actually soldiers."

"How do you know that they're not?"

"Those men over there." He pointed to a group of 20 or so men farthest west, all of whom were in the livery and armor of soldiers of the Holy See. "At least half aren't Etruscian."

She peered closer and realized the knight's observation made sense. No doubt all of the real fighters were from Etruscia, but half of the men in the party in question had the look of northern Surrey. Interesting.

"And look at their horsemen," said the knight.

"What of them?"

"Why, young miss, they've been running mounted patrols hither and thither since mid-morning. But to what purpose?"

She took some moments more to watch the nearest body of riders, and then another. Nothing occurred to her. These men all looked of a kind, dark hair, of middling height, and clean shaven. They appeared to be from a foreign land, cut from the same mold as those soldiers of Etruscia she'd first encountered at Westport.

"I don't understand," she said after a time more.

"The riders don't appear to be doing anything," said the knight, "except riding around in circles."

"Ah," she said. "To better hide their numbers." Deirdre was duly impressed. She'd come very much to like Armand, but never thought of him as having a keen mind. Generally, he had the reputation of being a great fellow with whom to drink and to ride to hounds. The man was no type of scholar, true enough, but he had a perceptive eye for military affairs. "How many do you think they are?"

"These folks don't have knights, not in the sense that we do in Albion or in Ghitland. But I'd say they have fewer than 20 mounted fighters. They hope to convince us they have twice that many. It's unlikely their foot soldiers number more than that. More likely, they have 12 or 15 men-at-arms, and only those few will be armed with bows."

"And not their horsemen?"

"No, young miss. In most parts of the world, a bow is considered an uncultured weapon. A true gentleman would never use one. And though these men be not knights, they certainly fancy themselves genteel."

"Pshaw!" she said with a smile. "Every knight in Albion uses a bow."

"That's the influence of your folk on we Ghect. The Surrey of this land long have been famous archers. Nowadays, every knight in Albion knows lance, sword, and bow. Even some few knights in Ghitland have taken up the weapon."

"But not Etruscia?"

"The grandees there see it as a weapon fit only for peasants."

"So we face 20 fighters and perhaps a dozen or more archers?"

"Indeed."

"But they have tradesmen as well. Won't they fight?"

"It's unlikely, Lady Deirdre. The tradesmen with us have fought alongside us because we are a single people."

"And because their lives depended on it."

"Indeed."

"Sir Armand, do you think we can trust the tradesmen?"

The nobleman didn't answer straightaway, as if pondering the question. "I think they have no love for me. But each and every one would fight and die for you and Lady Isabel. It was a kind and selfless thing you did this morning. Your generosity took me aback."

Her gift to the men cost her nothing, so it wasn't so generous as all that, but she found herself looking away, so the enormous knight wouldn't see her blush.

"When will they attack?" she asked.

"We'll find out soon enough."

"I can't be that patient."

"You'll not have long to wait, milady." The man made a gesture with is head. "Here they come now."

It wasn't the whole lot of them, thankfully. From the direction of the enemy camp, a pair of horsemen made their leisurely way toward the stockade. She'd come to find that parlay before combat was a perfectly normal part of warfare among the Gheet. It hadn't dawned on her that the men of the Holy See might seek the same accommodation.

The enemy camp was not far, only a hundred or so paces out of bow range, and the riders, one man armored and the other in clerical robes, reached the wall in no time at all. The clergyman, an older fellow, had been among those present at Westport and, later, at Mont Clair. She knew not his name, only that he seemed to be a fellow of some importance among them.

Neither man, it seemed, spoke the common tongue—or they pretended not to. After several failed attempts to communicate with the men, Armand called for Sir Bertrand to escort the men and informed her of what would happen next.

"These men are to be hostages, it seems."

"I don't understand." Deirdre had not seen parlay conducted in this way. Men usually met at a midpoint between the warring parties and made their various demands and threats, but only after certain cordialities were observed. There always was a certain surface civility among the Gheet. Even prisoners of war often were treated like guests, at least among the gentry. "This doesn't sound right."

"Don't fret, young miss. I've seen this type of affair before. These two will stay here, while I and one other proceed to the camp yonder to parlay. Such doings are common among folks on the Southern Sea."

It was only as the knight ordered the stockade gate opened that Deirdre first realized that neither of the two arrivals carried weapons beyond a dagger. It was a queer way of doing business.

"Who will you take with you?" she asked.

"Certainly not Lady Isabel."

"Do you fear treachery?"

"I trust none of those people farther than I can throw them," said Armand. "I'll not lay temptation before them."

"Who then?"

The knight again made a face as if in thought. It dawned on Deirdre that their leader couldn't afford to risk losing another fighting man, and she wasn't convinced he totally trusted any of the tradesmen to be at his side. The huntsman? Taking the creature along might be bad. This foreign magicker already had proven he could force the creature to reveal his true form. But would that be so bad? The creature running amok in the enemy camp?

No, definitely not a grand idea, at least not in broad daylight. And if this magicker were present, which he no doubt would be, the Fiend already had admitted that those same powerful magics could render him helpless. No, there had to be someone else. She toyed with the idea of just running away, grabbing Isabel and the creature, and bolting for the hills. But they'd only be pursued.

Better to get this done with. The stockade was well supplied, and Armand had convinced her that their party had a better than fair chance of beating these foreign soldiers. Even more, the Fiend had taught her enough about magic to know that most magickers posed little threat without soldiers to back their play. Let them bring on their fight.

No, even better.

"Sir Armand," she said, "you should take Lady Isabel along with you."

———

The faux huntsman spent some time helping Deirdre saddle and calm the Gelt, so they had a good reason to spend time chatting before she departed with Armand. It wasn't exactly an argument, but the creature needed some convincing on the importance of Deirdre's plan, even more than had the knight.

"I know I don't look like Lady Isabel," she said. The lass already had changed into some of her friend's clothing. "But as you often have told me, the eye sees what it expects to see. Their spies will have told them no one rides the Gelt but Isabel. In this dress and with my hair up, they might for a moment think I'm her."

"Child, that's exactly what I fear."

"They don't want Isabel dead. They could have done that at any time."

"True, but if they feel they've been fooled ... Deirdre, these are not forgiving people."

"I understand. My life has been nothing but danger this last year. I assumed the risk when I first traveled with you. But it's you who forever are telling me to strike my own path, to be my own person."

"That doesn't mean you have to...."

"The custom is hostage for hostage, and Armand shouldn't risk another fighting man. And the tradesmen...."

"I could go," said the creature.

"And the moment they force you into your true form, you'll have to gobble them all up ...."

The Fiend gave one of his undignified chuckles. "Undeniably."

"... and then you'll have to gobble up all the witnesses, including a number of people of whom we're fond."

"Ah, true," the creature confessed. "And you imagine that if Isabel shows up in their camp, they might try the same magic again? Doesn't that seem unlikely, when it failed to produce any effect on her the first time?"

"You wrenched the head from the man who tried it before. And no one else, including people standing right next to Chastity, noticed who genuinely changed that day."

"Perhaps."

"I know a proof more convincing," she said. "These scoundrels wouldn't still be here, if Isabel weren't the person who they sought. Besides, what's the worst that can happen? They cast one of those spells on me and it doesn't work. As you told me, it's harmless to humans, but as you also told me, it's a complex and difficult thing to craft. If they use it on me, what are the chances they have another ready at hand to later use on you?"

The faux huntsman smiled and adjusted the Gelt's halter. "You are very clever, Tuppence. I say it often, but not half often enough."

"Good. The whole idea of this guise is to get them to say or do something they shouldn't, at least to tip their hand in some way. I'm sick of not knowing what their intentions are and why they're here. If nothing else, I can keep my eyes open and let you know what I see there."

The creature nodded. "How'd you get Armand to go along with this?"

"No deep thinker, that one. I told him the truth ... or part of it. If they thought they had Lady Isabel, they might let down their guard for a moment. Are we ready to go?"

"You're not going anywhere just yet."

The creature waved its hand near her several times, as if he might be shooing away a fly, and a powerful tingling raced through her body. The sensation was not unlike when he'd magicked on her at Mont Clair, but stronger.

"That should protect you against most lesser magics they're liable to try on you. It's a minor cant. They won't be able to detect it on you."

She found her eyes straying toward the tent into which they'd placed their two hostages.

"Yes, the oaf in the robes probably heard me do that just now. That doesn't matter much. I convinced Bertrand to bind, gag, and blindfold both of the hostages when they got here."

"They're spies?"

"Of course, they're spies, child. Everything they see and hear is known to their master over yonder." The creature raised his hand again but paused. "I could do the same for you ... if you don't mind."

"What?" She hesitated a moment, uncertain if she wanted anything more of magics. "See what I see?"

"And hear what you hear."

She thought a moment more.

"Don't worry, Tuppence. It wears off in a short time."

"But until then, you can see and hear what I do?"

"Aye, as you see it and hear it."

She gave a short nod, and the ersatz huntsman made as if to wave away another pesky fly. The sensation that passed through her was different. For but a moment, she needed to blink away something, and a slight note rung in her ears. Then it was as if nothing had transpired.

On an impulse, she turned away from the creature and looked down at her right hand.

"Four," he said before she could ask him to name the number of fingers she held up.

"Oy. I'm not sure what I think of this."

"It'll wear off in no time. Until then, I'll know if you're in any danger."

They already had spent more time preparing the little horse than they needed, so they moved with the animal to the gate where Armand and Bertrand awaited them. There was nothing else left to say or do. Except one.

"Mr. Spears," she said when they reached the knights, "you have my permission to look in on Lady Isabel in my absence."

The faux huntsman knuckled his forehead. "I'll care for her like she's my own, young miss."

With that, she mounted the little animal, who to her delight felt not the least skittish under her, and she and the great knight headed for their meeting.

———

Of course, the butterflies in her stomach had butterflies. They were off to meet with villainous clerics and a wicked sorcerer, one so clever as several times to have humbugged the Fiend himself. But what was that to be afraid of?

As leisurely as they traveled, it was a short ride. Halfway there, a pair of armored horsemen road out, circled, and fell in behind them. Neither of the men were armed. Nor was Sir Armand for that matter, but he was a great heaving bulk of muscle compared to these men.

It was unlikely their new hosts would treat them roughly, but Bertrand had bound and gagged their counterparts. Might that irk the clerics who awaited them? Yes, probably. Her limited experience with the men of the Holy See was that they were arrogant and sneering, but they weren't fools.

They wanted something, and at the moment they might believe that they had it. Deirdre wore one of Isabel's traveling dresses, had her telltale red hair tucked up in a scarf, and a veil around her face. Women of Albion seldom wore veils as part of their daily attire, but such an article was common for women on the road, to keep off sun, dust, and unwanted eyes. She wasn't quite so tall as Isabel, but who would notice on horseback?

She watched everything, and she watched it with all the care and concentration she could assemble. Any little bit might be important, and even if there was something that she didn't recognize as being worthy of note, the Fiend might. She didn't want the creature missing something crucial because she hadn't troubled to look around.

Oh, that whole notion gave her the shivers. To be magicked upon, curious though she might be about such things, sent an unpleasant something through her. It wasn't what normal people did.

By the time they reached the edge of the enemy camp, it was clear a welcoming committee awaited them near a large central pavilion. It wasn't an enormous tent, but it was large enough to fit a dozen or more people comfortably.

Near the main opening to the tent stood four people, clerics all by the look of them. There was no sign of the cleric who'd come to visit them on the other side of the mountain, Massimo something or other. At the middle of the group was another of the men she recognized from Mont Clair, a wizened old toad by the name of...? Oh, what was that prune's name? ... Brother Hasenpfeffer, or something equally ridiculous.

"Well met," called out Armand when at last they reined their horses before the ecclesiastics.

"Yes," said the prune after an uneasy silence. The man made no invitation for them to dismount, offered not the least cordiality. Instead, he locked his gaze on Deirdre and looked at her in silence.

It dawned on her that everyone in camp either was looking at her or was trying far too hard not to do so. So much did this realization startle her that she realized that, without her having intended it, she already had stopped observing her surroundings. Such a thing was unlike her. She always strove to do what she set out to do. In compensation, she began to regard those around her with care, first the old prune and then those nearest him, noting every detail that seemed important.

But there was something terribly awkward about that moment. It had only been a scant few breaths since they'd stopped, but no one was saying anything. Even Armand. ... She stole a glance at the knight. He looked perfectly normal. But he just sat there complacent, uttering not a word.

Her eyes shot back to the clerics.

Was she mistaken, or...? She looked more closely and realized she was wrong about their number. There were five, and not all of the clerics were men. In the rear of the party stood a woman, short and slim in a grey cloak, and at that moment the woman in grey was the only one speaking. Deirdre couldn't make out the woman's words, but she appeared to be whispering to the men in front of her.

No. It wasn't that.

The woman simply was whispering, but to no one in particular. And her hands were making lively motions, the type that some people made while explaining something to a friend.

No!

The woman was casting some sort of spell!

But what kind exactly?

Deirdre looked around, so as to weigh what transpired about her. Nothing. People seemed perfectly normal save that they weren't speaking, or really doing anything. In those fleeting moments, Deirdre glanced back at the woman in grey several times. Each time, it was a challenge to find the woman again with her eyes, as if the woman had moved from the spot where she stood.

Except the female magicker, for she clearly was a sorcerer, hadn't moved at all, not a single span, not a touch. And then the woman stopped whispering.

It was as if the entire camp took a collective breath. The whole episode lasted scarcely a score of heartbeats. Afterward, people moved about, snatches of conversation erupted in the distance, and the prune began to speak.

"I see you've decided to surrender the prisoner," he said to Armand.

"No such thing. Be a good chap and quit this place. Trouble us more, and I'll be forced to shove something long and sharp up your elderly arse."

The prune moved as if to speak, but Deirdre, who allowed her gaze to slip from the thin woman, spoke first.

"What do you want from us?" she asked in a voice that was her nearest try at mimicking Lady Isabel's exquisite accent.

The prune's face clouded even more than it had at Armand's casual threat. The skinny old wreck looked as if he might bark some obscenity at her, but then seemed uncertain whether to reply to her or to the knight. The wrinkly old clergyman stood a faint moment with his mouth open.

Clearly, he wasn't accustomed to being spoken to thus, certainly not by a woman. Nor did he seem habituated to being in command. No doubt the Fiend had gotten his hooks into the man's predecessor. Woe unto them both.

"Do you need victuals?" asked Armand.

"Wh ... what?" the prune stammered.

"Do you need victuals?" the knight enunciated, "for your return trip. We're well provisioned. We can give you what we're able. I then suggest you return the way you came, and we'll depart another. No hard feelings. Best of wishes to all of you."

It was astounding. Sir Alexis several times had referred to Armand as an "insufferable peacemaker." It showed now. Even the knight's threats were couched in the friendliest of banter.

"'Twould be a shame to bury you all here, so far from your homes," the knight added. Butter wouldn't melt in the nobleman's mouth.

The outraged and trembling cleric waved a hand in Deirdre's direction and barked a command in his own tongue.

Deirdre guessed what it was the man had ordered and gave the Gelt a faint kick, causing the beast to lurch toward the group of clerics. The horse's motion wasn't an aggressive move, wasn't even all that sudden, but the youngest of the clerics reacted by yanking something from his robe and hurling it at Deirdre. The thing, which looked very much like the glass vial another cleric had hurled at Isabel a week before, shattered impotently on the ground to her right.

She looked at the thing and then looked at the young cleric. So far, none of the men-at-arms had hastened to seize her. They no doubt were afraid, deeply afraid of something. It showed in the eyes of some.

"That was bloody rude," she called to the young cleric. She pulled the scarf and veil from her head, revealing her thick red locks.

"Totally uncalled for," barked Armand, whose mount apparently had inched forward to come alongside her own.

They still were some five long paces from the clergy folk. Deirdre steadied her eyes and again searched for the woman who was standing not six paces in front of her. When her eyes again found the woman in grey, Deirdre was surprised to see that the woman was beaming. The magicker wasn't a pretty woman, but she had a beautiful smile, one that seemed at that moment chagrined and perhaps a hint of something else.

Deirdre took a long and careful look around her, pivoting in her saddle as she did. Sir Armand was scolding the prune and enquiring whether there might be someone younger with whom he could speak, but she paid that bit no mind. She was not the least interested in what the old man had to say in response. They'd come to the enemy camp, and she'd learned something important.

The lesson wasn't about magic or even duplicity. It was about fear. How perfectly obvious. This magicker, this woman, this sorcerer, no doubt could do wonderous things, could produce powerful and subtle castings. But those castings, those magics, weren't half so frightening as the prospect of being eaten alive. The soldiers of the Holy See were brave men, but the Fiend these past weeks had been slipping off most every night, gobbling them up one and two at a time.

No one wants to die, especially such a heinous death.

How close were these people to fleeing? How long before the clerics no longer could command their obedience? Was it just a matter of offering their tradesmen some coin, as Deirdre had feared the clergymen had offered their own workers and servants?

She knew one thing for certain. Despite not knowing the language of Etruscia, she knew the prune had ordered his soldiers to seize her. And not a single soldier had stepped forward to take her in hand. These terrified people were ready to break and run.

The yammering went on for some time longer, so long, in fact, that it was hard to pay attention, but Deirdre did her absolute best to mark every event and to make careful observation of all around her. She did this until the prune started shouting in his own incomprehensible language at Armand.

It was then that something caught Deirdre's eye. No, someone. Toward the back of the crowd, head down among some of the soldiers was a familiar figure. It was the very same cleric who, even at that moment, was bound and gagged in a tent back at the stockade. The fellow yonder could be only one creature.

An impulse struck her like a bolt from above. This wasn't a large camp, and the Surrey tradesmen employed by the Holy See were billeted in tents near at hand. Many, in fact, were milling about not too far away, watching what transpired at the pavilion. She stood in the stirrups and raised her voice as loud as she was able. In her native tongue, the only language she properly knew, she called out toward where the tradesmen were gathered.

"Five days food and three silver sovereigns for any man who quits this place and returns home today!" she shouted toward the Surrey men. "Five silver sovereigns and all the plunder you can carry for any man who joins us in the fight against these foreign swine!"

It was then that the gates of Perdition flew open.

43. The Battle of the Five Sovereigns

Powerful hands dragged her from her mount. Deirdre fought, kicked, and screamed to buy her freedom, until she realized the hands that had unhorsed her and dragged her across the front of a saddle were those of Sir Armand.

"Young miss!" the disgruntled knight growled around the reins in his teeth.

With one hand and the opposite foot, the soldier kicked and punched at those who meant them harm. Soon the knight's courser was bounding toward the nearest trees, some 50 paces away. Around them, she realized most of the enemy were dodging and ducking for cover as a lethal stream of arrows hissed into the camp. From somewhere, hidden archers assaulted the assembly.

This could only be the doing of the Fiend. What other mind would ponder violating the sanctity of a truce to launch a hidden attack? What promises and threats, what lies and blackmail, had the creature made Sir Bertrand to get the man to go along with this?

In a nonce, Armand's mount reached the trees, Deirdre found herself unceremoniously dumped on the turf, and the knight bellowed a defiant, "Show them no quarter!" before wheeling his mount around to charge.

It was a motley crew that stormed out of the underbrush, soldiers, servants, and tradesman, about 30 in all. Happily, nearly every man in Albion knew his way around a bow, and as the group rushed forward each would take a short pause to loose an arrow they'd knocked on the run.

Deirdre rose and charged after them. Finally able to yank the dagger from beneath her cloak, she rushed forward with a battle cry on her lips. It was time to put an end to this nonsense.

If Armand was correct, the enemy had fewer than 40 men left. True, those were fighters all, but it dawned on Deirdre that not all had been present when she and Armand arrived to make parlay. The enemy had continued to run mounted soldiers on their meaningless patrols, so fewer than 30 enemy soldiers were present to defend the camp.

By the time she reached the first tents moments later, the fighting was hot and heavy, and she'd been forced to cut away part of Isabel's dress to allow her to move. It took her scant seconds to take in the scene. Armand had snatched up an enemy spear, and most of their fighters had abandoned their bows for swords, cudgels, and axes. The enemy was making a great show of defending themselves, even when it appeared that many of their own tradesmen had taken Deirdre at her word and had entered the fight against them.

Before she could even think to join the fight herself, something tugged at her, something she never before had experienced. The thing was different, but somehow the same as the sensation she had experienced at the stockade with the Fiend and, later, when the magicker had whispered near the pavilion.

For a moment, a faint dread afflicted her and then passed. But at that same moment several men in their party dropped their weapons and ran.

It was magic.

With all the will she could muster, her eyes began to search the area nearest the pavilion. It took some moments, but she discerned the slim woman in grey standing a dozen paces outside the pavilion. As before, it took all her effort to keep her eyes locked on the woman. The Surrey lass wasn't going to let her go.

Deirdre knew little of war, but she knew panic was a death knell for an army. She would not allow that to happen today. No one stood between her and the enemy sorcerer, so she ran toward the woman at a sprint.

There was no plan to speak of beyond speed. The Fiend had taught her much of fighting. Attack first, attack without warning, and attack to kill. And she also knew something important about magic, a tiny and crucial element. The casting and conjuration of Source magic required great mental concentration. Marking where the woman stood in the path, Deirdre looked down, snatched up a field stool, and continued to run.

It took her a moment again to sight the woman, but by then the little woman saw her. The tiny magicker raised her hands and moved as if to say something, and when she did, Deirdre threw the field stool at her with all of the strength in her body. It was an ungainly toss, one made with her off hand, and it missed the woman completely. But the sorceress let out a shriek and turned tail and rushed back toward the pavilion.

Deirdre threw herself after the woman, not intending to let her reenter the fray or to cast her magics from afar.

When Deirdre burst through the opening of the pavilion, the first thing she encountered was the prune, a look somewhere between fear and outrage on his face. The shriveled thing made the mistake of reaching for Deirdre, and without her thinking the dagger slapped the man's hand aside. She left the poor fellow on the ground scampering for his fingers, and snatched up the nearest thing to hand and threw it at the closest clergyman.

For all she knew, they all were capable of sorcery, and she had no intention of being magicked upon anymore that day. So she ran at the nearest priest, the young man who'd cast the vial at her, and gave him a poke in the belly with her dagger before moving on to the next one. Soon she was chasing the three clerics that remained standing, the small woman included, in circles around the large tent's central dining table, screaming and throwing things at them, hoping that enough shouts and hurled fruit platters would render them incapable of concentrating sufficiently to make a casting.

It seemed to work. After a short time, the two male clerics, elderly codgers both, bolted out the main entrance, preferring to risk death on the battlefield outside rather than endure the teenage efreet who assailed them within.

The female hexer was remarkably quick and limber, especially for a woman who looked to be in her 40s, and she did a good job of staying away from Deirdre and her wicked blade. After a dozen more circuits of the tent, Deirdre swearing at her like a sailor and hurling anything that came to hand, the now frantic sorcerer dashed out a back entrance.

Deirdre tore after her, hot in pursuit until she spied a handful of mounted men approach at a gallop. The magicker barreled toward the returning Etruscian patrol, shrieking and yelling in their language.

The Surrey lass turned on her heel and raced with as much speed as she could muster in the opposite direction. Zipping back through the tent, she saw that the prune was gone and that the man who she'd poked with the dagger lay unmoving amidst an enormous pool of blood on the pavilion's rich carpeting.

She opted not to stop and enquire at the young man's health, but instead made her way back through the main entrance of the pavilion and into the open area beyond.

There were a great many bodies on the ground there, and a stream of armed men made their way from the stockade several hundred paces distant. Without any doubt, those were the tradesmen Sir Bertrand and the fake huntsman had been unable at first to recruit who now, having sensed the direction the wind was blowing, rushed to claim their share of booty from the enemy camp.

There wasn't much fighting left to do at that point, and she headed at a jog toward where the action still seemed hot, the place she most likely would find Armand and the creature.

The search didn't last long. There was no sign of the Fiend in any of the forms she knew him to use, but after some moments, she discovered Armand sitting on an upturned barrel. The man was attempting to stitch a deep and ugly cut on his own left shoulder and doing it poorly. He hadn't even properly staunched the bleeding yet. Without a word, she stepped over to help.

She decided not to think one bit more about the magicker. A few foreign soldiers still resisted near their makeshift corral, but most appeared either fled or dead, and the magicker posed no great danger without an army. The Fiend knew where Dierdre last had seen the woman, so let him worry about her. Besides, the Surrey lass had done her share that day and was not in the mood to poke anymore people in the belly.

"That was some mess," Armand observed after she several times had needed to slap his hand away from the needle and thread she'd liberated from his grasp. He cleared his voice. "You needn't have taken such risks, young lady ... or goaded the enemy the way you did."

"We won, didn't we?"

"Oh, aye. Some few of their horsemen remain, but I can't imagine they're in much of a mood for more."

"Where did you get this thread?" she asked.

"I always carry some with me."

"Hazard of the life," she agreed.

"Indeed. You know, these blokes didn't offer us a drink when we arrived. What sort of people are they? ... These foreign god-botherers aren't all teetotalers, are they?"

"You saw how that gang drank at Mont Clair," she reminded him. "Guzzled it like water."

"Thank heavens."

"Stop fussing so much, and I'll find you a keg when I'm finished here." She took a moment to think on how to formulate the next query. "I hope the huntsman is still looking after Lady Isabel."

"Spears? No, I think not. It was him that led Bertrand and the others through the woods to get here. Last I heard, he's off looking for enemy riders. ... Would you like me to have someone take you back to the stockade?"

"I would, the second I've gotten your keg."

"Excellent. That little horse must still be around here somewhere. He's a survivor that one."

It was a particularly good day for one that had gotten off to a somewhat bad start, and a fitting end to a silly and an abysmal quest.

44. The Road to Albion

It took them a few days to get on the road to Albion, but no one bemoaned the delay. In fact, affairs otherwise had gone quite well. The tradesmen of both camps seemed always to want more, but none grumbled terribly when the booty from the Etruscian camp at last was divvied up between them and the soldiers.

It helped a great deal that Sir Armand was liberal with the liquor stocks that the clerics had left behind and previously had hoarded to themselves. And there was a significant amount of coin abandoned at the main pavilion, more than enough to pay each tradesman their five sovereigns. Deirdre didn't ask what became of the rest of the money.

Though there were many wounded during the battle, none of those injuries were so serious as to threaten life, and Deirdre tended them as she was able. Of those, only Sir Bertrand was so gravely injured as to be unable to sit a horse, and they prepared a travois to transport the knight, much to his embarrassment.

Isabel was back on her feet not long after the battle was over, and after an additional day's rest was her regular self. The woman was stoic about the death of Deckard but was astounded to find Mr. Spears still alive and apparently uninjured. It surprised Deirdre, but it should not, when the fake huntsman produced a dented whiskey flask that he claimed had stopped the otherwise fatal arrow.

Neither Deirdre nor the so-called huntsman attempted to dissuade those who insisted Isabel's remarkable return and the party's great victory over the foreign magickers was attributable to the charisma of the Glaive. What would be the point? It was a victory, and Isabel's return did have the feel of a miracle, which was, in part, why Armand felt they could afford to be benevolent to their defeated enemy.

So they took no prisoners and sought no reprisal. Those foreign soldiers and priests who were not killed outright were allowed merely to flee unharried into the forest. It was for fate and for the loving mercy of the Walking God to decide if those men ever would make it back to their distant homes. Even the two hostages they'd held at the stockade were allowed their liberty, albeit without their mounts or any provisions.

Much to Deirdre's shock, the Fiend had allowed the foreign sorcerer to make her escape with several mounted soldiers. It wasn't an irksome thing. Truth be told, Deirdre was of two minds about the woman slipping away. True, the sorcerer had vexed them terribly, and in return Deirdre had tried to skewer the tiny woman with her dagger.

But there was something else. Deirdre had never fancied herself a tremendous judge of human character, but she found something agreeable about the woman's appearance. There just seemed to be a pleasant and likable quality about her. Perhaps that was just the lovely smile? ... Or the effects of some exotic magic?

For the life of her though, she couldn't imagine the creature being swayed by such earthly emotions. On the morning of the third day following the battle, after the party had settled into their first day's travel toward home, she broached the subject again with the Fiend.

"Aren't you worried she's still a threat?"

She and the faux huntsman were a fair number of paces ahead of the rest of the party, playing at being scout, and again were free to speak at their leisure.

"Your dance partner?" The creature several times had teased her about running around the great tent with the woman.

"You know who I mean. If she's a sorcerer of such great talent, why would you possibly wish her to survive? How do we know she won't yet try and cause us some mischief?"

"I hope that to be the case."

"You're not making any sense."

"She's that way," said the creature, pointing roughly east, "about two days travel from here."

"How?"

"I told you, child. In a great many ways, I am an appallingly bad magicker. But there are some things at which I excel."

"You put a cowbell on her?"

"An exceptionally good and subtle one, if I do say. Even if she's able to discover the thing, it's unlikely she'll ever be able to unknot it."

"And you'll always know where she is. Just the ... you know ... the same as that creature in Etruscia?"

"That Walking God of yours? Ah. That's a different matter, but somewhat the same thing. With this woman, I also got a taste of her."

"You took a bite out of her?"

"No, no. I managed to track down her and her escort the night following the battle and had a chance to look her over with some great care. I can't really explain it, but if ever she tries to touch the wind around me again, it won't work as well for her the next time."

"Because you've gotten a taste of her?" None of that made sense, but much the Fiend said didn't. Well, not all of it was nonsensical. "They're going to send more people, aren't they?"

"Without a doubt."

"And you hope they'll send the same person?"

The creature gave her a wink in response. "Sorcerers of her vast ability don't come along every day, once or twice a century at the most."

"And yet," Deirdre said, "we still don't know exactly why they sought Isabel, or what they have in mind for her."

"Hmm...," the creature murmured. "The fugitive clerics I tracked down were of no help. There was a very impressive and an immensely powerful compulsion placed on cach. Didn't get a word out of any of them."

"You could have asked the sorcerer you let escape."

"True, but it wasn't urgent. Now that the wind is back to normal, all the answers will come to me sooner rather than later. Especially now that I know what I'm looking for. As for the sorcerer, I have other plans for her."

"I think you're sweet on her."

"Yes, in a way." He hesitated a moment. "But in a way I doubt a human would understand."

Deirdre held her tongue. It was possible she understood simply fine. One thing she'd noticed was that the creature suffered frequently from simple boredom. Or maybe it wasn't so simple. She suspected it was the reason he often made it a point to do simple things with such flair. Life had to be about more than tedious efficiency, he'd often told her.

"What became of Brother Hasenpfeffer?" she asked.

"Who?"

"The talkative one, looked like a prune?"

"The one whose fingers you lopped off?"

"Ha! Yes."

"Father Hesperus."

"Yes, that doddering old fool."

"Those people use far too much garlic in their cookery."

"You didn't let any of the others escape, did you?"

"Tuppence, I'm not a glutton ... though I suppose I have been overindulging myself of late." A note of seriousness entered the Fiend's tone. "We need to keep a close eye on Isabel for the time being."

"What do you think?" she asked. "Do the people at the Holy See truly imagine she came from your world?"

"I'll have to think on it. Either way, they have their sights on her. We'll need to keep her close and be vigilant."

"But won't she be much in demand now that she's found the Glaive?"

"Bah, that thing," said the creature. "Give it a few months, it'll be forgotten about."

Deirdre found that extremely hard to believe. All the toil, effort, and pain. And she wasn't completely convinced that there wasn't some power in finding such an item, even if it otherwise was a fraud. She expressed those thoughts now.

"That's the tragedy, Tuppence. Even if this were a great and mighty holy weapon, it would be forgot about soon. The thing will be venerated for a time, much will be made of Isabel's piety and courage, but the weapon will end up stuck away in some reliquary somewhere, alongside the Bunions of Saint Bonaventura and the Fallen Arches of Archbishop Akbar. It'll never be seen again."

"Are you serious?" She wanted to argue with the creature, just on general principals, but he probably was right. Instead, she asked, "But in the meantime?"

"In the meantime, you're right. Isabel's celebrity will place her in demand for a time. But we can navigate that."

"You have a plan, I hope."

"There are some things in motion."

"Such as?"

The faux huntsman gave her a shy smile. "When word gets back to Baron William and the king of the goings on in Transom these last weeks, it's unlikely any delegate of the Holy See will be welcome in these lands."

"And then the Etruscians will turn their support to de Margot," she said.

"Of course, that was always to be the case. But through Birdy, Sir Alexis has exchanged a number of missives lately with his cousin the baron. It seems Baron William has convinced the king to forestall any Inquisition by appointing a Witchfinder General."

Deirdre nearly jumped out of her saddle in frustration. "But that's what those foreign scoundrels have wanted from the beginning!"

"True."

"But what of all the carnage you spoke of?" This was dreadful. "Didn't you call a Witchfinder a … what was it? A 'backdoor Inquisition'?"

"Aye, it'll be a bloodbath. Heads will roll, bodies will sizzle like meat, terror will grip the land."

"How can …?" she began. *No,* she said to herself. *Don't get angry. Think.* "Who is this new Witchfinder General?"

"Sir Alexis proposed your old tutor, Right Reverend Moorcroft Ainsley. It seems likely he'll get the appointment."

She reached over and smacked the faux huntsman on the shoulder. She then began to laugh. The Fiend was a scalawag, a miserable old scoundrel. "You could have opened with that fact!"

"Where would the fun be in that?"

By that point, her laughter had her nearly doubled over in the saddle. "Wait," she said after a short time. "What of the *gesh*?"

"That'll take some working around," the Fiend agreed. "But I'm confident it can be done. Reverend Ainsley will spend most of his tenure as Witchfinder General away on pilgrimage, walking the highroads and byroads of Albion while shrouded in prayer."

"Such a pious man."

"Yes," agreed the creature. "He's likely to be the only beloved Witchfinder in the history of Albion."

"With Beazley working the thumbscrews, I'd wager." It seemed perfectly obvious that this was all some tiny cog in one of the creature's many schemes, one that probably had been in the works for some time. She couldn't begrudge him that.

"It'll work out, one way or the other," he said. "In the meantime, the reverend should be able to take some of the pressure off you and Isabel."

"I can think of one other way to keep Isabel safe," Deirdre volunteered.

"You're determined to marry that lass off to Sir Alexis. Hasn't she suffered enough?"

"When will we see him again?"

"Very soon," said the creature. "The road is good. If we endure no delays, it'll be five days from here to the Vidin Pass in the Wols Marches, and then another three back to Albion proper. I happen to know Sir Alexis will be passing right along the border, through the town of Thirlby, at the exact time we reach it."

"Such a coincidence. To where do we go after that?"

"South."

"South? To where?"

"Along the coast some leagues north of Westport there's an early spring planting festival for the onion crop in a town called Pepperdine. It's delightful. They make the best bread there, and the local wine is a gem."

"We have no place else we need to be?"

"Do you not like onions?"

"I love them, but...."

"Ah, the war. According to the missives I've received through Birdy, the campaign season has just started. At this very moment, Sir Alexis travels to Westport to take delivery of the latest of 2,000 new war mounts for the army, and to receive three mercenary regiments that arrive within the month."

"We can see Vivian!" She almost said, "and the vicar," and felt a knot in her stomach for the loss.

"Look, Tuppence ... Birdy forwarded some other news about Westport."

"Vivian?" she whispered. Her heart nearly stopped.

"No, don't fret. William has had the governor check in on her family. They're fine. This is good news. Cousin William intends to keep the vicar's library together and to assign a resident librarian to the vicarage."

That was exceptionally good news, and she said as much. "Yet, it's still so sad. He was such a wonderful man and a great teacher."

"If it helps at all, he'll live on in his library. And the knowledge that was the center of his life will be shared with others."

A sudden impulse struck Deirdre. "What's to become of the vicar's printing press?"

"What? The one gathering dust in the shed? I suppose it'll continue to gather dust."

"I'd like to have it ... if that's alright?"

"I think the vicar would like the idea of you having it. What do you intend to do with it?"

"Print books."

"Tuppence, you are a source of endless surprises."

"And I want to learn more about walking the ways," she said. Even Deirdre wasn't sure from where that notion came. It was something they'd talked about before, but she soon had forgotten. Now she felt it was important. "I want to learn about the true and proper ways, that is. Like the ancients did to tap into the power of the world. ... Could you help me with that?"

"Child, I will help you any way I can."

"Do you know the location of any routes in Albion? True ones?"

"By merest happenstance, I do know of one not too far distant."

"Where?"

"Just south of the village of Pepperdine, nearby the road to Westport."

Another jolt ran through her, somewhere between ecstasy and annoyance. For the merest of moments, Deirdre wasn't certain whether to laugh or to reach over and punch the creature again.

"Happenstance, my eye," she whispered.

This was the Fiend's way. There always was a card up his sleeve, a scam in the offing, a long con he painstakingly was cooking up on the side, along with a dozen others he gently juggled well out of sight. And not for the first time she was reminded that things were never, absolutely never, as they appeared with the monster.

Case in point. A tiny thing had occurred to her earlier that day, and only now did the true import of that thing become clear to her. She'd scolded the creature not too many weeks past that they'd never be able to rely on angry servants to murder their way out of danger. It was a peevish jab at the time, a line she merely had cast at the creature because she was irked with him.

But was that not precisely what had happened three days ago in their final battle with the forces of the Holy See?

Damn. Double damn.

She'd flattered herself since then that it was she who had taken the bull by the horns on that day and had roused their party to victory, but was it not the creature who deftly and carefully had maneuvered every single piece into place for her to do that?

True, the Fiend had been at his wit's end at times these last weeks, and several times he'd appeared properly flustered. More than once he got everything wrong. It was precious easy to forget that even when the creature got everything wrong, he was always five steps ahead of his nearest rival.

No wonder the monster so often was bored, and no wonder he was generous to the rival who had given him such a close-run race.

The creature was a trickster, a liar, a cheat, and a fraud. But they'd prevailed on that day, in large part, because they'd relied on a frightened and an angry group of servants to rise up and murder their masters. And she was as certain as certain could be that the creature had arranged all of that, every single bit of it, as one of his many lessons for her. The highhandedness of the Fiend both appalled and delighted her.

And now he offered to teach her hidden secrets. No, even more. It dawned on her, perhaps for the very first time, that the Fiend was an open book to her, a teacher who would deny her nothing. In his orbit, there was no information too dangerous, no knowledge too sinful or too sacrilegious. If she asked the Fiend to teach her how best to murder half the world and to enslave the rest, he would do so without hesitation.

"Thank you for helping me," she said. The Fiend's kindness got her to feeling magnanimous. "So, I forgive you for killing Monsignor Krait without me."

"What?" The creature reined his horse to a stop, a look on his face like he'd been struck.

"Monsignor Krait," she said, her horse slowing to match his. "The fellow you tipped down the well at Mont Clair. How could you forget such a thing?"

"Tuppence, I thought *you* did that."

"Well, it wasn't me. And it certainly wasn't the baron."

By that time, their mounts had resumed their leisurely plod, and the fake huntsman's laughter resounded throughout the forest.

"Child, I've said it before, and I'll say it again, wells built along the style customary in Albion are death traps, and anyone...."

Oh, damn, she thought as the creature began to drone on about the inherent dangers and defects of the average Albion well. Five days to the Wols Marches, another three to Albion—eight long days, and there would be no hearing the end of this.

The End

www.ingramcontent.com/pod-product-compliance
Lightning Source LLC
Chambersburg PA
CBHW072056190726
48294CB00005B/1554